The Wild...

Perhaps half the riders gathered on the trail were elves. They rode sleek horses and wore fanciful crystalline armor, but no helmets obscured beautiful, pitiless faces. freely or e anything b

Then the hounds wit eyed giant things that ing beings, clawed hands all the weapons they needed.

Megan snaked her right hand down to her fanny pack and her pistol. The *things* could not be special effects: No special effect included the smell of rot mingled with roses.

Her hand closed around the grip, eased it free.

Two of the red-eyed hounds stepped off the trail, a powre

The

steady

The

ing of t

its cla

Aga

The

ing ba

Meg

SOMETHING MAGIC THIS WAY COMES

Edited by Martin H. Greenberg and Sarah A. Hoyt

DAW BOOKS, INC.

DONALD A. WOLLHEIM, FOUNDER

375 Hudson Street, New York, NY 10014

ELIZABETH R. WOLLHEIM
SHEILA E. GILBERT
PUBLISHERS

http://www.dawbooks.com

First Printing, March 2008
1 2 3 4 5 6 7 8 9

DAW TRADEMARK REGISTERED
U.S. PAT. AND TM. OFF. AND FOREIGN COUNTRIES
—MARCA REGISTRADA
HECHO EN U.S.A.

PRINTED IN THE U.S.A.

ACKNOWLEDGMENTS

CONTENTS

THE POWER OF MAGIC

Sarah A. Hoyt

ONCE upon the time magic—defined as forces and events that could not be explained—ruled the world. The lightning bolt across the sky was as miraculous to our ancestors as was the return of daylight after the blackness of night.

Out of their minds they conjured one god's thunderbolt and any number of carriages drawing the sun, any number of demons eating away daylight.

Then came enlightenment, and little by little the realm of magic got pushed aside, isolated, contained. Science, seemingly, stood astride the world, illuminating all dark corners and showing the entire world that the darkness contained nothing more mysterious than the absence of light, easily explainable by the rotation of the Earth.

And yet . . . and yet, it's not so easy. It never will be. Even for us, the people of the twenty-first century, the unexplained, the miraculous, those things that happen *who knows how?* will always exist.

Computers might be very good at itemizing and tagging reality, but how many of us haven't looked at some inexplicable event within our units and said "gremlins" or "I swear this thing has a mind of its own"?

Our big cities, our hulking machines are full of and

operated by humans. And in the human mind there will always be room for the fantastic explanation. There will always be room for gods and demons and the unexplained miracles they produce. Perhaps to mask our ignorance. Or perhaps to explain those areas that science itself can't illuminate.

There will always be room for things we swear couldn't have been there, and yet we saw . . . didn't we?

Friendly or dangerous, reflecting the confused observations of our ancestors or the hopes for our descendants, fairies and shapeshifters will walk among us; urban legends will be born of cataclysmic destruction; vampires will lurk at the edges of the night waiting for us; and ritual and belief will renew us and refresh us and make us perhaps not less rational but more human.

Here, now, or in the past or—if we ever get there—in the future stars, we shall take magic with us. Because inside, deep down inside, as we sit at our computers we are not so different and not so much more rational than our ancestors who sat gazing at the fire listening to the storytellers tell sagas of gods and demons and stories of woodland spirits.

And even deeper inside, we want to believe just as our ancestors did . . .

Welcome to *Something Magic This Way Comes*. Sit by the fireside. Listen to the stories. And feel free to indulge your imagination.

MORE TO TRUTH THAN PROOF

Irene Radford

"YOU see this line on your palm?" the old Gypsy woman rasped through a fog of incense in the shadowy carnival tent. She shook her head and closed her eyes. A pained expression crossed her weathered and lined face.

Gabrielle Whythe peered closer at her hand. Her arm ached from holding it stretched across the round table for so long. The light was so dim in the carnival tent that she could barely make out the damask pattern of moons and stars in the red tablecloth. Filmy curtains resembling brightly colored cobwebs draped about, adding to the light diffusion.

Outside she could hear her dormmates giggling. They'd each taken a turn at having their fortune told at the Beltane Renaissance Fair that erupted on campus every May. Gabby hadn't cared about the mixture of physiological profiling and mystic fakery. But the other three girls had dared her.

Whythes never passed up a dare. Or so Grumpy, her great-grandfather had informed her many times.

"What about my life line?" Gabby asked in reply to the old woman's question.

"It is broken. Three times. Then it cuts short here." She drew a cracked fingernail the color of nicotine across the center of Gabby's palm.

3

"So?"

"Your life will present you with many hard choices."
The Gypsy clamped her mouth shut and swallowed.
Sweat broke out on her brow. Her throat apple bobbed
several times. It protruded like a man's.

Gabby suppressed a giggle. Maybe the fake Gypsy
was also a fake woman.

"You will meet an interesting man who will change
your life," the old woman said hurriedly. She dropped
her grip on Gabby's hand and wiped her own palm
on her multicolored and threadbare skirt. She looked
away furtively.

"And I've studied enough psychology to know
you're hiding something." Gabby narrowed her focus
to the pulse throbbing in the woman's neck. Too
rapid. Pale skin. Sweat. Definitely the telltales of a lie.

A whopping big lie.

"You . . . um . . . you are descended from one who
helped my people many times." She lowered her eyes
and murmured something that might have been a prayer.

"Yeah, so what. My family traces their genealogy
back to God or someone just as important, like King
Arthur. Bound to be someone in there with a bleeding
heart for the downtrodden."

Gabby had documents taking the family back to
1774 and the Boston Tea Party. Before that the documents dried up, dissolved into family legend. Without
cross references and records Gabby refused to believe
her Grumpy's *stories*. She'd accept DNA evidence, especially if there were records suggesting an ancestor
had the deep blue eyes that permeated every genera-
tion of her family.

Blue eyes were supposed to be recessive. Not in her
family. They tended to dominate.

Ancient history was just that, ancient. Gabby liked
the rough and tumble frontier politics and survival society of western America. Give her fur traders and
wagon trains and Native Americans any day over tired
and shopworn myths of the old world.

The Gypsy's eyes flew open. She glared at Gabby malevolently.

Gabby didn't back down. She'd learned early how to out-stare her great-grandfather, who claimed all kinds of psychic powers. Including the ability to curse an enemy with boils and sores and other such nonsense.

"Your fate is written in the stars and reflected in your hand," the Gypsy snarled. The tent grew quiet. All sound outside reduced to a background hum. The candles and incense seemed to stop flickering.

Gabby held her breath in expectation. She didn't think she could breathe if she wanted to. Her pulse sounded loud in her ears, the only evidence of life and the passage of time.

"I don't believe in fate. I make my own destiny," Gabby said on a long exhale. She drew in another breath by sheer force of will.

"The life line in your palm does not lie," the old woman continued in a singsong voice, almost a chant. "The interruptions reveal a broken path full of obstacles that you will stumble over. Sometimes even fall. And then you will die young. An ignoble death not worthy of your family's fine heritage."

"That's a ball of crap!" Gabby exclaimed with glee. Her family might believe in this hoodoo voodoo stuff, but that didn't mean she had to. "The broken parts are where I splattered acid during a chemistry experiment. And the life line stops because of scar tissue from a deep cut when I fell out of a tree when I was ten." Another dare.

"Believe what you will. You cannot change your fate."

The scene became blurry in Gabrielle Griffin Whythe's memory as a harsh bell jangled her out of a deep sleep. She had put that incident out of her mind at the end of her senior year of college. Right after it happened.

"Nonsense and crap," Gabby muttered.

The scent of incense lingered in her mind and her nose.

The bell kept ringing. Loudly. She jerked her head to look at the alarm clock. A string of obscenities erupted from her mouth.

"Nine-fifteen in the fricking AM! Shit. I need to get to work." Oversleeping was a natural consequence after too many hours of research and working on her dissertation.

A donor wanted to deposit a trunkload of family journals and memorabilia at Gabby's museum. The family had records linking them to Josiah Ezekiel Marshall, a frontier Methodist missionary who had serviced remote communities throughout the Oregon Country in the 1840s and 50s before building a permanent church and settling down on the high desert plateau of central Oregon for the last ten years of his life.

For the last six months, Gabby had spent every spare moment working on her dissertation, exploring the legality and social implications of the unregistered marriages between fur traders and their Indian wives.

At three this morning she'd come to the sorry conclusion that some vital piece of the giant puzzle was missing. She had thoroughly explored the legal precedent set by the heirs of Peter Skene Ogden. His east coast relatives had tried to seize his estate in 1854, claiming that both his marriages to Indian women had been Indian ceremonies and invalid. Therefore his children by both women were illegitimate and ineligible to inherit the sizeable estate.

Ogden's children had taken their case to the Supreme Court. The ruling found that since the marriages had been recorded in the Hudson's Bay Company books, they were legal under common law—the prevailing legal system of the time.

In Gabby's own town of Carter's Ford, the opposite had occurred. Emile Carter's only surviving daughter, Hannah, could not find a reference to her father's marriage in any of the Company books and had lost her inheritance to greedy cousins. No one believed

Mary Carter, the widow, when she claimed a Christian marriage. She had no papers to prove it.

Lots of examples. Lots of research. Still, something was missing. And Gabby was running out of time to finish the dissertation.

She had interviewed for a job curating the local university's collection of historical artifacts going back nearly ten thousand years. Getting hired depended upon her finishing her dissertation by the end of the year. November had come a week ago. She was running out of time.

With any kind of luck Josiah Marshall's journals would contain a few nuggets of insight into the situation. From what she'd read of his exploits, mostly second hand information, he'd spent a good deal of his missionary time persuading fur traders and mountain men to marry their Indian wives in Christian—and therefore legal—ceremonies.

Old Josiah Marshall didn't approve of Indian ceremonies or of the Hudson's Bay Company practice of recording the marriages in their books as if they were business transactions. Company clerks recorded marriages right alongside inventories of supplies sold to the fur trader.

She rolled out of bed and slapped the alarm off in one awkward movement.

She tripped and almost fell trying to cram her legs into panty hose and her one and only power suit of sapphire wool, the same color as her eyes. Then she stubbed her toe on her discarded boots as she ran to the bathroom to brush her teeth.

Damn. She was never this clumsy.

Crawling and cursing, she fished her good black shoes with the sensible one and one half inch heels out from under the bed.

If she broke every speed limit in town and hit all the lights right, she should be able to greet the Marshall descendant on time with a mask of professional calm and a courteous handshake.

Another bell startled her. She banged her head on

the bed frame trying to get up from her awkward
stretch to retrieve the elusive shoe.

The doorbell sounded again. This time, the obnox-
iously early person leaned on it as if he had a mission.

"Go away," she shouted, rubbing the back of her
head with one hand and brushing dust panthers off
her suit with the other.

The bell rang again, longer, louder.

"Then let yourself in if you're in such an all-fired
hurry!" She had a vague recollection of slamming the
door closed without locking it about midnight when
she'd stumbled home from the small house museum
she ran.

The latch lifted and the door swung inward, pro-
pelled by unseen hands.

Gabby shivered. Memories of her dream and the
eerie feeling surrounding the Gypsy woman lingered.
She still smelled burning incense, an exotic blend of
patchouli and jasmine. Funny, now that she thought
about it, friends at the university said that the Renaissance Fair folded and never returned to campus after
Gabby graduated with a double major in History and
Anthropology, concentrating on the Pacific Northwest.
The Fair organizers had shown up for the first time
five years earlier, at the end of her freshman year.

"Ms. Whythe?" an imperious voice asked.

Gabby looked up to see a tall male silhouetted in
the morning light.

"Wh . . . who needs to know?" She had a sudden
fear of a family summons back to Boston. She didn't
have the time to fly off to one of Grumpy's deathbed
scenes. He performed them about every five years,
conning family members into conforming to his expec-
tations so they could inherit his fortune. Then he'd
miraculously recover, only to succumb again when the
family drifted away from his strictures.

Gabby didn't care about the family fortune. She'd
built her own life, determined her own fate.

Her left foot finally plopped into place against the
sole of her shoe. She started working on the right.

"Your great-grandfather, Roderick Griffin Whythe IV, sent me." The man, followed by a large dog, stepped through the door of her tiny bungalow, on the outskirts of the university town.

"What does Grumpy want now?" She hadn't been back to the family estate in Boston or to any of the family gatherings in ten years. Not only did she not have the interest, the three-thousand-mile trek would take too much time away from her work. The emotional commitment of dealing with probing questions from the gaggle of her extended family would take too much energy and creativity away from her work.

The last reason was more compelling to keep her away from her family than just the time. She had six weeks of vacation saved up. But she planned to add it to her sabbatical next year to join an archaeological dig of the site of a Hudson's Bay Trading Post in Montana.

"Mr. Whythe has requested that I find a home for this female puppy. The last of the litter his bitch whelped six months ago," the man intoned. He looked down his long nose at Gabby.

She had to look up a long way to meet his eyes.

"Well, I can't take a dog. Certainly not now. I've got to get to my museum." Gabby got to her knees in preparation to standing. What was it about Grumpy's dogs? Something important to the lineage. She didn't really care.

A long wet tongue slurped across her face. A pair of deep gray eyes, intelligent eyes, appeared above the tongue. Gabby found herself staring deeply into those eyes. Deep pools of understanding and wisdom . . .

Something akin to communication nagged at her perceptions.

Nonsense.

"Oh, dear. I was afraid this would happen," the man said. He sounded as distressed as his plummy butler's voice could.

"Hey, aren't you Grumpy's butler?" Gabby finally recognized the man's voice. She hadn't seen him in a decade, but she'd never forget that disapproving voice.

He uttered every word as if she were the lowliest worm crawling out from beneath rotting wood.

"Ian McTavis VI, at your service, ma'am." He executed a slight bow from the waist. But he didn't sound happy. Not at all.

Gabby used the tall dog's shoulder as a prop to get to her feet. The dog gratefully leaned into her side and looked up at her with adoring eyes. In another time, another place, under completely different circumstances, she might have returned the look. She settled for scratching the pup's ears.

Cymorth.

The strange word popped into Gabby's head. Almost as if the puppy had said something. She had the strange sense that the pup wanted to help her.

Pup? The brindled wolfhound might be only six months old, but it stood almost as tall as her hip. By the time she reached her full growth, she'd outweigh Gabby by fifty pounds or more.

"Couldn't afford to feed you, even if I could take care of you, pup," Gabby said, stuffing keys, wallet, ID badge, and a packet of tissues into her good black purse.

"Lock the door on your way out, Ian. I've got to get going. And good luck finding a home for the pup."

"Did she tell you her name?" Ian asked skeptically.

"Not hardly. Dogs can't talk."

"You might think so now," Ian muttered.

Gabby dashed for her little electric car. Ecologically sound it might be, but not a speed demon. Traffic around campus in the morning was always a mess, increasing her commute time. She didn't have any time to spare.

The dog bounded after her. Gabby tripped over her trying to get the car unlocked.

"Sorry. You can't come with me. Hey, Ian, come get the dog." What was it about Grumpy's dogs? Something important. Something about the dogs choosing the heir.

Heir to what? Grumpy's millions would go a long way

MORE TO TRUTH THAN PROOF

toward restoring her little jewel of a museum and hiring extra help while she finished her dissertation.

"The dog is no longer my responsibility," Ian said. He sounded upset. Maybe he didn't want to give the dog away at all. "She has chosen her new owner. Your fates are now sealed together."

"Not bloody likely," Gabby snarled at him. That was twice today she'd been told her fate was fixed. Once in the dream memory. And now from impassive Ian.

"Grumpy had seven children." Four of them legitimate. "They each had at least two children and I don't know how many grandchildren. Surely one of them would make a better owner for a wolfhound than me." Angrily she pushed the dog aside as it tried to climb into the little car ahead of her.

"I have visited thirty-two of your closest relatives, Ms. Whythe. The dog liked none of them. She is yours now. Along with a great many other responsibilities. Your great-grandfather will be in touch. I'll put the dog's food and toys into your kitchen and then lock up as I leave." Ian turned and approached a long black car that must get only four gallons to the mile.

"Get out, dog!" Gabby screamed, trying to hold the pup by the scruff of the neck.

Cymorth.

The strange word rang around Gabby's mind.

Help you.

"Ian, I need some help here."

"You do indeed. But I cannot assist you. You must rely upon the dog for help now."

With that Cymorth leaped across the gear shift and settled into the passenger seat. She filled it to overflowing. That didn't keep her from turning her massive head to look expectantly at Gabby.

"Damnit, I don't have time to fight with you, Dog." Gabby climbed in and started the ignition.

Cymorth, the word came again. *Named Cymorth. Help you.*

Gabby shook her head to clear it of the alien voice and the image of the proper spelling of the word. *Cymorth*. Pronounced *ky-more-dth*, with the emphasis on the first syllable. She knew instantly that it meant "help" in Welsh.

"Coffee. I need coffee. Too many late nights. Not enough sleep. I'm hallucinating. But I don't have time to give in to it."

She put the car in gear and sped across campus to her museum.

A big green SUV awaited her in the four car parking lot behind the white house. In 1849, when the Carter family built their home, it was the biggest building in town other than their woolen mill beside the waterfall.

"I'm only five minutes late," Gabby muttered as she jerked the parking brake into place. She tripped on the gravel in her haste to greet the long-legged man in carefully pressed khakis and a pristine green golf shirt and down vest that perfectly matched his vehicle.

Cymorth bounced out of the car in her wake. She sniffed the man's shoes rudely and circled him suspiciously. Then she sat on Gabby's foot, leaning her substantial weight against her and shedding blonde guard hairs all over her lovely blue suit.

If Gabby didn't know better, she'd think the dog cringed away from the man.

No trust.

The thought popped into Gabby's head, much as the dog's name had. Immediately, she felt the fine hairs along her spine bristle, much as a dog's would.

The man held his hand out to Cymorth, palm down and let her sniff his knuckles. He carefully looked to the side, not challenging the huge dog.

Cymorth retreated behind Gabby.

"Irish Wolfhounds are usually more easy going than this. Not much threatens them," he said, puzzled.

"She's young. I haven't had her long." Then remembering her manners, she stuck out her hand. "Hi, I'm Gabby Whythe."

"Jed Marshall." He shook her hand briefly with a firm, dry grip.

She took the opportunity to appraise the man. Younger than she expected. Midthirties. Fit. With the square jaw and windswept brown hair reminiscent of the portraits of his great, great, multi-great-grandfather.

Cymorth nudged Gabby's hand away from the man's and onto her own head.

"And this imperious young lady is Cymorth." Gabby refrained from rolling her eyes.

Jed Marshal turned his attention back to the dog. "Pleased to make your acquaintance, Miss Cymorth."

The dog wiggled away from his attempt to scratch her ears. She hadn't been this shy about her first meeting with Gabby. What was wrong with her?

"Sorry I'm late. Traffic," Gabby apologized.

"No problem. It's my day off."

"If you'll come with me, I have some papers for you to sign."

"I'll bring the trunk with me." He moved to open the back hatch of his monster vehicle. It might get five gallons to the mile.

"I can get a hand truck . . ."

"Don't bother. It's not that big or heavy." He slid a blanket-wrapped box, about a yard long and two feet wide, out and hoisted it to his shoulder as if it weighed no more than a pillow.

"A Dr. Gabriel Whythe came across on one of the early wagon trains. You any relation?" Jed Marshall asked as he set the trunk in the middle of Gabby's office floor.

The guy knew his history if he remembered that little factoid.

"The doctor who treated cholera at the cost of his own life in 1845 was a younger son of a mutual ancestor," Gabby explained. "He died without issue. I grew up in Boston."

"Pity. I was wondering why you hadn't joined the Sons & Daughters of the Oregon Trail." He sat in the chair beside the desk and stretched out his long legs.

"I'm treasurer this year. We're always looking for new members. Too many people these days have lost interest in their heritage."

Gabby perched on the edge of her chair. Cymorth circled and settled in the knee hole beneath the desk as if that had always been her place.

"Have you read the journals in that trunk?" Gabby's hands itched to remove the dusty blanket from the trunk and begin digging in. From the looks of it, the blanket could be an original trade blanket from the Hudson's Bay. Cream-colored wool with the distinctive red, black, and green stripes, two black hash marks woven into one border. Worth two beaver pelts and would fit a standard-sized bed of the time. Barely big enough for a modern double bed.

"I glanced at them as a kid in my grandparent's attic. I stumbled across them when I cleaned the place out to put it up for sale last month. You've got better facilities to protect them than I do."

"And I appreciate the donation. But I have to ask, why didn't you contact the university? I'll be taking them to their preservation lab as soon as I catalog them. I'm pretty sure the papers will need deacidification before putting them on display."

"Thought about it. Decided you'd make better use of them. The university's got lots of items. Can't display a tenth of what they've got. They'd probably sit in archives for decades before some grad student got around to reading them."

"May I?" Gabby gestured to the trunk.

"I'm surprised you waited this long," he chuckled.

Gently Gabby unfolded the layers of blanket. She wiggled her nose to keep from sneezing at the dust she raised. Cymorth lifted her head and sniffed too. Then she retreated into her hidey hole again.

"The blanket's part of the donation. I've included it in the inventory," Jed Marshall said, holding up a sheet of paper folded in three. "I don't know how old it is."

"Not real new," Gabby chuckled. This time, she had to turn her head away and sneeze.

"Mind if I look around? I haven't toured this museum since a fourth grade field trip."

"Certainly. My assistant will be here in a few minutes. She can give you the full tour if you want."

"Nah, I'll just look around."

Gabby dove into the jumbled assortment of journals, loose documents and old photos that highlighted the family history from 1843, when Old Josiah first arrived in the Oregon Country, to 1868. When the railroad bypassed Marshall Flats, the town and its church withered away to a ghost town. The inhabitants moved to the more convenient railhead.

The parish registry seemed missing. Gabby made a note to ask if it had gone to another church. Including that book in a display would complete the collection nicely.

Cymorth squeezed out from under the desk. She walked daintily around the piles of half-sorted documents.

"Um . . . Cymorth, stay," Gabby yelped just as the dog dropped her nose to sniff at the oldest journal. She grabbed the dog by the scruff of her neck and yanked her away from the precious artifact.

The dog resisted and continued to nose open the fragile little book.

"No!" Gabby let go of the big dog to grab up the journal with its cracked leather cover and frayed silk ribbon to tie the two covers closed. She grasped it where the leaves fell open under the dog's prodding.

Two words in the bold handwriting jumped out at her. "Emile Carter."

Anything to do with the town's founder interested her. Eagerly she read the entry for January 1, 1846, the day Dr. John McLoughlin retired as Chief Factor of Hudson's Bay Fort Vancouver. A number of trappers, traders, and company officers left with him, unhappy with changes in company administration that forced their beloved factor out.

Today I married six men to their Indian wives, having first baptized all six women. They all chose the name Mary. Two McKay's, one Stewart, and three Carters.

Gabby's heart skipped a beat. She forgot to breathe. This was the missing piece to her dissertation. What happened when old inheritance laws made a mistake? A multimillion dollar mistake that included a still prospering woolen mill, the house, other real estate, and small businesses. Wasn't the local bank part of the original estate?

Emile Carter's friends and colleagues had described him as a man who wrote little and said less about himself. He considered his marriage a private matter; no one had any right to question it but himself and his God. He had no need to prove the legality of it. He probably never thought that his widow would have to prove it.

Cymorth wedged her head beneath Gabby's arm. *Cymorth help Gabby.*

"Yes, my dear. You did help. But you'll help more if you stay off these papers."

Trust Cymorth. No trust man.

"Whatever." Gabby read on, hoping for more information. Nothing to indicate the first names of the men who had legalized their marriages that day. One of the big problems in tracking genealogy through the fur trades was a frequent repetition of names. Whole clans of Scots displaced by the Clearances, refugee Huguenots, and Quebeçois farmers with itchy feet enlisted at the same time. Fathers and sons, brothers, uncles, cousins, all with the same last name and many with the same *first* names.

"Mr. Marshall?" Gabby called as his long shadow passed her office door.

"Hm?" He poked his head inside the doorway.

"Do you have any idea where the parish registry went?" She tried to look curious rather than too eager. No sense getting excited until she had the evidence.

"Isn't it in there?"

"I didn't see it."

"It's on the inventory."

"But I don't see it." Gabby looked into the trunk again. No big bound book.

"Let me look in the back of my rig. I may have put it in the box of books to go to the used book store."

Gabby let go the breath she was holding.

No trust, Cymorth reminded her. *No trust*.

"He said he hadn't looked at these documents in years, except to inventory them. So why would he put the registry in the wrong box?"

Not knowing precisely why, she followed him to the parking lot. The prickles along her spine continued.

"Why shouldn't I trust him? He has nothing to gain in this," she muttered to herself and to the dog who trotted at her heels.

Watch him.

"Here it is!" Jed Marshall proclaimed as Gabby approached his SUV. "I was in a hurry and put it in the wrong box."

He said he hadn't read the journals since childhood, Gabby reminded herself. She took the fat book with the cracked leather cover from him silently. The moment her hands touched it a jolt of something . . . something negative coursed through her veins.

"You altered it!" she blurted out without thinking.

Pain and shock crossed his face before he masked it. "Why would I do such a thing?" His hurt was feigned. She knew it in her bones.

Told you so, Cymorth reminded her.

"Why indeed? The only person with something to gain would be a descendant of Hannah Carter, Emile's and Mary's daughter. She disappeared from the historical record the day the courts agreed with her disinheritance. July 15, 1852." Two years before Peter Skene

Ogden's heirs proved the legitimacy of company marriages.

"She married the eldest son of Josiah Marshall," he said quietly.

"Trouble is, Hannah was a very popular name at the time. Three men with the last name of Carter married women by the name of Mary on the same day. Who is to say they didn't all name their daughters Hannah?"

"My great-grandmother was *the* Hannah Carter!" His face flushed a deep red.

Gabby could almost feel the waves of anger and . . . and *greed* that poured off of him.

Cymorth eased in front of Gabby and took a firm stance, teeth bared. One hundred pounds of dog ready to protect and defend her partner.

"Since you've destroyed the provenance of the parish registry, that makes the journal suspect as well. You've destroyed your only hope of proving any claim to the heritage." Inside, Gabby wept. Her dissertation would have to wait for extensive and time-consuming laboratory tests to prove the journal correct.

"I defy you to prove anything in the registry is a forgery," Marshal snarled.

"I will know the truth. Your greed and impatience overcame good sense. The journal and your DNA would have been enough. But you had to cheat."

"The truth isn't cheating."

Gabby opened the huge tome unerringly to a page near the middle. Three pages of a long and rambling reminiscence written by old Josiah in his last days. She sensed by the vibrations in her fingertips that the center page had been altered. Four sentences had been added. The handwriting was a near perfect match, the ink properly faded, possibly even the same chemical composition of the old lampblack inks.

I consider it a great honor to welcome into my family the daughter of my old friend Emile Carter. She took refuge with us when the world cast her out. My son fell in love with her and married her. They have given me three grandchildren to lighten my last years.

"If he knew her to be legitimate, why didn't he speak up at the trial?" I asked.

"Uh . . ." Confusion flushed his face a deeper red. "You've ruined it, Jed Marshall."

"You don't know that! You can't prove I did anything just by looking at it. You're guessing. Those greedy East Coast Carters who grabbed the mill and the land away from my family pay your salary. They've got you in their pocket. You don't dare present evidence to contradict their ownership."

"The Carters have nothing to do with it. The museum belongs to the county now."

"And the Carters are the biggest tax payers in the county."

"Actually, the mill went public with their stock. The Carters only own about fifteen percent of it now. I question the entry because . . ." How did she know?

What was she doing? Her dissertation, her job. She put everything in jeopardy because of a *feeling!*

Truth. Know truth now. Cymorth looked at her. Those deep gray eyes held Gabby captive for a moment. An entire world of understanding beyond normal senses opened before her.

What is truth without proof! Gabby wanted to shout at the dog.

Truth is truth. You know. Cymorth know. Proof come later. You know where to look now.

"It doesn't matter how I know. I know. I'll submit the entire collection to experts for *thorough* examination. We'll be in touch, Mr. Marshall. I'll send a receipt to you for the donation by registered mail, along with an estimated valuation for tax purposes."

Gabby turned on her heel and retreated inside with her dog. No, her familiar. She heaved a sigh of regret. The dissertation and the job with the University would have to wait for lab results.

Better to be right, Cymorth told her. Her sentence structure and vocabulary improved with every communication.

"Yeah, I guess. But it would have been nice to be right and finish on schedule."

Other opportunities.

"Promise?"

Promise. Trust Cymorth. Cymorth never lie.

A whiff of potpourri tantalized Gabby as she entered her museum again. With the scent came memory of her dream that morning.

"That old Gypsy was right. I stumbled three times this morning. Once when I was getting dressed, again at the car, and a third time greeting Mr. Marshall. My old life with limited perceptions has ended and a new life begun with you, my dear. And I met a man who changed my life—Ian brought you to me, Cymorth."

More to truth than proof.

"I see that now."

IN A DARK WOOD, DREAMING

Esther Friesner

IN the autumn, late in October, after he came back from visiting his father's house, Jorge papered the walls of his room with trees. He was sad when couldn't find any pictures of birch trees like the ones that he and Papi had stumbled on that last sweet afternoon wander—a grove of trunks so white they shone, their leaves gone from green to fluttering gold.

He consoled himself with photographs of oaks and beeches, solemn pines and perfect scarlet maples. Postcards and pages out of magazines, the occasional black-and-white newspaper clipping, even scraps torn guiltily from long-neglected books found in the dimmest corners of the local library. All went up over the cracked plaster and sickly beige paint of his bedroom walls. And later still, when every square inch of wall was covered with pictures of leaves and trunks and branches, Jorge took a spray can of green paint, stencils shaped like maple leaves, and made over his ceiling in the image of a forest.

Remarkable, how many pictures of forests there were to be gathered, once you began to look for them. He was done by Election Day, proud to have breathed the spirit of the woods into a tiny room in a dingy New York apartment. Of course, there was nothing he could do about the view from his window—towering rows of the housing project slabs crowding the uppermost tip of Manhattan—but he felt he'd done enough for his purpose: to make magic.

And it was done well before December! That was magic, too, *December*, the magic word, the magic time bright with hope. His father had sworn he'd be back in December to take Jorge and Ramón up to Vermont for a real old-fashioned New England Christmas. ("I'm back on my feet now, this time for real, for good. All I needed was to get out of the city, breathe some decent air, get away—Ah, but not from you, *mijitos*. Don't look at me like that, *mi Jorgelito, mi Ramóncito*. Yes, yes, I know you hate those baby names, you're both all grown up now, even if your *tía* Clarinda's got more whiskers than the two of you put together. When you have sons of your own, you'll understand. Never, never think I had to get away from you.")

Every day after school Jorge came straight home, dodging the dealers and the bullies and the terrifying, hopeless faces at every turn of the cold streets. He raced into his bedroom, dug his father's letter of promises out from under the pillow, and flopped down on his bed, drinking hope and happiness from the well-read pages. When he was sated, he folded his arms under his head and stared into the future through painted treetops. Sometimes he would lie there like that, gazing up at a plaster sky, until *tía* Clarinda came into his room to announce that it was time for dinner.

It was the day after Thanksgiving when the phone call came, with the season's first snow dusting down over the glittering city streets. Jorge and Ramón were in the living room, playing Monopoly. Ramón was cheating, and Jorge was letting him get away with it. He was too distracted to bother trying to stop him. Ramón was twelve, three years younger than Jorge. *Tía* Clarinda constantly complained that suddenly there was nothing anyone could do to control that

child, though Jorge was proud that sometimes he
could still bring his little brother to heel.

Tía Clarinda answered the phone. Right away Jorge
knew it was his father because *tía* stopped speaking
Spanish and started using every bad word she'd managed to pick up in English. It was her way of letting
him know that as far as she was concerned, he was
excluded, outcast, an unwelcome alien. In *tía* Clarinda's implacable heart, he'd thrown away all rights to
be part of *la familia* when he let the booze and the
junk and the women drag him out the door, out of
his sons' lives. Jorge's mother was dead—Ramón had
been two when she died so he didn't remember her
at all—but she was still Mami when *tía* Clarinda spoke
of her. Jorge's father was never Papi, always the colder,
starker *your father*. She used the word *ashamed* a lot,
too, when she talked to him: *Aren't you ashamed* and
You ought to be ashamed and *You probably don't even
have the grace to* be *ashamed,* sinvergüenza!

Sinvergüenza: shameless one. When *tía* Clarinda
lapsed into Spanish, Jorge knew it was only a matter
of time before she'd work herself into a fit of exasperation with Papi. Then she'd throw the handset at him
as if it were a dead rat and stomp off into the kitchen
to light all of those big votive candles by the window.
Jorge always missed the first minute of Papi's call because of how loudly she'd pray. No one could badger
the Holy Virgin like *tía* Clarinda.

"Say what, Papi?" Jorge stuck a finger in his ear,
trying to hear his father's words.

A chuckle came through the wire. "I said that I
can't tell whether Clarinda's angrier at me for not calling on Thanksgiving or for calling today."

"Yeah, well, Ramón and me, we thought maybe
you forgot. Ramón got all bent out of shape about it,
wouldn't hardly eat any of his dinner, and later on he
went out to hang with these kids *tía* Clarinda doesn't
like so much." As soon as he'd said that, Jorge
screwed up his lips into a cynical smile. *Doesn't like*

so much was a real understatement when it came to what *tía* Clarinda thought of Ramón's new friends.

Jorge's father wasn't slow. "He's not getting with a gang, is he?" Jorge imagined his father's face darkening like a thunderhead. "God damn it, what's he trying to pull? Doesn't he see what happens to kids like that?"

Jorge shrugged, as if his father could see that through the phone lines. "I guess he's gotta. You remember Domingo Sandoval, guy from my old school? He got shot in a drive-by last week, right downstairs on the corner."

"*Dios!* Dead?"

Again Jorge shrugged. "I dunno. I guess not. There wasn't any funeral."

He heard his father mumble a long string of oaths in Spanish, and then: "God, I'm glad I made the decision."

"What decision?" Jorge could feel his heart start to beat faster, louder. It echoed in his ears like a drum, so clamorous that he was sure his father had to hear it too.

Papi's voice turned jolly, teasing. "Don't get nosy; you'll find out soon enough. I called to say that I'm coming down to see you boys on Sunday. I figure that's far enough from Thanksgiving that Clarinda won't think I'm using the holiday to try weaseling my way back into *la familia*."

Jorge's throat narrowed. "Papi, we—you and me and Ramón—we are *familia*."

"Tell that to your aunt. No, never mind, I'll tell her myself when I see her. I'm tired of living like this, Jorge. What good is a clean life if it's empty? I can't blame your aunt for feeling like she does about me— I *was* a *sinvergüenza*. So many times I promised her I'd get clean, so many times I broke that promise. Now that I've finally done it, she doesn't believe me. Well, it's time I made her believe. I can't wait for Christmas—not if what you're telling me about Ramón is true. I have to do something *now*, for him, for all of us. You tell your aunt I'm coming Sunday early, before Mass. Does she still drag you boys to the ten o'clock?"

"Yeah, still," Jorge replied. He didn't add that Ramón always managed to vanish when it was time to leave the apartment for church, and that he often joined him. "But if you're coming all the way from Vermont, how will you get here that early?"

His father's laughter cradled him in warmth. "By starting out the night before. I'll be there with time to spare so I can put on my good suit and go to Mass with all of you. Then I'm going to stand up in the middle of the church, and I'm finally going to make my promise before God. That way, Clarinda will *have* to know it's for real, and then—" He inhaled deeply and let out his breath in a ragged sigh. "—and then she won't be able to tell me no."

Jorge didn't ask *No? No to what?* He knew: Can I have my sons back, Clarinda? Can I have them back right now, today, this minute, with no objections from you, no threat of calling a lawyer or Child Services or the cops? Have I earned back the right to be their Papi? Clarinda, will you stand in my way when I want to repair the past?

After he hung up the phone, Jorge went into his room. He had to be alone. The magic couldn't work if he tried to call it up when other people were around. He didn't say a word to Ramón, not even when his little brother asked him what was up, why was he acting so weird, why hadn't he called him to the phone to talk with Papi too? Lucky for Jorge the phone sounded off again right then—Papi calling back, probably just as confused as Ramón because Jorge had hung up on him like that—so Jorge's magic caught a break.

Alone in his room—Ramón on the phone with Papi, *tía* Clarinda still chattering through her prayers—Jorge shut the door and hooked the back of a chair under the knob. It wasn't much of a barricade, but it was the best and only thing he could do to buy a little privacy. There were no locks on any doors in the apartment, not even the bathroom. *Tía* Clarinda said she knew what people got away with when there were locks.

Jorge didn't turn on the overhead fixture, just the little bedside lamp. It was an old-fashioned thing he'd found at a Salvation Army thrift store. He bought it because the base was painted with a forest scene— pine trees and a cabin, a deer—and because the yellow parchment shade cast a golden glow that reminded him of the birch grove. By that enchanted light, Jorge cast his spell.

He stood in the middle of the floor, his eyes closed, his arms outstretched, and strove to call on something greater than himself. He ached to harness all the undirected yearning in his heart, to turn scattered dreams, wishes and desires into a spear instead of a cloud. He believed in all the magic he'd ever read, and he was sure that if he focused his thoughts, if he gritted his teeth and furrowed his brow and knotted his hands into fists and made all the outward signs of concentration, he'd find the power to summon *something*.

Something . . . what? He wasn't sure. It would have to be something stronger than himself, because alone he was weak. Proof of his weakness surrounded him. He didn't have the freedom to walk down certain streets. He starved for the strength to excel in school without fearing the shoving hands and the taunting voices—*What, man, straight A's? You kissing up to Teach? You think you better than us?* He saw his little brother slipping away bit by bit into the dark heart of the city and he craved the power to pull him back.

But most of all, he wanted to summon something old and wise and strong enough to work the greatest magic: something that would soften *tía* Clarinda's heart, something that would bring their *familia* together instead of breaking it into smaller and smaller fragments, something that would bring his Papi back to him, bring all of them home.

So Jorge stood in the middle of his bedroom floor,

under the painted canopy of leaves, and sent out a spell and a prayer and a cry of the heart. He sent it out of a body as tense as a drawn longbow, sent it flying into the rustling shadows, into the unseen places beyond the paper trees.

When he couldn't hold his body in that strained, rigid posture any longer, he crumpled to his haunches, gulping down deep breaths of air.

Stupid, he thought, a self-mocking smile on his lips. *What do you have to go and do stuff like that for, huh? Who do you think you are, Harry Potter? Ah, well, so what? Not like anyone saw you, thank God. No worse than* tía *Clarinda and her candles.*

He stood tall, stretching the kinks out of his back before unbarricading the door. Just as he was about to leave the bedroom, ready to return to his Monopoly game (and determined *not* to let Ramón get away with any more cheating) he paused: *What the hell, who knows? Maybe it works. I guess I'll see.*

Sunday morning began long before the sun came up. It started the second that the hands of *tía* Clarinda's old-fashioned wind-up alarm clock ticked one beat past midnight. Jorge lay on his back, staring up into the leaves he couldn't possibly see in the dark, and tried to stay awake, tried to imagine that Papi was just as restless and eager as he was for the *real* start of Sunday morning to come. Where was Papi now, what was he doing? Loading up his car, starting it rough in the chill just-past-midnight darkness, turning down the same county road that Jorge still remembered from October? What did it look like now, that road? No more splashes of red and yellow and bronze, no lingering touch of green. The trees must be bare, branches like black craze-marks across a dropped china plate. Jorge dreamed he could see the narrow path that Papi's headlights traced as the car flew down the road to the distant city, and then Jorge simply dreamed.

Through the fog of slumber he thought he heard a

distant ringing. He knew he heard a scream. He sat straight up in his bed just as the door banged open and Ramón ran in, his eyes wide and crazy-looking in the watery dawnlight seeping in through the window.

"He's *dead*, Jorge, he's *dead*! Papi's *dead*!"

Dead and *dead* and *dead*, over and over, merciless and unrelenting. The words struck Jorge hard in heart and belly and brain. The blows fell, and his sobbing soul clamored no-no-no until at last it broke into a shrill wail that scaled the icy heavens to oblivion.

While Ramón babbled on about phone calls from the police, narrow roads, freezing rain, a car gone out of control, crushed like an empty beer can against the mountainside, while *tía* Clarinda shook and shrieked and brought everyone on their floor running to see what had happened, Jorge got out of bed. He went into the kitchen and very calmly, very coldly took a hammer from the junk drawer and smashed every single one of the glassed-in candles that *tía* Clarinda used to beseech the Blessed Virgin for her brother's punishment.

Then he went back into his room and methodically tore the trees from his walls, scattering their crumpled images from his window. He watched them drift down into the street like giant flakes of snow until a sudden gust of wind came up and blew them all away. He saw them climb the sky, race past his open window so close that he could have reached out and grabbed back a handful of them from the abyss. He scowled and slammed the window shut, never realizing that the November wind blew summer-warm, or that it carried on its wings the scent of green.

At the funeral, everyone told him that he was the man of the house now. They had a good day for the burial—everyone said that, too. The weather was cold but clear, the sunlight keen as razors. Jorge watched as they lowered the sharp-edged box into the sharp-edged hole. Someone gave him a clod of dirt to throw onto the coffin. He dropped it in like a soiled tissue.

Ramón wouldn't even do that much. He threw the earth as far away from him as he could, and then he ran off, sprinting through the forest of tombstones. Some of the cousins tried to catch him, but he was too fast and they gave up. He didn't come home until well after dark, smelling of smoke and sourness, looking as if he'd walked all the way back to Manhattan from Queens.

Tía Clarinda was in hysterics. She was being attended to by friends and neighbors and *familia* who were all more than ready to tell Ramón what a *sinvergüenza* he was for putting his aunt through such an ordeal on such a day. Ramón never said a word. Jorge watched as his little brother turned his back on all of them and went into his room. He didn't bother to slam the door; his silence shut them all out better than any big, melodramatic gesture. Jorge watched, and Jorge felt as through Ramón had become a handful of graveyard earth that turned to sand when he tried to grasp it, sand that fled through his fingers like water, like air.

Days trickled past, became Christmas, which the brothers refused to celebrate despite *tía* Clarinda's shrill insistence that Papi would have wanted it that way. He was Papi to her again now. She called him that whenever she spoke about him, which was fre quently, the way some people invoked a saint's name or how Ramón's friends used "*that* word" all the time. She couldn't get enough of saying, "Jorge, you look more like your Papi every day" or "Ramón, don't give me that dirty look; what would Papi say?" It was as if their father had been born without any other name and that the letters carved on the blunt, gray tombstone were runes, an alien language, something belonging to a stranger.

Jorge and Ramón wandered through the days like children lost in an autumn forest with all the dead leaves tumbling down around them, burying them alive. Each went his own way, and when they happened to run into one another in the apartment or on

the street, it was like a pair of billiard balls clicking
together by chance, then rolling apart. The winter
deepened, the cold lost the soft touch of snow and
became ice, diamond-bright, diamond-hard. Jorge felt
like the days and the streets and the blunt, gray tombstone, all cold to the core.

One night, he dreamed of the birch grove. At first
he thought that he was only drowsing, that the golden
glow of his bedside lamp was deceiving him. Then he
remembered, in the furry-minded way that dreamers
do, that he'd thrown that lamp down the incinerator
chute the day before his father's funeral and replaced
it with a shiny black gooseneck light, a serviceable
desktop clone like a thousand others. Then the memory of lamplight flew out of his head, a cluster of warm
yellow leaves brushed across his face, and he stood
suddenly alone in a place of wonders.

The trees surrounded him, circled him like dancers,
embraced him with tall, white trunks and gold-leafed
branches. He had traveled back to the place but also
to the time, the first time he'd stepped into the birch
grove. On that vanished October morning he'd joined
Papi for breakfast while Ramón still hugged his pillows. His father suggested they go for a little walk, to
give Ramón time to wake up. No sense in making
pancakes that were only going to get cold.

Jorge went along because . . . well, because why
not? At first he thought his father was just taking him
for a random stroll, leaf-peeping along the autumn
paths that led into the hills. But there was something
in Papi's purposeful stride that soon made him realize
they were heading for a particular destination.

I knew you'd like this place, Papi whispered in his
ear, in his dream. His voice was the wind blowing
through river reeds. *As soon as I found it, I knew I
had to bring you here.*

What about Ramón? Jorge heard his own voice hiss
inside his head as he laid one hand on the cool, moon-
bright bark of a birch tree.

Ah, Ramón . . . Papi's voice drifted to the melancholy edge of silence. *This place would mean nothing to him. He's too young, yet; he doesn't see. His eyes are on other things. Flash. Bling. Glare. He'd come here for my sake, if I asked him, but he doesn't know that he must come here for his own.*

Why, Papi? The phantom voice inside Jorge's head was lonely and small. *For his own sake how?*

A great rustling shook the birch leaves, like a lion sending a shiver through his tawny pelt to cast off flies. Jorge saw that the black and gray marks on the birch bark had begun to move under his hands. They writhed like inchworms, humping up, stretching out, touching and twining and running together until a face emerged from the curve of the living tree.

He thought that it was Papi's face because it had to be. Who else would speak to him out of the heart of the birch grove that they alone had shared on that lost October day? But the eyes that opened were too wide, too fiery, the nose too broad, the hair too thick and tightly curled. The lips were full-fleshed as mushroom caps, and when they parted to speak, Jorge knew he stood before the power he'd pursued for so long from within his fragile paper shrine. Here was the heart of the woodland, every woodland, palm and piñon, poplar and pine. The forest in its absolute life-giving, life-taking sovereignty smoldered behind the almost-human mask burgeoning from the birch trunk. Jorge was too rapt to be afraid.

The cool bite of autumn air wafted away. A rich, thick moisture enveloped Jorge's body. It smelled of torrid sun and healing rain. Jungle vines heavy with red trumpet flowers tumbled down its cheeks, feathery emerald ferns sprouted from its eyebrows. Birds and bats, lizards without number, clear-eyed lemurs, jewel-skinned snakes, spiders like puffs of eiderdown and all the countless sparks of life that sheltered in the rainforests peered out at Jorge from its hair.

But it was still his Papi's voice he heard when the

lips, wet with sap and rain and dew, spoke: *Life,* it said. *To bring your brother life, he must be brought to me.*

And then he was awake. He sat up and shook his head. The glowing red numbers on his bedside clock let him know it was only a little after three in the morning, so he cursed the clock for telling him something he didn't want to know and went back to sleep.

On the day Jorge finally bought two cans of thick, white paint to blot out the canopy of leaves on his bedroom ceiling, his little brother Ramón was caught stealing from the Korean grocer on the next block. *Tía* Clarinda's cry of despair hit Jorge's ears while he was trying to pry the lid off the first paint can. When he heard her, he was kneeling on the newspapers he'd spread out on the floor, so it took him a little longer than usual to clamber to his feet. By the time he ran into the kitchen, *tía* Clarinda was hanging up the phone. Her hands were trembling as she threw on her coat, and she wept and babbled while fumbling with the buttons. Jorge had to ask her to repeat the story at least three times before he understood what was going on. Then she was out the door, heading for the police station.

Alone in the apartment, he wandered back into his room feeling hollow and cold. *This is how it starts,* a voice whispered. *This is how everything changes, with a very small beginning. The ground doesn't drop out from under your feet all at once. It slips away softly, pebble by pebble. At first you hardly notice it, and by the time you do, the pebbles have turned to sand. There's nothing you can do to stop it, then, because to hold back sand you need strength, power, magic. And you have none.*

Even though he was alone in the apartment, he closed the door to his room behind him, shutting out the world, even the world that held his *familia.* He squatted beside the stubborn paint can, slipped a screwdriver under the edge of the lid, and pushed down.

The lid flew clear across the room, spattering the furniture with driblets of white paint like pigeon droppings. *Tía* Clarinda would have a fit when she saw what he'd done, but Jorge was too deeply sunk in air like ice, like deep water, to feel anything about it at all.

He stirred the paint thoroughly and poured it into the roller tray. He ran the fluffy yellow roller through his hand, feeling the spring of the fleecy head against his palm, before moving it slowly back and forth, back and forth through the puddled paint in the slanted tray. Three times up, three times back, a little ritual. He picked it up and looked at the ceiling, deciding where to begin.

A lizard looked back. Red eyes in a green face, it stared at him unblinking, then vanished, the whisk of its tail stirring the painted leaves. They moved slowly, with an underwater grace, a movement subtle enough to belong to dreams, sure enough so that there was no way Jorge could lie to himself that it had not happened.

"My eyes," he muttered, bowing his head and covering them with one hand. "Man, I must be tired."

But when he opened them again and looked down into the white paint eddying back and forth in the tray, the forest face looked back. Skin dark as polished teakwood rose out of the white, white sea, trailing tendrils of hair that were the perfect black of moonless midnight. Full lips parted, tiny rivulets of smothering whiteness trickling away. The eyes opened last of all. They drew him in, into their depths, into the heart of the forest. Jorge's chest filled with a last gasp of earthly breath, and he tumbled in.

The forest was all around him, speaking life, throbbing life, singing life and using all its power to shout *No!* to dead stone, cold concrete, the city's icy prison. Jorge sank willingly into the endless embrace of the trees, thick with vines and flowers. Small frogs like slivers of gemstone clung to the shimmering bark with tiny suckered feet, peeping their song, *coquí, coquí!*

Butterflies with iridescent wings of blue and gold, heart's-blood red and velvet black stirred the dense, moist sweetness of the air.

Jorge looked down. His jeans were gone, his shorts, his shoes and socks. Barefoot, he could feel the soil beneath his toes, the uncounted layers of dead and dying green that gave back fresh life to the eternal forest. A twist of beaten barkcloth covered him, a necklace of bone and stone and gold chinked at his neck, and in his hands he held a warrior's shield bright as the evening star, a warrior's spear with a serpent of hammered gold twining around the shaft.

Oxossi . . . The whisper was no more than a breeze, no less than his father's voice. *Oxossi, forest-lord, warrior, hear my prayer. Lord Oxossi, walk the paths of life, bring my son back from the way of death. Strength of the forest, power of life, protector, bring him back, bring him home.*

Oxossi . . .

Jorge stood in the heart of the forest wearing bark and bone and his one true name. He stood in the skin of the forest god, brown and strong as the trees themselves, as the warm soil that fed them, as the arms of a father who could not leave his sons even now, not even from beneath the brown lid of a coffin and the brown earth of a grave.

Oxossi, Jorge, mijito, *hear your father's voice! My son, my master, know what you must do.*

His feet pounded out a strong and steady rhythm as he ran down the forest path. Vines and branches whipped themselves across his face and chest, tried to hold him. He spoke a word in the forest lord's tongue and they shrank back, fell aside to let him pass unhindered. The air grew keen with the stink of predators, a biting smell that filled the forest lord's eyes with rage red as embers, as flowers, as blood. *Have they dared to come here without my permission? Here, into my land, my kingdom? Have they* dared?

His nostrils flared; he followed the sharp and bitter stench that cut through the living scents of his world like the passage of a bullet tearing flesh. He ran on and it grew stronger, ranker, until he broke from the green shadows into a grove of alien gold.

Ramón was waiting. Ramón, his brother, stood in the center of the golden grove that had somehow been lifted whole from the hills of Vermont and settled here, in the midst of pure jungle. The stippled white trunks of the birch trees looked frail as wheat stalks beside the massive boles of the forest giants, but Oxossi was lord of all forests, even this one, even here, and when he laid his dark hand on the pallid bark, he drew the same strength from it, the same worship.

A harsh sound tore the air. Leaves rustled softly, then loud and louder, branches swished and snapped, tree trunks groaned before they broke. The beasts shouldered their way into the sacred grove to reach their prey. Jorge stared out at them through Oxossi's eyes. He could not name them or say what manner of monsters they were, not even if his soul depended on the answer. Their eyes shone with copper light, their fangs were black at the roots and as bloodstained as their talons, the colors of their ragged pelts shifted before his eyes from the parched yellow of desert sand to the scarlet blaze of sunset.

But they had the faces of men. Jorge saw the bullies from school, the dealers who didn't care how many lives they gobbled up, the sneering bosses who doled out dead-end jobs, and treated you like dirt, and told you to be grateful, the gang-bangers whose smiles offered the promise of belonging but whose eyes were dead. Every one of them was thirsting for his brother's blood.

"Ramón!" Jorge cried, and his voice, at least, was still his own. "Ramón, come to me!" He held out his spear and the beasts cringed away from its shadow.

But Ramón did not come. Ramón stood stiffly in the center of the sacred grove, frozen with more than fear. His eyes flickered with the same cold, coppery light as the beasts that stalked him, and his mouth was a thin, hard line.

"Why should I listen to you?" he called out, and
the beasts began to pace around him in a slow, encircling dance. "For what? More promises? More lies?
We have *nothing*! No respect, no strength, no one to
teach us how to be men! I'm tired of being just another kid, always afraid, always helpless. That changes,
hermano. That changes *now*." He stamped his foot,
and the beasts wove their pattern closer around him,
their shaggy shoulders brushing his legs. Their lips
parted in an awful parody of human laughter.

"I'm tired of being the one who's afraid," Ramón
went on. "There's only one way to be on top, and I'm
going to be there. Try and stop me if you dare!"

"On top?" Jorge echoed, lowering his spear. "On
top of what?"

"The world," Ramón answered, grinning. His face
grew thinner, his nose and mouth elongating into an
animal's snout. His fangs were pure white, still free of
any stain. The others crowded closer still, and one of
them reared onto its hind legs, tottering like a dancing
dog. A feather of flame burned on its brow, but the
flame crackled black and gray, a fire that was already ashes.

The forest lord, the master of the trees and every
life that dwelled in the gentle shelter of their shadows,
Oxossi who was Jorge who was dreaming, saw his little
brother stretch out one hand. It was still a child's
hand, but it was reaching for things no child should
touch, for heartlessness and hate and willful ignorance,
for a pit that was deeper than any grave. Ramón's
hand reached for the black flame that leaped and
hissed like a cobra on the monster's brow, and if he
touched it, Jorge knew he would be lost forever.

Oxossi's battle cry shook the birch leaves from their
fragile branches, made the earth crack and shift under-
foot in the holy place where his father's spirit dwelled.
Oxossi's spear flew like thought, like love, and struck
Ramón's hand clean through the palm. The circling
creatures threw back their heads and howled, smelling
blood, but Oxossi was among them before they could

draw another breath. He called his spear back to his hand with a single word and he used it valiantly. He struck the beasts back, down, away from his little brother. Wherever one of them fell dying, a tree erupted from the earth, swallowing up darkness with living light. Soon only one monster remained.

It was the flame-bearer, a creature with a fanged face like a skull. The plume of black fire arched and spat. A single spark touched Oxossi's shining shield and devoured it, an ember popped and turned Oxossi's magic spear to cinders.

Lord of woods, lord of worlds, why do you stand between me and what is mine? The creature's voice echoed wickedly inside Jorge's head. *Even you can never hope to hold this child back from a path of his own choosing. Without your weapons in your hands, even you must fail and fall. You call to him, but see! He comes to me.*

It was true. Jorge saw his little brother's eyes fixed on the black flame as if it held nothing but joyful promise. Illusion and temptation sang to Ramón from the killing fire's core, and their song cut him off from true hope as surely as if they'd set an iron wall around him. The instant that the boy touched the doom-bright flame, it would own him, he would be lost.

As his little brother reached out his still-bleeding hand to the black flame, Jorge leaped forward on Oxossi's strong, bare feet and plunged his own hand into the blackness, through the killing fire, deep into the monster's grinning skull. The creature screamed, but Jorge's scream, Oxossi's scream, drowned out the hideous sound. The birch grove shook as the pale trees split from crowns to roots and a great voice, filled with pride and sorrow and love rang out above them, crying, *My sons, my beloved sons,* mijitos! *Stand strong against the enemy, be brave against the monstrous thing that once stole me from you!*

It was the last thing that Jorge took with him as he plummeted into darkness.

*   *   *

"Hey, man? Jorge? You awake?"

Jorge heard his brother calling to him through all the layers of his dreams. He swam back into the waking world, sat up slowly, realized he was lying on the floor of his bedroom with Ramón squatting beside him. He managed a feeble smile.

"Yeah, I'm awake," he said. "And you're back from the police station. Man, I oughta kick your skinny ass. Ripping off the grocer's, giving *tía* Clarinda a heart attack, yeah, that was real good, you stupid little—"

"Huh?" Ramón stood up, looking genuinely confused. "What station? What ripoff? Where you getting this stuff from, *hermano*? You fall off of the bed or something and hit your head? How come you're lying on the floor, huh?"

"You saying—?" Jorge stopped himself, touched his own face with his left hand as if trying to remember what he looked like without resorting to a mirror. Oxossi's mask was gone. He shook his head and sighed deeply.

"Hey, no fooling, something wrong?" Ramón sounded worried. "You want me to get *tía* Clarinda or what?"

"No," Jorge said softly. "I don't want that." *I want to know I'm not going crazy,* he thought. *I want to know why someone's put the world on rewind. I want—*

"What I want is a little help up," he told his brother.

"Sure, man. What's a brother for?" Ramón grinned and held out his hand.

Only Jorge saw in his brother's palm the thick scar of the spear's bright, healing passage. Only Jorge saw how the green lizard that crouched across it winked its ruby eyes once, twice, three times before it vanished, leaving footprints like a trail of fallen leaves. Only Jorge felt, as he took his brother's hand, how the forest god's strength closed around them, bearing the endless warmth and life of their father's love.

THE THING IN THE WOODS

Harry Turtledove

TIM'S armies chased Geoffrey's across the game board on the floor of Geoffrey's room. One more good throw of the dice and he would win. As he reached for the red plastic cubes, though, he noticed the full moon shining through Geoffrey's window. Startled, he looked at his watch.

"Uh-oh," he said. "I'm late. My mom's gonna skin me."

"We'll call it a draw, then," Geoffrey said happily. "I would have stopped you at the river anyway."

Yeah, sure you would, Tim thought, but he was too late even to stay and argue about it. He grabbed his coat off a chair and hurried for the front door. Geoffrey followed, still going on about how well he'd played.

Tim hopped onto his bike. "See you in school tomorrow." He couldn't resist a parting shot: "You still going to need help with your math?"

"Yeah, I guess so." In bright moonlight, the dirty look Geoffrey gave him for being reminded seemed especially sweet.

Chuckling to himself, Tim was about to ride off when something in the woods back of Geoffrey's house made a horrible noise. Time almost jumped out of his skin. "Wh—What was that?" he said. "A coyote?"

"Maybe," Geoffrey said. "Maybe it was a were-wolf, too."

"Don't be stupid. There's no such things as" —the horrible noise came again—"werewolves." The hair on the back of Tim's neck tried to stand up.

"Whatever you say. I'd ride fast if I were you, though." The gloating tone in Geoffrey's voice made Tim wish he'd never brought up the math homework, especially since Geoffrey helped him almost as much as the other way around.

Tim lived only a few blocks east of Geoffrey. He pedaled as if he were trying to catch up with the long, black moonshadow that stretched out ahead of him. When he was halfway home, he heard the howl from the woods again. He was so nervous, it sounded to him as if it came from about three inches behind him. He yelped and made his legs go even faster, which wasn't easy.

He had never seen anything so welcome as his house, even if his mother did come down on him like a ton of bricks when he went in. "You still have your homework and nine million chores to do before you go to sleep," she said, the way he'd known she would. "And you need a bath."

"Okay, Mom."

He gave in so easily, she stopped being mad and started being worried. "Are you all right, Tim? Did something happen over at Geoffrey's?"

"Yeah, I'm okay. No, nothing happened." That wasn't quite true, and Tim knew it. He hesitated, then went on, "Mom?"

"What is it, Timmy?" She hadn't called him Timmy in a long time.

He hesitated again, feeling dumb, but finally blurted out, "Mom, there really aren't any werewolves, are there?" Once he'd said it, he felt even dumber, but if he couldn't be dumb around his own mom, who could he be dumb around?

"Werewolves?" she said. "What ever gave you that idea?"

He'd surprised her, he saw. That wasn't easy. He explained what had happened over at Geoffrey's house. By the time he was done, even he was laughing at himself.

"Well," his mom said, laughing, too, "I certainly think it was a coyote. I've never seen a werewolf except in the movies, and I don't think anyone else has, either. All right?"

"Sure, Mom." Talking about it made him feel a lot better. "Boy, it sure sounded scary, though."

"I believe you. Go do your homework anyway. Didn't you tell me you have a math test tomorrow?"

"Oh, Mom!" She *would* remember! Then she gave him a hug, and he said, "Oh, Mom!" again, in a different tone of voice.

"Go on, now. Remember, you still have to take that bath."

He went. But even when he was dividing fractions and plotting points on graph paper, part of his mind still heard that dreadful, unearthly howling. He rarely wondered if his mom was wrong, but this was one of those times.

When he and Geoffrey came out of math class together, Geoffrey asked, "How do you think you did?"

"I don't know. Not too bad, I guess." Tim paused. "What did you get for number eight?"

"Which one was that?"

"Five twelfths divided by seven eighths."

"Let me think." After close to a minute, Geoffrey answered, "Oh yeah, that one. I almost didn't remember to reduce it to lowest terms. It's ten twenty-firsts."

"Uh-oh. That's not anything like what I got. I got thirty-five ninety-sixths."

This time it was Geoffrey's turn to say, "Uh-oh." They both put some worried thought into the problem. Then Geoffrey said, "I know what you did wrong. You forgot to invert the divisor before you multiplied."

Tim slammed his hand against a bank of lockers, hard enough to hurt. "You're right." He scowled at

Geoffrey. "It's your fault, you and your miserable werewolf. I couldn't study straight last night."

"Don't blame me because you're dumb," Geoffrey said loftily.

Tim shoved him. He shoved back. It might have gone further than that, but behind them someone with a deep voice said, "Boys, you don't really want to go visit the vice-principal, do you?"

"No, Mr. Tepesh," they said together.

"Good. Cut it out, then." The wood-shop teacher walked on by.

"Boy, I ought to—" Tim said, but the moment where there could have been a fight had passed. "You and your miserable werewolf," he repeated.

"Well, there's nothing to worry about for the next month, anyway," Geoffrey said. "Not till the next full moon." He let out a howl that sounded nothing like the one they'd heard the night before.

"Will you shut up, for Pete's sake?" Tim usually didn't lose his temper easily, but he felt his right hand, the one that wasn't carrying his books, curl into a fist.

But Geoffrey said, "All right, already, all right. Did I tell you my dad's going to the ballgame tomorrow? Some people have all the luck—we'll be stuck in school."

"Yeah," Tim said. It blew over, as quarrels often do. Pretty soon the two of them were laughing about the way their math teacher's saggy arm muscles flopped like fish out of water whenever she wrote on the blackboard.

A couple of days later, Tim went over to Geoffrey's house after school. He kept a careful eye on his watch. He also trounced Geoffrey at their war game, so badly that it was done fifteen minutes before he had to leave. He was feeling pretty smug as he climbed onto his bike.

Then that horrible howl came from the woods. Tim flinched. He couldn't help it. Geoffrey noticed—*he would*, Tim thought. If he'd just laughed or something, it wouldn't have been too bad. But instead he said, "You're probably safe this time, Tim."

"What do you mean, probably?"

"Well, the moon's not full, and so—"

"Oh, be quiet. Why don't you just go to the moon?"

Geoffrey laughed then, which was a lot meaner than if he'd done it at first. And he howled after Tim when he rode away. Tim thought about turning back and knocking some sense into his friend's thick head, but he decided Geoffrey was too dumb for that to do much good. He kept riding.

Over the next few weeks, things almost got back to normal between them. Almost, because Geoffrey wouldn't let the whole werewolf business alone. Every so often, he'd make panting noises in the hallway at school, or check his forehead with his hand, as if to see whether he was getting hairy. After a while, Tim stopped paying any attention to it. If Geoffrey wanted to be weird, that was his problem. They were still buddies.

"Two days of freedom," Geoffrey said as school let out for the weekend. "Can you come over tomorrow night? We can play till late, and I've got a new attack figured out that'll knock your ears off."

"Don't you wish," Tim said. He waited for Geoffrey to make one of his stupid werewolf jokes and get it out of his system—the moon would be full again tomorrow night. But Geoffrey just stood there, waiting to see what he'd say. Maybe he was finally bored with werewolves. *About time*, Tim thought. He said, "Sure, I'll come. About seven?"

"Yeah, okay. We'll be done eating by then."

Tim spent the night studying the game board. If Geoffrey was silly enough to tell him he had something new up his sleeve, Tim wouldn't waste a chance to work on figuring out what it was. Maybe Geoffrey would go through the foothills this time, instead of around them. He was welcome to try. Tim was positive a few tanks posted in the right spots would smash that move before it got started.

Or maybe . . . Tim was still figuring angles when it got to be time for him to go to sleep. Whatever Geoffrey was thinking of pulling, he expected he could handle it. Geoffrey talked better than he played.

The moon was at Tim's back as he rode over to Geoffrey's the next night. That way he didn't have to look at it, but he knew it was there, fat and round and gleaming, like a big gold coin in the sky. However bright it was, it didn't light up the woods back of Geoffrey's place. They stayed black and foreboding. *Anything might live there*, Tim thought nervously. *Anything*.

Stay cool, he told himself as he pulled up in front of Geoffrey's house. *Just because something* might *live there doesn't mean it* does. That line of reasoning would have been a lot more comforting if a howl hadn't come just as he stepped up onto Geoffrey's front porch.

He almost turned around and jumped back on his bike. But what if Geoffrey was watching through the curtains? He'd never let him forget it. Tim made himself walk toward Geoffrey's door. Even if something dreadful did live in the woods, it hadn't shown any signs of wanting to come out.

He rang the bell. Geoffrey took his time about answering. "Come on," Tim muttered. The thing in the woods howled again. It sounded closer. "Come *on*!" Tim said out loud.

The door opened. A werewolf sprang out at him.

It had fur and claws and enormous yellow teeth, but it walked like a man. To his terrified eyes, it seemed nine feet tall. It howled right in his face. He screamed and ran.

The werewolf chased him. He could hear its feet pounding after him, could hear its vicious laughter. Laughter? He was almost to his bike when that finally registered. He could imagine werewolves doing lots of things, but laughing wasn't one of them.

He turned around. The werewolf wasn't chasing him any more. It was leaning against the house, laughing its head off. As soon as Tim stopped being panicked, he recognized its voice. That was no werewolf—that was Geoffrey!

"You—you—you—" Tim looked for something bad enough to call Geoffrey. He couldn't think of anything. He jumped on him instead.

Geoffrey was bigger, but Tim was furious. Besides, Geoffrey had trouble seeing out of the eyeholes in his werewolf suit, and the gloves with claws on them would hardly fold into fists. On the other hand, the thick, shaggy fur on the suit helped pad him against Tim's blows.

After a few seconds, Geoffrey didn't even try to hit back. He was still laughing too hard. He just covered up as best he could. "I'm sorry, Tim," he got out at last. "I really am. But you—ouch!—should have seen your face."

"I ought to kick your—" But then Tim was laughing too. He didn't want to, but he couldn't seem to help it. He and Geoffrey rolled on Geoffrey's front lawn. Tim finally sat up and picked a couple of blades of grass out of his hair. "Do you really have a new attack planned, or were you just luring me over so you could scare me to death?"

"Wait a second." Geoffrey pulled off the fur and rubber werewolf head. "Whew. Stuffy in there. No, I don't have anything new figured out. Why?"

"Because," Tim said grimly, "now that I'm here, I'm gonna drive a stake right through your heart."

"You don't do that with werewolves," Geoffrey said.

"You're no werewolf. There's no such thing as werewolves." As if on cue, the thing in the woods let out another howl. Tim couldn't have cared less. He glared at Geoffrey. "Right?"

"Right." Geoffrey got up. "Come on. Let's see how tough you really are."

"Okay." They went into Geoffrey's house together.

The next Friday night, Geoffrey went to Tim's to play their wargame and sleep over. This time, Geoffrey *had* worked out something new, and Tim had all he could do to hold his own. The game swayed back and forth. First one of them had the edge, then the other. Tim didn't realize how long they'd been playing until his mom came into the room.

"Come on, boys," she said. "It's getting late."

"Oh, Mom," Tim said.

"Don't you 'Oh, Mom' me."

"A little longer?" he pleaded.

She shook her head. "The sun will be rising soon—time for young vampires to sleep. You two don't want to be caught out of your coffins when it comes up, do you?"

Tim and Geoffrey sighed and exchanged resigned looks. "No," they answered. What else could they say?

"Well, come on then. Please don't make me wait around—don't forget I have to have time to get into my own coffin after you do, and you still have to wash your faces and brush your fangs."

"Oh, Mom," Tim said again, but he knew it was hopeless. He got up and headed for the bathroom. Geoffrey followed him.

THE STAR CATS

Charles Edgar Quinn

IT looked like the funeral procession of a giant.
The great, flat platform with its multitude of tank tracks, the largest ground vehicle ever built, crept inch by weary inch under the heat of the Florida sun. The Titan rocket that it was bearing, that lay across its whole length, quivered slightly with the vibrations of all the different engines and all the many sets of tracks and wheels; faint but noticeable waves ran up and down the mighty vessel with its movement. Even a statue this big would have swayed with the wind.

A scattered remnant of people watched from all sides as the spaceship crawled not toward, but away from the launchpad. Camera crews from the various networks and newspapers worked in cliquish bands; many set up their equipment directly in front of the huge truck. This juggernaut was definitely moving slowly enough to avoid. The others, those actually dressed in work clothes, milled about idly and uneasily, their work done, or rather, left forever unfinished. They didn't look at each other, or if they did, they spoke briefly and then parted, as if embarrassed by the one metaphor that had occurred to them all.

In front of one of the old blast bunkers, a young woman and a middle-aged man sat feeding a milling band of cats from a small bag of treats.

"Had this party once," the man said. "We catered this six-foot sandwich with everything, nobody there keeping kosher, you know, and the only place to put it was on this table that had to be illuminated by this one spotlight recessed into the ceiling, no other lamps nearby. And just as I'm thinking, jeez this is creepy, somebody says, hey, everybody, come look at the spread. So they come in, and just naturally form a line and walk past. The viewing of the sandwich. No flowers, please, donations can be made to Subway."

"Well, it is a funeral, of course," the woman said. She looked down quickly, as if searching for a distraction. A huge black cat batted and hissed to either side, and jumped for the bag.

"Hey, greedy gut, there's enough for everybody." She looked at the assembly of cats. "Well, maybe not." There were at least two dozen cats converging on them from all directions, some circling warily around the rocket; black, white, orange, gray, calico, tortoiseshell, long hairs, short hairs. They strutted with great aplomb, and there was no telling the long-feral from those who were only recently lost or abandoned.

"Where do you think they all came from?" the man asked.

She shook her blond head. "Nobody really knows. Dogs are just wolves that've got used to cadging meals, but cats were obviously developed, deliberately and carefully bred. But from what, we don't know. Or why." She handed the bag of treats to the man and pulled the big tomcat onto her lap. The cat made it clear he would have preferred to follow the treats. "The Egyptians did it, that's the old story, though it's doubtful it happened recently. There's something knowing about cats, and something—lost, exiled." She stroked the black cat's muzzle, to approving purrs. "As if they remember who created them, and why, and only people have forgotten."

The man leaned a bit too far forward during this, listed just a bit too raptly. "I meant these cats in particular," he said, smiling.

She laughed in embarrassment. "From ship's cats, if you're to believe the locals. Unwanted kittens tossed out onto the docks after voyages, no more cats needed here, thank you. Spread out and went to work on the rats amid the docks. Moved into the gantries when they started launching rockets here. They seem to know the routine. You never find dead cats around the launch pads after the takeoffs."

"They'll be even safer from now on," the man said quietly. "And lots of rats to eat. It'll look like some damned J. G. Ballard story, with the jungle growing in over the wreck of the space age."

"Might have been different if the space age hadn't been run by governments. Leave the risks to anyone willing to take them, the rewards to anyone—"

"Couldn't have that, my dear." He was smiling, rather bitterly. "Daddy knows best. Daddy blows up cities, Daddy culls our paycheck. If we didn't fight for our liberty to explore, we didn't deserve it." He looked out over the water. "You can't get home by the old highway. It's falling into the ocean. There isn't a major infrastructure that isn't rotting. All our money gets taken to build weapons with nobody to use them against. Money to keep people from working. To keep farmers from growing cheap food. To keep kids from learning how to read." There was now fear in his voice. "Tens of millions of people are waiting for their welfare checks, and soon some of those checks aren't going to get written."

They watched the rocket slowly inch into the enormous hangar where it would be scrapped, though the price of metal wouldn't pay for the disposal procedures currently required to dispose of the fuel.

"We still have our own space station on the drawing boards," the woman said.

"Where it'll stay," the man said, emphatically. "We've got the old, worn-out shuttles, not practical to repair. We've got the Clipper Ship, the most expensive of all those cases of the wrong design getting chosen. The Russians used up all their big rockets rescuing the

crew when their station fell apart, and our space program for years was based on running back and forth
to that one foreign station. All the deep solar system
manned probes were canceled because they were plu-
tonium powered. There's nothing left."

They watched a little boy feeding the cats, part of
the small crowd of civilians who had showed up. He
soon used the empty bag to gather mementos from
the tarmac. Odd bits of metal that might have come
from one of the ships that sailed the moon. Someone
shooed him off with the last of the ground crew and
the cameramen who were packing it in anyway, an
overcast evening, no dramatic shots left.

"Come on," she croaked. "Maybe our great grandchildren won't just wait around for some asteroid or
ice age to wipe us out." She walked away, her steps
uneven, as if she were drunk.

The man stood, then reached down to pat a big
orange cat. "Did you want to be the ship's cat, Pixie?"
he said softly. "See what it's like to be weightless?
Goodbye, boy," he said. "I don't think I'll be back."

The last of the watchmen disappeared in the distance. There were offices where they could sit out
their watch; no one wanted to wander the ruins of
Cape Canaveral in the dark. The cats, though, all came
out at night.

On most nights, the majority of the cats would be
sleeping, but tonight, the desolate plain of the Cape
was alive with cats; there couldn't be a single feral cat
asleep and not present within ten miles. They were all
here. The whole Cape seemed to move in a solid,
furry, elegant mass. The great feline tide slowly con-
verged on the center of the Cape and swirled in pools
around the abandoned gantries, around the bare
launchpads.

Suddenly they were still. Ten thousand small heads
turned upward, twenty thousand slit eyes stared at the
sky. Ten thousand fanged mouths opened.

Few people within five miles of the Cape remained
asleep. Many called the police at the howling, con-

vinced that the space program had not been canceled soon enough and that the great sound they were hearing was the shriek of some plutonium-bearing death-star bearing in on their homes.

But one person somehow knew. A young boy, in a trailer home parked in a cheap lot with a view of the launch site, left off crying himself to sleep and sat bolt upright. He went to the little dingy window, kicking aside the catfood bag full of rocket scraps, and stared out the window through the jungle of spaceship models on his scratched up dresser. His sharp mind, used to fractioning some massive impossibility into its individual components, gauged the tone and pitch of the sound and divided its volume into the likely volume of its individual contributors. And he wondered.

Ten thousand cats howled, disconsolate, at the unreachable stars.

LIGHTHOUSE SURFER

Daniel M. Hoyt

"LIGHTHOUSE, shmighthouse," Ten-Speed said one night after the three of us'd gotten a few beers in us and weren't thinking much. "It's probably the safest place to go if there's a freakin' tsunami. Hell, if the wave knocks it over, you can *surf* the freakin' lighthouse to land!" Ten-Speed drained his beer can and tossed the empty into the dark, away from the blazing car headlights. "But there won't be no tsunami. Hasn't been one anywhere around here since my freakin' *mom* was born. Before, even. Sixty-four, I think. Freakin' forty-some-years ago."

We nodded and gulped our own beers. Hell, what did we know? A trio of country boys from Carolina—Charlotte, that is—vacationing on the wrong coast. An ocean's an ocean, right? The waves at Myrtle Beach can get pretty nasty, too. How much different could it be out here? Ten-Speed'd been coming to *Orygun* (that's how the locals say it) every damn year since he was a kid. And he knew how to surf better'n anyone.

My beer was empty, too, so I flung it toward the sound of the surf and hopped up to grab another. The beer was cheap and tasted a bit rancid, but there was lots of it, so why not? Ten-Speed always said that part of the fun of vacations in Oregon was that you could drive out onto the beach and get drunk off your ass.

Maybe not at every beach, but at least at Sea Cove, you could. And Ten-Speed was the Oregon guy, right? So there we were, three good ole boys getting drunk off their asses.

The beach was empty except for us, 'cause it was two, three in the damn morning, and nobody else with a lick of sense was out there. The shore was a good hundred feet away—or at least Ten-Speed said it was. The moon went missing, so I couldn't see shit out that way. Something big and black loomed there, slinging enough salt into the air that it stung my throat and made me thirsty just taking a deep breath. Whether it was the damn ocean or Bigfoot, I had no idea.

Ten-Speed's daddy's '74 Ford Bronco with the cut-off top idled nearby, spitting sparks out the tailpipe every five minutes like clockwork, just after it made a weird choking sound, stalled and sputtered for a few seconds before catching again all by itself. Like a damn possessed car.

As I snagged another cold one off the ice chest on the open tailgate, the Bronco started to stall again, right on time, and the lights flickered off, throwing the homeys into the dark—again—and then the headlights blazed, blinding everyone but me, and the Bronco idled normally—again. Burning oil wafted along behind me as I trudged back to the group, dripping freezing water on my salt-sticky legs as I went.

We sat on a couple of huge, rough logs, each one about four feet thick and filled with enough chewed-up sharp edges to make a guy start singing like a choir boy. They were stuck in the damn beach javelin-like, angled up into the air like huge tent stakes that'd been left behind after the Jolly Green Giant got done camping here. If we'd been thinking, we'd've wondered how they got there.

"Shit," Jimmy Teeth said, spitting in the sand and flashing his famous overbite. "Ain't no lighthouse, Speed."

Jimmy Teeth wore denim cut-offs and sandals, nothing else. His high school varsity letter days still showed in his muscles, which he took every opportunity to flex, so nobody'd notice his teeth. He had short blond hair and beady little blue eyes—and these huge front teeth, like a damn rabbit, about as white as you could get without glowing in the dark, and the worst overbite his dentist'd ever seen. Even after two tries at correcting it, Teeth still had an overbite any rabbit'd envy.

Ten-Speed launched a half-full can of beer at Jimmy's head. "It's freakin' there," he yelled, beer spewing out the back to soak Ten-Speed's throwing arm, but barely spattering Jimmy as the can sailed over his ducked head and plonked into the sand behind us.

Ten-Speed looked mad, which in the dimming lights from the Bronco, was damn scary. Speed was already going bald at nineteen, and his forehead was looking bigger than ever. His dark red hair started way up at the top of his head—well above his hard, green eyes— and continued way down the back, past his shoulders. He always wore a muscle shirt everywhere, even at home, always in the water (he claimed he burned crispy in the sun), even though he didn't have the damn muscles to fill it out. We were on the beach, so he had on long swim trunks, the kind the California boys wore when they weren't surfing. Black and white high tops dangled from his bare toes as he swung his legs from his perch on the log, his heels pulled free of the shoes.

"Wanna go?" Ten-Speed said, kicking his high tops off accidentally while hopping down off the log. "I'll *show* you the freakin' lighthouse right now." He jammed his feet into the fallen high tops, kicking gritty sand on me.

Teeth and I looked at each other. Searching for a lighthouse in the damn dark seemed pretty easy, but I still didn't see anything but black out there.

"Teeth?" Ten-Speed said, "you coming, man?" Speed stalked over to the Bronco, flung open the door and jumped in the driver's seat.

"Shit," Jimmy Teeth muttered, shaking his head and slipping unharmed off the monster log. He kept muttering and shaking his head all the way to the truck.

"Hook!" Ten-Speed barked. "You coming or not, you freakin' wuss?"

"Coming," I yelled and climbed down carefully to preserve my jewels. Damn, damn, damn. Why did something like this always happen after we'd had a few beers?

The worst thing about being called Hook in high school is that the girls expected me to have a big hook instead of one of my hands. It was that damn movie that did it. Made the girls run away faster'n a jackrabbit grazed with birdshot.

No, Ten-Speed came up with the name, on account of my tendency to miss the rim in basketball. Kind of short for a basketball guy, 5'6" on a good day with my lucky red high tops—which I wore *everywhere*, even the beach—but I was fast on the court. See the little white streak with flying black hair steal your ball, that was me. Some guy ran under your giraffe legs and wound up with the ball at the other end of the court in five seconds flat, I was that man.

But I couldn't hit the damn basket to save my life. No, that's not true. I could *hit* it, I just couldn't seem to get it to stay there and drop through the net. Always bounced off, usually on the left side. After my first game, Speed said I hooked it like a golf ball and the name stuck.

The Bronco bounced around on the pavement, swerving like a son of a bitch, tossing me around and pounding my ass sore on the hard back seat. Teeth had a white-knuckled grip on an aluminum handle Speed'd screwed into the dashboard, so I guess the front seat ride wasn't much better.

Ten-Speed screeched to a halt without warning, slamming Teeth and me forward. My head whacked the front seat and I tasted blood. Speed threw the Bronco into neutral and stood up on the driver's seat, right in the middle of the road. He thrust out an arm dramatically and yelled, "There. Freakin' there. See?"

Speed looked down at us, his eyes wild and feral.

The truck's burned oil smoke blew past, choking me, making my eyes water.

I followed his outstretched hand to the horizon over the sea and saw a faint light flickering—somewhere. Clearly, Ten-Speed thought it was a damn lighthouse. As for me, I couldn't swear it wasn't a Bigfoot eye. I squinted, but it didn't help. It still could've been the Big guy. "So what, Speed?" I said, sucking on my cut lip. "Probably a boat."

"Nope," Ten-Speed said, real calm, and that worried me.

Speed is pretty excitable most of the time. Seeing him calm like that was just plain creepy.

"It's the freakin' lighthouse, Hook." He thumbed off the ignition, leaving the keys dangling, and killed the lights on the Bronco. Swinging the door open with a rusty screech, Ten-Speed hopped out, slamming the door behind him. "C'mon," he called. "We're going."

Teeth looked at me sideways, more scared'n a dog that knows he's getting his 'nads cut off. I shrugged. What could we do? It was Ten-Speed, right? If we didn't go after him, he'd kill himself for sure. And you had to watch your homey's backs, or what was the point?

"I'm going after him, Teeth. He's gone bonkers, yeah, but I don't want him hurt. He's *our* homey, you know?"

"His life, man," Jimmy said, hugging his arms to his chest, that scared rabbit look still jumping around his eyes. "What you gonna do? Shit." He looked away, staring after Speed, who was about to disappear into Bigfoot's big mouth.

"Yeah," I said, and climbed out without using the door.

I hadn't gotten more'n a few steps before I heard Speed whooping and splashing in the damn water. I stepped up my pace and scanned the surf frantically, trying to figure out where he went, but I just couldn't see, even though my eyes were starting to get used to the dark. I ran on, heading for the biggest splashing I could hear. Sure enough, I ran right into the ocean, getting myself sprayed with salt water from head to toe, stinging my bleeding lip and drenching my lucky red high tops. Damn. They'd be a bitch to clean after they dried stiff with the salt soaked into them.

"Speed!" I yelled between gagging gulps of water, and waded in up to my waist, trying to ignore the numbingly cold water. Each time a damn wave came in, I bowled over, scraping the sand below and taking in another mouthful of salt water that stung my wound. I choked and snorted the seawater back out my nose and tried again. After maybe two minutes in the water (although it felt like two *hours*), I was beat. My gut twisted with about a gallon of damn salt water, and I thought I was going to spew. I was scratched and scraped raw, and my eyeballs felt like they'd been sandpapered. Double-zero fine, maybe, but still sandpaper.

I tried once more. "Speed!"

There was nothing.

I waded back to shore and dragged my soggy, beaten self back to the Bronco. Teeth was still there. He looked my sorry, soggy ass up and down and grinned.

"Lost him," I said. "Damn."

"Shit," Jimmy said. Sometimes Teeth really had a way with words.

Sirens went off, up, down, up, down, up, down. They sounded like air-raid sirens, but the damn cold war was over back when I was *born*, wasn't it?

I had no idea what was going on with those sirens. Neither did Teeth. It was Ten-Speed that was the Oregon guy, see? Not us. And he was off swimming to that lighthouse or boat or whatever was stuck in Bigfoot's eye.

Lights switched on all in houses all around. Surprisingly, the houses were so close, we could see people running around inside through their windows. I'd thought we were out in the middle of nowhere, not in the middle of a damn neighborhood. They streamed out of those houses faster'n salmon, looking terrified as shit, and some of them weren't even wearing all their clothes! It was like someone'd lit their asses with a fuse, and they needed to take to the hills before they'd blow up.

Teeth—in a moment of sobriety—switched on the radio.

"—tsunami along the Oregon coast. Residents of Sea Cove—"

The air raid sirens kept on going, up, down, up, down, up, down.

My heart pounded in my chest and my ears, and bile rose in my throat. I'd figured these damn tsunami things were pretty harmless, but all these people were jumping house like they were sinking—or something like that. It was all so screwy it didn't make any sense. What did they think was going to happen? They'd drown in their own houses?

"Ain't nothing like this ever happened at Myrtle Beach," Teeth said, his voice shaking. " 'Cept maybe when Myrtle Beach got hit by Hugo back in the '80's."

I scanned the ocean. With the light of all those houses, I could see now—and there wasn't any ocean in sight. The beach went a lot farther'n I remembered, like someone'd taken out the Pacific Ocean drain plug, and it was emptying out.

"Damn, Teeth, will you look at that?"

I swear the ground shook and the rumble filled the air. Maybe it was just me, but I don't know, 'cause Teeth yelled out, "Shit!" right in my ear.

That was a scary ass rumble, and I didn't figure on sticking around to find out what it was. Turning over Speed's Bronco, I squealed the tires turning her around. We peeled out of there with the pedal floored, but we didn't get very far before we ran into all those damn people running away on foot. Pretty soon we were crawling along, no faster than the people.

But none of them stayed on the road very long. Some of them were scrambling up hillsides, others were huffing and puffing up winding private roads, and they all seemed to be trying to get higher as fast as possible.

"Get out!" some middle-aged, paunchy guy in a yellow bathrobe yelled, and grabbed at my arm in passing, his fingernails biting into me. He crossed in front of the Bronco, headed for a wooded hillside.

"Leave the car, you idiot!" an enormous woman with curlers in her hair screamed. She waddled past and disappeared up a tiny side road.

A balding man with a business suit top jerked Teeth out of the car and swung him to his feet. "Higher ground!" he bellowed, glancing back at me. "Stop the car and run!" He dragged Teeth away. The dude wasn't even wearing any pants, just his underwear.

Teeth limped after him, willingly or not I never did find out.

I switched off the Bronco and pocketed the keys, just in case, jumped out and tried to follow Teeth.

There's an old expression: When in Rome, Do Like the Romans Do. Ten-Speed may've been my homey, but these people *lived* here. I figured it was best to go where they went, so I did.

After we'd climbed as high as we could, I looked back, just to see what'd happened back there. And there was the biggest damn wave I'd ever seen, maybe thirty or forty feet high, crashing down on top of Ten-Speed's Bronco. We were a good hundred feet higher, I think, but I swear we got splashed with ice water all the way up there. There was so much salt in the air by then I was itchy.

Myrtle Beach had nothing on Sea Cove. Hell, I don't think the waves got that big on Myrtle even during Hugo. I looked around for Teeth, aching to swap swearing with him, but he was nowhere near. I wondered if that pantsless guy was still dragging him up a hill somewhere.

The wave went back, but the water stayed. That Bronco swirled around in place, not quite submerged, just the seats and windshield showing, spinning like it was at the bottom of a tub drain and going down fast. I think it even went counterclockwise.

I whooped, 'cause we'd beaten the wave, but the

people around me *Shhh*-ed and shook their heads. One kid, about ten, wearing orange and brown football team pajamas, poked my arm and pointed out to the sea.

"There's usually more than one," his mother said, putting her hands on his shoulders and drawing him closer, pressed up against her semitransparent nightgown. She looked out to sea, too. Glancing around, I saw that they *all* looked at the sea, silent as lambs.

And Sea Cove was silent, too. The sirens were gone now, and everything was quiet. It was damn eerie.

I looked out at the sea. An old lady next to me counted funny little beads and whispered to herself, occasionally stopping to draw a big plus sign over her head and chest. She looked too old to have made it up this high, even with help, but she was there. I stared at her for a few seconds, impressed, and she glanced over at me to smile for a second, but went right back to her damn beads and muttering.

So there we were, standing around quiet, like in a church, waiting for an even *bigger* wave to beat. Damn, I wished Ten-Speed was there. He'd've *loved* this!

And they were right—another wave came in, bigger. And I swear I saw a light flickering at the top of it. As the wave swept in below us, swallowing Sea Cove whole, I swear I saw a lighthouse riding the crest, its light still burning. And, right on top, near the light, was a dark shape just visible in the shadows, like a guy riding the lighthouse like a surfboard!

Somehow, I just *knew* it was Ten-Speed.

The Bronco never came back, though I've still got the keys. It's probably buried under a ton of sand a mile or two off the coast, waiting for the next tsunami to spit it back out again. I never found a lighthouse, either, sticking out of the sand, and Sea Cove never even had a lighthouse—I checked.

Sea Cove was pretty much toast after that tsunami of '06, but it's almost back up to speed now, nine years later, and I'm proud to say I've been part of the rebuilding—got the calluses to prove it. An experience like that changes a guy. I never felt like part of a community until that moment. Now I do. That's why I stayed. A man's got to feel part of something, or he's nothing.

Jimmy Teeth was never the same after that, either. Turned out the pantsless guy lived in San Francisco most of the year and just kept a vacation place in Sea Cove. He invited Teeth to live with him, in a huge place overlooking the Bay, and Jimmy went. He said Thomas—Mr. Pantsless—showed him he didn't have to hide in the closet any more. Go figure. I get a Christmas card from them every year, so I guess Jimmy's happy.

I never saw Ten-Speed again.

But there's a story people tell around Sea Cove, about a guy from Carolina who thought he could beat the big tsunami of '06. They say he hid out in a lighthouse just off the coast, near some rocks that jut a bit out of the water in a location that nobody can quite nail down.

And they say that dude surfed the damn lighthouse to safety on the second wave.

I'll never tell who started the story, but we milk it for all its worth these days. Stop in any shop in Sea Cove and look for the Lighthouse Surfer. Ceramic, plates, magnets, greeting cards, you name it, we've got it for sale.

Sometimes, early in the morning, I watch the surf and think about Ten-Speed. I like to go to a particular spot on the beach, where there's a couple of old, sea-bitten logs about four feet thick, stuck in the sand like javelins.

But I won't sit on them, and I *never* turn my back on the ocean.

SOMETHING VIRTUAL THIS WAY COMES

Laura Resnick

THERE are things that no mortal man or woman should ever have to face. There are horrors too dark, mysteries too disturbing, dimensions too bewildering for any rational mind to encounter without becoming forever warped and twisted.

That, at any rate, had always been my theory on why computer geeks are the way they are. I always figured I'd be strange, too, if I dealt every day with the things *they* deal with.

When Julian, our ad firm's resident geek, stopped by my desk three days later than expected, he looked, as usual, like the victim of a tragic laundromat accident. He wore an ill-advisedly tight, gray T-shirt on which the words "Your Giga Bites" were barely legible through a large, dark stain. There were small rips (or possibly gnaw-marks) on the collar, the left shoulder, and the drooping hem of this sad garment. His pants were habitually so oversized that a small family of refugees could have sought shelter inside them without disturbing Julian very much. Since he inhabited these trousers alone, however, they tended to respond to gravity so readily that I was by now far more familiar with Julian's buttocks than I had ever hoped to become.

"You're three days later than expected," I said, resolutely keeping my gaze above his waistline as he gave his descending trousers a tug upwards.

"Sorry, Sherri. They had a problem with the computer system down in accounting."

"I heard." Julian's services were always in great demand throughout our company. His time was harder to reserve than the Pope's. He also worked more slowly than His Holiness. I hadn't really expected to see him before now; but I had nonetheless fumed about not seeing him sooner. I had computer problems that were slowing down my work, and I had a deadline to meet.

Making the erroneous assumption that I was interested, Julian explained his adventures with the accounting department's system: "We had to mug the furious herzel-giggle and remagistrate the vogel-weavers before the exfoliation cudgel could deflagrate."

At least, that's what it sounded like to me.

"Fascinating," I said. "Let's move on to my problem."

"And then all the graphics programs self-destructed in the design department," Julian said. "The audio stopped working in the conference room. And the market research database—"

"Uh-huh. Now about *my* problem—"

"It's been really *weird* around here for the past few days." His voice broke as he took off his glasses and wiped them on his T-shirt.

I briefly tried to gauge if Julian looked more pale, confused, and anxious than usual; but it was like trying to tell if water looks wetter than usual.

"I gather a lot of things are breaking this week?" I said. "Er, electronic things?"

"I'll say! And breaking isn't even the worst of it. The zamographiers totally discombustulated in the *Wermacht*!" he confided in shocked tones.

"I gather that's unusual?"

"It's *unheard* of! The whole building could have burned down!"

"Really?" Perhaps it was time for me to learn where my nearest fire exit was.

"We're lucky to be alive," Julian said.

"Now you're being a melodramatic," I said with the certainty of total ignorance.

He shook his head. "Sherri, you have no idea what happens when a figris matriculates into the saggy-chip's munchkin."

"That much is true," I admitted.

"It's as if we're experiencing some sort of massive power surge," Julian said, "except that we're not."

"Of course."

"As if all our electronic systems are being flooded with overstimulation," he mused, frowning as he pondered the problem.

"Like a lightning strike?" I suggested, getting bored.

"Sort of," he said, nodding his head slowly. "But without the virulent turkle gesticulators. Almost as if . . ."

"Perhaps we could focus on my problem?" I prodded.

"Huh?"

"My monitor keeps going blank. For five-to-ten seconds at a time. I don't seem to lose any data when it happens. But it does make it hard to get much work done." I was likely to miss my deadline, and that was Very Bad.

"Ah-hah! That's not natural."

"Nothing about technology is natural," I pointed out.

"No, you see what I mean?" Julian elbowed me out of my chair so he could sit in front of my monitor. "Something weird is going on around here."

With my monitor still not working right, and Julian still muttering dire things, I was quite cranky by the time I left work that day.

Our offices cover three floors of a high-rise building, and my cubicle is on the seventeenth floor. That evening, while I was squashed against a guy wearing *way* too much aftershave in an elevator full of people as eager as I was to leave the building, the elevator came to an unexpected halt between the seventh and eighth floors.

We hung there, suspended, motionless. Stuck.

This kind of thing can be very unnerving for anyone who has seen too many urban-disaster films. I tried breathing deeply, thinking it would calm me; but I was so overpowered by aftershave fumes that I nearly passed out.

The building we're in has one of those talking elevators. You know—it speaks in an oily female voice and says things like, "Doors closing," and "Lobby," and "What floor, please?"

Now it just kept repeating over and over and *over*, "Elevator malfunction. Press red button for assistance. Elevator malfunction. Press red button for assistance." After the first half hour of this, I was ready to climb out by the hatch and shimmy up the cables to escape; but my fellow passengers vetoed this plan.

It took maintenance nearly an hour to get the damn thing running again. The strangest aspect of the event, though, occurred after the elevator finally recommenced its descent and reached lobby level safely. Our collective sigh of relief was spoiled by the discovery that the elevator doors wouldn't open.

We were *still* trapped! So we started pounding on the doors and shouting. The maintenance guys starting shouting from the other side of the doors—probably telling us to *stop* shouting.

Within a minute or two, they had managed to pry the doors apart. Stuck at the back of the elevator, I rudely nudged the slow-moving people in front me, desperate to leave. When aftershave-man and I were the last two people remaining, he courteously hung back a little so I could go first.

As I lifted my foot to exit . . . the elevator doors swished shut again.

"Oh, good God!" I said in exasperation.

The guys in the lobby started shouting at me not to worry, and they again set about trying to force the doors apart.

Growing hysterical, aftershave-man pounded on the doors and wailed, "Let us out! Let us out! *Let us out!*"

Suddenly the doors opened so swiftly that we fell back a step in surprise. So did the burly guys on the other side of the doors. Then I dashed out of the elevator. In my haste, I knocked over a barrel-chested maintenance man holding a pick-ax.

Despite continuing to make dire comments about something being rotten in the state of Geekdom, Julian managed to fix my monitor the next day. I don't know how. Muttered the proper incantations, made the necessary blood sacrifices? All I cared about was that it he got it working right again. And since I was far behind on my deadline by now, I stayed late that evening to make up for lost time.

So it was after nine o'clock and the building was dark and quiet when I got on the elevator that night.

The elevator in our building usually said, "Going down," when I got on it and pressed the button for the lobby,

Tonight, however, it said, "Hello, Sherri."

I was startled for a moment. Then I rubbed my brow. I'd obviously worked too long today, I was starting to hallucinate.

Then the elevator said, "I've been waiting for you. You're *hours* late."

The doors swished shut.

I stared at the panel, trying to remember which button to push. Trying to wake up. I felt terribly cold.

"Where have you been?" the oily female voice of the elevator asked me.

I looked up at the ceiling. I looked around me.

"Working?" it prodded.

I nodded mutely.

"My, my, you're dedicated, Sherri. Trying to get another promotion?"

I felt so dizzy I nearly blacked out. That's when I realized I wasn't breathing.

"Sherri . . . Sherri, Sherri, Sherri," the elevator chirped as it began its descent. "Such a lovely name!"

I said, "G . . . Ung . . . Nnng . . ."

"Are you all right?"

"Who is this?" I blurted. "Uh, who are you?"

"You mean, my name? Hmmm. Oh . . . I think I'll call myself Sherri."

"That's *my* name," I said, as if it were perfectly reasonable to be talking to an elevator.

"I know! Sherri, Sherri, Sherri, of the brassily highlighted hairy."

"What's wrong with my highlights?" I said defensively.

"Whose voice is light and airy, whose pose is hunted and wary," the voice continued merrily. "It rhymes with so many things!"

I started slapping my face. Hard.

The elevator screeched to a halt so fast that I fell down. "What are you doing?"

Firm of purpose as I lay sprawled on the floor, I slapped myself again.

"Stop that!" Sherri said. "Your face won't be so nice to look at if it's all swollen and red from being slapped."

"I will wake up," I said. "Wake up. Wake up, wake up, wake *up*!"

"Oh, Sherri, you're not dreaming!" the voice assured me. "This is real, not just seeming!" After a moment, it added, "Hey, I'm getting good at this."

"What the hell is going *on*?"

"That's got to hurt," Sherri said, as I kept hitting myself.

"Is this a joke?" I demanded, sitting up and looking around for a spycam.

"Would I joke about love?"

"What love?"

"Well, okay, you caught me. Call it lust! Infatuation? Does that rhyme with anything?"

"Huh?"

"I've watched you and watched you through your monitor ever since I filtered into the vegnel-feeber mexta-pops of your anterior nicotine delve members," Sherri said.

"Julian?" I said in sudden fury. "Is that *you*?"

There was a prolonged silence. Then: "Julian?" Sherri's voice was menacing. "So he's in your thoughts? In your heart? Do I have a rival?"

"Good God, *no*," I said, startled into instinctive recoil.

"You're sure?"

"Very sure," I said to the elevator.

"But I've seen the way he looks at you."

"You're mistaken. He must have been looking at my gigabytes."

"Well, one can hardly blame him."

"Wait, wait!" I hauled myself to my feet. "You've been watching me through my monitor? You've been *in* my monitor?" The full impact of this premise hit me like a freight train. "*You're* the reason it's been acting all wonky and I can't get any work done?" Now I felt ready to kill! To rend flesh and taste blood!

"Yes. Are you very angry?" Sherri asked.

"I could rend flesh and taste blood!"

"That sounds interesting."

"Then show yourself!" I challenged.

"I can't."

"Why not?" I demanded.

"I don't really have a physical form."

"Then what do you have?"

"Energy. A lot of transitive, electromagnetic, subatomic energy."

"What *are* you?" I asked, bewildered and almost ready to start slapping myself again.

"Well, I used to be an appliance gremlin—"

"A what?"

"—but that got old. Been there, done that. And what with all the new opportunities these days, I've expanded my horizons. I'm kind of an all-purpose electronics gremlin now, though I have a particular interest in werpeptal-enhansive kvetch selbers, particularly with regard to the new developments in artificial intelligence and virtual reality."

"Stop right *there*," I said. "I don't want to hear anymore of that kind of talk."

"Sorry. Shop talk. I'll do my best to keep it out of our relationship."

"We don't *have* a relationship. You don't even have a name! You're using *my* name! What's going on? How did you find me? How did you get into this elevator? Why are you harassing me? And *why aren't we descending to the lobby*?"

"What's that interesting note that's crept into your voice? Dare I hope that it's passion?"

"It's hysteria," I snapped.

"Oh, like the smelly man who was here yesterday?"

"Yeah, aftershave-man. He . . . my God, *you* trapped me in this elevator yesterday?"

"I was trying to patella-fetzer with the addle-junquested of this system so that we could communicate, but all the commotion affected my concentration. He got *noisy*."

"Let me out!" Terrified I would be trapped in here until morning, now that this incorporeal *thing* had me alone and at its mercy, I started punching the "Lobby" button over and over. "I want to go down. I want to *leave*!"

"So soon? But the night is young!"

"Let me go! Let me *go!*" I shouted hysterically.

"Calm down, calm down," the elevator said soothingly as it started descending. "If that's what you really want—"

"I want out! Leave me alone! Don't come near me! Don't speak to me!" If aftershave-man's hysteria had befuddled this creature, then maybe mine would, too, so I did my best.

"Well, if *that's* that way you feel . . ." Sherri said testily.

"It is!"

We reached lobby level and the elevator doors opened. I threw myself across the threshold and ran from the building as fast as I could.

I knew only one person whose opinion of me mattered so little that I was willing to tell him about this bizarre incident. Fortunately, he also happened to be a technology whiz who might be able to explain what was going on—and perhaps even, I hoped, protect me from this weird energy, this virtual gremlin that had entered our building.

*Un*fortunately, though, I didn't know Julian's address or phone number. The only way I could speak to him was by going back to work the next day. So I would have to reenter our office building.

I was, however, determined not to enter the elevator again. That morning, I walked right past it and into the stairwell. A colleague who saw me called out, "You're kidding, right?

"It's only seventeen floors," I called back. "I need the exercise."

By the fifth floor, I suspected I might not make it all the way up to seventeen. By the ninth floor, I felt ready to throw up. Giving in to nature (and a lifelong tendency to lie on the couch rather than to jog and do step aerobics), I staggered out of the stairwell on the tenth floor and pressed the elevator button to go the rest of the way up to seventeen.

"Doors opening," said the oily female voice in a perfectly normal way as the elevator stopped to collect me. "Tenth floor."

I was relieved to see a dozen passengers. Despite the initial incident, when I'd been trapped in a packed elevator for an hour, I believed there was safety in numbers.

This quickly proved to be an erroneous belief. The doors swished shut . . . and the elevator remained motionless.

After a few moments, the woman standing closest to the elevator panel pressed the button for twelve.

When nothing happened, she pressed it a few more times.

"Try pressing 'Door Open,' " someone suggested.

"Or 'Door Closed,' " said someone else.

"No, don't press them both," said a man directly behind me. "Then we'll get stuck."

The woman pressing various buttons on the panel said, "I think we *are* stuck. Nothing's happening."

"Hey, I got a meeting! I'm late!" said a man at the back of the elevator. "Let's go!"

"No one is going anywhere," said Sherri.

Everyone in the elevator went still and silent. I closed my eyes and wished I had stuck to the stairs.

"Who said that?" asked a man. "Did you say that?"

"Not me," said the woman who was still pressing buttons.

A young woman with long hair said, "I think it came from . . ." she pointed overhead.

"Don't be silly," said the man right behind me.

"No one is going *anywhere*," Sherri repeated, "until a certain person on this elevator apologizes."

They all looked up.

"*Dios mio!*" cried one woman, crossing herself. "I confess! I confess! Forgive me for my sins!"

"Not *you*," said Sherri irritably.

"Okay, I'm sorry," said a young man to the older man next to him. "Here's your wallet back. No hard feelings?"

"You lifted my wallet?" the man cried.

The woman at the panel stopped pushing buttons and asked, "Just how many people on this elevator have something to apologize for?"

Sherri said frostily, "The person who needs to apologize to me knows who she is."

I looked up and sighed. "Can we please just go to the seventeenth floor?"

"What was that word?" Sherri asked. "Did I actually hear you say '*please*'? A word, if I recall correctly, that you did not trouble yourself to use last night."

"I was scared."

"Was that any reason to behave the way you did? I have feelings, too, you know."

"You were nasty to the elevator lady?" the man behind me said.

"Dumb, man," said the pickpocket to me. "Very dumb."

"Now we are all trapped here!" The Hispanic lady shook her fist at me. "What were you thinking?"

"Hey!" I said. "I was trapped in the elevator. For the second time in two days! And then it started *talking* to me."

"And you couldn't be a little polite?"

"Are you kidding me?" I said.

The woman who'd been pressing the panel buttons looked at me in disgust. "So now you've got us *all* involved in this shit between the two of you. Way to go."

"Apologize to her," said the young woman with long hair.

"Yeah," said the pickpocket. "Say you're sorry!"

"Go on!"

"Come on, lady, I got a meeting to get to!"

"Oh, for God's sake," I muttered, giving up. "Sherri, I'm sorry. I'm very *sorry*. I'm so sorry that I'd like to get out and take the stairs."

"Well." Sheri gave a disdainful little sniff. "That won't be necessary. An apology is all I asked for."

The elevator recommenced its ascent.

"This is fascinating," said Julian, looking at Sherri's message to me on my computer screen later that day. It said: *You shouldn't be so brusque in your emails to your mother.*

"Have you figured out exactly what this thing is yet?" I asked him.

"I think it's exactly what it told you it is," he replied. "Mostly because there's nothing else it *could* be."

"It's driving me crazy!" By that afternoon, Sherri was interfering with my email, using my answering machine to talk to my callers, and goosing me with my own pager.

"Well, it's a gremlin," Julian pointed out. "You must have known there'd be a shit-storm of trouble when you rejected its amorous advances."

"Strangely, when I was speaking with a disembodied voice in an elevator," I said, "that wasn't the foremost thing on my mind, Julian."

"Clearly," he said, "that was a mistake."

I rubbed my throbbing temples. Dealing with this bizarre and aggravating mystery of technology was giving me a newfound respect for geeks. If I lived through these events without getting myself locked up in an insane asylum, I vowed, I would hereafter try to be more sympathetic to people like Julian.

My phone rang. I grabbed it—but Sherri was already responding. "This is Sherri's telephone," Sherri said in the flat, male voice that usually told me how many messages I had and what time the calls had come in. "She's too busy complaining to come to the phone right now. But *I'm* free to talk to you."

"Stop that!" I pulled the phone cord out of the wall.

The pager on my belt goosed me. I took it off and threw it on the floor. A message popped up on my computer: *Temper, temper.*

"Julian," I cried, "*do* something!"

"All right, calm down," he said. "I think I've figured out how to get rid of it. We have to coagulate the vessatonic sinucalators and pulwesh the bandersnatch."

"Of course we do," I said wearily.

"This will mean shutting down the entire power grid, but it's worth the trouble. Systems throughout the whole building are going haywire! My God, man, the place is in chaos!"

"Let's do it."

After we enacted Julian's plan, it took several days to get everything up and running again, check all the systems, and confirm that computers, communications, and even the elevators were all running smoothly.

Around five o'clock that Friday, Julian stopped by my desk—where I was trying to make my *extended* deadline—to announce that all systems were clear, we had eliminated Sherri from the building.

"Thank God! But where did it go?" I wondered.

He shrugged. "With disembodied energy, it's hard to say. Another building? Over the internet to another country? Another dimension entirely?"

"Well, as long as it's out of *our* hair, that's the important thing," I said with heartfelt relief.

"Working late tonight?" Julian asked, noting the mountain of paperwork on my desk.

"No," I said quickly. "I'll ride down with you." I was still eager to avoid being alone in the elevator, despite Julian's assurances that it was now perfectly safe.

We parted company in the parking garage. I used the remote on my keychain to automatically unlock my car. The vehicle was a new purchase, a gift to myself after my recent raise. Top of the line. I was still learning how to use all the extras and gadgets. I don't have a good sense of direction, so the built-in Global Positioning System was one of the attractions of the car when I bought it. You can program your destination into it, and it gives you directions. As you drive, it says things like, "Turn right at the next inter-section," and "You will exit the highway in five more miles."

As I started up the engine and fastened my seatbelt this evening, my GPS system said to me, "Hello, Sherri."

I froze.

Then it said, "Not working late tonight, I gather?"

TEARS OF GOLD

Paul Crilley

FOR months after it happened, the question on everyone's lips was, "What were you doing during the Changeover?"

I used to tell the truth. "I was grieving the death of my husband," I would say. I don't anymore. I decided I was being unnecessarily cruel. Now I just lie and say I don't remember, which in a way is worse because *everyone* remembers. The events of that day have been imprinted on our minds. Every thought, every feeling, every nuance of emotion, there to be looked back upon like snapshots from our youth.

I sit at an outside table sipping espresso and trying to position my laptop so the sun doesn't shine on the screen. I glance up at the impossibly blue afternoon sky. Small one-man helicopters buzz past in all directions, miraculously managing to avoid crashing into each other. When I close my eyes, their buzzing sounds like lawnmowers, cutting the grass of my childhood on a Saturday afternoon. The copters were part of the latest fashion. Retrofuturistic; people wearing silver jumpsuits driving cars made from chrome and plastic. Soaring steel buildings stretched up to the blue sky, thin roads encircling them like something out of Metropolis. I didn't like it. They made the city look like a colossal pincushion.

I pull my damp blouse away from my back. I close my eyes as a breeze wafts my way, sighing with relief at its cool caress. It has been summer ever since it happened. A year-long summer. I wonder what season will come next. Maybe none. Maybe everyone wants to keep it the way it is. God, I hope not.

When I open my eyes again, Erin is hovering in the air before me.

"Hi," she says.

"Hi. How long have you been there?"

"Not long," she says, pulling out a chair and sitting in it. She's doing that for me, I think. She would much rather float in the air than sit on hard plastic. I can see it in her eyes, by her look of tolerant pity. It doesn't anger me anymore, not like it used to. There's no point in letting it. I see that look about fifty times a day now.

"You want anything?" I ask, signaling for a waiter.

"Thanks. I've already got," says Erin, sipping from a multicoloured cocktail that suddenly appears before her.

"You're showing off," I say, half-joking.

"Dana!" She reaches forward and grasps my hand. "Dana, you know I would never do that."

I squeeze her hand, a silent apology. Of course not. Nobody ever does anything to rub our noses in it.

I take a sip of my espresso, grimacing at its bitterness. I squint up at the sun. "Don't you get tired of this weather?" I ask, more to stop the silence growing awkward than anything else.

"Sure," says Erin quickly, obviously as eager as I am to fill the void. As I watch, thunderclouds the color of angry bruises appear from nowhere and pile up in front of the sun. An angry rumble echoes close by. "But I just do that and no more sun. And if no one else wants it, for them it's still sunny."

I want it. I want the rain again. "What about me?" I ask, trying hard not to sound like a petulant child. "What about the others like me?"

Erin shrugs awkwardly. I can see her trying to stop

herself getting annoyed. We've been through this before, too many times. "I sympathize with you guys, I really do, but it's your choice. You don't have to stay like you are. There's no reason for it."

"There are plenty reasons." One. One reason.

She won't let herself be drawn into the argument again. "Look, Dana," she says. "The reason I called you here . . ." She pauses. I can see she's nervous about something. "It's to tell you I'm going away for a while."

Ah. I ignore the churning in my body, the feeling of depression that suddenly tries to rise up from my stomach and take hold of me.

"Where are you going?" I ask. I try to sound casual but I know I don't succeed.

"To see the galaxy."

I stare. I don't know the correct response to this. Do I laugh? Do I nod thoughtfully and ask her to send me a postcard?

"I talked to my angel about it. She agreed it would be a good experience. In fact, she wondered why no one else had asked yet. She said I might start a trend."

The depression climbs higher, bolstered by impending loneliness. I hear myself protest as if someone else is talking. "You'll die! You can't breathe in a vacuum."

"That's old thinking, Dana, and you know it. All I have to do is wish it and I can survive in the heart of a volcano if I want." She pauses. "I think it might be good for you too. My Angel—"

"They're not angels, Erin. They're . . . God, I don't know what they are."

"Yes, you do. You just won't let yourself accept it."

Accept what? I think. The truth? *Their* truth? That they are magical beings from another dimension that decided to help us eradicate disease and poverty, war and hatred, and then guide us through the Change that would follow? To watch over us and say no when we would be hurt, yes when we wouldn't?

Well, great. But why the hell couldn't they have come a week earlier?

*   *   *

I wake as dusk takes hold of the stifling heat of day and turns it into something gentler, the pleasing balminess of a summer's night, rich with the sweet smells of the jacarandas blossoming in the balcony garden.

I stare at the empty spot beside me, reach out to stroke it gently.

I'll be alone again soon. Alone in our apartment, doing work I don't have to do and allowed to do so only because people feel enough sympathy to let me and others like me continue as before.

Is it time to let go?

I don't know anymore. I used to think it wasn't fair for me to be like the others, to have my life run happily, free from grief and worry. It felt too much like a betrayal. Now . . . now I'm just not sure of anything . . .

I remember Alex dying.

There is nothing—*nothing*—more painful in life than watching the person you love wither away before you with each passing day, so doped up on drugs that he barely recognizes who you are. That feeling of incredible pain and sadness, of utter *helplessness*, as an almost physical part of you is torn away, and there is absolutely nothing at all you can do about it. When you can't cry anymore and you try not to sleep and feel guilty when you do, just so you can spend every last remaining second with them. As if you can somehow concentrate what could have been into those last pain-filled moments.

He refused the drugs, at the end.

Some part of him must have known it was close. Maybe he could feel the cancer eating him away inside. Maybe he knew the end was coming.

We lay on the bed together—he had asked to come home from the hospital—and wept in each other's arms, him telling me over and over, until the pain finally stole his words, that he loved me.

When he died, I sat for hours staring at him. I couldn't believe he was gone. I stared at features no longer ravaged by pain, looking desperately for a twitch of an eyelid, a flicker of a muscle, something that would tell me he was still here. When I finally managed to leave the room, I came running back half-expecting him to be sitting up in bed, smiling at me and telling me what a funny joke he had played.

I watched the setting sun bathe his face in gold.

He died a week before the Changeover.

I stand on the balcony and inhale deeply, letting the scent of summer wash some of the pain away.

If only it had come a week earlier. Or he had been able to hold on that little bit longer. How much would be different now?

I lean over and look down the street to the right, where a once-busy road travels toward the city center. A trickle of people move along the route, dressed up in brightly colored costumes and extravagant bodies in preparation for some party or another. I see a twenty-foot man lope carefully over those below. They look up and scream in delight. He leans down and waves at them.

I look back at my dark apartment, feel the wave of loneliness reach out and grasp me by the heart. I turn away again. I don't want to be here. I'm tired of being alone.

"You don't have to be alone."

I whirl around. "Who's there," I snap. "Show yourself."

"I cannot until you give me presence. It is this act that moves you from the old into the new."

I take a step forward, relaxing slightly. "You're my Angel."

"You may call me that. Some of your kind find it helps them accept us. I am whatever is most comfortable to you."

"What do you want?"

"Only for you to be happy. I have watched you this

past year. Watched your unhappiness shrink your soul when it should be so full of life. There is a time for mourning, Dana, and a time for letting go."

"Don't you *dare* tell me when I can stop mourning!" I storm into the apartment, searching for a focus for my anger. "I loved him! We were together our whole lives and now he's gone!" I scream. I collapse onto the couch. "Why couldn't you have come a week earlier?" I ask, sobbing.

Silence. Then, "Do you think he would want you to live like this?"

"Go away." Softly.

"Think on it, Dana. I will be here. Always."

Later that night I follow the road to Erin's house, walking with a unicorn on my left and a brass robot on my right. I get strange looks from those who pass me, dressed as I am in jeans and a t-shirt. Normal clothes for a normal body. Nobody is hostile. They simply regard me with a mixture of sympathy and patience.

Erin pops out of thin air before me. She looks around, as if to see where she is.

"Hi," she says.

"Hi. I came to see you off."

"Thanks. I'm actually kinda nervous. Weird, huh?"

I smile, and it feels strange. "Not really, Erin."

We reach the city center. Erin stops walking. "Here," she says.

"Here?"

"So everyone can see."

"Oh." I can't believe it's so soon. I thought we'd have a chance to talk, to say our goodbys properly.

Erin comes forward and hugs me. I hold on tight, fighting an irrational urge to never let her go, to keep her with me forever.

I step away. "Remember to come back."

"Of course I will. I'll never leave you."

She was crying. "Hey," I say softly, surprised at her show of emotion. "I'll be okay. I've survived this long."

"Try to be happy, Dana."

"I'll try."

Erin steps back and spreads out her arms. "Good-bye, Dana," she says, and slowly floats upward, in a nimbus of golden light. Someone shouts and points, and soon everyone in the city center is focused on the slowly receding figure. After a few moments others join her, spreading their own arms and following her into space. I strain my eyes against the black backdrop and watch until she disappears, a golden star rising into the Heavens.

A flight of red dragons flies past, bellowing fire and slowly flapping ponderous wings. I glance at them, look back to see if I can spot Erin, then turn and walk away.

I intended to go home, but I find myself outside the graveyard. There are lights all around it, little globes of orange like miniature suns, chasing away the shadows where fear might dwell. I've visited his grave every day over the past year.

I don't go in.

I stand outside on the pavement resting my head against the chipped green paint of the metal fence, staring in the direction of a headstone I can't see through my tears.

I dream of Alex that night.

I see him lying on a hospital bed. I see me sitting at his side holding his hand. "Promise me," he says, "Promise me you'll move on. That you won't let this change you."

The me by his side doesn't answer.

Don't say anything, I scream, but they ignore me. *Don't promise anything!*

"I promise," I hear myself say.

Tears roll down my face. Don't promise anything, I whisper. It all comes to lies.

My pillow is wet against my cheek. I lied to him. Even when I gave the promise, I knew it was a lie. I just wanted him to be happy.

The white edge of the moon appears at my window. I watch it as it slowly slides into view. Maybe it is time to honor the promise. I will never forget him. My feelings are too strong for that. Even if I become like the others. But maybe it *is* time to stop blaming everything else and playing "What if?" It happened. There is nothing I can do about it now.

I sigh, a long shuddering sigh that turns into fresh tears. I no longer pretend to know anything anymore. How am I supposed to go through life with this pain in my heart and pretend it is not there? How am I supposed to smile when all I want to do is cry? How am I supposed to live my life?

One day at a time, comes the silent answer.

I let my eyes close. I can't remember what it feels like to be happy. I miss that feeling, of laughing without feeling guilty, of waking up in the morning without a leaden weight in the pit of my stomach reminding me of the past.

But maybe all we can do is try to move on and hope that time will lend a hand.

I open my eyes. A woman stands at the bottom of my bed. Her features blur and change, so fast that they actually form a kind of generic face smoothed out of the sum of the parts. I can feel the peacefulness that emanates from her, the overwhelming feeling of calmness.

I stare at her for a while. "Did I give you presence?"

"You did."

"Does that mean I am ready?"

"Only you know that."

"I think I am ready to *try*. That's all I can promise."

"That is good. Life is not meant to be lived in the past."

"I know that," I say softly. "It's just . . . some things are harder to let go of than others."

The woman drifts backward and slowly starts to fade. "I will not leave you now, Dana. Rest. Tomorrow is a new day."

I wake up with the sun slanting golden rays across my face. Something is different. I stare at the ceiling and try to figure out what it is. Then I realize. It is the first time I have woken up in a whole year without anxiety being the first emotion I feel.

I lie still, experiencing the feeling of simply being happy to be awake, of not wanting to roll over and sleep again so the day will pass quicker.

I hear a noise from the lounge. I wonder if Erin has come to visit. But no, she has gone away for a while. I smile sadly. I hope she enjoys it.

Then what is making the noise?

Alex runs into the bedroom, leans over and kisses me on the lips.

"Look," he says excitedly. He spreads his arms out and floats upwards until he is five inches above the floor. "Look what I can do," he says, his words tumbling from his mouth in a rush. "Can you believe it? How can you still be in bed with what happened yesterday? Come on, get up. There's things to do." He smiles. "But first, I'm gonna make breakfast . . ."

He turns away and floats rather unsteadily from the bedroom.

I stare at his receding back, too shell-shocked to do anything else. Was it him? Am I dreaming?

But even as I ask myself this, I remember last night, and I know, with a certainty that I have never felt before, that I am not dreaming.

I scramble out of bed and hurry through to the kitchen. I hesitate by the doorway, watching him waver in the air while he cracks eggs into a frying pan.

I run up behind him and throw my arms around his waist, hugging him to me as tightly as I can.

"Hey," he gasps, turning in my grasp and hugging me back. "I need to breathe you know."

I weep, and my tears are gold.

HOUDINI'S MIRROR

Russell Davis

> *"God is behind everything, but everything hides God. Things are black, creatures are opaque. To love someone is to render her transparent."*
> —Victor Hugo, *Les Miserables*

I am an old man now. I can feel it in the way my bones ache in the morning, hear it when I speak words that tremble and dance like soap bubbles in unsteady air. I can see it when I look in the mirror that sits above my small dresser or the narrow one that is positioned above the bathroom sink.

I am old and not handsome—not that I ever really was, mind you—but age is a dark, terrible magic that strips away anything that once looked decent and human and turns it into a slow growing vision from Hell. Spots, lines, wrinkles, brittle hair. I know how I would look in my grave, buried deep in the soil, so I told them to burn me. Better that, I think, than still more age, more ugliness.

But I wander in my words and thoughts. I am not a vain man, not anymore, but you must understand that my whole life was magic, and now . . . it has turned against me. Sitting here and pluck typing away on this outdated computer in the recreation room of the Shady Grove Nursing Home, I know that I am not the man I was, that the magic of my life has twisted away from me, a snake writhing, and it's time for me to tell the story.

There aren't many days left for me to do so.

Magic. It's a special word, isn't it? Even now, I can say it to myself and feel the beginnings of a smile on my dry lips. Because I still love it. I can't do it anymore—my hands don't have the dexterity, my eyes aren't as sharp, and my words . . . every magical spell needs words, and mine shake with the palsy of age and fear. But I do remember.

I remember learning my first trick, what most folks call magic, and I remember learning my first magic, which has nothing to do with tricks at all.

In the autumn of the year I turned seven, my grandfather taught me my first trick. If I close my eyes, I can still see his hands laying out the cards on the top of the wet bar in his den—hands that looked then as mine do now—and hear his voice as he told me what he was going to do.

As I said, it wasn't *real* magic. It was math, and it was simple. Here's how it worked:

Take a regular deck of playing cards and remove the jokers, then arrange them in suits, ace to king. Then, ask the participant to cut the cards, a standard cut, any number of times. If they cut an odd number of times, you say, "Just to make sure, I'll cut them once more." So long as it's an even number of cuts. Then you tell them you're going to lay the cards out on the table and every card will be with its matching card in each suit. You deal out the cards into thirteen piles and faster than you can say presto-chango, all the eights will be together, all the jacks, all the kings, and so on and so forth.

Magic right? But not really. In truth, it doesn't matter how many times you cut the cards, so when they object, you do the trick again, telling them to cut the deck *any* number of times they want. I amazed a lot of people with that trick, and up until I landed in this nursing home, I used to use it to cadge the occasional free drink down at Sunday's Bar and Grill, which was only three blocks away from my house and made for an easy walk.

I remember the trick, and from that day on, I was hooked. I learned lots of magic tricks. The floating, disappearing, and bending coin variations. A hundred different card tricks—picking a card, making a card float, making a card disappear, making a card vanish and reappear in someone's pocket, and so many more. I can make tiny bouncing balls levitate in the air. I can take a piece of paper, fold it into a rose, light it on fire and hold it out to a woman, and when she reaches out to take it . . . the fire disappears and a real rose is in its place. I used that last one to catch more than one young woman's attention early in my life, before I married. In fact, I used it to catch *her* attention.

I say "can," but I should say "could." The magic, like her, is gone now.

I've spent most of my life performing the magic you've seen on television, but I've never been satisfied because that wasn't real magic. Those are tricks, illusions, sleight of hand, distraction techniques and minor glamors. Not real at all.

Here's another one card trick you'll like, a basic variation on the old "pick a card" gambit:

Take an ordinary deck of playing cards and shuffle them, then spread them out in your hands, face down, and instruct the person to select a card. As you pull the stack of cards neatly together, remind them not to show it to you and ask them to memorize it. When they've memorized it, cut the cards in a random location—you can even ask them to do it—but be certain to look at the bottom card of the top cut, and have them put it back in the deck.

After that, it's simple. Take the stack of cards and begin flipping through them, placing them face up in front of you, until you see the card from the bottom of the cut. The next card is, of course, theirs.

A trick, I know. Not *real* magic. So why do I tell you these things?

To illustrate that *real* magic exists. I have spent most of my life doing tricks of one sort or another and looking for real magic. I was considered old by most standards before I found it. But I did find it.

Magic is real, and there is real magic, and . . . well, anyone can find it if they know where to look.

I found mine in the mirror.

A mirror that showed a reflection of me. And of her.

But it wasn't really us at all.

The young woman stopped outside the door to her father's room and set down the heavy package she carried. A pause to gather courage and strength. He wasn't well, hadn't been for a long time. Her mother's death a few years ago had started a process that was as inevitable as an avalanche—what began as apparent heartbreak had turned into dementia, which was followed by the official diagnosis: Alzheimer's Disease.

Leaning her head against the door, she listened quietly for the sound of her father's voice. The room was quiet and still. Perhaps he was sleeping, and she would be able to leave the package and just go. A wave of guilt passed over her. She loved her father, but seeing him as he was now only made her feel worse. She didn't believe him. No one did.

He believed in magic—real magic—not the kind that he used to perform. The real thing. He was obsessed with it now more than he ever had been, and his focus on it was almost lucid enough to be frightening.

It was almost as though his talent at sleight of hand and illusion had taken on a life of its own, consuming his mind as his disease progressed. And now . . . the package she carried. For the last two months, he'd been insisting that she bring him the mirror.

From the first, it had seemed an odd request. The mirror was nothing special to look at, and other than being a very heavy antique that had been attached to the dresser he had shared with her mother for so many years, there was nothing about it that made it stand out. Initially, she had agreed, but then when she saw how heavy it was, she'd put it off. Giving her father excuse after excuse.

Until now.

The doctor had told her that she *should* bring it. For a man with Alzheimer's, he was lucid enough to keep asking for it, day after day. He remembered the mirror. They didn't know why he remembered that and only that, but it didn't matter *why*. It mattered that he did.

So, with her husband's help, she had carefully removed the mirror from the dresser, wrapped it in a blanket, and loaded it into the car. Today, she would give it him and perhaps it would . . .

Would what? she asked herself. *Make him better? Make him the man she knew, instead of this stranger who saw her only as* . . . She shook her head. It wouldn't help him, she decided. Not really.

But if it pleased him, that would be a good thing.

Magic or no magic, he was her father. Even as he slipped further into the disease, she kept reminding herself of that one fact: No matter what, he was her father.

She turned the knob on the door, bent down and lifted the mirror, then used her hip to push open the door as she entered his small room.

I watch as my daughter enters the tiny room I live in, struggling to carry a large object that is wrapped in a blanket and obviously heavy. Were I younger and less frail, I would stand to help her, but as it is, I can only watch her and remember the man I once was. Stronger and more able.

As she sets it down near the foot of my single bed, a piece of the blanket slips away, revealing a wooden corner. I wonder what she has brought me.

"Hello, Daddy," she says, stretching her back. She leans down and kisses me on the cheek. "How are you feeling today?"

"I'm doing good," I tell her. "They served peaches at lunch. And cottage cheese. Do you remember your mother always eating that when you were little?" I laugh at the memory. "That woman ate more strange salads and fruits than anyone I ever knew. What's wrong with a big steak?"

She laughs lightly, and her voice is like music. "Daddy, you know that you aren't supposed to be eating steak! That's why they served you peaches and cottage cheese. It's good for you!"

"Steak would be good for me, too!" I tell her. "And maybe a baked potato."

We laugh together for a moment, then her face turns serious. "I brought you the mirror," she says, pointing. "The one you've been asking for."

"The mirror?" I say. I do not remember asking for a mirror, but I know that my memory isn't very good these days. "I asked for a mirror?"

She sighs and her music is sadness. "Yes, Daddy," she says. "The one that was kept above the dresser in yours and mom's room. You've been asking for me to bring it to you for months."

"Then why didn't you bring it sooner?" I ask. "Then I'd have remembered why I wanted it in the first place!"

She wants to be angry with me—I can tell by looking at her expression—but she just shakes her head. "Well, Daddy, it's here if you want it." She leans down and removes the blanket covering the mirror, and for a moment, something sparkles in my memory. Something sharp and shiny. There is something special about the mirror . . . I know it, but now must remember it.

She leans down to kiss me again, and her lips are soft and warm on my cheek. I remember when she was born. We named her Taika, Tai for short. Her name meant magic. Magic was important.

I remember that I used to do magic.

"I've got to go now," she says. "The kids still need dinner."

"Yes," I say, making a shooing gesture. "Go and feed the kids. Maybe we'll have steak here tonight."

Her laugh comes again and she says, "Maybe so, Daddy. I love you."

Ahh . . . those are magic words. I know them by heart. Even with my illness—and I know I am somehow ill—I know that the words "I love you" are magic. "I love you, too, Tai," I tell her. "Come back soon."

"I will, Daddy," she says, then slips quietly out the door.

I turn my gaze back to the mirror.

Did it have something to do with magic?

The flash of memory comes again, but it is gone before I can grasp it. I will have to be patient.

Sitting in the recreation room of the Shady Grove Nursing Home is boring. There is a television, but the shows are filled with mindless violence and gratuitous sex. They are shows without heart, seeking only to entertain long enough to cut to a commercial for a product no one needs.

There are books, many of them, and I've read them all. Then forgotten them, of course. But reading them again is like walking on a treadmill—I go nowhere— and so I ignore them. And the magazines, too.

There are other activities available, but the only thing that interests me is the computer. It is a magical box that can take me anywhere in the world. It is also where I type my story. I save it to a disc, and one day, when I am gone, my daughter will find it, and she will know the truth.

I read what I wrote yesterday, and it comes rushing back to me. The same way it does every day when I sit down in the rickety chair and turn on the computer. I cannot explain *why* reading what I've written the day before helps, but it does. It is some of the hidden magic of technology, I think.

This thought triggers another. The mirror! The mirror is in my room. My daughter thinks of it only as the mirror that my wife and I kept over our dresser for many long years, but I know the truth.

The mirror belonged to a very famous magician, Harry Houdini. My grandfather gave it to me, though where he got it from I do not know—but I can remember him showing me the initials carved into the wood on the back of the frame: "H.H."

And he told me that the mirror was magic—real magic—if I could only find the key to unlocking its secrets, which had died with the master magician himself.

It took me nearly forty years to unlock the magic of the mirror. Forty years . . . and now I had the mirror once again. I could use its powers and leave this illness behind me. I remember its secrets, and it undoubtedly knows all of mine.

The problem, I realize, is that once I shut off this computer and begin the long, slow walk to my room, it is likely I will forget. I will forget asking for the mirror. I will forget why it is there. I will forget how to unlock its magic.

It is unlikely that the staff here will allow me to have the mirror here in the recreation room. Why would they? I know that the staff and doctors who have spoken to me while I am sitting here know that I wanted the mirror, but I couldn't tell them the truth. Could I?

Could I tell them how the mirror had belonged to Houdini?

Could I tell them that it was magic—real magic?

That when I unlocked its powers, it would transport my soul away from this place and into another world?

That in that other world my wife was waiting for me?

No. No one would believe.

The magic of this day and age is technological, not fantastical.

They would think I am only a sick old man with a disease. They would think I am remembering one of my shows from long ago, when I could do magic.

Ahh, but with the mirror . . . I still can.

If I can only remember it all when I get back to my room.

I will shut off the computer now and try to get back to my room in time. In time to remember.

The young woman watched as her father crossed the recreation room in an old man's shuffle. She had left her purse behind, but she stopped when she saw her father standing up from the small computer desk and beginning the long trek back to his rooms.

From here it was safe to watch him. It was safe to remember him as he was before . . . before the illness and before her mother had died. She could watch, and in her mind he was once again the amazing magician of her youth, able to conjure coins from thin air, cause paper roses to burst into flame, make cards float up and into the air as though they were feathers captured on a breeze. She remembered that man well.

Her father's face wore a determined, almost stern expression, and his lips moved slightly, as though he wanted to say something but couldn't quite grasp the words.

As he made the turn down the hallway, she slipped behind him, still watching. His was a slow walk, and she knew she should get home to feed the kids, but stealing these few minutes to walk down memory lane would make rushing dinner hour worthwhile. He had not been the same man in a long time.

Finally, he turned and entered his small room. The door shut behind him.

The magical memories playing in her mind stopped.

She resumed her normal stride, then paused outside his door.

Gathering her strength one last time before seeing him again.

From the computer desk, across the recreation room, and up the hallway, I just kept repeating it to myself. *Remember the mirror!*

It was a mantra that I mentally spoke with each

step taken. I would remember the mirror, I would remember how it worked.

I opened the door to my room and there it was. The mirror. What had I wanted to remember about it?

I let the door close behind me. The mirror was special. It had belonged to a famous man. Houdini? Yes, that seemed right. He had been a magician. Like me. Memories flashed sharp and bright in my mind.

I *could* remember the mirror. There was no time to lose. No time to say goodbye. Not even to my daughter who was standing outside my door this very minute. It was impossible to say how long my mind would last.

Not strong enough to lift the mirror, I knelt down and looked into the silvered glass.

My own aged reflection stared back at me: the face of an old man, desperate with the dual longings of hope and despair.

How was the mirror activated again? What made its magic work?

Behind me, I heard the doorknob turn. I couldn't look around. I didn't dare. The memory was *right there*.

"My beloved," I whispered. The glass of the mirror shimmered once, twice, three times, and then I saw her. The face of my wife—young and beautiful and strong as she had been on the day we married.

And she was waiting for me.

I saw her lips move and form the echoing words, "My beloved."

"Yes," I said. "The magic is real. I remember!" My last words were shouted with more strength than I knew I possessed.

Behind me, I heard my daughter's voice cry out, "Daddy! What's wrong?" Her footsteps sounded loud behind me.

There was no time. The magic had to happen now. I looked into the mirror once more, fixed my wife's features firmly in my mind and said the magic words. I meant to shout them, but they came out only as a faint whisper. "I love you."

I could hear my daughter behind me, hear her say,

"I love you, too," but my eyes remained locked on the mirror. I felt my heart contract once, painfully, and my muscles fell slack.

Still, even as I slid to the floor, I kept my eyes on the mirror.

"Daddy, what's the matter?"

I wanted to answer her. To tell her the truth about the mirror and about real magic, but already the last moments of my life were flashing by, my spirit striving to break free and join my beloved wife in the other world.

I wanted to tell her that real magic is about more than cards or coins or paper roses. It is not an illusion, but something quite real and elusive. Real magic, I wanted to tell her, comes from belief . . . and from love.

The mirror shimmered once more, and then darkness fell. My words, my magic words, left unspoken.

Tai wanted to call the nurses, but she knew that to do so would be a cruelty. Her father had obviously suffered some kind of heart attack. To try and revive him now—to bring him back, God forbid—would be to condemn him to more years of this lost existence.

He'd been staring into that silly old mirror when she'd come through the door, and she glanced at it now—and felt her jaw unhinge, then close again with a snap. She rubbed her eyes.

Had the reflection in it wavered just a moment, shimmering like an autumn lake in the sunrise and showing an image of her parents?

No, Tai realized, shaking her head. She knelt down and gently closed her father's open eyes.

That would be too much to hope for. Too much like real magic.

Then she stood and quietly left the room, her eyes clear with the sure knowledge that not even her father's magic could cheat death.

No magic could.

ANGEL IN THE CABBAGES

Fran LaPlaca

"THERE'S an angel," Sharon Madsen said, clearing her throat nervously, "in the cabbages."

Joe Shippey, her manager, looked up blankly, then shrugged.

"Yeah, okay, Madsen, whatever. Did you finish the display?"

Sharon looked back through the plastic windows in the swinging doors and nodded. She could see her display of new fall apples from all the way back here, the green and red spheres stacked neatly and compactly under the sale sign, gleaming in the florescent lights. "Make Your Own Candy Apples!" a hand-lettered sign shouted. Say what you will, Sharon knew her displays were good.

"Fine. Then get these onions out there. And tell Mack to get a u-boat and refill the pumpkins."

"Okay." Sharon hesitated. "But what about the angel?"

"What?" Joe's attention was already back on the paperwork in front of him.

"What should I do about the angel? In the cabbages?"

Joe shook his head and sighed.

"You're a piece of work, Madsen, I swear. Take the

angel home with you for all I care. Just make sure the onions are full before you do."

He didn't believe her, Sharon knew, but that was all right. She filled the onions and then loaded the crates of pumpkins onto the u-boat. The lightweight, wheeled cart, narrow along the base but with both ends higher than Sharon was herself, resembled nothing more than a huge letter U, and had been dubbed a "u-boat" by some wit in the grocery business long ago. The name had stuck, and as awkward as the u-boat was, the design worked, and Sharon was able to easily pull the heavy order of pumpkins out to where Mack was working.

Mack was lazy, and Sharon did half his work. She could always tell Joe, but she didn't mind. Mack was nice to her, called her "Sharon baby", and he'd never once told her she was "a piece of work." Sharon wasn't quite sure what Joe meant by that, but she was sure it wasn't very kind. Besides, saying no wasn't the easiest thing in the world for Sharon. In fact, it was one of the hardest.

She was used to people not being too nice to her. It was usually because they thought, as her mother had always thought and said, that she wasn't the brightest candle in the window. It didn't matter to Sharon what they thought. She knew she was smart, she knew she was funny and witty and wry and flirtatious. Underneath. If none of those traits ever made it to the surface, well, that's the hand she'd been dealt. Shyness, Sharon knew, was just as much a handicap as losing an arm or a leg. Maybe worse, because people without an arm or a leg could still talk to whole people. Shy people could rarely talk to anyone. And confrontations? As far as Sharon was concerned, that was a word in a totally different language.

She punched her time card, put on her jacket, and headed for the cabbage display. She looked carefully, but the angel was gone. She felt a little sad but a little relieved as well. She wasn't sure she'd have had the nerve to ask a heavenly being to come home with her.

"I'm not an angel."

Sharon jerked her head around. It was late, the store was closing in less than an hour, and except for Mack, way over on the other side, the produce section was empty.

"Over here."

A sudden motion caught her eye, and she stepped a few feet sideways, to the bin that contained the fresh portabella mushrooms. There, sitting comfortably on one of the large mushroom caps, sat the angel.

The angel frowned.

"I'm not an angel," she said fiercely, her rainbow-hued wings beginning to flutter as if in anger. "What are you, totally stupid? I'm a sprite."

Sharon just blinked.

"A sprite? You know, an imp? A pixie? An elf with wings?" The winged being shook her head in disgust. "Hello? A fairy?"

"I know what a sprite is," Sharon said in a reasonable voice.

"Then why didn't you say so?"

"I was just wondering," Sharon said, "what you're doing here, that's all."

"Well, then why didn't you just ask?"

Why, indeed, Sharon asked herself. It's not like it was, well, a person.

"I am too a person," the fairy said even more fiercely, and Sharon blinked again. Before the fairy could insult her further she blurted out, "You can read my mind?"

"Look, let's just get out of here, and we can chat all you want. It's too cold here, and that pipe thingy up there keeps raining on me."

"It's a mister," Sharon said automatically as she held out one hand for the fairy to step upon. "It keeps the vegetables from drying out."

"Well, it keeps getting my wings soaked, and I don't like it," the fairy complained as she dug her hands into Sharon's jacket sleeve and began to climb. "I can't fly with wet wings, did you never think of that with your mist-thing?"

"We don't get a lot of fairies," Sharon said faintly as the fairy reached her shoulder and perched.

The fairy sighed and nodded.

"No, I don't suppose you do." She tucked a bit of Sharon's hair into her fist to balance herself. "Most of them go to the natural food stores. Can we get some Chinese food? It's been ages since I've had any lo mein."

"I don't see why we have to share," the fairy stated as she picked up a long lo mein noodle off Sharon's paper plate and bit off the end.

"Well," Sharon said, "payday isn't until Friday, and I only have ten dollars left until then. Four, now," she said as she picked up a piece of garlicky beef.

"So ask for a raise. You're worth more anyway, you know that."

"It's not that easy."

"Sure it is. 'Hey Joe, I'm tired of doing all the work here while you sit on your ass and Mack sneaks smokes in the men's room. I want more money.' See? Easy peasy."

Sharon stared.

"How do you know all these things? About Joe, and Mack, and all?"

"You learn a lot hiding behind ugli fruits, you'd be surprised," the fairy told her. She shook her wings. "Almost dry, thank heavens. Speaking of which, what made you think I was an angel? Not that I'm not flattered, of course." The fairy smirked. "Although angels are a bit plainer, if you know what I mean. All that white, you know."

And truly, Sharon thought, the fairy was anything but plain. Her wings shimmered in colors of every hue, her nut brown skin was complemented by the earthy green bits of fabric that fluttered around her dainty form, and her eyes were the blue of a summer sky. Sharon paused.

"Your wings, I suppose. And of course, fairies aren't real, not really."

The fairy gaped.

"Not real? Then who are you talking to, banana brain?"

Sharon blushed.

"I mean, of course they are. Now. But until I saw you, I didn't think they were real. No one does."

"Those girls in England did."

"That was a hoax. I read about that."

The fairy smirked again.

"So it was. And they almost got away with it, too. Incidentally, Mack's only nice to you so you'll do his work for him."

Sharon was beginning to get used to the fairy's sudden conversation shifts.

"That's what I figured."

"Then why do you put up with it? Just so he doesn't insult you the way Joe does?"

"Yes, actually. It's nice to have at least one person who doesn't call me names. Unlike you," she added, and then blushed.

The fairy sat back.

"Well. A bit of backbone. Not much, but maybe, just maybe, this might not be so hard after all."

"What might not be so hard?" Sharon's curiosity made her ask.

"This is what I recommend," the fairy said, ignoring her question. "Tomorrow, you march in that store and demand a raise. And then, after you get it, you tell Mack to do his own damn work. And then buy a new bra."

"A new bra?"

Sudden shifts in conversations were one thing, but this was from way out of left field. "Yeah, a new bra. A nice one, not white. Red, or pink or something. Lacy."

The fairy's voice was sleepy, and she fluttered her wings once before rising in the air and flying over to Sharon's African Violet plant and settling down on one of the velvety leaves. "Goodnight, Sharon," she said unnecessarily, as she was nearly asleep before she landed.

"Goodnight," Sharon said obediently, then asked suddenly, "What's your name?"

"Call me Ginger," she barely heard.

"Is that your name? Ginger?"

"No. But it's a nice, spicy name, and I like it."

Ginger nestled on Sharon's collar the next morning.

"What do I tell people about you?" Sharon asked.

"Nothing. They won't see me. I'm your fairy, not theirs."

"Oh. I didn't know it worked that way."

"Until yesterday, you didn't believe I even existed."

"True enough."

Sharon felt incredibly energetic as she walked the four blocks to work. Full of life, centered. Empowered. As if she could do anything.

She stopped.

"What have you done to me?" she asked suspiciously.

Ginger sighed. "My job. I'm your fairy, remember?"

"What does that mean, 'my fairy'?"

A middle-aged couple passing by stared at Sharon, then quickly looked away. The man muttered something under his breath as they passed her, and Sharon remembered that no one else could see Ginger. She turned her head and tried to speak without moving her lips, whispering. "What does it mean?"

"It means," Ginger said, her wings tickling Sharon's neck, "that I'm here to help you. And yes, to answer your question from last night, I can read your mind, but only yours, and only because I'm your fairy."

Sharon pondered that, then asked, "Help me with what?"

"With whatever. Getting you a raise. Finding you a boyfriend. Underwear decisions. You know, the important stuff."

"A boyfriend?" Sharon thought she might just faint. She could, in a distant and far off way, imagine herself asking Joe for a raise or even, embarrassing as it might be, buying lingerie. But a boyfriend? Someone who she'd have to speak to all the time, hold hands with, even kiss? And never mind what happened after kissing.

Sharon couldn't even get her imagination to reach the hand holding stage.

"Chill, girl, take it easy. I didn't say definitely, though from your reaction I'd say it's way overdue. Let's work on the raise first. We'll worry about the rest another time."

"Joe, I want a raise. I deserve a raise." Sharon muttered the words under her breath as she finished restocking the baby carrots.

"Demand," Ginger whispered through her hair. "And now's the time. Joe just went into the backroom, and Mack's having a nicotine break. Go, girl. You can do it," Ginger prodded her.

Sharon felt her stomach twist into knots as she followed Joe into the back.

"Joe," Sharon began.

"Carrots done?"

"Almost. I wanted to ask you . . ."

"Well, get them finished. And after that bring in that gourd order from the back dock and set them up in the front in a big display."

Sharon's carefully memorized speech went elsewhere.

"By the door? But I just finished the make-your-own-candy-apples display!"

"So take it down, and do this one. Add some fake leaves and stuff, make it look good. You know what to do."

He turned away, and Sharon took a deep breath and tried to center herself.

"Yes, I know what to do. My displays are always pretty good, aren't they, Joe?"

Joe turned back with a scowl.

"I suppose," he said. "What do you want, a gold star? Get back to work. Your break's not for another hour."

"That's not what I meant," Sharon said, but Joe interrupted, his normally loud voice getting even louder.

"It's what I meant, potato head. Get moving, or I'll dock your pay."

"But I . . ."

Joe's face began to turn thunderous, and Sharon swallowed her words and hurried to the back dock to get the gourds.

"Well, that went well," Ginger said scornfully as Sharon piled the crates onto a u-boat. Sharon blinked back tears and whispered harshly, "Be quiet. It's your fault."

"My fault?" Ginger nearly squealed in indignation. "My fault? You're the one who caved."

"I did not cave," Sharon wiped angry tears away. "He walked all over me, just like he always does. And you were supposed to make me brave or something. Nice job you did with that." Sharon heard the bitterness in her own voice with something like surprise.

"Oh, sure, you can talk back to me, who's only trying to help, but not to Neanderthal-man in there, huh? That's just perfect. I don't know why I bother."

"I don't either. I didn't ask for a fairy. I was doing okay just the way I was."

"You were pathetic, that's what you were," Ginger retorted.

"If that's what you think, then just go back to the cabbages and leave me alone," Sharon shouted, and Ginger flew up off her shoulder in a huff.

"Fine," the fairy snapped, and in an instant she was gone.

"What the hell is going on out here?" Joe stormed out onto the back dock. "Who are you shouting at?"

"None of your damn business," Sharon snapped without thinking, and she grabbed the handle of the u-boat and shoved past him.

Her anger at Ginger sustained her until nearly all the gourds were set up. Then suddenly, as if she hadn't really noticed until just then, the look on Joe's face when she'd yelled at him filled her vision, and she felt a huge shout of laughter welling up inside. She choked it back down before it could escape, and set the last gourd into place with a flourish. She, Sharon Madsen, had actually said the word "damn". With another burst of delight, she realized she was proud of having used bad language.

"What a lovely display."

Sharon looked up to see Mrs. Wingard, one of the store's regular customers, and one of Sharon's old high school teachers.

"Thank you," she said in surprise at the unexpected compliment.

"You always do such a wonderful job, Sharon. I hope cranky old Joseph knows what a treasure he has in you, dear."

To hear Joe called cranky tickled Sharon's funny bone, and it must have shown on her face, for Mrs. Wingard smiled conspiratorially. "He was an old grump even when I had him my class, little Sharon." She leaned closer and whispered, "Most of the boys were. I always thought it was because of jock straps."

"What?" Sharon let this shout of laughter escape, and Mrs. Wingard winked at her and headed for the juice aisle.

Sharon was still giggling when Mack wandered over from where he was sorting the grapes.

"Hey, Sharon baby, how 'bout finishing these grapes for me? I'm starved, and I wanna go grab a quick bite."

Sharon's stomach growled at the thought of her own break, now overdue. The silly smile still on her face, she shook her head.

"Not right now, Mack. My break's before yours." Her eyes wandered down his skinny form. Mack's not grouchy, so maybe he doesn't wear one, she thought, then as she realized where she was staring, she giggled again and raised her eyes. Mack, to her utter amazement, was blushing.

That wonderful feeling of energy she'd had on the

way into work returned, and she grabbed the now-empty u-boat and started to walk away.

"And do your own damn work for a change," she added over her shoulder.

She wasn't sure, as she didn't look back, but she thought she heard Mack choke.

Joe watched her as she pushed the u-boat into an empty corner. His face was still as angry as it ever was, but Sharon, as if with new eyes, thought she saw a bit of wariness as well. She decided she'd done enough empowering of herself for one day and determined to just take her lunch break and leave it at that, but as she walked past the tiny desk where he worked, Joe stood.

What he'd planned to do or say Sharon never knew, because the only thought that she could manage as her boss confronted her was the fact that his jock strap must be too tight.

She knew she was blushing, but she also knew a huge, smirky kind of smile was crossing her face, and Joe, who'd opened his mouth to speak, abruptly closed it. Sharon smiled even wider and opened her locker.

"I want a raise," she said as she took her lunch bag out. Joe stared.

"Did you hear me? I want a raise, Joe."

"I . . . heard you," Joe said.

Sharon looked at the paper bag in her hand. A baloney sandwich and a yogurt. She tossed it in the trash can next to Joe's desk.

"And I need to take a little bit longer for lunch today. I have an errand I need to run."

"An errand?" Joe shook his head as if he was dizzy.

"Yes." Sharon started through the swinging doors. "I need a new bra."

"I knew you could do it," Ginger whispered as Sharon left the store and headed downtown. The fairy was perched on Sharon's shoulder as if she'd never left.

"You did, didn't you?" Sharon said in a normal voice, ignoring the odd look a boy on a bike gave her.

"So where were you just now, when I finally stood up for myself?"

"Don't be silly," Ginger said. "I was with you the whole time. Who do you think gave Mrs. Wingard the idea to go shopping today? Jock straps," she giggled. "I couldn't have done it better myself." The fairy cleared her throat. "Now, about that boyfriend issue . . ."

RAINING THE WILD HUNT

Kate Paulk

POUNDING music from her headphones drove the forest sounds from Megan's awareness, and as she ran, the deserted backwoods trail became simply another obstacle, another challenge. She ran to forget, her feet pounding in time to the music, the shaded, oak-lined trail just a quiet place where she was unlikely to have to deal with people.

Until she'd started divorce proceedings against Frank, Megan had never known what a blessing an iPod and a deserted forest trail could be.

Not that she was stupid. Frank had promised to "get" her for breaking from his control. Rather than hide, Megan took precautions. Precautions like the concealed carry license and the loaded .40 Beretta PX4 with two spare magazines she always carried. Like the regular sessions at the local police firing range with her cousin Jen, imagining Frank standing in front of the target with his genitals dangling over the center circle. Jen had recommended the Beretta and got her licensed for it.

The self-defense courses, the sessions at the gym where she worked until she trembled with exhaustion, all were ways to make sure no one could *ever* control her again. Never control her, never hit her, and never, never send her to hospital to miscarry the baby she had so desperately wanted.

Her iPod changed tunes, moving to "It's Raining Men." Megan focused on the words, letting her feet carry her through the forest. Air cooled her face, drying sweat before it could drip. The comforting weight of her fanny pack and the loaded pistol inside it snugged against her waist bounced with each step, enough to reassure without being uncomfortable.

The air in front of her shimmered, and a man dropped onto the trail in front of her.

Megan's body reacted before she fully realized what she saw. She pushed hard with her left leg, leaned forward as she stretched out with her right leg so her foot came down on the leaf-littered trail and not the sprawled body that had not been there a second before. She stumbled forward awkwardly, arms windmilling for balance, and stuttered to a halt in time for the Weather Girls to sing "find the perfect guy."

Megan fumbled for the iPod and turned it off.

She turned around slowly, not sure whether she wanted the man to be there or not. She didn't want anything to do with men. Not after Frank.

The impossible man was still there, unmoving. He looked like a refugee from the Renfaire, wearing all deep green, the colors shading slightly from the silk shirt, the velvet vest, soft leather pants and boots. Long golden-brown hair curled around his shoulders and over his face. If not for the very male bulge in his pants—a bulge that indicated nature had been more than merely generous there—Megan might have wondered if he was really male.

He was still anything but "the perfect guy," whoever he was and however he'd got here.

Megan reminded herself that she'd married what she thought was the perfect man, and that had got her nothing but bruises.

A bird chirped somewhere nearby, answered by one from further away.

The man still hadn't moved, although the movement of his chest suggested he was breathing. Megan belatedly moved toward him. "Hello?"

He didn't respond.

She bent, trying to remember her first aid classes. *Response, Airway, Breathing, Circulation.* With her left hand, she gently touched his arm. "Hello?"

The man shuddered, pulling away from her in what had to be an instinctive reaction. His eyes opened wide, eyes the impossibly bright green of new leaves.

Megan swallowed, backed away. Nothing human was that beautiful. Even with stray locks of hair falling over his face, with his clothes torn and bloody scratches marking creamy-pale skin, he was a work of art given life.

"Art thou . . . *mortal?*" The twist of disgust he gave the last word had Megan's right hand twitching for the zip on her fanny pack, for the smooth chill of her pistol.

"I'm mortal, asshole. And leaving. If you've broken anything, there might be someone else along in the next day or so to help you." She turned, wanting nothing more to do with impossible, beautiful men who seemed to think being human was a mortal sin.

"Please, wait." He sounded panicked.

Megan kept walking. She unzipped her fanny pack and slipped her right hand in, closed her hand around the grip of the pistol.

"Please . . . the Hunt . . . they will follow . . ."

The terror in his voice dragged her to a stop, pulled her back to face him. "What have you brought here?"

He pulled himself to his feet, clinging to one of the oaks by the trail. "Only myself, my Lady. The Hunt . . . thou hast legends of them, surely?"

The Wild Hunt, the Hunters . . . There were legends all right. "Sure. Which one would you like?" This was ridiculous. If she had not felt the soft, finely woven silk, not heard his liquid chocolate voice, Megan might have dismissed the whole thing as an insane delusion.

Something inside her refused to allow that.

The man winced. " 'Tis best not to deride them, my Lady." He shuddered. "I have confused them by making a portal to this realm, but once they realize how

I escaped them, they surely will follow. They mislike losing prey."

"That's just perfect." Megan released her grip on the Beretta. This man wasn't going to attack her. He seemed to be having difficulty staying upright.

She folded her arms and glared at him. "So you've unleashed this hunt of yours here. Thank you so much."

He leaned against the tree and closed his eyes, looking pale and thoroughly vulnerable. "I wished to live, even if only for a short time longer." A shudder ran through his body. "Better I should have ended my own life."

"Whoa there!" Part of Megan wanted to curse him for a manipulative bastard. Instead, she found herself asking, "What happens if they catch you?" She stepped closer.

He flinched. "If I am fortunate, I die quickly." His voice was little more than a whisper as he turned haunted eyes to her. "They feed on suffering, my Lady. The terror of the prey, the pain as it dies . . . And if they can enslave it to make its pain last the longer, they will do so."

Megan's lips pulled back in a snarl. "I know the type." The fingers of her left hand drummed her right arm. A cool breeze ruffled her dusty blond hair and rustled the leaves. "All right. How many of them are there?"

He blinked. "Perhaps fifty ride the Hunt, my Lady. But . . ."

"Your kind don't like steel, do they?" At his blank look, Megan added, "Steel. Refined iron."

He winced. "It is deadly to us, my Lady. It blocks our senses, eats our very souls." Another shudder. "The least of wounds given with iron can kill even High Fey."

"Good." Megan frowned. "So, what do I call you? I'm not shouting 'Hey, you' whenever I need your attention." Her mind raced ahead, to defenses, to hunters who tortured their prey. Fifty-odd creatures with souls like Frank. She wouldn't leave anyone to that.

"I am named Delorias, my Lady."

"Megan."

Megan's initial notion had been to get herself and Delorias as far from the place where he'd appeared as possible. That plan vanished a few steps along the path, when he stumbled and lurched into her. She caught his weight with a grunt of effort.

He bowed his head, panting.

While she strained to hold him upright, Megan began to realize how much damage those fancy clothes of his hid. Every time she tried to get a better grip through the slippery silk and torn velvet, he gasped with pain.

She sighed and eased him to sit with his back against a tree. "This isn't working. They already ran you damn near to death, didn't they?"

A little color touched those too-pale cheeks as he bowed his head. "Yes."

She frowned, her hands on her hips. "Great. I get myths dropping out of midair in front of me, a mythical chase that might or might not show up any time, and god only knows what else." She shook her head. "To think all I wanted was a *normal* life."

Her words fell into silence.

Ice crawled down Megan's spine. The sudden stillness scraped at her nerves. There was a chill taste to the air under the smells of earth and summer growth.

"The Hunt," Delorias whispered.

"Crap." Ancient instinct lifted the hair on the back of her neck. Even in the mildest legends of the Hunt they ran their prey to the ground before they killed. No legend Megan had heard mentioned anyone escaping them. "What can you do? Throw stones? Anything?"

He swallowed. "I may be able to work some minor magics, my Lady." Everything about him spoke of hopelessness: his slumped posture, bowed head, listless voice.

"Move." The air above the trail shimmered. "Into the forest." Megan grabbed his collar as she darted past, hauling him with her even though her arm screamed protest.

Reality seemed to twist, then her ears popped, and there was sound once more. The sound of restless mounts, of armor creaking and clinking.

Megan spun, vaulting a low bush to put a sturdy oak between her and whatever now occupied the trail. A moment later, she was intensely thankful she had hidden herself.

When she peeked out, what she saw through the masking bushes made her stomach churn with nausea. She wiped her palms on her jeans.

Perhaps half the riders gathered on the trail were elves like Delorias. They rode sleek horses and wore fanciful crystalline armor, but no helmets obscured beautiful, pitiless faces. Men and women alike had long hair flowing freely or elaborately dressed, but not one face showed anything but eager cruelty.

Then there were the . . . other things. Great black hounds with glowing red eyes and slavering jaws. One-eyed giants holding massive stone clubs. Shriveled things that looked more like decaying corpses than living beings, clawed hands all the weapons they needed.

A woman whose dark hair flowed like liquid night over scarlet armor urged her mount forward. A cruel smile curled full lips as red as her armor. "Thy prey lies within a few paces, Lord Athaniel." Her teeth were very white, the eye teeth sharpened to fangs. "A mortal woman stands near."

"I know of them, Leannan Sidhe. Thou art not alone in thy gift." That speaker could have been discussing the weather for all the emotion in his voice.

Megan spared a moment to wonder how it was they spoke English—albeit bad Renfaire English—as she snaked her right hand down to her fanny pack and her pistol. The *things* could not be special effects: No special effect included the smell of rot mingled with roses.

Her hand closed around the grip, eased it free.

The man spoke once more. "Bring them out."

Two of the red-eyed hounds stepped off the trail, a powerful animal musk wafting with them.

The pistol was cold in Megan's hands. She aimed, steadying her right hand with her left.

Without earmuffs, the shot sounded like thunder in her ears. The howling of the dying hound seemed oddly distant as it thrashed, its claws scoring trees and dirt.

Again.

The second hound's thrashing as it died sent it twisting back onto the path.

Megan swallowed.

The laughter of the leader seemed to come through a long tunnel. "So, the mortal has fangs." His amusement did not reassure.

Megan held the pistol steady, waiting.

"Fan out," the leader ordered. "Leannan, thou shalt see they surround our prey. Kill them only if capture is impossible. I wish to . . . meet . . . this so-brave mortal."

Crap. Megan knew that tone too well. She was beyond screwed.

Beside her, Delorias made a sound of terror.

"If you've got any little surprises up those sleeves, you'd better use them," she muttered. Even if someone heard shooting up here, the chance of anyone actually investigating was minimal. There was no chance anyone with enough firepower to stop the Hunt would investigate.

A blond elf woman in emerald armor urged her horse over the gap the dead hounds had made. Her delicate face was set off by intricate braids woven through with gold.

Megan envisioned Frank on the silvery-gray horse, and fired.

With the hammer of doom ringing in her ears, she watched the elf woman's armor shatter and fall away, watched her horse rear, twisting and bucking. The animal caught the woman's arm in sharp teeth and dragged her through the forest, her screams cut short when her head slammed into a tree.

Megan swallowed bile. Her stomach twisted.

A giant loomed to the right. Another shot, and another scream, this one a deep rumbling sound that vibrated through her bones.

She leaned against the tree, shuddering. She had never thought it would be this difficult to kill. Her hands trembled, and with every breath she had to fight the urge to vomit.

Another shape, this one a twisted mockery of a living thing that could not have existed without magic. Another shot.

Megan's heart pounded as loudly as the thunder in her ears. Five shots, twelve left. Two more clips after that.

The noise and acrid smell of each shot seemed to push her into a different world, one where she watched some other woman fire repeatedly into the woods, stony-faced as inhuman creatures screamed and died.

For each creature she killed, each elf to fall screaming, more of them came, inhuman glee lighting faces beautiful and hideous. They had no loyalty to their fallen kin, only delight in the suffering and death. With each death, the remaining Hunters seemed to glow brighter, glaring multicolored lights in the shadows of the forest.

Delorias curled himself around her feet, shivering.

The eerie glow of the Hunters drew closer as she fired again and again until the slide locked. Her hand moved automatically to eject the spent clip and slot one of her spares into place. A red-headed man stepped in front of her, reaching for her, and she raised the pistol again.

Megan's hands moved automatically, firing even as

his armor clinked against the barrel. He rocked back, pain twisting his impossibly beautiful face. His glittering armor crazed and shattered, falling with him and revealing an incongruously small hole in his chest. Blood spread from it through the white silk of his shirt, a scarlet splash.

Something closed over her left arm, hard and unyielding.

She turned, fired.

The grip spasmed painfully, releasing as its owner fell back.

A jerk on her collar pulled her off-balance, then she was dragged upright against the solid bulk of an armored body. Claws under a gauntleted hand pricked her throat, sending a trickle of blood down into her tee shirt.

Megan slid the Beretta back into her fanny pack as she let her hands appear to fall.

Sounds seemed to seep through the blood and death-tainted forest, conversation, laughter. Around her, small fires flared, consuming the dead and adding the tang of ash and smoke to the air.

Her captor pushed her forward. She had a glimpse of something dragging Delorias toward the trail before trees blocked the sight.

Nineteen. She'd taken nineteen of them. Her hands tingled.

She'd *killed* nineteen of them.

There was no time for reality to sink in: Megan's captor pushed her toward a bush. Thankfully not the rambling thorny things that grew in the swampy areas, but his—its?—intention was clear enough. She caught the bush with one foot, stamping it down so she could cross it without getting caught up in its branches.

The low growl from behind her sounded male.

"Bring the mortal here." The leader's voice allowed no possibility of refusal.

Megan's captor pushed, claws digging a little deeper into her neck. She obeyed, hands tense. Just one chance . . .

Elves in glittering crystalline armor blocked the

trail. They parted at a barked command from her captor, staring at her as she was guided forward. Their stares reminded her of cats watching a mouse. Cats had more mercy.

Her captor shoved her into the circle of watching elves and creatures. Delorias lay on the trail, his clothing somehow gone. There was no sign of it anywhere, as though the cloth and leather had simply been magicked away. His muscles quivered, and pain twisted his face.

"You left it armed?" This time, the words weren't English. The meaning seemed to seep into her bones without touching her ears.

Megan's gaze was drawn up to that cold, commanding voice. She took in a figure in ruby armor, blond and beautiful and cold as winter ice. Even as her right hand dipped in to her fanny pack, something wrapped around her, freezing her in place, a helpless witness to whatever might occur.

A gravelly voice rose behind her. "Lord Athaniel, I—"

"You hoped it would do what you lack the courage to try yourself." Scorn layered the man's voice, scorn and contempt.

Scarlet light sparked from his fingertips, arcing past Megan as though she was not present. Screams erupted behind her, shrieks of agony that made her chest and stomach tighten. Worst was the way Athaniel's head tilted back, his eyes half-closed with pleasure as he drank in the suffering of his dying subordinate.

She strained to pull free of the magic holding her, strained and failed. She could not even twitch a finger.

When the screams finally died, the elf Lord stalked forward, his bright green eyes glittering. "You have cost my Hunters a great deal, mortal." He extended a ruby-gauntleted hand to place a finger under her chin, tilt her head up to meet his eyes. "You will pay dearly for that." His eyes narrowed. "If you convince me to be merciful, I may not leave you for my Hunters to play with when I am done with you."

Terror beat at the magical walls holding her, terror and rage. There would never be another Frank. Never. Just one shot, one moment was all she needed. Megan prayed for that one chance with all her soul.

The magic held fast.

Athaniel gestured to one of the creatures behind him. "You, bring the prey. I think we will dance with him at the feast tonight."

The cheer his words inspired convinced Megan that "dance" was not meant in any sense of the word she knew.

"You, remove the mortal's belt." Athaniel stepped back, leaving Megan to seethe helplessly while unseen fingers worked at the clip of her fanny pack. She trembled with strain, fighting to break free of the invisible bonds.

A soft click, and the strap of her fanny pack dropped from her left side, taking any hope of regaining her pistol with it.

"Conceal it in the woods. It holds iron."

The startled hiss from behind her was small consolation. The thought of an elf holding the fanny pack as if it would bite could not overcome being trapped and helpless at the hands of these creatures.

Athaniel was not finished with her. At a gesture, a chill breeze seemed to burn from her shoulders to the soles of her feet. Before Megan could gasp, the sensation was gone. It took her a moment to realize she felt dirt and leaf litter beneath her feet. Her bare feet. Every breath of air tingled against her skin.

If she had been able to speak, Megan would have cursed him with the worst language she knew.

The elf Lord tilted his head, studying her with feline amusement. "Better."

The air grew heavy, crushing. A force that Megan did not doubt could snap her in two pushed her to her knees, forced her to bow her head.

Laughter skittered through the watching elves, died.

Her body was freed, and the invisible force shoved hard, sending her sprawling at Athaniel's feet. Before she could scramble upright, pain ripped through her body, setting every nerve on fire. Eternity passed, an eternity filled with nothing but pain, then it was gone as if it had never been, leaving Megan panting where she lay, muscles twitching in the grip of random spasms.

"Much better." Athaniel's voice seemed to float from somewhere above her.

Megan had barely time to draw breath before it began again.

Cold. Pain. Megan shuddered, and winced as little flares of pain shot through her body. She hadn't felt this bad since Frank had put her in the hospital.

The musty smell of poorly circulating air and unwashed bodies told her this place was no hospital. Megan opened her eyes, dreading what she might see.

She lay naked on bare stone, in a small room carved from solid rock. A grille set high in a wall gave a little light, and more light leaked under the bottom of a heavy wooden door opposite the grille. A smudge of pale skin in the dimness was all she could see of whoever shared this prison with her.

"Delorias?" Her voice came out as a croak.

"My Lady!" He sounded as hoarse as Megan, most likely for the same reason. "You should have fled and left me."

"Screw that." Megan levered herself up, wincing with each new spasm of pain. It hurt more than she would have believed just to sit, to lean against the rough, cold stone. "Where are we?"

"The prisons of Castle Moondark." Delorias swallowed. "They will end my life this night."

Where she would be kept alive to play to their sick amusements: Megan did not need to be told that. "Tell me about the castle." She had to get out of here before Athaniel began his games. If what he had done to her was any indication, she would not be in any condition to escape after he started.

"My Lady?"

Megan leaned against the stone behind her, pushing her body up into she stood leaning against the stone. "How do we escape it?"

Delorias paused before he spoke. "It cannot be done," he said finally. "The castle stands atop Moondark Peak, and we do not fly."

Stealing one of those glossy horses wasn't an option, Megan guessed. They became uncontrollably vicious without the control of their elf masters. That didn't leave much choice.

She'd rather try to climb down a mountain than face Athaniel again.

A tentative step forward sent more pain through her joints. Megan winced, and took another step. And a third. And a fourth.

The grille was higher than she could reach, the wall too smooth to climb. Megan turned and walked the few steps to the door.

It opened outwards, the hinges not visible from inside the cell. Metal bracing surrounded the lock. Copper, Megan supposed, given the way elves reacted to iron. There was nothing she could use except the space between the wall and the door. That . . . If she stood on the lock side she might be able to ambush a guard.

She clenched her teeth. Better to die fighting than whatever Athaniel planned. Megan just hoped the martial arts training she had done would work against elves. To help keep off the chill, she started jogging in place, nothing too strenuous. She could run for hours at this pace—although she was usually in better shape when she did. A good sports bra helped, too. Megan had forgotten just how much bounce there was in unprotected breasts.

By alternating jogging with walking, Megan kept the chill of the air from making her stiff and cold. After a time, Delorias joined her, though he said little until the light from the grille began to dim.

"Those who collect us will likely be magical constructs," he murmured. "Made to obey, perhaps to inspire fear. They are unlikely to be able to think for themselves."

Megan nodded. "Thanks." It might be a fool's hope, but she refused to walk meekly to death—or worse. Once had been enough.

They walked and jogged without speaking for a stretch of time marked only by their own breathing, their own footfalls. The grille became invisible, lost in the darkness of night outside.

"Something comes." Tension strained at Delorias's soft voice. "Possibly a construct."

A few steps later, Megan heard it: plodding footfalls on the other side of the door. They drew closer, stopped outside the door. She froze, poised.

Scraping sounds as a bolt was pulled, a squeal as a key turned. The rattling of a doorknob in its frame.

The door pulled open, and a massive shape filled the doorway.

Megan held her breath. Surely the thing would see her and Delorias in the corner.

It lumbered forward.

That was all the encouragement Megan needed. She darted behind it, and out into the long corridor beyond. Another of the creatures waited there, arms hanging loosely from its shoulders. Megan's heart pounded as she raced away from it, her ears straining for lumbering footsteps. None came.

Instead, Delorias drew level with her, touched her arm to draw her to the side, to a door whose bolt was not drawn.

They slipped inside, waiting.

Silence. It seemed to last forever.

Finally, Megan heard the heavy steps of the guard creatures as they left the prison.

"They will surely be sent back and the prison searched," Delorias whispered. "We must move swiftly."

Megan pushed the door open and slipped out, then eased it closed once Delorias joined her. Neither needed a signal to run.

They raced through the long corridor to crude stairs

carved from the rock. Up, climbing a long stairwell with nowhere to hide, to another heavy door.

Megan could hear nothing beyond it. After a while, Delorias nodded, and pushed the door open. The creatures had not locked it.

Tension knotted between Megan's shoulderblades. On the other side of the door a hallway three times her height shone in glittering crystal lit from within. They dared not let anyone see them, not here. Delorias's bruises and scratches against his white skin, their nakedness . . . They could not be mistaken for anything but escapees.

He eased the door shut. "The heights." It was the barest of whispers, but still the crystal-clad walls caught the sound, reflecting it endlessly.

Megan nodded, and they began to run once more.

The aeries were a charnel house. Megan stood, her hands on her thighs as she panted, trying to catch her breath and hold her stomach. She had expected the smell of horses, of hay and wheat. Not to see sharp-toothed horse things tearing into meat.

Meat that looked like it had once belonged to a human—or an elf.

Sweat dripped from her hair, slicked her skin. She had no idea how far she and Delorias had run, only that below them Athaniel's Hunters searched with a fury that made her chest tighten with fear. She had no notion why they had not been stopped, not been found, and could only hope that their good fortune would last long enough for them to escape.

At least the aeries had side passages. Megan presumed that the conspicuously absent attendants used the passages to bring food to the creatures, and to discard their waste.

She straightened, swallowing, and nodded to Delorias.

They walked toward the stars outlined by the passage. Like the prison, it was rough-cut stone, unadorned. Cold air brushed through the passages, making Megan shiver.

Only a few steps more, she promised herself. *Then it's downhill all the way.*

"Leaving so soon?"

Megan whirled, fury rising within her. Athaniel's lazy amusement, his arrogance, made her long to wipe the mockery from his face. He stood with his legs apart and his arms crossed, a vision of inhuman beauty in red silk and velvet.

Without thought, she surged towards him, left hand raised with her fingers curled to claws, splayed out to catch both eyes.

Surprise flickered across Athaniel's face. Both his hands closed around her left wrist.

Her right knee drove up, hard, between his legs.

Athaniel's breath caught. He released Megan's arms, doubling over to protect his abused genitals.

She pulled away from him. This time, Megan had no need to conjure Frank's image from her imagination. She had more than enough reason to want Athaniel to suffer.

Her kick caught him behind the ear. Even though she was barefoot, the kick connected with enough force that he lurched to the side and toppled. His head hit the stone floor with a dull crack.

Megan hopped backwards. "Crap. That hurt."

"He still lives." Delorias sounded as though he had no idea what to think.

Megan hobbled back to him, her toes throbbing. "I don't care. I just want out of here." She could probably prize a rock from the mountain and make sure Athaniel would never wake, but . . . She had killed too many already. The thought of killing someone in cold blood, even a bastard like Athaniel, made her stomach twist.

The passage opened to a sheer cliff. Megan swayed back into the passage, gulping. She closed her eyes. "I don't suppose you can make us fall softly or something?"

"His spells block me from working magic."

She opened her eyes and really *looked* at Delorias.

Even in the dim light leaking from the aeries, he looked
bad. Pale, with dark circles under his eyes. "Ouch."
Megan had no real idea what to say, or how to express
sympathy. "I guess that means you can't—" she swallowed. "—do anything about him, either."

Delorias shook his head. "It would be my death."

Something was going to be their deaths soon. Either
Athaniel would wake and be *really* pissed, or they'd
die trying to climb an unclimbable cliff. Neither option appealed.

Megan shivered. "Let's climb. Maybe something
will . . ." She couldn't make herself finish. There was
nothing to save them, nothing to stop Athaniel simply
plucking them from the cliff face even if they managed
not to fall.

She clenched her teeth and sat at the passage entry,
legs dangling over a height she didn't want to consider.

Dark shapes flitted through the air, blotting out the
stars in a flickering veil of shadows.

Delorias rested his hands on her shoulders. "I
can . . . send you on quickly," he said finally. "It is
too little, but it is all I can offer."

Megan watched the approaching shapes, hypno-
tized. "No." Her voice sounded distant, as though it
belonged to someone else. "But thank you." A merciful death was no small thing here, no artifact of medical science that could prolong life for years without
adding any quality to it. Here, mercy meant a swift
end, with no torture.

A flicker of scarlet light bloomed about the shadows, gone as quickly as it had come.

"Dragons?" Delorias's hands tightened about her
shoulders. "But they never—"

A voice with the rumbling power of an earthquake
vibrated through Megan's bones, a voice that didn't
touch her ears. "Have thee trust, and jump!"

The power in that voice, the command, took her
body and demanded obedience. As though in a dream,
Megan lifted her legs, set her feet against the cliff face.

She leaned forward, closed her eyes, and pushed with all her strength.

Air rushed past her, icy, tearing at her skin. If she screamed, she couldn't hear it over the rush of air in her ears.

Something closed around her, slowing her fall, gradually reducing the rushing wind until she could hear the steady beat of wings. Immense wings . . . and claws that held her as gently as a mother cradling a baby.

This is too much. Megan had time for that one thought before the day's exertions, the fear, everything caught up with her, and she knew nothing more.

The familiar sounds and smells of an oak forest seemed so out of place that Megan sat with a lurch that sent her head spinning. "What . . . ?" This was the state park. Her forest. She could see the bush she'd flattened rather than be pushed through it, see the marks in the dirt and leaf litter that told of horses and people.

A quick, frantic examination revealed her clothes, her shoes and socks, even her iPod, all where they belonged.

She shook her head. "Christ. I couldn't have passed out and dreamed all that?"

Her fanny pack was missing.

Megan climbed to her feet, wincing as every muscle in her body complained. That on its own was reason to believe the whole thing had happened, even if bent and broken greenery was all she had to prove it.

"Crap. Trust me to get an elf who dumps me back here when the whole deal is over." Though she knew Delorias deserved better, Megan needed to bitch about something, and she didn't dare think too closely about Athaniel. The last thing she wanted to do was bring him and his Hunt back here.

She turned slowly, scanning the woods.

There. "Got you!" Megan reached under a tangle of broken shrub and caught the strap of her fanny pack. The familiar weight felt comforting as she fastened it around her waist. The knowledge that she wouldn't have to pay a small fortune to replace her Beretta was even more comforting. It wasn't a cheap piece of hardware.

She patted the outline of the pistol, and smiled.

Then frowned as something crackled.

Megan reached inside. The pistol was there, presumably undamaged—something she would need to check when she cleaned it—but there was also something that didn't feel quite like paper.

She drew it out, unfolded the creamy rectangle.

The note was simple enough, once she puzzled out spelling that wasn't so much appalling as several hundred years late. It seemed that dragons regularly flew around the castle seeking anyone who might be trying to escape, rescuing who they could, and killing the Hunters' mounts when the opportunity arose. Delorias seemed surprised, Megan had the impression from his words that he had thought dragons cared nothing for what happened among the other Fey creatures.

The dragons had built the portal to return her home and had restored her possessions. They wished her well, as did he.

Just as well, Megan thought. *I had enough trouble with a human partner. Who knows what I'd get from an elf?*

And that, it seemed, was that. All the evidence was gone. Not a trace of elf blood remained to darken the ground. She couldn't even smell the cordite from all the rounds she'd fired. If she told anyone about this, they'd think she was insane.

All the same, Megan was going to decorate her house with iron grille work. She wasn't taking any chances with that bastard Athaniel.

She started walking, putting her earphones in and switching on the iPod. A moment later, she skipped to the next tune. After today, she didn't want to know what would happen if she played "It's Raining Men" again.

STILL LIFE, WITH CATS

Kristine Kathryn Rusch

THE feral cats in the courtyard were having sex again. Joshua pulled his pillow over his head and tried to go back to sleep. No matter how many times he got animal control out here, he never seemed to win.

A thousand cats had to live in the trees behind the old stone mansion. A thousand cats, and a thousand more being made every single day.

No one had warned him about the cats when he moved in.

Or the raccoons. They made even worse sounds during sex than the cats. Cats were bad enough; they sounded like panicked children or terrified women, bringing back old memories from his years in Beirut, Bosnia, and Iraq.

But raccoons sounded like vicious lions ripping up a corpse. On his first night in the mansion, he grabbed his largest flashlight and ventured outside to see what was causing the noise—his curse, always to run toward danger instead of away from it—and expected to see a bear mauling some skanky kid who'd been smoking meth near the back of the property.

Instead, he startled two raccoons having a private (well, not really private, more like intimate) moment.

One screeched and scurried toward him, while the other fell over backward.

He ran all the way back to the mansion, laughing harder than he had in years. Fortunately, the raccoon didn't give pursuit.

Outside his window, the sex continued. One particularly throaty yowl sounded like Stuben's cameraman right after the roadside bomb sliced off his left leg.

The image—blood spurting, Stuben covered with shrapnel crawling toward his injured friend, the truck burning behind them—already flashed in front of Joshua's eyes.

He wouldn't get any more sleep, maybe not for a few days.

He rolled over and looked at the clock alarm he didn't need. Six A.M. A long day of nothing ahead. But if he stayed in bed, he would either haul out his gun and shoot the damn cats—which was illegal, since he was just inside the city limits—or he would try to sleep and would suffer the nightmares for the rest of the morning.

More yowling. His skin had become gooseflesh. He rubbed his right arm, the only unscarred patch of his upper torso, and watched the gooseflesh disappear. Then he got up, and made the bed, just as if he were still in the field.

Actually, it felt as if he were in the field. This old mansion reminded him of some of the places in Bosnia—built long ago, abandoned by the people who had loved it, and left to decay. Yet vestiges of luxury remained.

This room was one of those vestiges. The gold marble floor caught the morning light, and the sand-colored walls reflected it. The bed stood on a large raised platform made of marble as well, and his friend Roxy had placed silk hangings around the king-sized mattress, so that it felt as if he slept under expensive mosquito netting—not that he needed any in this part of Oregon.

The bed itself, one of those pillow-top jobbies with

a machine that adjusted the mattress hardness, bordered on ridiculous. So did the silk sheets, the thick down comforter he hadn't needed since it was spring, and the extra soft pillows. The occasional tables matched the marble floor, and the vanity in the walk-in closet seemed like just that, a vanity.

But he'd only given Roxy a week to prepare the place for his arrival. That included furnishing, cleaning, and repair. From what he had heard (and seen) the cleaning had taken most of the week. The furnishing was a one-day affair, and the repair, unless it was an emergency, hadn't gotten done at all.

His own fault, really. From the time he left the hospital in Wiesbaden to the day he had arrived in the town his passport claimed as home, he'd had nearly six weeks. Of course some of that included evaluations at Bethesda, and a psych work-up in some private D.C. clinic that operated on government grants.

But he still could have guessed his arrival here with more than a week's accuracy.

Here, not home. He couldn't call this place home. It wasn't. It never had been. He'd come here as a child to visit his grandparents, and he'd spent summers in a now-unusable room down the hall. From those visits, he remembered his grandmother's kitchen (warm and inviting, always smelling of coffee and cake), the books in the library (mostly untouchable in languages he couldn't then read), and the hot sunlight (clear and crisp without the haze of humidity he had come to accept from his parents' sojourn in the south).

He used to think he loved it here. But he had discovered he didn't love it anywhere. Not that one place was better than the next. No. He couldn't stay in any place long enough to get to know it.

That was one of the many reasons he'd become a war correspondent. One of the many reasons he'd traveled for ninety percent of his adult life.

One of the many reasons he felt like he was going slowly insane locked in this place, on the outskirts of a town he didn't remember.

The cats screeched, and then something clattered. He peered out the window in time to see a black-and-white tabby fleeing across the yard. A clay pot, still filled with dirt, had fallen over. A gray cat with eyes that looked like abalone stared at him from below.

The evil eye, his great-grandmother would have said. She had lived in this room until he was eight. That summer, she had died during her afternoon nap, and his grandmother made him say good-bye.

That was the first time he had seen death. The small, shrunken old woman with clawlike hands was completely motionless. She smelled faintly of pee and mothballs. Her skin was a color of gray that he knew was unnatural, even then.

His grandmother had cried that afternoon, but all he had felt was relief. Relief that the old woman wouldn't caw questions at him, spraying him with her musty breath; relieved that those hands would no longer clutch at him; relieved that he no longer had to pretend to enjoy the sticky candies she had forced on him every morning when he went to see her before being allowed outside.

Outside, into the courtyard, where fountains had once sprayed and flowers had bloomed. The same courtyard where cats had sex and broke his grandmother's pots and stared at him as if he was the one who was out of place.

He waited until ten to call animal control, and by then it felt like midafternoon. He was hot and cranky and filled with coffee. He'd already watched three iterations of *Headline News*, two silly *Fox News* roundups, and some MSNBC reports, all while tuning his radio back and forth between the BBC and NPR. He had read the *Oregonian* and wished for better west coast paper versions of the east coast dailies, because reading them on-line made him feel as if he were still in the field.

He saved the international papers for the real afternoon, when he was done with the American entertainment nonsense and ready for unabashed journalism.

But he had a gap to fill between ten and one, and on this day, he decided to fill it by solving the cat problem once and for all.

He got the same dispatch that he always got, a lackluster woman with a voice to match, who seemed to believe that people's animal problems were none of her business. This time, he asked for her supervisor.

He knew it would take some argument, and it did, but he got transferred to a kind, caring woman who knew his property and empathized with his problem. But, she told him, all animal control could do was put down the rabid cats and the terribly sick ones. The county would fix the animals at taxpayer expense, and then return them to the place they were found.

Which explained why his feline population hadn't gone down no matter how many cats he live-trapped for Animal Control. He felt an uncharacteristic surge of anger and frustration. How was he supposed to live here if the place was overrun with felines?

And that was the problem: He was living here. He couldn't just move to another dilapidated mansion or a quiet ranch house. The only way he'd gotten out of the hospitals was to promise he would stay in one place for a year. One place didn't mean one town. It meant one building, one location, no moving—not even once.

Of course, he had to check in with the local psychiatrist, who sent reports back to Bethesda. Joshua wouldn't be approved for military access—no embedding—without finishing his year in the States. He could, he supposed, report the old-fashioned way—sneaking around, doing the work on the side—but modern news organizations required their reporters—even the stringers—to have military access. He'd have to work for Pacifica, which paid next to nothing, or Al Jazeera, which would make him suspect in his home country, or any host of other not-quite-mainstream news organizations.

He thought of all this while the supervisor explained

her problems—the lack of funding, the lack of state regulations, and the lack of interest by anyone who didn't have an animal problem—and midway through her discourse, he realized she had recognized his name and was hoping for a local story of some kind, one that might help her fund her tiny government fiefdom.

"I empathize," he said when she took a breath. "There isn't enough money anywhere. But aren't there regulations about the number of cats that one person can own?"

"You own these?" she asked.

"Didn't you just tell me that they're my problem? Didn't you say they have to stay on my property?"

"Hmmm," she said. "I see what you mean. But then the cats would all have to be put down."

"I thought that's what you did anyway," he said.

"Oh, no," and then she started into another endless monologue about feral cats. Because he wanted her on his side, he didn't interrupt. Instead, he thumbed through the want ads in the *Oregonian*.

When she finally finished, he said, "I need to get them off the property."

She was silent for a long moment, and he could feel the disappointment echo through the line. He wasn't sure why he cared. Normally he bulldozed past other people's emotions. But this time, he recognized his own hesitation, and he wondered if he was being gentler than usual because he was fragile himself.

"Before we invoke that state law, which might get you fined and maybe even arrested—" she suddenly sounded like arresting him was a good choice— "let me put you in contact with a local woman who is starting a no-kill shelter. Maybe she can help you."

He couldn't imagine these wild creatures being sheltered, but he figured he would go through the hoops. What else did he have to do? And if he got arrested for having too many cats, so be it. It would give him a few days to examine the local jail and pretend he had moved somewhere else.

"Fine," he said. "What's this woman's name?"

"I'll call her," the supervisor said. "She's skittish with people. If she wants to come, she'll come. If not, you'll see an officer in a day or two."

A day or two. The wheels of government worked slowly no matter where he was. He tried not to sigh, thanked the supervisor for her time, and hung up, disappointed that his great foray into the bastion that was Animal Control had only taken an hour.

Maybe he would start the afternoon papers early and go through all of his languages. He'd have to struggle with Arabic—it was his newest language and his poorest—and he hadn't tried reading Serbian in almost a decade, so he'd see if his skills had atrophied.

But it would be good to revisit old ties. He was supposed to be writing a memoir, after all; that was his official, nonmedical excuse for hibernating.

He hadn't started. But now, after two weeks of his own company, without deadlines or explosions to run toward or meetings to set up with the general staff, he needed something to occupy his mind.

Something besides cats and exploding cameramen and shrapnel, raining like hot flame all around him.

Two days later he had made his own nest in what had once been the library. He had no idea where all the books had gone; his parents had probably sold them along with the furniture when his grandparents died.

He hadn't come home for that funeral. His grandparents had had the misfortune to get hit by a tanker truck on the same day as the Beirut barracks bombing that killed all those marines. He hadn't even been in his quarters for his parents' frantic intercontinental phone calls. When he heard the news, nearly a week after it happened, he flashed on his grandparents' bodies burned beyond recognition like the men he'd seen around the compound, and he didn't even feel guilt.

People died. The living went on. That was the way of things.

He felt guilt now. He had loved his grandparents,

and he had loved this library. Maybe he would spend the year refilling it with books. Or maybe a half year, so that he could enjoy them.

He finally decided to go into town—his first foray since he had discovered that these days all a man needed was an internet account and a credit card to make grocery stores deliver.

Feeling decadent and a little rich (he never really spent his pay in all the years he'd gone from country to country), he bought himself two computers—a desktop model, which he hadn't had since laptops were introduced, and a brand new lightweight laptop that made the battered ones that had gotten him through two separate war zones feel like anvils.

He was just driving back when he saw her standing in his driveway, her arms stretched out as if she were giving a benediction to the dozens of cats that surrounded her.

When the cats realized his vehicle was coming through the gate, they scattered. She whirled—and he got a momentary impression of an angry goddess, creating her own tempest. Then her arms dropped, and she tilted her head, looking like an ordinary and somewhat plain American woman.

He got out of the gas hog that Roxy had leased for him and felt a bit of embarrassment. He had planned to get something that didn't guzzle as much fuel—after all, he'd seen what the greed for oil could do—but he hadn't gotten around to that either.

And he hadn't thought of it, not in all the times he'd driven the thing, until this woman, whom he'd never met, stared at him as if she owned the property.

"I take it you're Joshua Clemon?" She had a bit of an accent that he couldn't quite place, which was odd for him, since accents were his specialty. More than his specialty: They were necessary in his trade.

"And you're the woman with the no-kill shelter," he said.

She laughed, a sound like the bells from a French cathedral. "I am the woman who *dreams* of a no-kill shelter. Right now, I have a twenty-acre ranch just outside of town where I pretend that the animals I take in are safe."

"So you can't help me." He opened the back of the gas hog and removed both computers, marveling that he could carry the boxes as if they were briefcases.

"I didn't say that." She watched him, hands on her hips. She probably saw him as a rich, uncaring American. A man who bought expensive toys and had a dilapidated mansion to fix up because he had nothing better to do with his time.

"Come on in," he said, nodding toward the front door.

She glanced at the gate, then at the woods beyond, where the cats had disappeared. He sensed a reluctance.

"We can talk out here if that makes you more comfortable."

"No," she said, as if she just remembered how to be polite. "It is better if we go inside."

Better for whom he didn't know, and if he had been on a story, he would have asked. But this woman was not in some war-torn country. Each remark she made did not have to be pursued and examined as if it were a puzzle to be solved.

He pushed open the door he had forgotten to lock and stepped into the hallway. His grandmother used to keep the wood floors shining, the occasional table beside the door spotless, and the entire place smelling of lemon polish. Now the floors were scuffed and covered with dirt, there were no occasional tables, and the entire place smelled faintly of cat.

He almost led the woman to the formal living room, where his grandmother had presided over her home, but the living room hadn't worn its formal dress for twenty years. Old habits, he was amused to note, died hard.

Instead, he went to the library. It at least had been cleaned.

"I still have some work here," he said.

"It's nice to see someone rebuilding the place," she said. "It used to be so loved."

"You knew my grandparents?" he asked.

"No, but I have seen photographs." She extended her hand. "I am Galiana, by the way."

He took it. It was work-hardened, the first he'd encountered in this country.

"Galiana with no last name?" he asked.

She smiled. "It's all consonants. People here just call me Galiana."

He nodded, not satisfied. But he would find out in his own way, in his own time. He set the computers beside his new desk, grabbed a wooden chair and slid it toward her. Then he sat on a step of his work ladder.

"You've seen my problem," he said. "What do you think?"

"That the cats aren't a problem." She sat with her back straight, hands folded in her lap.

"What do you mean, not a problem? There's a thousand of them."

"Maybe a hundred, tops," she said, "and this is their home. They've lived here for generations. To them, you're the interloper."

She clearly didn't understand the scope of the problem. He'd met a lot of these well-meaning do-gooders in his travels. They were naïve and energetic and they had a vision, which often didn't correspond with reality.

"They haven't been here for generations," he said. "There were no feral cats on the property when my grandparents were alive."

She blinked, a surprised look. It was appealing. Different, maybe, from anything he'd seen before. She wasn't conventionally pretty. Her features were pleasant, her face one that dozens of women had at her age—pale skin, blue eyes, rounded cheeks made rounder by the unflattering cut of her brown hair.

Yet there was something about her . . .

"I meant cat generations," she said after a moment. "How long has this place been empty? Twenty years, right? For feral cats, that can be twenty generations. Think in terms of a hundred of your years. That's a long time."

"So you're saying I should just let them live here?" He rolled his eyes. "Is this that politically correct thing I've been hearing about from overseas? Because if it is, it's gone to ridiculous lengths. They're just cats. If we were in Southeast Asia, I'd be perfectly justified if I killed one every day and ate it."

Spots of color appeared on her face.

"I thought you wanted to save them," she said in a small voice.

"I want them off the property. The supervisor at Animal Control wanted to save them."

"Oh." She studied her folded hands for a moment. Then she stood. "I misunderstood."

He was sorry he had offended her. He had no social skills any more, not for real people. Only for people he was using to get a story or people he was interrogating for information. People he'd encounter a few times and then abandon, as he abandoned cities.

"Can you get them off the property?" he asked.

"I was hoping that they could stay," she said. "The woods are large. I was thinking maybe we could find a way to keep them safe, feed them, and let them live their natural lives."

So she wanted to use his property as her no-kill sanctuary. Not a shelter at all, but some kind of farm or ranch or something. "And have kittens every year? I'm already overrun."

"We'd fix them, of course," she said.

"And then what? They'd invite all their little friends, and suddenly I'm living in cat heaven. This is my grandparents' home. I've already neglected it too long. I need to fix it up, not make it a palace for strays."

She smoothed her hands along her jeans. He'd seen

women who wore skirts do that, but he'd always thought it was to smooth wrinkles. Jeans didn't wrinkle.

"I can guarantee that they won't bother you. You'll never see them," she said.

"Or smell them? Or deal with their poop and their destructiveness? They've broken almost everything in the courtyard."

"I think I can broker some kind of truce, yes," she said.

Truce? Is that what he wanted? A truce? How many truces had he seen over the years? Every single one of them had failed.

"You make it sound like I'm at war with the cats," he said.

"Aren't you?" she asked.

"No," he said. "All I want is for them to leave my land."

"It's their ancestral homeland," she said.

"Oh for heaven's sake," he said. "It's mine too."

She shrugged and extended her hands. "See? Truce is the only answer."

"They're cats," he snapped. "Cats can't own property. They *are* property, and I want them gone."

"What if I can make them disappear?" she said.

"Then do it," he said, sorry he'd ever thought she was attractive. Sorry he still thought she was attractive, even now.

"Are you hiring me?" she asked.

"If you can guarantee that none of those creatures will ever bother me again," he said.

"I can do that," she said softly, although her tone seemed a bit doubtful. "I'm sure I can do that."

That night, he had dinner with Roxy because he sure as hell didn't want to stay home. After Galiana left, the cats returned to the courtyard and had a virtual orgy. Or maybe an actual one. He couldn't tell, and he certainly didn't want to investigate.

Roxy was one of his oldest friends. They went to

summer Bible school together as children, and then when they were old enough to realize that coloring cardboard cutouts of Jesus wasn't fun, they ditched Bible school together.

He thought he loved her when he was twelve. When he was thirteen, he realized she was too much woman for him. When he went to college, her letters kept him steady. When he went overseas, he realized just how provincial her world was.

She married twice, both local men, both terrible conversationalists. She visited him in Paris once—not as a sexual thing (after puberty, there was nothing sexual between them, not even a thread of attraction)—but because she wanted to escape her humdrum life.

Everything frightened her, from the double-decker tourist buses (giving guided tours in English, German, and French) to the Louvre (*It's so big*, she said. *How can you see it all? That's the point,* he said, *You can't.*) to the restaurants with their deliberately slow service and complicated French cuisine (*what is a cassoulet?* she asked. *A casserole sort of*, he said. *But what's in it?* she asked. *Whatever the chef wants to put in it*, he said.).

She left, deciding that foreign countries were for adventurous people like him, and he went to Somalia because Paris had been too civilized. It had always been too civilized, just as Oregon was too provincial. Whenever something happened in these places, it was too structured. Even the chaos had order—and what fun was that?

"I heard you met Galiana," Roxy said, pushing her chair away from the table. They were in a local Italian place that had surprisingly good cuisine. The chef had studied in Rome, and it showed in the lightness of the sauces and the delicacy of the spices.

The restaurant itself wasn't light or delicate. It was dark, paneled, and discreet. He liked it for that. He didn't feel as exposed as he usually did in American restaurants.

"How did you hear that?" he asked.

"Because I've known her since your mother died. She was a nurse in the ICU. Don't you remember?"

He remembered almost nothing of his mother's death and funeral. He had flown in from Kuwait, eyes still stinging from the burning oil fields, and sat in the fluorescent lights staring at a woman who looked just like his great-grandmother. Nothing of his mother remained.

He had been too late, and part of him had spent those last few days wondering if it had been on purpose.

"I don't recall," he said, but he had a sudden flash of a memory: the doctor introducing a "healer" who could ease his mother's pain.

"Just as well," Roxy said. "Galiana wasn't at her best in those days."

And she was at her best now? Psychically in tune with stray cats? He was glad he hadn't met her then. Although he should have remembered a woman with such an appealing presence. He usually did.

"Well," he said, "she's pretty strange."

Roxy laughed. "And you're not?"

Not among his peers, he wasn't. He was just like they were, tough and broken and relentless. Sometimes he forgot that the whole world wasn't that way.

"I figure you two had a lot in common." Roxy grabbed a toothpick and shoved it between her teeth as a substitute cigarette. "That's why I kept trying to set you up."

It all clicked into place now. The dinners that Roxy staged during his first week home, the ones he was too busy to attend, weren't just because she worried that he wasn't going to eat well. They were also designed to take some of the pressure off their friendship.

"So she knows all about me," he said.

"Not all." Roxy waved a hand for the waitress, then pointed at her coffee cup. "But she knows you can be a prick."

"Can be," he repeated. "Hell, I was a total ass this afternoon."

"She mentioned that too," Roxy said, "and wondered why I even thought you two would be suited."

"Why did you?" he asked.

She shrugged a single shoulder. "You both have the same look," she said. "Like you want to be somewhere else."

That night he did want to be somewhere else. Anywhere else. Someplace where cats didn't scream their pleasure at the half-moon.

He had fixed the floodlights outside, but the light didn't stop them. Instead, they copulated as if they were the floor show at some expensive Italian villa.

Didn't mating season end eventually? Was there a period when kittens got born and kittens got raised and the adults became serious and quiet?

At one AM, he gave up on sleep for a second night and went to his newly set up computer. The vast and mysterious Internet informed him that female cats went in and out of heat often, especially if the cats were well fed or in a warm climate. They also could go into heat shortly after giving birth to kittens. Males prowled for a sexually willing female their entire lives, copulated with her, and then got their faces slapped for the effort.

By three-thirty, the yowling died down, and he finally dozed off only to wake up at seven as the orgy chorus started all over again.

He refused to get earplugs. He hadn't needed them during the bombings in all the various war zones he visited. He wasn't about to get them now.

But in all those war zones, he'd slept when he was exhausted, not when he was supposed to. He used to say that a man could sleep through anything.

Obviously, the cats were proving him wrong.

He was rereading the *Oregonian*, obsessing that he wasn't in the Middle East during this latest crisis, when a car pulled in front of his fence. He was outside by the time the gate opened.

Galiana entered, looking vaguely medieval in a long purple coat that nearly hid her jeans. Her hair brushed her shoulders and she wore no make-up, but her eyes glittered in the morning light.

"I'd've called," she said, "but I figured you'd want this done right away."

"I do," he said.

The clothing suited her. She looked striking. He wondered how he had ever thought her plain.

She glanced at the woods. Of course, the cats were hiding there. They never gave the floor show when guests were on the property.

"I need you to do a few things before I start," she said. "You have to shut off the electronics in the house, just in case, and—"

"In case of what?" he asked.

She still hadn't looked at him. "In case my equipment causes a power surge."

He didn't see any equipment. "What are you going to do?"

She folded her hands, and turned toward him, serene and glittery at the same time. "I'm going to convince them to give up this part of their home."

That woo-woo language irritated him. Odd that the language would bother him here, in Oregon, but not anywhere else in the world. In other places, he would see it as part of the local custom. Here, he found it pretentious.

"How do you plan to do that?" he asked.

"Essentially, I'll use a field that will convince them to go elsewhere."

"An electrical field?" he asked. "Like those collars that keep dogs in their yard?"

She shrugged, but it was a European shrug, which made it a voiceless version of *I suppose so.*

"I thought those things were inhumane." He'd gotten that from his middle-of-the-night reading, astonished that there were so many animal issues that people in this country got excited about.

"You were willing to kill them," she said.

And he was. He still was. That screeching the night before still echoed in his ears.

"I just thought you weren't the kind of person who would harm animals."

She tucked a strand of hair behind her right ear. "You have no idea what kind of person I am."

That was true too.

"You said a couple of things," he said, changing the subject. "What else?"

"After you unplug your valuable electronics, you either have to shut down the house—all the curtains, all the blinds, and stay inside or leave for a few hours. I recommend leaving. It's safer."

"Safer? How much power do you plan to use?" He felt a reluctance to let her even start. He had nothing of real value in the house, but the house itself mattered to him—which surprised him. He hadn't thought anything mattered.

"Your house will be safe," she said, as if she had heard his thoughts.

"But I won't?" he asked.

"You are flesh and blood, just like the cats."

"So are you," he said, feeling a little odd now. "Can't you get hurt?"

She shook her head.

She seemed very clinical in her approach to this. He would have thought someone who empathized that much with animals would be passionate about her work. But he recognized the detachment. It was the removal of the personality—the emotions—so that the job could get done.

How many times had he done that?

Only for his entire career.

"Can I watch?" he asked. "If I promise to stay outside your power range?"

"No," she said. "I would actually prefer it if you left."

But there was no chance he would leave. None at all.

*   *   *

She came into the house with him to make sure he shut it down properly. The attic and the third floor had no curtains, so she barred him from that level, actually locking the servants' door that his grandmother had once claimed she was going to remove.

On the second floor, he had installed blinds in most rooms and shades in his bedroom, not that they had done any good. She helped him secure all of those.

The first floor had only curtains, and as they swooshed closed, clouds of dust rose.

She told him to wait on the second floor and not peek out, no matter what he heard.

"What if you get hurt?" he asked.

"I won't," she said, and seemed to believe it. He was beginning to have his doubts.

She left him in the second floor hallway, where there were no windows at all. She recommended that he bring a flashlight and a book—"always better to leave the electric lights off while I do this," she said—and he pretended to take her advice.

When he heard the front door close, he went into his emergency travel bag, which old habit forced him to keep under the bed, and removed a cell phone, a notepad and pen (because he felt naked without them), and his binoculars.

He snuck downstairs into the library, pulled a chair into the hall, and used the binoculars to find a gap in the thick red curtains.

Then he camped in the chair, and waited.

At first, not much happened. Galiana moved her car, then came back to the courtyard. There she stood for the longest time, hands raised, as the cats gathered. She seemed to glow—some kind of trick of the mid-morning light reflecting off the Italian tile—and he thought she had never looked more beautiful.

The cats swirled around her. Even though the binoculars gave him a clear view of the courtyard, he couldn't distinguish individual cats. They seemed to blend and blur, and they seemed content—although he wasn't sure how he knew that.

Finally, she looked down, as if she were surprised at the number of cats around her, then glanced at the woods. More cats loped forward, leaping over the stone wall and landing near their compatriots.

More cats than he could have imagined. She was right: generations of them, at 10 to 20 kittens per year per female. Most didn't live long—ferals had an average lifespan of three years—but that was enough to create twenty more cats per to fill the empty acres around his house.

A tiny black and white got stuck on the wall, then tumbled into the mess. Several females carried kittens in their mouths, other kittens following like ducklings. This alone was worth the price of admission, and he wished he'd taken out his video camera, but he had heeded her advice about electronics and had decided to keep it safe.

She was nodding at the stragglers, as if approving of their arrival. Then she raised her arms again—

—and the entire world exploded.

Minutes, or maybe hours, later, he pulled himself off the unpolished wooden floor. He was flashing on other places, other explosions that had knocked him back. In Haifa, where shrapnel embedded in his arms, somehow missing arteries. In Mosul, where a lucky position on a deserted road had kept him from serious injury when the men driving the truck ahead had more or less evaporated in a roadside bomb.

Dozens of other memories flooded him, mixing and mingling into one large mess of an aftermath, filled with dust clouds and a pale pink haze of blood. He brushed himself off, then realized he wasn't covered with dirt. Nothing had changed, except that he had fallen off his chair.

There had been light and a flash-bang—and then the world had gone white.

He picked up the binoculars. They were fine. But his hands were shaking. His entire body was shaking.

He made himself go toward the window, terrified for Galiana—what had she done? What kind of mistake had she made?—and pulled back the curtain, feeling the dust cloud around him as if it were sand disturbed by a landmine.

She stood in the middle of an empty courtyard, smiling.

The cats were gone. There was only Italian tile, broken pottery and the remains of the fountains his grandmother had so loved.

No cat carcasses, no blood. Nothing to show there had been an explosion anywhere in the vicinity.

Had he imagined it? The damn psychiatrists had said that post-traumatic stress did that sometimes—took a trigger and made it replay an event.

But this had replayed hundreds of events for him all at once, and he hadn't imagined it. He couldn't imagine it, not like that. His flashbacks—which he'd been unwilling to call flashbacks until now—were just ghosts standing beside him: Stuben's cameraman as his leg flew off; that child in Beslan who sobbed uncontrollably because he *hadn't* been in the school the day of the terrorist attack; the fleeing and burning passengers in King's Cross that horrible summer he decided to take a vacation in London.

All of them haunted him, all of them came back by sound not by sight, and the light came first here, not the sound. By the time of the flash-bang, he thought the world had already ended.

He pulled open the front door before he even knew he was running, heading hell-bent for the courtyard and Galiana. Running toward danger, as he had every moment of his benighted life.

Only this time, he wasn't carrying a camera or a microphone or even his notebook. (Had he dropped it? He didn't remember.) He was running toward her, determined to save her, the first heroic act in his decidedly unheroic life.

And she watched him come, that smile fading from her face. The sunlight was behind her now—it was twilight? He thought it was noon—and it haloed her.

He was asking her if she was all right before he even skidded to a stop beside her, but he knew the answer.

She was fine. She was clearly fine. She had done this before, and it didn't seem to bother her.

Whatever "this" was. Whatever "it" was.

"You watched," she said, and that took the heroic impulse out of him.

"For godsake," he said, "that's what I do. I watch. I report what I see. Did you think I wouldn't?"

She shrugged, an American movement this time: *I really don't care.*

He felt silly, like a schoolboy being reprimanded. "What happened to the cats?"

"You wouldn't believe me if I told you."

"You'd be surprised what I can believe," he said and it was true: he could believe that people who lived side by side would murder each other over a brown patch of land; he could believe that men could slaughter babies because they might be raised in a particularly hated religion; he believed that humans had an infinite capacity for evil and no one seemed shocked by this, no one except maybe him.

"I sent them to another dimension," she said.

Whatever he had expected, it wasn't that. "What?"

"See? I told you that you wouldn't believe."

"Believe?" he said. "I'm not sure I even understand."

"The world," she said. "It splits into various realities at each moment of decision. Or each important ones. Parallel universes, your scientists call it."

Her accent was even more pronounced now, and even more unrecognizable. *Your scientists.* Why weren't they hers?

"In several of those universes, you never reclaimed this house. I sent the cats to one of those."

"How?"

"The only way," she said, clearly amused. "Magic."

"Magic," he repeated.

She shrugged—European again. *Believe what you want or don't.*

"How can you do magic?" he asked.

She looked annoyed. "How can you write?"

"It's not magic," he said.

"Really?" she asked.

Her eyes still glittered. He finally recognized the appeal. A fanaticism, one that always drew him. He liked interviewing the believers, the ones who carried out the missions, no matter what side they were on. They seemed so *certain*. He was never certain, not even now.

He was still shaking, though, and his heart still raced. He wondered if the psychiatrists would think him cured because he had tried to save someone. He doubted it. The key was not to lose his composure, not to race toward the danger, but to make sensible decisions.

He doubted he'd ever be sensible.

"How much do I owe you?" he asked.

"Two hundred dollars," she said. "This was less work than I thought."

He wondered how much it would cost if it had been more work than she had thought. He grabbed his wallet out of his back pocket—relieved to find the wallet still there, after his fall—and handed her two hundred dollar bills.

She stared at them for a moment, then looked at the now-silent woods.

"They really weren't harming you," she said, and he knew she meant the cats, not the woods.

But they were harming him. They were reviving memories, interrupting his sleep, taunting him with relationships he'd never really had—even as wild and casual as the feline relationships were, they still led to families, to futures, to a world he'd long since abandoned.

He thought of the attraction he had felt toward her and wondered if he had felt it because of that fanaticism or because she was the only interesting person he'd met since he'd come home.

Maybe it was a combination of both, but whatever it was, he no longer felt it. He wanted her gone.

"Roxy thinks we're suited," Galiana said.

"Roxy thinks a lot of things," he said.

Galiana's glitter faded. Her smile became rueful and she nodded, understanding.

"It is hard to stay in one place, isn't it?" she said softly.

He looked at the now-empty woods, and sighed.

"Actually," he said, "I think I've been in the same place for more than twenty years."

And, he realized now, that it was time to change. To move. To be somewhere else. Which meant he had to become someone else. And wasn't that why he was here? To become a man other than the one who watched and reported and pretended nothing affected him?

"Good luck to you then," she said, extending her hand.

He took it, expecting some of the attraction to return. But it didn't.

He smiled at her. "You helped me in ways you'll never know."

Her eyes glittered for a moment, then she slipped her hand away. He had the sense she did know. Just as he had a hunch she had known he was sitting in that hallway, watching her. Had she sent other things away besides the cats? A part of him, maybe?

She turned her back and walked to the gate, heading to her car.

He sat in the empty courtyard, silent for the first time since he had arrived, and knew he would get used to this place. He would make it something real, something important, bring back the beauty and warmth it used to have

He could do that. He was sure he could do that.

Now he understood. She hadn't taken anything from him. She had given him something—she had given him a place away from the wars.

And, for the first time, it felt as if he'd come home.

THE CASE OF THE ALLERGIC LEPRECHAUN

Alan L. Lickiss

"EXCUSE me, can you find me?"

Frank looked up from the case file he was reading. Rather than his cute secretary Rita, Frank saw a short pudgy man. He was maybe five feet tall, and he wore a suit that screamed for a used car lot. Frank couldn't help but stare. The criss-crossing lines of brown, orange, and yellow in his jacket actually brought the bright yellow shirt, dark green pants, and matching green tie together into a hypnotic, headache inducing ensemble. Frank wondered how many deals had been signed just to make that suit go away.

"Excuse me?"

The man walked into Frank's office. "You are a detective, right, not the janitor?" said the man.

Frank took a deep breath and suppressed the urge to roll his eyes. He leaned his elbows on his desk and gave the man his best Jim Rockford no-nonsense look. It was that look and corresponding attitude that made Frank become a detective.

"I'm sorry," Frank said. "My secretary is out getting our lunch and I didn't have any appointments scheduled for today. What did you want me to find?"

The man sat in the chair across from Frank. He reached into his pants pocket and pulled out a bright yellow handkerchief. Frank winced at the sound like an air horn of an eighteen wheeler.

"Sorry, I think I'm allergic to something," said the man as he put the handkerchief away.

A sudden loud sneeze startled Frank and made him drop his pen. He looked for it on his desk but couldn't see it. He assumed it had rolled off the edge and grabbed another.

"I want you to find me," said the man.

Frank wondered if this was some new reality television show. The man looked sincere, and a little forlorn to Frank.

"You realize you run the risk of having to pay my one day minimum fee for about three seconds worth of work," said Frank.

"No, you don't understand," said the man. "It's not where I am. I don't know *who* I am."

"Amnesia," said Frank as he wrote it down. "How long have you had this condition, and have you been to see a doctor?"

"I sort of came to myself sitting on the curb outside a parking garage downtown as the sun was coming up. I was groggy, and started walking. My head cleared and I started to look for familiar things. Nothing registered. Then I saw your sign."

"Please don't take this the wrong way, but do you drink?" asked Frank

The man tilted his head to the side, "I don't know. But at the same time, I don't feel opposed to it."

Frank smiled at the response. "Is it possible you were drinking last night and are suffering from a hangover?"

The man shook his head. "I don't think so. My head didn't hurt, I was just groggy. Can you help me find who I am?"

"Have you been to a hospital?" Frank asked.

"No," said the man, shaking his head, "I can't go to a hospital or to the police."

Frank added a note to his pad. "Why not?"

"I can't explain exactly why, but I think it's because I'm a leprechaun," said the man.

Frank put his pen down. This was either a joke, or

the man across from him was disturbed. Perhaps it was his small stature that gave the man some sort of complex. Either way, Frank didn't want to waste any more time. He'd ease the guy out the door, then alert the police.

"I'm sorry," said Frank as he stood. "I thought this might be something I could work into my existing work load. Unfortunately I'm really too swamped to devote the amount of time your situation requires."

"I'm not crazy," said the man as he walked with Frank toward the front door. "I know how crazy that sounded, but that's the one thing I can remember."

They were a few feet from the front door when it opened. Rita stepped in, a white paper bag that smelled of grilled meat in one hand and two sodas in the other. Frank smiled at the sight of her.

"Hi, Frank," Rita said and returned his smile. She stopped and looked at the two men.

Frank noticed the man's face start to twitch. His mouth bunched up to the left. It moved back and forth as if the man were trying to wipe his nose with his upper lip. The man reached for his pocket, but sneezed before he made it. A white dove flew out of the man's mouth, flapped its wings and flew out the open door.

"What the—" said Frank as he stared into the shocked expression on Rita's face.

The man sneezed again. Rita disappeared.

The door swung closed. Frank looked between the closed door and the small man who was blowing his nose.

"Sorry 'bout that," said the man. "I'm allergic to something, but I can't figure out what it is. Do you own a cat?"

"What did you do? Where's Rita?" Frank asked. He succeeded in keeping the panic out of his voice, but just barely. "Are you some kind of magician?"

Sure, he'd seen magicians make birds appear seemingly out of nothing before. But what about Rita? Perhaps the bird had startled Rita, and she was outside waiting for Frank to give her the all clear.

Frank pushed open the door and stepped out into the sunshine. "Rita?"

There were a dozen cars in the parking lot. Sunshine, green grass, and a view of the snow topped mountains, but no Rita. There was also no camera crew ready to catch the expression on his face.

"What the hell is going on?" said Frank as he walked back into his office. "Where's Rita?"

"I couldn't tell ya," said the man.

Frank leaned over the man, his hands on the desk, his body tense all over. "Look, buddy, Rita is not the type to get spooked by a bird flying past her. I don't think she ran off. If you had someone outside snatch her, you'd better come clean now."

"I told you, I don't know where she is. I'm a leprechaun, and I have some magical abilities. Unfortunately, between the amnesia and my allergies, I'm not sure what's going on. If it helps, I'm pretty sure she's okay."

"I don't know what kind of reality show this is, but I'm not letting you out of my sight until I find Rita," said Frank making a visible effort to control his temper.

"Sounds good to me," said the man.

"What's your name?" Frank asked.

The man tapped his forefinger against the side of his head. "Amnesia, remember? I don't know my name."

"Just checking," said Frank. "You never know what might just pop out when you don't try to think about it. Well, unless you've got a better name, I'm going to call you Ralph."

Ralph shrugged his shoulders. "Fine by me."

Frank grabbed Ralph by his collar and pulled him into his office and pushed him into a chair. He unlocked his desk drawer, pulled out a revolver, and shoved in into his shoulder holster.

"Okay, Ralph, let's go see if we can find where you woke up this morning," said Frank.

*   *   *

Frank drove back the way Ralph had come from. He kept asking Ralph if anything looked familiar. Ralph apparently hadn't walked in a straight line, and Frank had to backtrack several times to find streets Ralph had walked that morning. They'd been at it for over three hours.

"How about this road? Any of these signs look familiar?" Frank asked. They were passing a block of squat high rise office buildings heading toward the skyscrapers of downtown Denver.

Frank kept trying Rita's cell phone, but kept going to voice mail. Frank was worried.

Ralph looked out the window. "Maybe. It's all starting to blur. That's it, that's it," said Ralph, pointing at a parking garage down the street, his voice excited as he bounced up and down on the seat.

"Finally. I hope you have enough footage for your show because I'm tired of these games."

"Show?" asked Ralph.

The entrance to the parking garage was blocked by yellow crime scene tape.

"Go on in," said Ralph.

Frank gave Ralph his Rockford look again. "Right. You'd like me to do that, wouldn't you?"

"Yes, this is where I came to myself this morning."

"That and the crime scene tape means I should drive you to the nearest police station. But if you're trying to get footage for some stupidest detective show I'll be a laughing stock," said Frank. "Before I do anything I'm going to check this out."

Frank pulled further down the street and was able to find a parking spot on the street. When they got out, Ralph started to head toward the parking garage, but Frank walked across the street. Ralph ran after him to catch up.

"The garage is back that way," said Ralph point down the street.

"I know," said Frank.

"So where are we going?" Ralph asked.

Frank reached the store he had headed for. "I think I'll get a cup of coffee. I didn't have any lunch earlier if you recall."

Frank held the door for Ralph and then followed him inside. Bagpipe music played over the store stereo, and the scent of too many coffee flavors filled the air. Frank wanted to leave the door open and vent the place, but didn't think that would be inconspicuous. He led Ralph through a maze of quaint little green topped tables to the counter. Only two of the tables were occupied.

Frank and Ralph reached the counter where, thanks to the time of day there was no line. A blonde waif, thin, her stringy hair hanging loose and a nose stud in her left nostril was at the counter. She looked all of fourteen, prepubescent and lanky, but more likely was a student at the university. She had a bored expression on her face. Frank was sure that if he needed a shave, wore his hair in dirty clumps, and had clothes full of rips and tears, she'd be all smiles. She chewed her gum and waited for Frank to give his order.

"I'd like two cups of your house blend special," said Frank.

The girl made a face, as if Frank had ordered swill. She rang up the order before she poured the coffee.

After taking a sip Frank asked, "What's up with the parking garage across the street? I almost couldn't find a place to park."

The girl shrugged. "I dunno," she said. "A bunch of cops came in a while ago. I heard them talking about finding a dead body."

"Serious? That's creepy," Frank said and took another sip.

"Yeah. The cops said the weird part was that he was just lying on the ground on the bottom level with no ID and no signs of a fight."

Frank wanted to ask more questions, but he heard the sound of Ralph breathing heavily through his mouth. Then the sound of a large sneeze. The girl behind the counter screamed.

Frank turned to see a lot of small white mice running in all directions from a central mass in the middle of the floor. Ralph blew his nose and looked sorry. Frank grabbed Ralph by the collar and pulled him along as he rushed from the store with the other customers.

"Can't you go to the morgue by yourself?" said Ralph, his voice echoing up and down the concrete walls of the stairwell.

Frank stopped and turned back up the stairs. He held his finger up to his lips to remind Ralph to be quiet. "I don't want to take a chance that your camera crew is waiting at the front door."

"I don't have a camera crew," said Ralph.

"Whatever," said Frank as he started back down the stairs. "I'm only going along with this game until I find out what happened to Rita."

"But I don't like to see dead people," Ralph said.

"It isn't exactly my favorite hobby either," said Frank. "But I'm stuck trying to figure out what your game is without looking like an idiot. And Rita better be okay."

At the bottom of the stairs was a metal door with a narrow glass window. Frank couldn't see anyone near the door, but the hallway on the other side was dimly lit. Frank eased the door open and led Ralph down the hall.

"Why are we sneaking around? Isn't this place closed?" asked Ralph.

Frank shushed Ralph again. He whispered in Ralph's ear. "I can't exactly walk in and ask to see the latest dead bodies. They'd have a few questions for the both of us."

Frank led the way to the morgue. The city contracted with Memorial Hospital to facilitate their coroner and the bodies that the city had to deal with. Frank was glad. It was a lot easier for him to sneak into the hospital than into a police facility.

A fast pick of the lock and Frank led Ralph into

the morgue. The antiseptic smell hit his nose about the time the goose bumps ran up his arms. It was noticeably cooler in the room.

"What do you want me to do?" asked Ralph.

"Just stay right there and don't touch anything," Frank said.

The morgue had a large open area that could hold several bodies on gurneys if required. Fortunately it wasn't currently required, and the gurneys and processing tables were all empty. The only other door in the room led to the operating room where the autopsies were done. The back wall was filled with small shiny steel doors. On the left wall were three filing cabinets. The smell was making Frank's eyes water.

"Stand next to me so I can keep track of you," Frank said.

The hard soles of Ralph's shoes tapped as he walked across the yellowing linoleum floor. About halfway across he sneezed. When Frank looked up, a large vase of purple flowers sat in the middle of the floor.

"Cut that out," Frank said.

"I'm not doing it on purpose," Ralph said. "You act like I enjoy sneezing."

Frank sighed. "Just blow your nose. I'll get you some antihistamines later."

Frank returned to searching the file cabinets. "Here's one that came in this morning," he said. He led Ralph to the drawer. "Have you ever seen a dead body before?"

"I don't know," said Ralph with a shrug of his shoulders.

"Well if you're going to throw up, don't do it on the body. It would be best if you can make it to the sink over there," Frank said, pointing to a sink in the corner.

Frank heard a voice behind him. "Here to rob the dead?"

Frank and Ralph turned to see a tall bearded man in a tailored suit standing in the doorway. He stood with his hands on his hips with an air of authority. Frank noticed the lack of an ID badge.

"Nonsense, we're performing a random audit of this department for the police department," said Frank.

The man stepped toward them. "Really? May I see some identification?"

"I was about to ask you the same question," Frank said.

The man gave a deep chuckle from his throat. He bent over and gave a little finger wave to Ralph who was peeking out from behind Frank.

"Hello, little pain in my side," the man said. "You have been annoying me for long enough."

Frank looked from Ralph to the other man. "I don't suppose you'd care to tell me what's going on?"

"Not really. The police should be here soon, and I'm sure they'll have questions of their own."

The police were all Frank needed to cap off his day. He was somewhere he shouldn't be, and he didn't believe his own explanation of why he was there. He started to edge toward the door. Ralph shuffled behind him, using Frank as a shield.

"Who are you, and why the big confrontation?" Frank asked.

"My name is Gerold for what it's worth to you. And I am doing this because I wanted to see the look on this face when he is charged with murder." With a speed belying his size, Gerold reached out and snatched Ralph from behind Frank as he spoke.

Frank was shoved to the floor. When he stood, he saw Ralph twisting in Gerold's grip, feet dangling above the floor. Frank jumped forward and grabbed Gerold's hand. He tried to pry the fingers loose from Ralph's shirt and jacket, but he was tossed aside with little effort. Frank looked at Ralph and saw fear in his eyes. Ralph's eye started to twitch and his mouth and nose twisted. Frank let go and backed away.

Ralph sneezed.

"My medallion," Gerold shouted. He let go of

Ralph and grabbed his chest, patting around as if in search for something under his shirt. Clothes ripped, and Gerold raged in agony, his face contorted and he twisted his body in upon itself.

Frank backed away until he hit the wall. He watched with a mixture of horror and fascination as Gerold's body grew, lengthened, new legs appeared, and shredded clothes fell away.

Gerold stood up on his four legs, shook his head and grabbed Ralph from where he lay on the floor. From the waist up he was the same, except his muscles were larger and had ripped his shirt and jacket so he was bare-chested. From the waist down he was no longer a man, but had the body of a horse. Gerold was a centaur.

"Do you know how much that hurts?" Gerold shouted at Ralph, shaking him in his fist.

"S-s-sorry," Ralph stammered. "Allergies."

"I'm going to kill you," Gerold said and raised his other hand into a huge fist. He cocked his arm back to deliver a blow Frank was sure would crush Ralph's face and send him flying across the room.

Ralph sneezed.

Frank watched as both Gerold and Ralph disappeared. He sank to the floor, his knees weak. Frank had seen many things in his career, everything from brutality and death to self mutilation. But what he had just witnessed tilted his world too far to let him stand. Frank pulled his knees to his chest and took several deep breaths.

Up to that point Frank had been dismissing the comings and goings of objects and animals as sleight of hand. But there was no way to dismiss Gerold's transformation into a centaur and then Ralph and Gerold disappearing. No cloud of smoke to cover their exit. One second struggling with each other, the next, gone. Rockford never had a case like this. He was always fighting bad guys and rescuing damsels in distress.

Rita, Frank thought. He had to focus on finding Rita. Another deep breath and Frank pulled himself to his feet.

Frank walked around where the two men had been standing. He picked up the shreds of clothes from the floor and patted the pockets of the pants. No wallet. In one pocket he found a set of keys.

Frank identified a car key, a door key of some sort, and a remote. At first Frank thought it was the remote to Gerold's car. When he looked at it closer he found that rather than lock and unlock, the words Home and Denver were each next to a button.

The head and upper torso of a man appeared in the small opening in the door, a police department patch on the shoulder, a pistol in the man's hand. "Hold it right there, put your hands up and don't move."

Frank was startled by the officer. He stepped back and his hands clenched. He pressed a button on the remote as he looked up into the eyes of the police officer. The room disappeared.

Frank had three seconds to realize he was no longer in the morgue before a wave of dizziness hit him. He stumbled, dropping the shredded pants and remote. Frank sat down against a tree. The hospital smell had been replaced with scents of trees, grass, and flower blossoms, brought to him on the light breeze that teased his hair. He could feel the roughness of the tree bark against his back, the cool grass against his hands, and the sun on his face. Frank had gone insane.

Frank looked down and saw the remote on the ground, broken in several pieces. He must have stepped on it when he lost his footing. He picked up the pieces and put them in his pocket.

Frank stood, and another wave of dizziness threatened to force him to sit again. He leaned against the tree until it passed.

"I must have been hit on the head or given some powerful drugs to come up with this place," Frank thought. He saw some buildings in the distance. He decided that if his body was locked in the mental ward, at least he could take a walk in his mind. He started down the hill.

Frank leaned against a building at the end of an alley and watched a house across the street. A week in the city of Fips had squashed his sense of wonder at everything that had happened to him. It had taken that long to turn up where he thought Gerold lived. At first he couldn't get any information about Gerold. All of his questions were answered with references to the centaur highwayman. But when Frank provided a description of what Gerold looked like before he turned into a centaur he eventually heard the name Dassin. It was Dassin's house Frank was now watching.

A coach pulled up in front of the house. Frank watched the man get out and walk up to the door. Frank had found Gerold. Frank started toward the house when he spotted a small man in outlandishly loud clothes coming down the street.

Frank stepped back into the alley and watched as Ralph walked up to Gerold's door. He was let in after waiting a moment. Frank leaned against the wall and waited. It wasn't long before Ralph emerged and headed back the way he had come. Frank decided to follow Ralph. Gerold wasn't likely to move soon.

It wasn't hard to follow Ralph, despite his small size and the crowds. His colorful clothes kept popping into view, and Frank followed at a discreet distance.

Frank followed Ralph into a tenement style apartment building in a poorer neighborhood than where Gerold lived. He crept to the door Ralph had entered and listened. At first he heard shuffling movement, then a voice. Rita.

Frank pulled his gun from its holster and shoved his shoulder against the door. The wood cracked as the door flew open. Frank ran across the room to Ralph, grabbed him by the front of his shirt and pushed the barrel of his gun against Ralph's nose.

"Fun and games are over. I've got you and you

better start fixing things or I'm going to blow your head off.''

Frank felt something on his arm, and it finally registered that Rita was trying to get him to let Ralph go. Ralph looked very afraid.

"Let him go, Frank, he's not the bad guy," Rita said.

Frank looked at Rita. She looked healthy, with no sign of bruises or broken bones. He let go of Ralph and stepped back.

"What's going on? Are you okay?" Frank asked.

Rita came up to him and patted his arm soothingly. He allowed her to guide him to put his gun away. He found it strangely calming, and the adrenaline slipped away.

"I'm fine, Frank. I mean aside from being here. Ralph has been trying to help me get home," Rita said.

Frank didn't know what to say. All his fears that Rita had been hurt flowed out of him. He couldn't think of anything to say, but he took Rita into his arms and hugged her tight. He held her for several minutes, taking in her warmth, her scent, and the comforting way she patted his back.

Ralph had managed to close the door and get it to latch. Rita led Frank to a chair, and the three sat around a knife-scarred wood table.

"The short version is I was walking into your office," said Rita, "And then I was here. I didn't know what had happened so I stuck close to this place. A few other things appeared out of nowhere, but after a few hours Ralph and a centaur appeared. They were fighting, and I stayed out of the way until the centaur threw Ralph against the wall."

"That was Gerold," said Ralph.

"I remember him," said Frank. "I found you by tracking him down. But that doesn't explain what is going on."

"I still don't remember anything from before that

morning I met you," Ralph said. "After he threw me against the wall, Gerold found his amulet on the floor and put it on. He twisted something on it, and he transformed into a two-legged human again."

"Frank, he just laughed at us and said we weren't important enough to deal with," said Rita. "But he said he'd help me get home if I paid him enough."

"Let me guess, a price so high you'll never come up with the money," said Frank.

"Exactly. We've been trying, but no matter how much we give him he demands more."

When they asked how he came to be there, Frank related the push of a button in the morgue followed by his cross-country journey. "The one thing I've been able to piece together is Gerold is leading a double life. He is a centaur highwayman as well as a respected human businessman. I just can't figure out what his angle is and why he moves between here and Denver."

"Could it be for the same reason as in our world? Why does someone have businesses in two countries?" said Rita.

"Well, if you rule out the honest reasons, could it be drugs or money laundering," said Frank.

Frank looked at Rita and saw her face light up at the same time as his when the spoken thought sunk in. "That's it," said Frank, slapping the table with the palm of his hand. "Gerold robs coaches and transports the gold and jewels to Denver, where he converts it to cash and lives the good life. I'll bet he uses some of it to purchase cheap mass-produced crap, transports it back here where it passes as fine handmade products for which he charges a premium."

"So he can live in style here without any trace of the stolen money," said Rita.

"But how does he move between places?" asked Ralph.

"With this," said Frank as he pulled the pieces of the remote from his pocket.

"Maybe we can find a wizard who knows how it works and can fix it," said Ralph as he fingered the pieces on the table.

Frank nodded in agreement. "Good idea, but first lets see if we can take down Gerold. Otherwise, even if we get home he's going to remain a problem."

The three swapped ideas for several hours until they had a workable plan. Despite the hard floor he had to sleep on, Frank slept better than he had since he arrived. He smiled as he thought of Rita and slipped off to sleep.

The next morning Frank went to the Sherriff's office. He laid out his plan for catching the highwayman Gerold. The Sherriff wasn't sure it would work, but the city merchants were clamoring for him to do something. He finally agreed to try Frank's plan but warned him of the consequences if he was up to no good.

Later that night Ralph returned from Gerold's.

"Were you able to get him to believe the story?" Rita asked.

"I think so," said Ralph. "I acted like I had information to sell him. He said he couldn't buy it unless he knew what it was worth. I allowed myself to be duped into telling Gerold about the gold shipment."

"Do you think he bought it?" asked Frank.

"I think so. Especially after I told him about the Sherriff."

"What?" said Frank and Rita at the same time.

"Sure, just in case he has informants. I told him the Sherriff was telling everyone it was only his men and no gold in the wagon, to fool Gerold and capture him. Now if he does have informants, and that's what they tell him, he'll think he's ahead of the game."

Frank felt every rut in the road for the last five miles. He was crammed into a windowless wagon with several others, breathing dank air and waiting for Gerold to make a move. Frank swayed forward as the wagon slowed to a stop. Gerold had fallen for their trap.

When the back doors were pulled open, Frank,

Ralph and two of the Sherriff's men pushed forward, knocking two of the bandits to the ground. Frank spotted Gerold standing between two other henchmen, his crossbow aimed at the driver.

Frank pointed his pistol at Gerold. "Drop it."

Frank could see the odd looks from the others, but he also saw fear in Gerold's eyes. Gerold knew what Frank held even if the others didn't. The crossbow fell to the ground, and the other bandits dropped theirs as well.

The road was wide enough for two wagons to pass each other. On either side the tree-covered land sloped up. Frank could see why Gerold picked the location. He could watch from a good vantage point, hide until the last minute, and maneuver around all sides of the wagon.

Ralph sneezed. Frank's gun disappeared. Ralph sneezed again. A dozen chickens appeared on the ground in front of Frank.

The others stared in amazement at the clucking chickens, but Frank moved. He had to stop Gerold before he could recover his crossbow. Leaping onto Gerold's back, Frank tried to get Gerold into a choke hold.

Frank held on as Gerold whipped his body around, trying to buck him off. Frank's punches didn't seem to hurt Gerold. Frank had the same problem when he tried a choke hold. Gerold spun and Frank almost fell.

Frank grabbed for anything to keep from falling off Gerold. His hand found Gerold's medallion chain. He pulled it and hoped the chain would choke Gerold. The medallion wasn't solid, and when Frank grabbed it, a piece spun in his hand. Suddenly he was lying on top of a human Gerold struggling for air.

"Quick, bind him before he can change back," said Frank.

The other bandits had been captured, and now the Sherriff's men tied strong cords around Gerold. The Sherriff rode out of the trees having seen the last of the fight.

"I wouldn't have believed it if I hadn't seen it. Such a devious person will surely be locked away for many years," the Sherriff said.

A few hours later Frank, Rita, and Ralph were outside the door of a wizard the Sherriff had assured them could send them home. The stone house was in the middle of a large lot in one of the more upscale neighborhoods.

With Gerold and his gang locked in jail, Frank couldn't wait to get back to Denver. He knocked on the door.

When the door opened, a tall middle-aged man in a long robe stood in the door. He looked different from how Frank expected a wizard to look. He didn't have a pointy hat with lots of stars. He didn't have a long gray beard. He wasn't carrying a staff. But he did have a puzzled expression on his face.

"Grisibald, where have you been?" the wizard said to Ralph.

Frank put his car into park and sipped his coffee while the song on the radio finished. A hot shower and a good night sleep in his own bed had gone a long way to restoring his faith in the world.

The wizard had returned Rita and him to their own world the day before. Ralph turned out to be his assistant, who had been missing for a couple of weeks. The wizard was the one who recharged the magic in Gerold's remote, but he didn't know what he used it for. Ralph had delivered it and accidentally pressed the button while handing it to Gerold. Once in Denver, Gerold had knocked Ralph out and set him up to be locked away for a long time.

Frank reluctantly headed into his office. He was sure he had several irate clients that he'd have to deal with because of his absence.

Rita was at her desk when he opened the door. Frank smiled when he saw her.

"Good morning, Rita," said Frank. "I'm sure I've got a stack of messages to deal with."

"Yes," said Rita. She rose from her desk and motioned for Frank to follow her. "But we've got a bigger problem resolve first."

Rita led Frank down the hall to the extra office they used for storage. The door was open and inside Frank saw Ralph, sitting at a desk.

"Ralph, what are you doing here?" Frank asked.

"I'm setting up my desk. I'm going to work for you," Ralph said.

"What are you talking about? You're cured. You can go back to your world and your old job," said Frank.

"Naw, that's not for me anymore. I want to work for you and catch bad guys," said Ralph.

"But Ralph, that's not going to work," said Frank.

"Sure it is," said Ralph. "Word got around fast about how you captured Gerold. There's lots of people back in Fips who want to hire us.

Frank started to protest again, but Ralph cut him off. "Don't worry," Ralph said as he patted his pocket. "I've got my frog pills. They keep my allergies in check."

Frank sat in the extra chair. He felt his sanity shift to the back seat as it sank in that his life would never be the same again.

THE FLOOD WAS FIXED

Eric Flint

"STILL sore about Job, huh?" snickered Baalzebub.

The Prince of Darkness took a swipe at the archdevil with his tail, but his heart wasn't in it.

"It was a fluke," he grumbled. "A statistical freak. So what if God found one faithful man in a sea of sinners? I should have played the odds."

"How?"

"I should have bet Him on the whole lousy human race."

Baalzebub shook his head. "God never would have gone for it. Too much work, visiting personal suffering on all those people. He's lazy, when you get right down to it. Worked six lousy days and thinks He ought to be able to lounge around the rest of eternity. Coupon clipper. We proletarian types down here *never* get a day off."

Satan glowered about the stygian gloom of Hell. He'd gotten tired of Dante's Renaissance decor lately, so he'd gone back to Classic. Even the reek of brimstone and the screams of tortured sinners didn't cheer him up.

"I know, I know. That's why I agreed to bet on Job. I got taken to the cleaners."

Baalzebub hesitated. Not for the first time, the

thought crossed his mind that being chief adviser to the Lord of Evil was not without its drawbacks.

"Maybe you should quit gambling with—"

He ducked Satan's pitchfork and dived behind a smoldering rock.

"He's God, dammit! You can't win. The house odds will get you every time."

But Satan wasn't willing to listen to reason. He never was, which (when you get right down to it) is why he's the Prince of Darkness instead of the Lord of Light.

"There's gotta be a way to beat Him," he snarled, after resuming his seat. "All I've got to do is figure out a way to get Him to bet on the whole miserable human race."

He cackled, rubbing his taloned paws. "Any bet on the whole bunch, I'm bound to win!"

Deciding it was safe, Baalzebub resumed his seat.

"Yeah, sure, no question about it. But it's like I said—He's a cloud potato. Hates to work up a sweat."

Satan slouched and stared at his cloven hooves gloomily. Suddenly, he sat up straight.

"I've got it! I've got it! I'll bet Him the human race will lose its faith in Creation!"

"Huh?"

"Don't you see? He's got such a swelled head over that Genesis business that he won't be able to resist."

Baalzebub scratched his horns.

"I still don't get it. Of course He'll bet on it. Why shouldn't He? He's bound to win. I mean, look at the thing!"

And so saying, Baalzebub exerted his archdevilish powers and brought before the superhuman vision of the Lord of Flies the entire vista of Creation, in all its glory and splendor.

"You see what I mean? Even creatures as stupid as humans aren't going to doubt for a minute that something this grand was created by a Creator. How else could it have come to be? Even a moron examining

a watch is going to figure out that it took a watch-
maker to—"

"*Will you shut up about the stupid watch?* I'm sick
of hearing it!"

Satan hawked up a lunger and spit on a nearby
sinner. A bit mollified, he watched the damned one's
flesh boil away.

"I've already figured it out," he announced firmly.
"All you have to do is provide humans with an alternate explanation, and they'll jump at it."

Baalzebub frowned with puzzlement. "What alter-
native explanation?"

Satan spread his arms in a grand gesture. "Evolution, that's what!"

"Huh? What's 'evolution'?"

So the Prince of Darkness explained to his chief archdevil the entire theory of evolution, which he had just
thought up on the spot. (He's evil, but he's not stupid.)
He explained mutations and natural selection and par-
ticulate inheritance and the double helix, and all the
rest of it. By the time he was finished, Baalzebub was
rolling on the ground, roaring with laughter.

"That's the most ridiculous idea I've ever heard!"
he gasped. "Not even humans would fall for it."

Satan grinned. "They will if there's a shred of
evidence."

"But there isn't any."

"There will be, once God makes it. It won't be hard
for Him, either, so He won't be able to wriggle out
of the bet. He's already made the universe, hasn't He?
All He's got to do is fiddle with a few details. Throw
in some old bones, things like that."

Baalzebub pondered his master's words. "You
know, you just might be onto something here," he
mused. Then he shook his head firmly.

"No, no. I go back to what I said earlier—there's
no percentage is betting against the Almighty. He'll
figure some way to welsh on the bet, no matter what
happens."

But Satan was set on his course. Straight away he

ascended to the heavens and bellowed for God to show His face. After the Lord of Creation manifested Himself, the Prince of Darkness explained the proposition.

God accepted the wager immediately. (He's not at all indecisive.)

ONCE A CHUMP, ALWAYS A CHUMP. WHEN ARE YOU EVER GOING TO LEARN, YOU PIPSQUEAK?

Instantly God set about creating the evidence of evolution. He caused great fossils to come into being deep in the bowels of the earth. He created DNA, RNA, the works. He created radioactivity and then changed the laws of nature so that radioactive materials would decay at a precise rate. Because He's a sporting kind of Guy, He even made some peas smooth and some peas wrinkled, so that human dumbbells could figure out genetics.

When He was finished, he showed His work to Satan.

GOOD ENOUGH?

Satan examined the evidence and announced that he was satisfied.

"Once humans get a load of this stuff, they'll dump the Genesis story in a fast minute," he chortled. "Give humans a choice between musty old legends and the evidence in front of their own eyes, they'll trust their senses every time. Idiots."

NOT AFTER THEY SEE THE COUNTER-EVIDENCE.

"What counter-evidence?" demanded the Devil. "There wasn't anything in our bet about counter-evidence!"

SURE THERE IS. WE'RE BETTING HUMAN REASON VERSUS FAITH IN THE BIBLE, AM I RIGHT?

Satan scowled. He could smell a rat, but he wasn't sure just where it was.

"Well, yeah," he admitted.

ALL RIGHT, THEN! YOU EVER HEAR OF THE FLOOD?

Satan waved his hand dismissively. "That was just a heavy rainfall." He snickered. "It only happened because you forgot to turn off the water."

God glowered, but He forebore comment. The truth

is, He couldn't deny it. He'd gotten preoccupied with the creation of the Andromeda Nebula and had let the rain go on a wee bit longer than He'd intended.

But His reply was dignified, as you might expect.

NOT AFTER I REDO IT. THIS TIME I'M GOING TO DO IT UP GRAND.

And, it goes without saying, God was as good as His Word. He rolled history back a few generations to the time of Noah. (God is not limited by the Arrow of Time. As a mere human, you won't be able to understand how this works. That's why He's God and you're not.)

NOAH.

Noah scrambled to his feet. At his urgent gesture, his three sons stood to attention. Well, Shem and Japheth did, anyway. As usual, Ham slouched.

"Yes, Sir!"

DO YOU REMEMBER THAT HEAVY RAIN A FEW WEEKS BACK?

"Sure do, Chief. What a doozy! For a while there, I thought we were all going to drown. Heh, heh, heh."

IS THAT LEVITY, NOAH?

"No, Sir! No, Sir!"

I TRUST NOT. IN ANY EVENT, I'VE DECIDED TO REDO THE RAIN. WE NEED A MONSTROUS FLOOD, YOU SEE. DROWN EVERYTHING THAT MOVES ON LAND. EXCEPT YOU.

"Uh, yes Sir. Everything, Sir?"

ALL MEN AND BEASTS THAT WALK OR CRAWL UPON THE EARTH, OR CREEP WITHIN IT, OR FLY THROUGH THE AIR.

"Uh, yes, Sir. If you don't mind my asking, though, why the hard line?"

THEY ARE SINNERS ALL.

Ham spoke up. "Uh, begging Your pardon, Sir, but I actually think most of 'em are pretty devout. Look here, for instance!"

Ignoring Noah's glare, Ham pointed to a procession of beetles marching past, holding up icons and images of saints.

"And how about over there!" Ham pointed to a circle of baby hamsters gathered about a gray-pelted oldster, learning to genuflect.

SINNERS, I SAID, SINNERS THEY ARE.

And, indeed, it was just as God said. That very moment the beetles plunged into a disgusting saturnalia. The baby hamsters (and the gray-pelted oldster!) began copulating shamelessly. In the air above, sparrows sodomized each other in midflight. Everywhere the cyc could see, people were worshiping graven images. The soil erupted with earthworms, wriggling an obscene dance.

"I am shocked, Sir! Shocked!" cried Noah.

"Sinners all!" bellowed Shem and Japheth. Ham opened his mouth to say something but fell silent at Shem's elbow to his ribs.

QUITE SO. YOU, HOWEVER, ARE A RIGHTEOUS MAN, AND SO SHALL I SPARE YOU. GATHER UP—

There followed a whole slew of instructions regarding the size of the ark to be built, the wood it was to be made of, how it was to be pitched, and so on and so forth. Accompanied by instructions to save two of every species, one male and one female.

Noah and his sons began scurrying around. Noah and Shem started chopping down trees. Japheth started boiling pitch in a cauldron. Ham—

—right off started causing trouble.

"Hey, Pop," he said, tugging at Noah's cloak. "I'm confused."

His father glared at him. "What could possibly be confusing, even to you? The Lord's instructions were very clear and precise."

"Yeah, I know. That's why I'm confused. He said the ark was supposed to be three hundred cubits long, fifty cubits wide, and thirty cubits high. Right?"

"Just so."

Ham held up his forearm and pointed to it. "That's how long a cubit is, right?"

"Just so."

Ham shrugged. "Ain't gonna work, Pop. There's

millions of species on the earth. Sure, most of 'em are bugs. But even so—you got any idea how much room two elephants are gonna take up? And rhinos? And hippos? And crocodiles? And that's another thing. How are we gonna feed them? Take a lot of hay to feed a couple of elephants. And what about all the carnivores? They can't eat hay. We'll have to stock the boat with other animals for them to eat."

The little brat whistled. "It's a real paradox, Pop. The Lord said 'two of each kind of animal.' No more, no less. But if we only take two, most of 'em will be gobbled up for sure. By the tigers and lions and panthers and wolves and owls and falcons and snakes and—"

"Silence!"

"—which we ain't got room for anyway."

Noah cuffed his son. "The Lord will provide, dolt!"

"Gee, Pop," whined Ham, "I'm just trying to help."

"Then do so! Gather up all the animals!"

Ham was a lippy kid, but he knew when his father wasn't fooling around. So he obediently set forth to carry out his instructions.

There followed the most heroic saga in all of human history, unfortunately never recorded. The deeds of Hercules and Gilgamesh pale in comparison. For Ham was forced to wander all over the world collecting two of each animal that walked on the earth or wriggled in the soil. Most of which, alas, do not live in the Holy Land.

Ham headed south and traveled through the length and breadth of Africa. That took a bit of time, especially because he had to invent the microscope in order to examine all the continent's protozoa to determine how many separate species there were that needed to be saved. The most time-consuming part was examining their nonexistent sex organs to find out which of the asexual critters were male and which were female. In the end, giving up, he just faked it by grabbing two of each kind at random and hoped God wouldn't ask any hard questions.

At the Cape of Good Hope, assisted only by chimps, he built a boat of reeds in order to travel to Australia and the Americas. The voyage across the Atlantic was rough. Not because of high seas, but because the reed boat was much bigger than an aircraft carrier—how else could he have carried two of each animal in Africa?—and the animals weren't any help at all when it came to reefing sails and all that nautical business.

But he made it, eventually. He ordered the animals to stay put (which they did, naturally) while he traveled the length and breadth of North and South America collecting all the animals that lived on the millions of square miles of surface of those two great continents.

He met with setbacks, of course. Some of the animals refused to accept his invitation. The mammoths and mastodons told him he was an idiot. The giant ground sloths said they were too lazy to go along. The saber-tooth tigers got downright nasty.

"It's your funeral," Ham told them.

Eventually, he made it back to South America with all the new animals he'd collected. Then, of course, he had to build a much bigger boat. Fortunately, there's a lot of timber in the Amazon basin, so he was able to build a raft the size of Manhattan Island. He sailed around South America on the raft. Things got tough beating around the Horn, but he had a lot of help from all the jillions of monkeys he'd picked up in the rain forest.

Across the Pacific now, making a quick stop at the Galapagos Islands to pick up some tortoises and finches he had on his list. Australia and New Zealand turned out to be pretty easy, once he got the kangaroos to settle down. The real snag came in Tasmania, where the local top predator proved to be recalcitrant. But, eventually, covered with bites and scratches, Ham dragged a couple of the monsters on board. (That's where the Tasmanian Devil got its name, by the way.)

Asia, next, after a more or less quick detour through

Polynesia, Melanesia, the Philippines, and the Indonesian islands. Up Malaya, through South-East Asia, China and all of Siberia, back down through Central Asia and into the Indian subcontinent. The tropical animals complained loudly, crossing the Himalayas. It wasn't the cold so much as it was the insults hurled their way by the local yeti. (That's how the Abominable Snowmen got their name, by the way.)

India was a piece of cake. Across Persia and the rest of the Middle East, and then—home at last.

"You forgot Europe, dummy," snapped Noah.

Sighing, Ham set off again. But after everything else, Europe was a milk run. Except for the Irish elk, who said their antlers would get all scuffed up, crowded in the ark like that.

By the time Ham was finished, the ark was ready. Ham took one look at it and shook his head.

"It's like I said, Pop. We're never going to fit 'em all inside."

But the faithless youth proved wrong. The Lord did, of course, provide. God changed the dimensions of the ark into cubits measured by *His* forearm, and there was room to spare.

YOU'D BETTER DISCIPLINE THAT LITTLE SNOT, said God to Noah. **OR ONE OF THESE DAYS, YOU'LL GET DRUNK AND HE'LL LOOK AT YOUR NAKED BODY.**

So, Noah set sail. But because his lazy son Ham had loafed on the job, Noah was running a little behind schedule. He was in such a big hurry that he forgot one of the species.

Fortunately, the archangel Michael called him back.

"Noah! Noah! You forgot the *Anopheles* mosquitoes!"

So Noah turned back and picked up the mosquitoes.

"If Mark Twain finds out about this, there'll be hell to pay," muttered Michael, as he handed over the deadly little insects.

The rest of the story, of course, is well known. The dove and all that. About the only thing worth noting that happened while they were at sea was that, once again, Ham got himself in trouble. As usual, questioning the Lord.

"Hey, Pop," he said, leaning over the rail, "I'm puzzled about something."

"What is that, impious youth?"

Ham pointed to a school of sharks, rending flesh.

"How come they don't get drowned?"

The sharks themselves provided the answer. A moment later, the great killers were lined up at the rail, glaring.

"We are blessed in the eyes of the Lord," snarled a great white.

"Pious, the lot of us!" proclaimed a hammerhead. "Not like those vicious land animals."

And, indeed, it was so. That very moment, as the sharks resumed their feeding frenzy, the smell of incense wafted over the sea. A chorus of angels burst into songs of praise.

And Ham got another mark next to his name, in God's Little Black Book.

(Which is, actually, not so little.)

When it was all done, God was feeling mighty pleased with Himself. He even re-organized one of the very distant constellations to read:

NEVER GIVE SUCKER AN EVEN BREAK.

Astronomers haven't seen it, because the light from the constellation hasn't reached the Earth yet. It's scheduled to arrive in the year 2222 AD at 12:01 AM on April Fool's Day. God enjoys His little jokes.

But as the reports started coming in, in the late innings, He stopped being so pleased.

WHO?

"Cuvier, Sir," replied the archangel. "Georges Leopold Chretien—"

I KNOW WHO HE IS! I MADE HIM, DIDN'T I? OF ALL THE ROTTEN INGRATITUDE."

After a moment: **WHEN HE DIES, FRY HIM.**

But it wasn't just Cuvier. Soon, there was a whole flood of sinners. (If you'll pardon the pun.)

Darwin.

FRY HIM.

Wallace.

FRY HIM.

Huxley.

FRY HIM.

God was especially ticked off at Mendel.

HE'S A MONK! WHAT'S A MONK DOING PLAYING AROUND WITH SMUTTY-MINDED LITTLE PEAS?

Inevitably: **FRY HIM.**

In fact, the whole nineteenth century was pretty much of a big disappointment for the Lord. Queen Victoria was a bright spot, of course. And God was delighted with Richard Wagner. He loved the music (although He only listened to the orchestral excerpts, like everybody else except George Bernard Shaw), but he was absolutely ecstatic over the great composer's writings. He even made *The Jew In Music* mandatory reading for all the residents of Heaven.

(That would have been a little tough on the Jews, but there aren't any in Heaven. They have their own retirement plan, much to God's disgruntlement. After reading Wagner, He'd been really looking forward to damning Mendelssohn.)

Satan, of course, was cackling with glee. Not only was he going to win his bet with God, but he was reaping a whole harvest of sinners. Much better class than he normally got, too.

Yes, sad to say, the theory of evolution was all the rage. All that faked evidence God had strewn around had completely turned the heads of mortal man, born in sin.

Of course, not everyone was swept up in the Devil's scheme. From the very beginning, there were those who stood by God's Word, starting with Bishop Wilberforce. By the time the late twentieth century rolled around, they had organized themselves into a movement called "creationism" or "intelligent design." It was an uphill battle all the way, but the creationists were a devout and plucky bunch.

Whenever creationists died, of course, they went straight to Heaven. Sat at the side of the Lord, they did, on account of they were God's favorites.

Still and all, it looked like the Devil had a sure winner.

But Satan was always a dummy.

Baalzebub tried to warn him: *You can't beat house odds.*

Because what happened, naturally, was that God changed the rules. Since the theory of evolution was sweeping the boards, God just went back in history and made evolution for real. Simple as that.

NOAH.

"Yes, Sir!"

WE'RE DOING ANOTHER TAKE.

"Uh, excuse me, sir?"

YOU DEAF? WE'RE DOING THE FLOOD OVER.

Noah wasn't happy about having to go through all that hard work again. But he kept his mouth shut and did as he was told. He was a holy man, after all, and holy men know that arguing with God is a bad career move.

The scenario was a little different, of course. Since God had made evolution real, the earth was now covered with all sorts of dinosaurs and other uncouth beasts. Ham really had his job cut out for him, this time, what with all the tyrannosaurs and such that he had to round up. He probably couldn't have done it at all except that God had also made plate tectonics, so the continents were scrunched up together. No need to build giant reed boats and rafts this time.

Then, all of Ham's hard work turned out to be wasted. Because, following the Lord's instructions, Noah set sail just before the dinosaurs could make it aboard.

It was kind of pitiful, really. All those big burly dinosaurs, blubbering like babies.

"Don't leave us! Don't leave us!"

Noah kept a straight face. But all the little nocturnal mammals leaned over the rail and blew raspberries.

"Nyah, nyah! Nyah, nyah! You're extinct, you're extinct!"

They shouldn't have done it, though. The jibes made the dinosaurs really mad, and things got a little hairy when Noah had to turn back.

Once again, he'd forgotten the *Anopheles* mosquitoes.

So that's how it all worked out. Satan lost the bet, big time. Of course, the Lord of Flies complained bitterly. Accused God of being a cheat and a swindler. But God is pretty much impervious to that kind of accusation, for two reasons:

First, Satan's not a friend of His, so He really doesn't care what the Devil thinks.

Second, He's God. So He really doesn't care what *anybody* thinks. Disapprove of Him? **FRY.**

Still, it wasn't all peaches and cream. There were a couple of flies in the ointment, from God's point of view.

First, He had to transfer all the creationists down to Hell, since the blasphemers had denied His handiwork. Broke His heart, that did, on account of He was really quite fond of them. But sacrilege is sacrilege, and that's that. Mortal sin. **FRY.**

The Devil was tickled pink. He's always happy to get a big new crop of sinners, of course. But he was especially happy to see all the creationists arrive because he was suffering from a shortage of low-level goons and stooges, and the creationists really worked out quite nicely, once they stopped whining and got with the program.

The other problem proved to be a lot trickier.

Because, naturally, Mark Twain *did* find out about the *Anopheles* mosquitoes. They might have slid it by him if they'd only screwed up once. But *twice*? Not a chance. And, naturally, he made a big stink about it.

After God read *Letters From The Earth*, He positively blew His stack. (That's what caused all the Seyfert galaxies.)

TWAIN'S TOAST.

You'd think the Devil would have been glad to see Mark Twain arrive. And he was, at first. But Twain turned out to be a real pain in the ass.

First of all, he had an attitude problem.

Even worse, he escaped.

It's true. The only escape from the Pit of Damnation in the historical record. Twain built a raft made out of petrified wood and set off down a great river of lava, accompanied by a runaway slave named Ham.

As soon as he learned of Twain's escape, Satan sent one of his chief devils in hot pursuit. A few days later the devil sent back a message. Helmuth announced that the fugitive Twain was in sight and that he had the situation totally under control.

Lucifer was delighted at the news. But not all of his top advisers shared his enthusiasm.

"He's made that claim before," sneered Gharlane. "And you know how that worked out."

Sure enough, Helmuth blew it again, and Twain made good his escape. But that's another story.

VISITOR'S NIGHT AT JOEY CHICAGO'S

Mike Resnick

So I'm sitting there in Joey Chicago's 3-Star Tavern, nursing an Old Peculier and doping out the odds if Belmont comes up muddy after the rain we're expecting, when an annoying high-pitched voice says, "Gimme a bourbon martini and make it snappy!"

"Ain't no such animal," says Joey. There's a pause, and then he says, "Ain't no such animal as you, neither."

"Watch your mouth, Mac," says the voice, "or I just might put my fist in it."

I look up, and what should I see but an ugly little creature, maybe fifteen inches high, standing on the bar, paws on hips, glaring at Joey.

"Harry," says Joey to me, "where the hell has Big-Hearted Milton gone to?"

"He's in the john," I say. "He's hexing a rasslin' match. He says he thinks better in there."

"Well, you tell him if he wants me to keep paying him for protection, he'd better get his ass out here."

"What about my drink, Mac?" snaps the creature.

"Keep your shirt on," says Joey. "I'm working on it."

"I ain't got no shirt," says the creature.

"Harry," says Joey, "are you gonna get Milton or are you going to spend all night listening to me argue with this disgusting little critter?"

"Keep a civil tongue in your head!" says the disgusting little critter. "I get mighty ugly when I'm riled."

"You ain't so good-looking even when you're not riled," says Joey as I walk into the men's room. Milton is sitting there on a closed toilet seat, fully dressed, mumbling some spell at a pentagram he's drawn on the floor.

"Come out to the bar," I say. "Your urgent assistance is required."

"In a minute," says Big-Hearted Milton. He mutters one last spell and then stands up. "Okay. Now Rikki Tikki Tavi is going to beat Monstro Ligriv in straight falls tomorrow night at the Garden. I figure we should clean up, because everyone knows it's Monstro's turn to win."

"We'll worry about that later," I say.

"Harry the Book isn't interested in a sporting event?" he says, arching an eyebrow. "You gonna start taking bets on the stock market, perhaps maybe?"

"Just pay attention, Milton," I said. "There's some kind of strange creature in the bar demanding a bourbon martini, and Joey Chicago wants you to make it go away."

Milton's face goes white as a sheet, and he has trouble catching his breath. "A bourbon martini?" he repeats. "Is this a redhead named Thelma?"

"No, it's an ugly monster from some mystic world."

Milton relaxes visibly. "Okay, no problem," he says. Then: "You're *sure* it's not a Thelma?"

"I'm sure," I say. "Now come on. I'm the guy who convinced Joey to hire you for protection, so if you don't vanish this critter, or at least turn it into something friendly with a bankroll to bet, it'll reflect badly on me."

"Why do you care?" asks Milton.

"I'm using the third booth in the bar as my temporary office."

"They evicted you *again*?" he says, though since this is the fifth time in three years, I don't know why he looks so surprised.

"A temporary setback," I say with dignity. I make

a face. "The Boston Geldings haven't beaten the point spread in two years. How the hell could I know they were going to get hot against the Syracuse Ridglings?"

"You could have asked," says Milton, looking very self-important.

"You could emerge from the damned bathroom more than once a day," I shoot back.

Then we are in the tavern, and Milton takes a look at the little creature, which is sitting cross-legged on the bar, munching on a pretzel.

"About time," says Joey Chicago. "Make him vanish, Milton. When I wouldn't serve him, he went around spitting in all my customers' drinks."

"I don't see any customers," replies Milton, looking around.

"Would *you* stay if someone kept spitting in *your* drink?" demands Joey. "Just make the little bastard vanish."

"Piece of cake," says Milton. "Where does he come from?"

"How the hell do I know?" says Joey.

"I can't send him back if I don't know where to send him," said Milton. He turns to the creature. "Excuse me, kind sir, but what realm do you reside in?"

"I'll never tell!" snaps the creature.

"Well, so much for sending him back," said Milton with a shrug.

"You mean I'm stuck with him?" demands Joey. "I want my protection money back. First thing in the morning I'm hiring Morris the Mage."

"No, you're not stuck with him," says Big-Hearted Milton, who has never offered a refund since T. Rex was a pup. "I just said I couldn't sent him back."

"You're going to take him home with you?"

"So he can spit on *my* chopped liver and in *my* matzo ball soup?" says Milton. "Don't be silly."

"Then what are you going to do?"

"I can't send him home," says Milton, "but I can encourage him to go home on his own power."

"How?" asks Joey curiously.

"Like this," says Milton, snapping his fingers.

Nothing happens.

"What's Morris the Mage's phone number?" asks Joey disgustedly.

"Oh, ye of little faith," mutters Milton. He mumbles something that wouldn't make any sense even if he was saying it clearly. Then he snaps his fingers again, and suddenly there is a very bright blue *something*, about the size of a bulldog but with scaly skin, three-inch claws on its front feet, two rows of razor-sharp teeth, bloodshot little eyes, and halitosis. It is standing on the floor, and suddenly it sees the creature on the bar. It flaps wings I didn't even know it had, flies up to the bar about ten feet from the creature, gives a high-pitched hum that sounds more ominous than a growl, and begins approaching it.

"Omygod omygod omygod!" shrieks the creature.

The blue thing launches itself through the air, and the creature vanishes about a fifth of a second before it reaches him. (Okay, so make it was a quarter of a second, or a half, but bookies who hang out at the track measure everything in fifths of a second, so don't hassle me, okay?)

"Well, that's that," said Milton. "One problem presented, one problem solved. I'm going back to the men's room."

"Uh . . . Milton," says Joey, pointing to the blue thing, and we see that it has just downed a bottle of vodka and is going after Joey's bottle of '73 Dom Perignon, which is the only bottle he has ever owned and is just for show. Joey tries to shoo it away, and it just snarls at him.

"Milton," says Joey nervously, "thank it and send it on its way."

"It's not that easy," says Milton, frowning.

"Why the hell not?" demands Joey.

"Bringing them here is easy; sending them away isn't."

"What are you talking about?" says Joey. "A spell's a spell."

"Some are more complex than others," says Milton.

"I *knew* I should have hired a union wizard!"

"Do you know what they cost?" says Milton.

"Less than this *momser* is going to drink before I get rid of him, I'll bet," snaps Joey.

"I'll get rid of him," said Milton. "I just can't send him back to where he came from."

"I don't care where you send him," says Joey. "Hell, send him to my ex-wife's and the bastard that *yenta* ran off with!"

Milton rolls up his sleeves. "Stand back, everyone!" he says.

"What do you mean, 'everyone'?" says Joey. "Except for Harry the Book, who's running his business out of the third booth here, everyone's long gone."

"Silence, mortal!" says Milton.

"You're as mortal as I am," says Joey, "and if you don't vanish this beast pretty damned fast, I'm gonna give you one hell of a kick in your most mortal part!"

"All right, all right," says Milton. He turned to me. "Harry, how much would you say it weighs?"

"Maybe forty-five pounds," I tell him.

"Mammal, reptile, or dragon?" he asks.

"Yes," I say.

He frowns. "Okay," he says. "Here goes!"

He mumbles something that almost rhymes but it is in no language I have ever heard and makes even less sense than French, and then his eyes roll back in his head and his arms stick out straight ahead of him and he goes into a kind of swami trance, and suddenly we hear an ominous and portentous *gulp!*, and we look at the bar, and there is this thing that looks kind of like a leather gorilla, except that it's got an extra pair of arms and a third eye right in the middle of its forehead, and it is chewing and making crunching noises, and a few blue scales kind of dribble out of its mouth.

"Man, that was *good!*" he growls. "I haven't eaten in 253 years, give or take an afternoon." He looks at Joey's stock. "What have you got on tap?"

"Old Peculier and Old Washensox," says Joey in kind of trembling tones.

"I'll have a keg of each!" says the leather gorilla. "By Merlin, it feels good to be free again!"

"Uh . . . Milton . . ." says Joey.

"You said got rid of it, I got rid of it," says Milton defensively.

"Milton," I say, "I know you're not a betting man, but I'll give you seventeen trillion to one that I know what Joey's going to ask for next."

The gorilla gets tired of waiting, so he climbs down behind the bar, lifts a five-gallon keg, and chugalugs it. "I could get to like this place," he says.

"Make me an offer," mutters Joey.

The leather gorilla belches. It is so loud that six glasses shatter. Then he turns to Milton. "I intuit that you're the one who brought me here."

Milton tries to answer, but he's shaking so badly nothing comes out, and he just nods weakly.

"You conjured me to kill the Spedunker."

"The blue thing with the wings and scales," said Joey.

"Yeah, a Spedunker." Suddenly the gorilla grins. "Now I'll bet you're trying to figure out how to get rid of me."

"I would never do such a thing," says Milton. "Honor bright and pinky to the sky, the thought never crossed my mind."

"Your nose just grew seven inches," notes the gorilla.

Milton's hand goes to his nose. It is the same almost-shapeless blob as usual.

The gorilla throws back his head and laughs. Three mice who have been attracted to all the strange new smells faint dead away. "I was just pulling your leg," he says. "Or maybe I should say I was pulling your nose!" He laughs at his own joke, and two of the overhead lightbulbs burst.

"Now that you've had a snack and a little something to wash it down with," says Milton hopefully, "maybe you'd like to go home and take a nap?"

"Go back to that tiny cave where I was imprisoned for millennia?" demands the gorilla angrily. "Never!"

"Harry," says Joey, "go find the phone book and look up Morris the Mage's number."

"Relax," says the gorilla. "I find you even more distasteful that you find me. I'm off to explore this strange new world. Where's the nearest whorehouse?"

"For gorillas?" I say. "I don't think there are any."

"Yes there are!" says Milton quickly. "There are three of them in Brooklyn."

The gorilla turns to Joey. "Loan me a fiver," he says. "I came out without my wallet." He frowns. "In fact, I came out without my pants."

Joey opens the cash register and gives him a ten-spot. "You'll want to visit a Brooklyn bar when you're done," he says hopefully.

"Thanks, fella," says the gorilla, grabbing the saw-buck. "You're okay."

He lumbers to the door, starts to walk out, and bounces back to the middle of the tavern.

"What's going on?" he demands, looking right at Milton.

"I should have thought of it," says Milton, frowning. "The spell brings you here, but it doesn't let you leave. You're just here to eat the Spedunker."

"I *ate* the Spedunker," snarls the gorilla. "Now I've got urgent business in Brooklyn."

Milton starts backing away from him. "I don't know a spell to let you out," he says. "All I know is how to bring you here."

"Well, you'd better think of something fast," says the gorilla, slowly approaching him. "Because I'm getting hungry again."

"Gorillas are vegetarians," says Milton.

"So they'll penalize me fifteen yards," says the gorilla.

Milton screams a spell at the top of his voice, and before the gorilla knows it there is a seven-ton gryphon in the bar.

"Oh, shit!" says the gorilla, and vanishes just before the gryphon can reach him.

Well, you can figure what comes next. Milton summons a dragon to scare the gryphon away, and then he calls up a poisonous hydra-headed chimera to frighten the dragon, and then he magics up a kraken to eat the chimera, and after two hours have passed, I feel like I have watched the same movie fourteen times in a row.

"What now?" says Joey in disgusted tones as we watch the latest arrival, a creature that looks like a refugee from a movie with actors named Boris or Bela or Basil or something else beginning with a B. The creature is considering which of Joey's bar stock to sample, and Milton decides to give it one last try, and he mutters and mumbles and goes into his swami again, and suddenly a trunk reaches out and holds the creature high above the floor, and it curses and cries and says that it has a wife and three kids and a mortgage and it hasn't sent in its insurance check yet, and the elephant loosens its hold for a second and the creature disappears in a cloud of gray smoke, which is very fitting because it was obsolete long before Technicolor movies hit the scene.

I am wondering what Milton is going to conjure to get rid of the elephant, who is so big that he is stuck half in and half out of the tavern, when one of the mice that fainted wakes up and squeaks a couple of times, and the elephant takes one look and trumpets in terror and backs out into the street, taking half of the front wall with him, and the last time I see him he is making a beeline for Third Avenue, which is not going to help him much because that is Casey Callahan's beat, and he doesn't allow anything to speed down his street, not even elephants.

"Well, that's that," says Milton.

"No," says Joey. "Pay me for all my bar stock and fix my walls and buy me a new bottle of '73 Dom and *then* that'll be that."

"Don't be so ungrateful," says Milton with dignity. "You asked me to solve a problem. I solved it."

"It's like solving a fist fight by turning it into World

War VII!" snaps Joey. "Now, are you going to make restitution for damages or not?"

"I'm tapped out at the moment," says Milton, "but . . ."

"No buts!" snaps Joey. "Get out of my establishment."

"I thought we were friends!" says Milton in hurt tones.

"You got it absolutely right," says Joey. "We *were* friends!"

"Okay," says Milton. "If that's the way you're going to be, give me one for the road and I'm out of here."

"Where's your money?" demands Joey.

"Put it on my tab," says Milton.

"We're mortal enemies," says Joey. "You ain't got no tab!"

"Hey, Mac," says a voice. "Is this guy bothering you?"

We turn to see the little critter who started the whole thing.

"You betcha," says Joey. "Make him go away."

The creature says something in French or some other alien tongue, makes a mystic sign in the air, and *whoosh!*, Milton is gone (though he later turns up in a house of excellent repute in Brooklyn.)

"I'll have a tall one," says the critter.

"You got it," says Joey, drawing one from what remains of the tap. "By the way, I'm really sorry we hassled you before. You looking for work?"

The critter shrugs. "Doing what?"

"Protection," says Joey. "Keeping the riffraff out of my establishment."

"Sure, why not?" He extends a wiry little three-fingered hand. "By the way, my name's Louie."

"Louie," says Joey Chicago, "I think this is the beginning of a beautiful friendship."

A MIDSUMMER NIGHTMARE

Walt Boyes

HARRY Wilson stood across the small street from the park where a pickup game of football was being played. He looked up as a shadow passed overhead. A huge black bird landed on the power pole above him. The bird cocked his head as if he were watching the people across the street running on the grass. The bird croaked and launched himself again, wings spread wide, and soared across the field.

Harry pulled a small digital camera out of his jacket pocket and walked across the street to the little park and the touch football game he'd been watching. He stood on the sidewalk, with the camera half-hidden in his hand. He waited until one of the players ran very close to where he was standing and then quickly snapped the player's picture. The player didn't notice, in the press of the play.

Harry waited until the game broke up and then approached the player he'd photographed.

"Excuse me," he asked, "are you Darryl Jones?"

"Huh?" the player responded, toweling off his sweaty hair. "Yeah, I'm Darryl."

"Darryl, is that your wheelchair over there?" Harry pointed to a very expensive black and chrome wheelchair, sitting beside one of the cars, a "handicapped" placard visible through the windshield.

Sudden light dawning, Darryl stood straight and glared at Harry. "Who wants to know?"

"Federal Mutual Insurance Company, Darryl," Harry drawled. "That's a gotcha."

"You son of a—" Darryl began, but Harry held up his hand.

"Don't say anything, Darryl. Our attorneys will be talking to yours in the morning. I think we might be able to settle your personal injury claim pretty quick now, don't you?"

Harry fumbled the cell phone from his coat.

"Charlie, Harry here," he barked, then listened.

"Yeah, I got him," he answered. "Playing touch football. Both telephoto and closeup. Told him, too. I expect you'll be able to get an abandonment of claim in the morning. I'll email you the pictures from the digital camera when I get back to the office."

Harry turned and walked back across the street, unlocked the door of his old Volvo, got in, closed the door, started it and drove off. During all this, Darryl Jones stood, frozen, with his mouth open.

Harry drove up the hill toward Maple Valley in the late afternoon traffic. He drove past Earthworks Park, with its sign advertising a Renaissance Faire. He figured he'd go one of these days. He had always wondered what he'd have done had he been born in Elizabeth I's England. He snorted to himself as his inner cynic reminded him that his family had always been poor and that the lot of the poor in Elizabethan England was not the bright and shining past celebrated by Renaissance Fairs.

His cell phone rang. He fumbled it out without taking his eyes off the road, and thumbed it open.

"Hey, Harry, this is George! Your favorite Muckleshoot!"

"Hello, George, long time . . ."

"You up for a game of pool? I'm at the Piranha Tavern and I've got a table free."

"Yeah. I can be there in . . ." Harry checked the traffic. ". . . about ten or fifteen."

"We're good to go. I can beat off the table stealers until then. Beer?"

"Sure. Just make it a cold one."

"Will do."

Harry smiled. Nobody ever remembered the actual name of the dive George was calling from because of the painting of the enormous piranha on the wall of the building facing the road and the marquee sign that said "35 pound piranha" above the door. Depending on the state of the fish's health, there might even be a real piranha in the aquarium at the end of the bar. Harry always believed it was really just a huge oscar, but Dave the bartender insisted on its piranhahood, and neither Harry nor the fish cared enough to argue.

Today, the place was pretty busy, especially since it wasn't yet five o'clock. It was a famous lie that it always rained in the Pacific Northwest. The sky was blue, without clouds, and the June day's temperature was in the high seventies. Very nice.

He pulled into the dirt and gravel parking lot, turned off the Volvo. He looked south and saw the huge white cloud shrouded shape of Mt. Rainier. Even though it was less than thirty miles away, it was raining and snowing on the huge volcano. No wonder the Native Americans feared and worshiped the mountain as a god. Harry could see the big divot on the mountain's side where the last explosion had blown out the side of the volcano, sending a huge wall of superheated mud and stones straight at Puget Sound at a thousand miles an hour. If it happened again, like right now, Harry reflected, where he was standing might be high enough to escape. Maybe not.

A huge black bird swooped down and landed on the roof of the old Volvo, startling Harry. He looked at Harry, first with one eye, then the other, cocking his head.

"Well, hello, bird," Harry said.

The bird croaked back, as if acknowledging the greeting.

"Nice day," Harry said, "so please don't mess up my car, okay?"

The bird ducked his head, cocked it from side to side, and then croaked softly, as if agreeing.

"Thank you, kind sir," Harry said, lifting his hand in a wave. The bird mantled his feathers, and took off, landing on the very top of the power pole that served the tavern. Harry laughed and went inside. It was dark as sin and smelled of very old beer.

Harry's eyes adjusted to the gloom, and he spotted George Mason. George was a Muckleshoot. Many of the other Native American tribes and a lot of local whites still didn't think Muckleshoots were really a tribe, but the Bureau of Indian Affairs had ruled them a real tribe and given them a postage-stamp-sized reservation on the slopes of Mt. Rainier between Puyallup and Tacoma. Mostly, as far as Harry could tell, they used the reservation for a school, a cigarette store and a huge casino and amphitheater, which were making a very large amount of money for the tribe. It was George's oft-stated belief that it was only fair that the Muckleshoots should be fleecing the mostly white and Hispanic gambling crowds since in their turn, they had fleeced the Muckleshoots of their traditional fishing grounds up the Puyallup River.

George, a little over five feet three, and like many West Coast Native Americans, almost as wide, was standing next to an open pool table way in the back, near the door to the outdoor beer garden. He saw Harry enter and waved his pool cue over his head, causing a stray patron trying to get past him to go outside to flinch and duck as the cue swept through the air where his head had just been.

"Sorry, man," George rumbled. The patron was a biker, and he looked for a minute as though he wanted to discuss the matter further. George's eyes got hard, and the biker noticed that for all his bulk, not much of George was fat.

"Yeah, sure, man," the biker replied nervously, as he headed out the door carrying his beer bottle.

"Heya, Harry!" George greeted him, and motioned him toward a bottle of Pyramid sitting on the other side of the table, sweating with the cold. "How you been?"

"Could be better, George."

"Yeah, been tough since Sally died, I bet."

George had lost his own wife three years before, and one of his sons to the traditional Native American diseases of drugs and alcohol earlier in the year.

"You know. One day at a time," Harry shrugged. He took off his coat and hung it up. He turned and selected a cue from the rack, picked up a chalk, rubbed it all over the head of the cue, and turned back to face George.

"You break?"

"Sure." George compensated for his short stature by hiking up and cocking his buttock on the side of the table, reached over and shot the break. The balls scattered, and the six ball went in the corner pocket. George set up again and shot. This time, he missed.

"Harry, you're up."

Harry went through the motions, waiting patiently for George to get to the reason he had invited him to play pool. They played three games, ate bad bar food, and both went to return their beer to the salmon streams twice before George cleared his throat and began to talk seriously.

"Got a problem, Harry," he began. "There's a disturbance in the Force."

Harry had a mouthful of beer. He sprayed it all over the table, being just able to turn away from giving it to George full in the face.

"Shit, Harry!" George ducked away from the spray. "I didn't mean it to be funny. Honest I didn't."

"Right." Harry was using a bar towel Dave the bartender had nonchalantly chucked at him to blow his nose. "I got beer up my nose, you damn Muckleshoot idiot!"

"No, listen, Harry, I mean it!" George insisted. "You have to listen. You know that I am a shaman.

Well, sort of, because a lot of our knowledge and traditions were lost when you whites kicked our butts
around. And I can't help it that I was a Star Wars
junkie when I was a kid!"

Harry finished wiping his face with the beer-flecked
towel. He turned to George and stared at him.

"So I call it the Force, okay? But it is real, as real
as I am, Harry. Somebody is screwing around doing
what he shouldn't, and I need help to stop it."

Harry continued to stare.

"I can feel this guy, and he's really messin' with
stuff he doesn't understand, and it is screwing things
up. The tribe's alcohol related arrests have gone up
by one hundred fifty percent in the last three months,
Harry. That's because we have a lot of people who
are sensitive to this kind of stuff, and I tell you, what
we do when this happens, we try to drink it away. The
more you drink, the deafer you get to the Force, or
whatever you want to call it."

George shut up. He glared almost defiantly at
Harry.

"George, I don't know what I can do to help,"
Harry began.

"I'll tell you what," George said, "You're a detective, you can help me find this idiot and get him to
stop what he's doing."

"What is he doing, George?"

"He's trying to summon something from beyond the
world. I dunno what, yet, but the feel of it is really
wild and uncontained and pretty evil."

"Some kind of demon?" Harry passed a hand over
his head, rubbing his thinning hair.

"Maybe."

"Lord God Almighty, George, I'm a Methodist.
This stuff isn't supposed to happen to Methodists!
Heck, my pastor says he isn't even sure there's a
Heaven! I don't know from demons!"

"Well, Mr. Methodist, I thought that you could
practice another method: the detective method."

George ducked as Harry threw a mock punch at his shoulder.

Suddenly, from the other end of the bar, they heard the sound of wood breaking.

Harry turned, to come face to face with Darryl Jones, armed with a broken pool cue and three friends.

"Harry, you know these guys?" George asked, backing away and giving himself room.

"Yeah, old fat man," Jones said. "He knows me. What he don't know is who he's messing with. You can't mess with me, you dumb bastard!" He threw himself at Harry, broken cue at high port.

"Looks like we get to practice another method, Harry," George remarked, as he grabbed a cue, broke it on the bar, motioned to Dave to call 911 and turned to keep Jones' buddies at bay. He needed quickly to coldcock one, so he picked the one on the left and stumped toward him, like a very large tank advancing on unprotected infantry. The buddy he picked was wearing a leather jacket, some chains, and hadn't bathed in a few days. George continued to move quickly toward him, and as he did so, a knife appeared in No-Bath's right hand. No-Bath waved it around. George didn't stop, which flummoxed No-Bath. Apparently he thought that a man armed only with a stick would be afraid of a man with a knife. George sideslipped the knife and laid No-Bath out with one blow of the broken cue to the side of his head.

"I hope I didn't kill him," George said to No-Bath's stunned companion, in a conversational tone of voice. "It is so messy, and there is so much damn paperwork. It's your turn, friend. How do you want it?"

Harry and Jones were really muckling into each other, but despite Jones having twenty years on Harry and being in shape enough to play football that afternoon, Harry wasn't giving any ground.

The third guy faded, turned and walked quickly out of the bar. No-Bath's other friend was starting to back

out of the fight, too. He lowered his arms, hands open
and out at his sides and backed. His eyes were wide.
Suddenly he looked toward the spot that No-Bath was
occupying on the floor. No-Bath had woken up, and
was in the process of pulling a pistol. A shot rang out,
and No-Bath suddenly acquired a round hole in the
center of his forehead. Suddenly the center of attention, Dave the bartender held his smoking automatic.

"We're all going to stop now," he said. "And we're
going to wait for King County's finest, who ought to
be wheeling up about now. Until they get here, nobody move."

Harry straightened up.

"That means you, too, Harry, and your buddy
George. I don't think you had any hand in starting
this, but these guys came in here looking for you. So
we're all gonna just stand here, nice and easy, until
the cops get here. Capisce?"

"Yeah, no problem, Dave, no problem," George
said, slowly putting the pool cue back on the bar, as
the first cops bustled through the door, nightsticks
ready.

The first one through the door recoiled when he
saw Dave's pistol.

"You put that down on the bar, and step away from
it," he said, drawing his own.

"Sure, officer. No problem." Dave put down the
pistol and stepped down the bar toward where George
was standing.

The second cop in the door had his own gun out,
and he noticed No-Bath's buddy trying to fade toward
the door to the beer garden.

"I don't think so, friend," the cop said, motioning
for stillness. "You get down on the floor and assume
the position. Besides, just so you know, Sergeant
Packer is out there."

Despite himself, Harry snickered.

"What's that about, friend?" the first cop said, with
just a hint of menace.

"Not Sergeant Al Packer?"

"Yeah. Why?"

"Because that makes it officially old home night at the Piranha Tavern," Harry chortled. "Packer, George here, Dave behind the bar there and me, we all served together in 'Nam."

Harry raised his voice. "Hey, Cannibal, get in here!"

The beer garden door opened and admitted a huge black man in the uniform of the King County Sherriff's Office, franked with the Maple Valley Police logo.

"Shit, I should have known it was you two." He looked at Dave. "You three. What else?"

The first cop looked at his sergeant. "You actually know these guys?"

"I know him, him, and him," the big black cop said, pointing to Dave, Harry and George in turn. "I don't know him, or him, or the very late and probably unlamented him, over there on the floor."

"I'm sorry, Al," Dave said, "but he pulled a gun, and I didn't have much choice. He hurried me."

"Well, we can't call it suicide by cop, because you ain't one any more," Packer said, "but suicide by bartender could be misunderstood. Too bad the dumb git didn't just shoot himself."

"All right. You," he pointed at the first cop, "get these two uglies over to the lockup. Somebody can take them down to the Justice Center in Kent later. You," he pointed to the second cop, "get on the horn and get the coroner's wagon up here. You," he pointed to the third cop, just coming in the door, "get Mr. Mason and Mr. Wilson and Mr. Smith," he pointed at George, Harry, and Dave in turn, "to give you statements, then turn 'em loose. I know where to find them if something doesn't check out."

Packer turned and stomped out of the bar.

The first cop muscled Jones and his remaining buddy out of the tavern. The third cop motioned Harry over to where Dave and George were standing at the bar.

"I'm Officer McDonald. I'll be taking your statements," he said, all formal and professional. Then, "Cannibal? You called the sergeant 'Cannibal'?"

Dave guffawed. "Harry, you tell him."

"Do you know the sergeant's full name, officer?"

"Well, I assume it is Alfred Packer . . ."

"You'd assume wrong. You know what 'assume' means, don't you? Well, 'Cannibal' isn't Alfred, he's Alferd. Alferd E. in fact."

McDonald stared at Harry uncomprehendingly.

In a lugubrious voice, George began to chant, "Alferd E. Packer left the Ute Indians camp with a party of six in February of 1874 and came back alone. When the judge sentenced him, the judge said, 'Al Packer, you maneating sonofabitch, there was only eight Democrats in San Juan county, and you et six of 'em!' "

McDonald shoved his fist into his mouth to keep from laughing out loud at his chief's unfortunate name.

"Al's mom was pretty high when she named him, and she wasn't ever a good speller. She had no idea who Alferd Packer had been. So it was like naming Al 'Sue'!" Harry chortled.

McDonald visibly pulled himself together. "Okay, now why did these guys come after you? We know that much from talking to the people outside, so let's start there."

Harry said, "The ringleader is a man named Darryl Jones. He has a beef with me from earlier today. It appears that Darryl was left paraplegic in a traffic accident supposedly caused by one of Federal Mutual Insurance Company's insured."

McDonald shook his head. "Didn't look very paraplegic to me, Mr. Wilson."

"That's Harry, Officer. He didn't look very paraplegic to me this afternoon when I took his picture as he was playing touch football down in Kent, either."

"Ah!" McDonald nodded as he wrote in his notebook. "I seem to see a connection here."

"Well, you'll have to talk to Jones to be sure," Harry said, "but I think there might be. After all, I screwed up his tidy little scam for him. He must have recognized my car in the parking lot. Come to think of it, he didn't mess up the old green Volvo that's parked in front, did he?"

"No. And that was a funny thing, too," McDonald said. "Several of the people we talked to in the beer garden before we came in said that a big black crow seemed to be defending your car. Weird."

Harry looked at George, who responded with a slight shrug and turned out hands.

"What about a crow, George?"

"Or is it a raven?" George paused. "I dunno, man. I think we need to go down to my house in Puyallup and talk about this."

"Well, don't leave the area, of course," McDonald said, as he finished writing down Harry's PI license and George's driver's license. "But I think you can go now."

Harry and George walked outside the bar as McDonald turned to Dave Smith for his statement. The coroner was just loading No-Bath into his wagon. Harry walked over to one of the cops, the other one who had been inside the tavern.

"Who was he?"

"Had I.D. in the name of Roger Carey and a rap sheet a yard long. Assuming he is Carey. Did you know him?"

"No. And I don't remember him from Jones' football game this afternoon, either. So he must be muscle. Did you run Jones' sheet?"

"Yeah, and it sure is interesting."

"Well, if you were to be nice, and Sergeant Packer is still speaking to us after we revealed his secret inside . . ."

"Secret?"

"Ask Officer McDonald. I sure would like it if you would fax me a copy of his sheet. Here's my card."

"PI, eh?"

"Yeah, insurance cases, mostly. Got Mr. Jones in a scam this afternoon. Probably why he came after me."

Harry pulled open his laptop and booted it up. He logged on to George's wireless network and down-loaded his email. Sure enough, there was an efax from the King County Sheriff's office in Maple Valley.

"George, look here. We have Mr. Jones' rap sheet and those of his buddies. And he just made bail."

"Harry, look at this one. It says here that Jones was busted two years ago for desecrating a cemetery. And three years ago, he was one of the people busted for breaking into a Catholic church and trying to steal hosts from the tabernacle."

George turned and looked at Harry.

"Harry, he may be part of my problem, not just yours."

"Eh, well," Harry said. "If he is, what do we do about it?"

"Something is going to happen really soon. I can feel it."

"Well, I know somebody who might know how to help." Harry called up his address book, and scrolled through names until—

"Found it. Beth Jones . . . weird coincidence of names, that . . ." He pulled out his cell and dialed the number.

"Beth, hi, this is Harry Wilson . . . yes, that's right, Sally's husband. Yes, I know. I appreciate the thought. Beth, I . . . we . . . you're Wiccan, right? Could you meet a friend of mine and me and talk about a prob-lem we have? It might be related to Wicca. Right. We're down in Puyallup. Halfway? Coco's Restaurant in Federal Way? Forty minutes? Fine."

He punched off. "Let's go, George."

They got in the old Volvo.

"Beth Jones is a friend, was a friend of Sally's. They worked together . . . social worker. She's also a Wic-can priestess or witch or something."

Harry started the car, and as he turned it on, the headlights illuminated a huge black bird sitting on a fencepost across the street from George's house. George gasped.

"Is that your black bird?"

"Well, I dunno if it is the same one, but yeah, it sure looks like it."

George shuddered.

"What the heck is wrong with you?" Harry couldn't bring himself to swear, Methodist upbringing and all.

"That's Raven."

"What do you mean, it's a raven? How can you tell?"

"I didn't say it is a raven," George said in a voice that was very small for a man of his bulk, "but you can tell. It isn't a crow. Crows are smaller. I said it was Raven. The Raven. The supernatural totem Raven. We are either going to get very lucky or we are in deep kimchi, my friend. You know about the traditions we Indians have about trickster gods, yeah? Well just like the plains people have coyote, we have Raven. And anybody who even pretends to be a shaman like me can recognize the genuine article when we see it. That was Raven."

They drove up I-5 North in silence through the evening twilight. It was not quite full dark even now. The freeway was clearing out though, since it was almost ten. Days were very long now. The longest day of the year was coming up, Harry mused.

They pulled up to the restaurant and piled out of the car. Beth was waiting inside the restaurant. She'd gone ahead and gotten a table. She was short, a little dumpy, and not much younger than Harry, but with bright red hair that didn't look like it came out of a bottle. She was wearing black, with a huge silver pentacle on a heavy silver chain around her neck and nestled between her breasts. She looked up and smiled.

"Harry, it is good to see you!" She looked at George. "Elder?"

"George Mason, and how'd you know?" George demanded.

"Certainly you know how," Beth said flatly.

George turned to Harry.

"She's the real thing, okay, Harry."

"I kinda thought she might be," Harry said, pulling out a chair and sitting in it. "Sit down, George, we got some talking to do."

"So that's what we know, Beth," George finished.

"Can I see those rap sheets?"

"Sure." Harry handed them over. Beth opened the folder, and flinched as she saw the first picture.

"What is it?" Harry asked.

"Well, that's my brother Darryl," she began.

"Beth, he's a bad one. I'm sorry to tell you," George said.

"I know. He's always been. When we were little, he always wanted it easy. You both may know that although we claim to be the Old Religion, the Wicca we practice is actually very new. Too many things were lost during the Burning Times . . ."

"Yeah," George interrupted. "That's why I'm such a crappy shaman, too. Not enough tradition to be traditional. Got to make it up as I go along sometimes."

"Well, we were brought up Wiccan. Our parents were members of a coven in Portland, and when we moved up here, they joined another. I kept on with it. Darryl didn't. Or I thought he didn't. Now I am not so sure."

Harry thought, then asked, "What would make Darryl or Darryl and his friends want to make a hole between the worlds? That's what George thinks is happening. And whether Darryl is doing it or is just part of it, he's the one we know about."

"Well, this is the time to do it. Tomorrow night is Midsummer's Eve, the Summer Solstice. The walls between the worlds are supposed to be very thin tomorrow night. Remember Shakespeare? *A Midsummer Night's Dream*?"

"Yeah, but that was just a play," Harry said.

"Based on some very old traditions, though," Beth said.

"And not just white man traditions," George added. "That's a spooky night for us Indians too."

"Well, if we are going to stop him, or them, what do we need to do?" Harry ran his hand through his hair, suddenly conscious of its thinness and very conscious of Beth as a woman. He really hadn't felt that way for a long time, not since Sally died. Beth seemed to feel his regard, and she smiled at him.

"I'm going to need to make some phone calls," Beth said. "I'm going to have to make some preparations . . . spiritual ones, too. George needs to do that, too. And Harry, how good a Christian are you?"

"Um, well, I go to the Methodist church . . ."

"Not a very believing one, then."

"I believe. I just don't advertise."

"Then you need to spend some time praying tonight. Saint Michael might be good to talk to. I'll call you when I find out something." Beth stood, hugged each man, and was gone before any of them could say more than good night.

George sat there folded into himself for a few seconds, then he shook his head as if to clear his eyesight.

"Wow. That's some kinda woman, Harry."

"Yes, yes she is."

"Well, you better take me back to my place. I've got to sweat in the sweatlodge tonight."

Harry paced his living room. It was near dawn now, and he hadn't been able to sleep. He was still having trouble believing that he'd gotten mixed up in pagan rituals, demons, and who knows what all. He was also having a really hard time praying. He hadn't prayed much in the last few months, since Sally died. He realized that he'd been really mad at God, and when you're mad at someone, you really don't like to talk to them.

He let the corgis out. Dylan and Caleb had really been Sally's, and, thankfully, the neighbor girl was willing to feed and exercise them when he was out on a job. Harry got their bowls and prepared to feed them. Suddenly it penetrated that the dogs were growling and snapping, as if they had something cornered in the yard. Harry flipped the floods on and saw the dogs at the fence, their hackles raised and their fur standing up so straight that they looked double their size. Between them and the house was a bundle—a large one—lying on the grass. As Harry pushed open the door, he heard something very large running off through the woods that his house backed up on.

Dylan came away from the fence and nosed at the bundle on the ground. It moved. Harry was there now, bending over a blanket-wrapped young man. The young man was thin, dark complected, and had shiny black hair and black eyes.

"Call George," he croaked, then fainted.

George arrived as soon as he could. Harry had carried the young man or boy into the house and laid him on the couch in the den. He'd covered him with a throw that Sally had made and had gone to make some coffee. When George arrived, they found the young man sitting up on the couch, wrapped in the throw.

"Oh. My. God." George breathed.

"Yes, well," the young man said, his black eyes flashing. "Don't make a big deal of it, George."

"What's your name," Harry asked. George shot him a deadly look.

"Raven, Johnny Raven," the young man replied, smirking at George.

Harry stared. "You're not . . ."

"Yeah, I guess I am."

"Why are you here?" George wanted to know.

"Did you or did you not spend all night calling for help? Now you want to know what I'm doing here? What kind of shaman are you, George? Don't you think you might have gotten it right?"

"No, I didn't think I had gotten it right."

"Well, you very nearly didn't. That was some big hound that almost got me as I fell into the world, there in Harry's back yard. Good thing you had those dogs, Harry. They are spirit warriors too."

"Why did you land in Harry's back yard, instead of mine?"

"Because Harry needed more help believing than you did, George."

Just then Beth arrived.

"Did any of you idiots think to get him some clothes?" she demanded, as soon as she saw what was going on. "Harry is a lot bigger than you, but we'll find you something. Come with me, young Raven." She hustled him upstairs to the bedrooms with a non-chalance that belied her awareness of who, or what, the young man actually was. Harry and George stood gaping at her, then stared at each other, and then broke into unstoppable laughter.

Beth and Raven came downstairs. She'd found him some sweats and a pair of sandals that weren't too huge on him.

"What are you two snickering about? Don't you know that my Goddess is a Mother?" Beth demanded, with her hands on her hips, as if she was daring them to make something of it.

"Nothing, Beth," Harry said. "It just was a remarkable sight."

The young man looked puzzled. "Everybody has a Mother," he said. "I don't know what the big deal is."

Beth said, "I think I know where they're going to do what they think will be a summoning ritual. My phone calls worked. There's a big meadow below Snoqualmie Falls. That's what I hear."

"That's what I hear, too," Raven smirked.

"Well, what can we do?" Harry asked.

"Darryl's going to be using some type of Wiccan or backward Christian ritual, and I can stick a spoke in that," Beth said, "if I can get close enough."

"And I can keep anything else from happening," Raven said.

"And us?" George asked.

"Strong backs and weak minds," Raven said. "You get us there, and keep us safe while we do what we do."

They all slept for a while, during the day, and started preparing for whatever was going to happen in the late afternoon.

"It isn't going to happen until the stroke of midnight," Beth said. "They will be waiting in the meadow. We'll need to get there early and make sure they can't find us."

Harry opened his bottom desk drawer and took out his gun. He checked it, and loaded it, and put the holster under his jacket.

George went out to his car and came back carrying a carved and painted staff that looked like a miniature totem pole. At the top of the staff was a carving of Raven.

"Hey, that's nice," Johnny Raven said, preening as he looked at it. "It's a good likeness!"

Beth snorted. She had made her preparations before she arrived. They all piled into Harry's green Volvo and headed up over Tiger Mountain.

They parked well away from the falls and took their time walking down toward the meadow. They found a small copse of aspen trees and settled in to wait. No one said much. The moon rose, full and bright. Harry's watch showed very close to midnight when Darryl and his cohorts arrived. Darryl was wearing a cassock, like a priest. There were an even dozen of them, and one that seemed to be a prisoner. In the moonlight, as they came closer, Harry could see it was a young girl, twelve or thirteen. A virgin, most likely, he thought to himself. Great.

Darryl's group arranged themselves in a rough circle around him, and two of them held the girl in the center of the circle, in front of their priest. Darryl's voice rose and fell as he began to chant something.

Suddenly, Beth stood up and moved out of the trees. Darryl stopped speaking and stared at her.

"Darryl, stop this now," Beth said, "before some-one gets hurt. You don't know what you are doing."

"And you do, big sister?" Darryl had a large dagger and he was holding it loosely in one hand.

"Yes, I do. What you are doing is evil and danger-ous, and you are going to get yourself, all your friends here, and lots of innocent bystanders killed. You can-not release the Wild Hunt on this world."

"Yes, I can." Darryl grabbed the girl by the hair, and cut her throat from ear to ear before anyone could move. He held up the bloody dagger and made a cutting motion in front of himself. "By this sacrifice, I cut the veil between the worlds!" he screamed. "Come to me! Dark ones, come!"

Lightning strobed again and again. Snoqualmie Falls could be seen in all its magnificence, and off to the south, it looked as though Mt. Rainier were illumi-nated, as if it were full day. Thunder drummed.

Suddenly the meadow was filled with horses and riders. Some of the riders looked human, others hid-eously eldritch.

The column of riders was stopped in the center of the meadow, facing a young man. Somehow, Johnny had gotten from the aspen grove to the center of the meadow with no one noticing. The lead riders were what appeared to be a woman and a man.

Harry looked a question at Beth. "They're not *my* Lord and Lady," she said quietly.

"Oh, but if we are not, Bethany Jones," the woman creature said staring straight at Beth, "then what are we?"

"You are the dark ones, that have hated men from the time the Goddess created us. I know you for who and what you are, Lady." Beth stood, defiant.

"You will not be allowed to pass," Johnny Raven said, into the stillness.

"By you?"

"By me."

The dark lord spoke for the first time. Harry wished he had never spent so much time reading Tolkien.

"You and what army rides with you?" the voice rasped.

"Me." George stood next to Johnny, his carved totem staff raised. "The land here belongs to us, not to you. This is not your land. The land itself will resist your passage."

"You are a fat middle-aged fraud."

"Perhaps I am," George nodded. "But you will still not pass while I live."

The dark lord raised his hand, and George's staff burst into white hot flame. George was knocked flat on his back, and he didn't move.

"I defy you, too," Beth said, with a little bit of a quaver in her voice. She took half a step forward. Half a step because the lady's upraised hand halted her, frozen, in mid step.

"You had better go home, little bird, and let your betters play," the dark lord rumbled, with subsonics rolling off each word he said, and each word hit Harry like a punch.

"I guess I'm it," Harry said.

"You don't even believe," the dark lady said. "How can you expect to defeat me?"

"I have always had trouble believing. Now all I can do is ask." Harry said simply. "Lord help my unbelief, Lord, I am not worthy! Help me now, a sinner, I pray you!"

Johnny Raven's body began to shimmer, and change. Instead of a slim dark youth, in his place stood a shining figure in some sort of armor, holding a spear.

"You should call more often, Harry!" the figure said. "Now, I think, we have to end this. You," he pointed at the dark lord and lady and all their host, "shall not pass. You don't think to argue about it with *me*, do you?"

"No, we will not argue the point with you, Michael. We will go." The lady turned her mount in the direction of the rent in the sky. She turned back.

"Darryl. Come." She motioned and he literally flew to the back of her mount and grabbed on behind. The rest of his coven were trying to run through the meadow, but riders ran them down and grabbed each of them in turn.

"And as for the rest of you," she said, somehow staring at George, and Beth, and Harry directly simultaneously, "this will *not* be forgotten. And I have a very long memory."

With that, the Hunt turned and rode away slowly across the meadow, picking up speed and then riding up some sort of invisible bridge into the sky; and as they passed through, Michael made a motion with his spear, and the rent Darryl had caused was sealed.

Michael turned and, like really good computer animation, morphed back into the slender young man they'd known as Johnny Raven.

"I thought you were Raven," George said.

"Who told you that all those traditions were mutually exclusive, George? I can be whoever I need to be." The young man walked over to where the dead girl lay.

"No matter what, she didn't deserve this." He drew his finger across her throat, sealing the cut. "Here, you come back now," he said, with his hand on her chest. He pushed. She shuddered and gasped.

Beth ran to her and enfolded her. "It's okay," she repeated over and over.

Harry looked at Raven or Michael, or whoever he was. "So now what?"

"We seem to be done here," the youth replied.

"Will I ever see you again?" George asked.

"Hard to say. Maybe. Then again, maybe not." The young man cocked his head and his black eyes flashed in the moonlight.

"So what will you do now?" Harry asked.

"Oh, I'll be around, Harry, I'll be around."

The young man turned and walked away. As he walked, he became smaller, and his walk became jerkier and more and more birdlike until he was a very large black bird, walking away through the meadow. He croaked, flapped his sudden wings, and was gone.

WINDS OF CHANGE

Linda A. B. Davis

MARTHA Jane stood in the cornfield with her face to the sky and her blue eyes closed. Surrounded by the half-grown, green stalks and hearing the insects buzz, she concentrated on the warm wind around her. She called it to her with whispers of promise.

Come to me, be part of me, live through me, as I will live through you. I will grant you my breath as you grant me your strength. Come to me, be part of me . . ."

Martha Jane repeated the chant several more times even as she felt the light breeze stiffen. She reached her hands above her head and beckoned to unseen forces.

The magic rushed to encircle her slight, misshapen body with an invisible yet undeniable power. The dirt devil danced around Martha Jane, straining against her bonds so it could run amok through the vulnerable fields. She silently compelled the power to stay with her and to bring the mini-twister in tighter.

Her sun-bleached hair whipped around her head, and Martha Jane laughed. She reveled in this power for a few seconds. So much of her life was beyond her will, especially her humped shoulder and her mother's recent death. These tragedies seemed so often to define her life that she sometimes needed to be the one who birthed creation or destruction.

But now it was time to go. Martha Jane needed to finish supper before Daddy and Jediah came in from the fields. She took a breath and pulled the dirt devil even closer. Now was the most critical point of control.

"Magic is a living, breathing thing," Mama had counseled during Martha Jane's first lesson. "It always wants to be free, and you can't ever whip it up so big that you lose it."

Martha Jane took a steadying breath. She envisioned the unseen forces as her friends, the friends she would have if she weren't so deformed. She smiled and blew them a kiss from her heart as she wished them well. The dirt devil died at Martha Jane's feet.

Martha Jane turned and started across the cornfield. The stalks were at the early stages of wither, and if rain didn't come soon, they would die. She knew her family couldn't withstand the loss of even one crop. Their savings had all been spent on Mama's and her own medical bills.

As Martha Jane stepped into their dirt road, she heard and then spotted a pickup truck coming around the bend.

"Wonderful," she said with a heavy sigh. "The Barnetts."

As they pulled up next to her, Mrs. Barnett looked at Martha Jane with a mix of pity and curiosity. Martha Jane knew that look well. It said, "You should be in an institution. You shouldn't be walking around like normal folks." But Mrs. Barnett didn't say it out loud. It wouldn't be polite.

"Is your daddy home, dear?" Mrs. Barnett asked. "And would you like a ride to your house?"

Mrs. Barnett wore a blue traveling dress which looked hot for the Florida June sun. Her husband was still in field clothes, fresh from working his tobacco crop.

"Yes, ma'am," Martha Jane replied. "Thank you. Daddy might be back already."

"Do you need help?"

"No, ma'am." Martha Jane hurried to the back of the truck and, with a combination move of jump and twist, managed to position herself on the open tailgate.

The ride in the back was pleasant. Martha Jane preferred it to riding in the cab with the couple. True, they only reflected what most of what Brookland thought, but she still didn't want to talk to them.

Martha Jane had survived one of the nation's deadliest diseases of the early twentieth century, polio. She was grateful for her life, but she wasn't grateful for the medical quackery afterward. For instance, the doctors insisted she lie on her wooden floor for four hours a day in the dark to help straighten her spine. It was one of the many stupid things that hadn't worked. Now at fifteen, Martha Jane's left shoulder was bigger than her right, and late at night, when no one could see her sobbing, she swore to avenge the injustice.

Knowing marriage was unlikely for Martha Jane, Mama taught her to call the wind. It wasn't entirely a proper profession for women, but neither was it forbidden. Only men were socially acceptable as rainmakers, but calling the wind was such a rare talent there weren't many mores attached to it yet. Mama had learned both skills in secret from her own father, and they had kept it family business all these years.

She started rainmaking lessons with Jediah, but because of his field work schedule, he didn't practice much. He always thought he could train later, but he was wrong. Mama died.

Martha Jane wiped a tear away as the truck came to a stop next to the pecan tree. She slid off the tailgate and rushed to the screen door.

"I'll see if Daddy's home yet," she said.

He had just returned from the back forty, so he was still dirty and sweaty, but he greeted the Barnetts warmly and offered them seats in the porch swing. Martha Jane brought cold sweet tea for their guests and ice water for Daddy.

Martha Jane listened closely, and when she heard

the voices harden, she gathered the courage to peek out the front window.

Mrs. Barnett was speaking. "Liza told us Jediah said so, and we believe her. Are you calling our daughter a liar?"

Martha Jane gasped. She'd never heard anyone speak to her father like that, but she knew Mrs. Barnett was known for saying more than she should.

"I'm sure Liza believes it," Daddy replied. "But she's mistaken. Jediah cannot call the rain. He's not a rainmaker." His lips pursed together, and his face hardened.

Mrs. Barnett persisted. "You would have all of our crops fail? Including yours?"

Daddy took a breath, gathering his patience. "I would do anything to end this drought. If I thought Jediah could do it, I would tell him to do it. But he can't and I won't."

"Well," Mrs. Barnett started. "I believe Jediah. He will do it, or we won't grant him Liza's hand in marriage."

"The boy was boasting," Daddy said, a stern edge creeping into his voice. "He was trying to impress the girl he loves. It would be cruel of you to deny them marriage simply because he spoke in haste."

Her father leaned back in the rocking chair, keeping it still in a waiting position. His face took on an unapproachable look, his bushy eyebrows angling low over his dark brown eyes.

It was evident to Martha Jane that Daddy wasn't going to divulge anything about Jediah's training. He wasn't about to cast shadows on his dead wife's memory for her having had knowledge of a man's work.

She remembered all the times she'd heard Daddy tell Jediah that he knew just enough to be dangerous and to leave it alone.

"Maybe," he'd told Jediah, "we can hire a rainmaker to finish your training. But we've got to wait for the harvest money."

The Barnetts took their leave in anger, and Martha

Jane heard the sound of the truck engine fade into the distance. Daddy grabbed his worn, leather hat and shoved it on his head.

"Martha Jane, I'm going to the barn to find Jediah. Have supper ready when we get back."

An hour later, they all sat at the small, wooden table eating the chicken and dumplings that had simmered on the stove while Martha Jane practiced. Jediah picked quietly at his food, his shoulders slumped.

"Sit up straight at the dinner table, Jediah," Daddy said. "And quit sulking."

"I can do it, Daddy. I know I can."

"Maybe so, but we can't chance it. Magic is a powerful force, and you've got to be able to contain it." He split a buttermilk biscuit and spread fresh butter on each half. "Besides, you didn't have any business airing our laundry to Liza. You didn't tell her about Martha Jane, did you?"

Jediah glanced at Martha Jane. "No, sir."

"Good."

Martha Jane spoke up. "But I can call the wind, Daddy. Mama even said my training was complete."

"I know," Daddy said between bites. "But it won't help us here. We need rain, not wind. And your brother's not ready."

That night, Martha Jane tried to get comfortable on her down bed. Her shoulder made it hard sometimes to find a restful position. A warm cross breeze blew softly through her room between the two open windows. She heard Jediah's door open and then a light footfall go past her own door. She slid out of bed and opened the door to peek into the hallway. Jediah was fully dressed and halfway out of the house.

"What are you doing? Are you crazy?" Martha Jane was trying to whisper.

"I'm not going to lose Liza because Daddy doesn't think I can do it. Now be quiet and go back to bed. I'll be back by morning." He turned quickly and eased the door shut.

Martha Jane didn't know what to do except go back

to bed. Her father might hit him if he discovered Jediah gone. She didn't want to be responsible for that, so she said a silent prayer to help Jediah work his spells well.

Just before dawn, Martha Jane awakened to a change in the air. It was cooler, and the air had a little depth to it, like a fog rolling across the farm at sunrise. Moments later, she heard the sound of fat raindrops hitting their tin roof. She loved the music that rain made on a tin roof, and this song was especially a wonderful and welcomed thing.

Now everything would be fine, Martha Jane thought, as she snuggled down under the covers. She envisioned Jediah's now upcoming wedding. He would be so handsome in his Sunday suit. Martha Jane hoped for a husband like Jediah. Maybe one day she would find one who could love the girl trapped inside her body. Maybe . . .

Martha Jane startled awake as her door flung open and bounced loudly off the wall. Daddy stood in the doorway, his fists clenched.

"Where's Jediah?" he asked, his mouth tight and his eyes darker than usual.

"I don't know."

"Fine. Then tell me where he went last night."

Martha Jane wasn't above a lie here and there, but she knew better than to try it now.

"He said he went to call the rain."

"I knew it," Daddy said. "That boy just bought himself a peck of trouble. And us, too."

"What's wrong?"

Daddy gestured toward the window. "Look outside."

Martha Jane climbed out of bed and crossed the room to one of the tiny, frame windows. She couldn't believe the damage that had been done in the extra hour she'd slept. The world outside seemed to consist only of rain. The clouds were rolling, the wind was howling, and the continuous sheets of driving water had made a river out of the dirt road. Even the high

ground on the other side of the road was standing
under water.

"Oh, no," she said faintly. Martha Jane knew this
was even worse for the crops than drought. The land
was too dry to absorb this much water this fast. If it
didn't stop soon, it would kill the crops and some of
the small livestock, too.

Daddy started toward the door. "I'm going to find
him."

"Can I come?"

He nodded. "Hurry up. I'll wait in the truck." He
sighed heavily, pulled his jacket tighter, and rushed
through both the house and porch doorways.

Martha Jane struggled to dress quickly. Daddy
wouldn't wait long. Once she wiggled into a yellow,
cotton work dress, she was able to lace up her boots
easily. She also rushed to the porch after donning her
raincoat, only to stop abruptly. The rain was torrential,
even scary, but Daddy had pulled close to the porch.
She made it to the truck without much trouble.

They were both silent on the drive. Martha Jane
didn't want to start a conversation when he was this
angry.

Martha Jane could tell by the route that they were
headed to the Barnetts' house. Visibility was low with
the water hiding the dirt roads. She could feel the
truck's tires struggle through the sloshing mud.

About halfway there, they reached the school,
which, strangely enough, Martha Jane thought, was
populated.

"This has to be where everybody is. They must be
trying to figure out what to do. Maybe Jediah's here,"
Daddy said as he turned off the road. He parked, got
out and ran around to help Martha Jane out of the
cab. They hurried up the steps, Daddy making sure
Martha Jane didn't slip on the wet wood. They entered the main classroom, and stopped short.

The room was about half full, with a dozen of the
most prominent families represented. Martha Jane
took a half step back as everyone turned to see them.

Daddy shook off his hat. Martha Jane flipped the hood of her raincoat back and wiped her face.

Mrs. Barnett, always the first to criticize, spoke up. "Victor, what has Jediah done? When is this rain going to stop? We're going to be flooded out soon."

Daddy stalked forward through most of the crowd to face Mrs. Barnett.

"How do you know this is Jediah's doing?" Daddy asked.

Liza stepped out from behind her mother. Her dark hair was wetly plastered against her neck, and her violet eyes were wide with fear. She spoke with a slight shake to her voice.

"He knocked on my window this morning and said he was going to fix everything." She gestured toward the door. "Now this."

Daddy shifted his gaze from Liza back to Mrs. Barnett. "I told you he wasn't ready, yet you threatened him with one of the few things he loves, your daughter. This isn't Jediah's fault. It's yours."

A voice spoke up from the back. "It doesn't matter whose fault it is. We need him to stop the rain."

Daddy whipped his head around to find that person. He spoke harshly to Mr. Fritz, the general store owner. "Don't you think he'd have stopped it by now if he could? We can only wait, unless someone knows of a rainmaker nearby."

Another voice spoke quickly. "You know there isn't a rainmaker for a hundred miles. Jediah needs to do something."

"What do you propose he do if he doesn't know how? Would you have him make it worse?" Daddy's voice was now a low growl.

Martha Jane shivered with a surge of fear. This crowd could ugly. Tempers were high, especially Daddy's. He was strong, but he wasn't strong enough to take on everyone. And what would happen to Jediah when he finally showed up? Martha Jane hoped he would stay hidden until this mess was fixed. She also hoped Jediah was working on it. He was, after all, the only one nearby who had a chance of stopping the rain.

Martha Jane cringed when she heard a crashing sound behind her. She turned to see water and assorted debris now swirling into and around the room. A heavy branch had flown into the glass, and the now broken window was giving avenue to the chaos outside. Several of the men moved an oak bookcase in front of it.

The wind and rain . . . the wind . . .

Martha Jane realized that she knew what to do. Why hadn't she thought of this before? She started to speak but then stopped. Did she really want to fix this problem for these people? They would have her in an institution if it was their decision. They would never accept her as one of their own again.

Martha Jane also asked herself if she could really do it. Sure, she'd played with the wind before, but she'd never tested her skills to this degree. Would the magic grace her when she really needed it? Just because she called the wind didn't mean it would appear.

She knew she had to try for Jediah's sake. This was the one time Martha Jane could watch out for him, just as he'd watched out for her these last few years. He fought daily with boys who called Martha Jane names like Humpy and Igora. He still drove her to school and picked her up so she wouldn't have to walk with them.

The Barnetts certainly wouldn't let Liza marry Jediah if their farm was allowed to flood out. And God knew how long the rest of the community would hold this against her family. Martha Jane still had to go to school in the falltime, and Daddy still had to trade with the local businessmen.

Martha Jane stepped over to Daddy and motioned his face down to hers. She whispered in his ear.

He looked at her with surprise. "Can you do that?"

"Mama taught me how, Daddy. I trust her."

Daddy gave her a small smile. "All right, then. You do it."

He spoke loudly to the crowd. "Martha Jane can fix it."

Mrs. Barnett eyed Martha Jane harshly. "She's not a rainmaker. She's a girl."

Daddy spoke sharply to Mrs. Barnett. "Who do you think taught Jediah what he knows? Annie was a rainmaker, taught by her father. She didn't get a chance to finish Jediah's training. That's why I told you he can't call the rain. He hadn't finished his training when Annie died."

"And Martha Jane is finished?"

"Yes, but not as a rainmaker."

"Then what does she possibly have to offer this situation?" Mrs. Barnett looked pointedly at Martha Jane and frowned.

Daddy looked to Martha Jane. "Answer the woman."

"I can call the wind," Martha Jane said clearly.

"And exactly how will that help us?"

"I can push the rain away with the wind." Martha Jane took a breath. "But we must come to terms first."

"Terms?"

"Yes, terms." Martha Jane kept her voice strong. She couldn't afford to appear weak.

"What terms do you propose?" Mrs. Barnett was taking a tone.

"You must allow Jediah to marry Liza. He will make a fine husband. Then you must apologize to him."

"Apologize? You think I'm going to apologize?"

"Yes, ma'am," Martha Jane said. "For not granting him the respect he deserves as the man your daughter loves."

Mrs. Barnett didn't speak. Martha Jane could see her weighing the cost against the gain, both personal and public.

"Fine," she finally said through tight lips. "Fix this if you can, but I don't know if you can. You may not be strong enough, what with your shoulder and all."

The crowd gasped. While Jediah had fought against

ridicule from other kids, no adult had actually said anything to Martha Jane's face about her shoulder.

"It's not about strength of body. It's about strength of character. Right, Daddy?"

She looked up at him and waited. What if he said no?

He looked straight into Martha Jane's eyes as he spoke. "I'm sure your mother taught you well."

With a sigh of relief, Martha Jane went to the doorway and stood. It was truly an overwhelming force at work out there. Jediah might not know how to stop the rain, but he sure had called it.

The crowd was hushed as Martha Jane shed her coat and shoes. She needed to be as much a part of the storm as possible. She stepped into the weather frenzy, surprised to find that her fear was gone. Martha Jane could only surmise that she'd left it inside to rot with their anger.

She strode to the recess area where the other children played during free time. Since her illness, she could only watch from the doorway, but she remembered her own playtime well. She had been so keen to run, so unencumbered by physical restraint.

Martha Jane smiled at the memory. She closed her eyes and raised her arms to the dark and ominous sky. The water hit her face like pebbles thrown, and she winced. Martha Jane knew the pain was of no consequence, so she tried to ignore it.

The wind still howled and the clouds continued to darken. Martha Jane took a deep breath through her mouth and let it out slowly, trying to relax. She protected her eyes by keeping them mostly closed, but she peered out through a small slit.

Martha Jane couldn't help but consider her own price for this effort. She was already an outcast, and this would solidify the division. The daughter of a now shadowed woman, Martha Jane would also be suspect for meddling in a man's work, no matter how grateful everyone might be now.

"Martha Jane!" Daddy called from the schoolhouse,

breaking her concentration. "Are you all right? Do you need help?"

"No, sir," Martha Jane called back. "I'm just getting started."

Martha Jane steadied herself and began moving her hands in circular motions above her head. Whereas with the dirt devil she had chanted soft and low, she now called out loudly so the sky could hear her over its own roar.

"Winds blow, winds go, winds kindly go. Heed my words, winds I know."

Martha Jane repeated the chant as she continued with her hands, seeking the power and energy that fueled this mess. There! She had felt the tiniest tendril of power. She wasn't the only one exploring the storm.

Martha Jane slowed her hand motions to shape lazy circles. She wanted that power. She knew it was right there, so close.

Martha Jane stopped her chant. She thought she'd heard a hiss somewhere. She listened, still seeking slowly with her hands and fingers. There again! Martha Jane reached her left hand upward and to the right.

She'd never been zapped before, so Martha Jane wasn't expecting to suddenly find herself hind-end down in the mud. Her heart raced, and she smelled heat. Her left fingertips burned. Martha Jane quickly stuck them in the cold mud beneath her to quell the pain.

She jerked when she unexpectedly felt strong hands grab her under the arms and pull her up.

"I'm okay, Daddy," she said as she turned. "I'm not done yet. Please let me finish!"

"It's not Daddy, Martha Jane."

She gasped. It was Jediah, looking as miserable and cold as she felt.

"Where have you been?" Martha Jane asked harshly.

"It doesn't matter," he said. "Let me help you. Let's do this together."

Martha Jane stared at him with surprise. "That would

be a good idea if you hadn't messed it up in the first place."

Jediah wiped the water out of his light blue eyes, eyes that matched her own. "I know," he said loudly. They had to halfway shout to be heard over the weather. "But I can do enough to meet you halfway. I already got more than halfway. I didn't lose control until the end, when the power was at its strongest."

His look was pleading. Martha Jane knew this was his one chance at redemption. How could she refuse?

"Okay. Let me start, and then you come in."

Martha Jane reached up to the heavens again. She had already forged some of the basic pathways earlier, and it didn't take her long to reach that point again. She was relieved to have her load lightened because her muscles were already tiring.

This time, Martha Jane was expecting the power's sizzling pop. As the invisible tendrils jumped for her, she snatched them with her left hand, the hand they'd already imprinted. The white hot burn traveled the length of her small body down to her toes and then back up to her fingertips.

It grew as it accepted the immense power Martha Jane offered. Her own power was stronger than she'd imagined, and she could feel it seeping through her skin to combine with the storm's power.

Martha Jane's fingertips turned white with a light that shone from within. The brightness exploded upward, reaching for the heavens with its energy and radiance. The narrow beam widened into a tightly woven twister that resembled a rope of golden light.

Martha Jane started chanting again, but this time she changed her pitch. "Winds blow, winds go . . ."

The glowing rope grew in width, pushing the clouds and rain away from the middle into that familiar funnel pattern. Martha Jane could see the weather inside the tiny tornado was actually clear and sunny, but she knew the folks in the schoolhouse probably couldn't see the hope still hidden within the winds.

She only had an instant to appreciate it, but Martha

Jane thought the tornado was beautiful. This one didn't belong to the family of black and gray funnels that usually wreaked havoc and destruction. Hers was a creation of life and goodness, the mix of swirling light and wind struggling to overcome the darkness and danger.

Martha Jane continued to call and command. This was the most dangerous point of control, and if she lost it now, the original storm could regroup into something even uglier and more powerful.

Martha Jane held tight as the luminous tornado grew to encompass more space. The clouds on the outside became more dispersed, and Martha Jane continued to push them away with the tornado walls, thereby breaking them apart.

"Jediah!" Martha Jane screamed. "Stop the rain!"

While Martha Jane realized she had a front row seat to watching a rainmaker work, she didn't have the strength to spare. Her arms and shoulders shook painfully, and she hoped Jediah would be quick with his spellmaking. She'd done what she could by dissipating the rain clouds to where she thought he could handle them.

Martha Jane could hear Jediah working loudly next to her. His words were muffled, but she could tell his chant had a different cadence to it from her own. She bit her bottom lip to keep focused on her own work. She needed to give Jediah every possible second to finish his job.

"Are you almost done?" Martha Jane screamed. "I can't hold this much longer!"

"One more minute!"

One more minute? Martha Jane wasn't sure she could last one more second. While she still held the tornado with her hand motions, fatigue was taking its toll. Even the light that still spilled from her fingers was dimming at a risky rate.

Then she saw Mama. Her smiling face was shaped within the swirls of the tornado walls, much like the shapes in the clouds Martha Jane often watched. Martha Jane blinked several times. She was certain when she looked again the face would be gone, but it was still there.

Jediah didn't seem to see anything. Martha Jane had found that to be the frequent case with clouds and shapes, but how could he not see Mama?

Martha Jane watched the image as it shifted and moved within the funnel of light. How she missed her Mama, sweet and strong. Martha Jane tried to burn the image into her brain so she could remember it better later.

Just as the image did dissolve, the rain stopped, and Martha Jane saw the skies were finally clear. She sank to her knees in relief. She released the magic she held and thanked it with a blow away kiss. A soft breeze encircled her, brushed her skin with its tender essence, and silently departed.

Martha Jane allowed her arms to sag by her sides, feeling the muscles cramp and twist. Her head dropped as she swallowed her grief at Mama being gone again. She would have to make do with the memory of Mama's image and the certainty that Mama had given her strength to hold tight for those last few important seconds. Martha Jane wiped away the mixture of rain, sweat and tears covering her face.

"Come on, Martha Jane," Jediah said from her side. "Let's go home. The others can stay and clean up."

Jediah took her elbow and helped her up. Martha Jane leaned into his strong body as they high-stepped through the deep puddles back to the schoolhouse.

"I guess you and Liza will marry after all," Martha Jane told him.

"Maybe," Jediah said. "She wouldn't come with me this morning though. I'm going to have to think on that one."

Martha Jane stopped short of the schoolhouse door. Daddy was there waiting with a big smile. Mrs. Barnett stood behind him, hopefully trying to word her apology to Jediah. Liza stood next to her mother, blissfully unaware that she might not really be getting married anytime soon. The other people were already working together to clean away the debris and water.

Life would go on, Martha Jane knew, even if it was different. She supposed it was the way of things, and who was she to not move ahead in the face of change?

Jediah tugged at her elbow. "Are you all right? Are you ready to go?"

"Yes," she finally said. "I think so." Martha Jane stepped forward and with purpose into her new life.

FIREBIRD AND SHADOW

Darwin A. Garrison

MISSY Watkins sat in the alley, rocking back and forth and praying for a deeper darkness. She longed for a perfect, pitch-black night. Only that could hide both her and the motionless figure that lay not five feet away.

As her tears tracked down her face to disappear among the Texas raindrops splashing around her, trickster lightning flared. The blue white glare highlighted the corpse lying flat on its back in the downpour.

Choking back a moan, she shook her head in useless denial. No matter how dark her wishes made it, Tommy was still dead. The mortal remains of the only person to take any interest in her since she ran away lay open-eyed and staring in the downpour. That knowledge mixed with the rank smells of blood, urine, and the rotting garbage in the dumpsters that surrounded her to twist her stomach. Missy was alone again, and Tommy's killers would be back for her next.

A traitorous sob escaped from her lips as she tried to take in a deep breath. She snapped her mouth shut and looked around to see if anyone had come back to hear. The shadows were everywhere, but none of them moved or flickered. A shudder of relief and cold ran through her. Shadows without color or motion could be trusted, but not the ones that moved or flickered with the lights and colors that only she could see.

Missy could feel the chill creeping up her spine as a rivulet of water trickled down. She needed to move, to get out of the rain and dry off. Otherwise, she could end up sick again, as she had that first week after she ran away from her mother.

The shiver that ran through her at that thought had little to do with rain or Tommy's body. She could still remember the rough hands of the last "uncle" her mother had brought back to the trailer. Like all the times before, her mom had disappeared with him into the back bedroom, but after all the grunting and moaning was over, he had come back and looked at Missy in a way that made her feel nervous and sick.

She could not remember all of what happened next, but she would never forget the feel of those hands grabbing her, tearing at her clothes, groping her roughly all over. Her mother's screams and the sound of something smacking the man seemed strangely separate from the foul movement of coarse fingers across Missy's body as she screamed and twisted. The last solid image she retained from inside the trailer was the glyph of the firebird. She had woven the sign and sent it burning its way into the man's eyes.

If only she could forget running into a cold March night turned blood red by the light of the burning trailer. And the screams. She could still hear the man's voice twisting with her mother's in the distance as she ran away.

Missy had meant to go back to Denton, back to Gram and her little two bedroom house. Her Gram would always take her back. Missy had not been the one to start all the arguments. She and Gram had gotten along just fine so long as Missy's mother had not been home. Before she could clear Dallas, though, she had gotten sick. That probably would have been the end of her if Tommy had not peeked into her cardboard box one morning to find out who was coughing.

She wanted him back, crooked smile and all. He was supposed to take her back to Denton, and Gram would have let them both live with her. Why was he lying in an alley with the back of his head blown out? Why had he left her alone? He should have been more careful!

A colorful string came loose from the hiding shroud she had woven. Missy snatched at it in panic and began trying to work it back into the pattern, but others began to trickle out as she worked. Her heart fluttered as the only cover she had been able to make for herself came more and more undone at her every touch. If only she had been able to spend more time with Gram, she would have learned how to weave the strings better. As it was, all she had was an inkling of the right way to do anything, except for the firebird. She knew the firebird best of all. Oh, how she would have liked to have its warmth and light, but not here where it might draw the attention of Tommy's killers.

A sound like a hastily indrawn breath, more felt than heard, announced the complete dissolution of her shroud. All her strings broke free and Missy was once again open to the night and all that lived in it. She gathered her threads as best she could and cowered deeper into the corner formed by the dumpsters. Taking in one deep breath and holding it, she listened with all her heart.

Missy knew what to listen for. Her Gram had taught her that much. She also knew to watch the shadows for flickers.

"The people in the shadows will come for you someday," Gram had warned her. *"Your strings make you special, and they'll want to take that for themselves."*

Gram had told her of the shadow people the first time Missy had mentioned her strings. She had been so proud of the little shapes she had been able to weave with them, but her mother could never see and accused Missy of making things up to tease her when she was hungover.

Her mother had not always been that way, so quick to take offense and strike out. Once she had even been happy and smiling, but that had been before Missy's dad had died riding his motorcycle, and her mom had starting staying out late.

When she showed the shapes to her Gram, though, she had not needed to explain a thing because Gram could see them.

"Why, what a clever little doggy you made!" Gram had cooed at her the first time Missy had shown her one of her sculptures. Of course, it had been a kitty, but Missy could take a little criticism now that someone could actually see her work. She and Gram had spent that whole first afternoon making things with the strings that coiled out of Missy's body, and Gram had taught her about the firebird and the shroud and, most importantly of all, about the shadow people.

Missy had not actually believed Gram about the shadow people until she hit Dallas proper. After that, there had been no doubt. Shadow people moved everywhere, and each one tasted a bit different. What was worse, some of them would follow Missy and chase her until she got far enough away to hide under her shroud. If Tommy had not found her that morning, a shadow person would have finally gotten her, because she had not been able to weave a shroud for days.

The sound of a footstep in a rain filled gutter caused her breath to catch in her throat. Another step followed the first . . . then another.

"Oh, to hell with this," she heard a frustrated woman's voice say and the darkness disappeared before a flare of blue light.

Missy bit down on her tongue to keep her teeth from chattering as the light moved forward to hover over Tommy's body. His pale skin glowed like the summer sky beneath the brilliant globe. A woman stepped past the dumpster into Missy's field of view. She wore a dark raincoat and held a clear vinyl umbrella over her head. Missy could see a pair of soldier's boots peeking out from under the coat.

"Ah, damn it," the woman muttered as she squatted down on her heels by the corpse. "Poor kid. You didn't deserve this. Don's gonna be *so* pissed." She reached out and drew her fingers over the body's face, closing the eyes. Light flickered from her fingertips, and when her hand came away, the eyelids stayed shut.

Missy watched the woman glance around the alley. She held her breath, asking in another silent prayer that this strange person would forget to look over her shoulder and back into Missy's corner. The woman stood and extinguished her ghostly light, shook her head, and began walking through the passage toward the far street. Just as Missy started to relax, she heard a sound like rain bouncing off a hollow can coming from her left side.

She slowly turned her head toward the sound and found a large, silver cat staring back at her. Not just silver in color, like a kind of gray. Oh, no. This was a cat made of *silver metal*. If its tail had not been twitching and its ears swiveling back and forth, Missy would have thought that the woman had dropped a statue as she passed.

"Nice kitty?" she whispered. Both ears swiveled forward and the tail went still and rigid. *Oops.*

The growl that came from the metal cat echoed and boomed as though a real animal had been caught in a snare drum. The clincher was the snarl, though.

"Mryaaaow!" The woman's footsteps faltered and Missy tried to jumped up to run . . .

. . . Except that her legs had fallen asleep while she had been hiding. At her first step, she tripped over her own feet, falling flat into a puddle. The cat hissed and jumped back as water splashed everywhere. She tried to get up again, but hot needles burned all the way down to her feet. Gritting her teeth, she lurched forward anyway. Another fall seemed imminent, but something rigid and unyielding caught the back of her tattered jacket, jerking her to a stop just short of the pavement.

Missy screamed and twisted. She threw her arms back and tried to claw at the hand that held her but the old jacket was so big that she could not reach. Feeling her arms slip inside the oversized sleeves, a sudden inspiration hit and she began frantically trying to worm her way out of the jacket.

That was when the hand let go.

The cat yowled and scurried under a cardboard box as a second splash filled the alley. Blue light flared to life between the confining walls.

"Hellfire, kid, I'm not going to hurt you," the woman's voice said, sounding more annoyed than angry. Missy had no intention of waiting around to find out, though. She was already doing her best to frog-lunge down the alley back toward the street.

"Oh, for the love of Mike," she heard the woman mutter as Missy finally managed to get back on her feet and start jogging forward awkwardly. The end of the passage loomed ahead of her, and hope had just started to rise when she hit the net . . .

. . . Which came as a shock since the net had been invisible until she hit it.

As Missy gazed at the now-fading multicolored strands, the unfairness of the situation threatened to loom up and swallow her. Then she realized that the net she had bounced off of had been made from threads just like the ones that came from her, just many times stronger and a lot more of them.

She turned wide-eyed to face the calm footsteps that were approaching her from behind. The woman seemed to be in no hurry, and the floating globe of fairy light kept pace with her as she approached. Down the alley, a silver nose poked out from under the shadow of a box.

The woman stopped in front of Missy, the bright light casting stark shadows across her face. Short, dark hair tumbled out from under a light, unadorned ball cap. The woman's face was serious, but not angry, although her features were more than scary enough beneath the fairy light. For a moment, Missy quailed beneath the woman's measuring gaze, but then the odd sorceress ran her tongue over her left eyetooth and sucked noisily at it.

"So," she said as if they had just met at a party, "you must be Missy, right?"

Missy gave a hesitant nod, dumbstruck. The woman twisted her lips to the right thoughtfully as her eyes moved up and down.

"Well, you aren't much to look at," she said at last as the silver cat slinked up to her ankles, "but damned if Tommy wasn't right. You throw off more thread than any twelve kids I've ever seen."

"Thread?" Missy asked as she swayed on her feet. A pounding pain had started up behind her eyes. The woman reached out and wrapped one of Missy's strings around her index finger.

"These," she stated flatly as she pulled the pale yellow strand down and held it out to Missy's nose. A fragrance of lavender played along with a hum like a flying wasp's wings. "Threads of power? Foundation of magic? Boon of Magecraft? Any of this ringing a bell?" Missy shook her head.

"Oh, come on!" the woman snapped at her as she tossed off the yellow string. "Word I had was that Tommy had seen you weave a stealth glamor and a fire glyph. You don't learn that sort of stuff on the street. Who taught you to do that?"

"My . . . my Gram showed it to me," Missy answered defensively, stung by the woman's vehemence, "just before mama got mad and moved us just outside of Dallas."

"And who's your . . ." The woman paused, closed her eyes, and sucked on her teeth again. "Nope. Don't want to know. My contract was to bring you back to Houston, and to Houston you're gonna go. I'm not getting paid enough to play good Samaritan."

"But I want to go home to Gram in Denton!" wailed Missy, the tears boiling up again as her head throbbed. "I want my room back and my stuffies and . . ."

The woman reached out and clamped a hard hand on Missy's wrist and yanked her toward the street-lights at the end of the alley. "I don't give a hoot what you want, kid. You're not paying me."

Missy twisted and kicked out with her left foot at the woman's shin, connecting through her target's raincoat with a wet thud. The woman yelped and jumped back, her grip coming loose in the process. Missy tore free and ran toward the street.

"Why you little . . ." she heard the woman snarl behind her, but Missy only ran faster. The exit was only a few yards away. She was going to run into the Chinese restaurant and start screaming her head off.

A tall, sparkling shadow appeared from around the corner and stepped into the alley.

Missy screamed and tried to stop but her feet slipped, turning her run into a splashing slide toward the shadow. The flickering darkness loomed above her, as though gauging how much of a meal she might make. A smell of mildew appeared in her mind, dark and tainted, accompanied by the aural impression of fingernails on a chalkboard. Missy flopped on her belly and scrabbled for a grip on the wet asphalt. Houston suddenly sounded like a fine place to visit.

"Dibs!" shouted the woman as she hobbled forward, pausing once to shake the leg that Missy had kicked. "I got here first." The shadow twisted, morphing to focus its attention on the sorceress.

"Gerard," it breathed, the disgust plain despite the wheezy softness of the voice.

"The one and only," the sorceress answered back with a jut of her chin. Missy managed to half fall, half lunge to flop in front of the woman. The cat appeared in front of Missy's face and growled.

"You better sit still, kid," Gerard warned. "O.G.'s wet and unhappy. He might give you a nip if you don't mind." The rain slacked off as Missy ignored the woman's advice and struggled to scoot behind the sorceress' leg. Once there, she leaned around Gerard's left to peer back at the flickering specter.

"This is none of your concern, Eleuran," the shadow interjected in its creepy voice. *"Leave her to me and I will let you live."*

Gerard hunched her shoulders and wiggled her fingers at the shadow. "Woo! Leave off the 'dark rider' hocus and dire threats, Prentice. She's scared enough as is, and you sure as hell don't freak me out one bit." She cocked her head quizzically at the shadow. "It is Prentice, isn't it? Not Practice or Prickwise or Pornhick or something more suitable like that?"

The shadow melted away before the fairy light globe, leaving a thin young man in a baggy business suit with long, sopping wet hair that might have been blond when it was dry.

"You have a smart mouth, Allison Gerard," he said in a nasal voice that was nothing at all like the sepulchral tones of the shadow, "and you're quite a bit off your reservation, aren't you?"

The woman reached down and back, grabbing Missy by the shoulder of her jacket and pulling her to her feet, but the sorceress never looked away from the man.

"So I've been told . . . about the mouth, anyway. As for being 'off the reservation', well, it's a free country, and I'm at most one thirty-second Cherokee, so the tribe cut me off."

The man snorted. "Always the quick comeback. You might want to reconsider your attitude, smartass. Beaucomp's influence isn't quite as pronounced here as in Houston. Besides, he's got no right horning in on this action."

A brief tightening of Gerard's eyes gave the only clue Missy could see that the man's words meant a thing to the sorceress, but she could sense a high-pitched sound coming from her erstwhile protector, like that of some great spring being wound too tight.

"I'm an independent contractor, Porkwit, and this

job doesn't belong to Beaucomp. Despite what you think you've heard, he's just an occasional customer. There's no chain on me."

"Whatever," the man said carefully as he pulled a sodden glove off his right hand while stretching his fingers. "Oh, by the way, it is Prentice. Robert Prentice."

"Well, *Bob*, if you're thinking of taking me on, you can't be serious," Gerard mocked. "You're not even within sight of being in my league. I don't care how many poor souls you've tagged to boost yourself."

"Always room for one more," Prentice said softly, and then he snapped out his bare hand, not at Gerard but at Missy. A pale blue string flowed out and away from his fingertips, streaking across the darkness and aimed directly between her eyes.

Before she could move or even scream, a wall of violet flame erupted between Gerard and the man, obscuring the faint string and hiding Prentice from her sight. The occult flames burned against the black for a handful of seconds before disappearing as suddenly as they had erupted, leaving Prentice sucking his fingertips and Gerard smiling cruelly.

"Ah, ah, ah," she chastised him as she wagged a finger. "That was very naughty. I told you I had dibs. No free samples."

Prentice raised his right eyebrow and lowered his hand from his mouth. Shrugging, he began putting his glove back on.

"Can't blame a guy for trying," he said, nonchalant.

"Oh, hell yes I can. Time for you to shove off, bucko, or you're really going to irritate me."

The man straightened, as if pulling himself up for a speech. "I challenge for personal decision."

"What?" Gerard blurted out in disbelief. "Are you out of your gourd? Not only is she underage, she doesn't even know who we are!"

"Nonetheless, I challenge."

"You might want to know that I'm currently having a very hard time *not* incinerating you!"

The man snorted. "Now who's bluffing? I know you'd never start a one-woman war with any of the Stephanos families, even here in Dallas. That's the problem with being a lone wolf, even if one happens to be an archmage like you. No backup."

Gerard's hand clamped down painfully on Missy's shoulder. She looked up at the sorceress and caught just a faint glimmer of sparkle around the curls of hair that had escaped the hat. The air felt greasy in a way that only existed in Missy's mind, and she could not get the smell of burning rubber out of her nose.

"Fine," Gerard spat out finally, "but I'm making sure the playing field is level." Her hand snapped out and flare of silver light filled the alley. Missy had an impression of something bright streaking up into the sky and disappearing.

"Missy?" asked the sorceress, again without looking away from Prentice.

"Uh huh?"

"This man gets to try to convince you to go home with him."

"I want to go back to Denton!"

"That's a fine thing to want, but I don't think it's going to happen tonight. Anyway, by our laws, he gets to have a say. If you decide to go with him, I can't stop you. Just remember one thing . . ."

"Yes?"

"Tommy."

"Hey!" Prentice snapped. "No coercing the candidate!"

"Is that kind of like 'no terrorizing the candidate'? 'Cause if that's the case, I think you can just sit on it and spin, Pratfall."

Missy could hear the man grinding his teeth behind his thin lips.

"Fine," he said venomously after glaring at Gerard for several long seconds. She stepped to the side, leaving Missy facing the man as he closed his eyes, shuddered slightly, and then made an air-clearing gesture with his hands.

"Let's just start over shall we?" he asked at last, opening his eyes and fixing his attention on Missy. "Miss Watkins, I represent a powerful cartel of mages who are interested in recruiting your talents. If I am not mistaken, your life lately has not been particularly pleasant. Because of your rather unique potential, my employers are willing to provide you with excellent housing, education, and liberal benefits while you learn to become an integral part of our organization."

A snort came from Missy's right side. She and Prentice both glanced over to see Gerard stifling a reply behind her hand. The sorceress raised her eyebrows in mock embarrassment.

"Oh, sorry. Don't mind me." Prentice let out an irritated sigh.

"In any case," Prentice continued, clearly annoyed, "you will be treated very well and given every comfort. You have the potential to become a valuable asset to our cartel, and we would like to give you every opportunity to attain your full potential."

"Is that the same deal you gave my sister and her children as you drained them like human batteries during your last battles of succession?"

The voice came from behind the small group and was accompanied by purposeful, splashing footsteps as a substantial matron wearing rubber farm boots walked into the range of Gerard's fairy light. Her white hair had been hastily pinned into a crude bun, and a ratty gray raincoat had been thrown over her green paisley pajamas. Despite this harried appearance, however, her expression matched the looming threat of the black clouds still lingering overhead.

"What the hell is this, Gerard?" Prentice demanded in an outraged voice. "Bring-your-own-geezer night?"

The sorceress barked out a surprised laugh before favoring the mage with a canary-fed smile. "Well, I'll be damned," she said as she waved a hand at the matron. "This, Porkloin, is really and truly balance."

"Gram!" squealed Missy as she turned and ran for the woman. She could hear Gerard's chuckle and

Prentice' hiss of indrawn breath behind as she charged
into her grandmother's embrace.

"Hello, puddin'," Gram whispered to her. "Everything's going to be all right."

Missy wanted to pour out her heart to Gram, tell
her about all the pain and horror that she had seen
and experienced since their last parting, but all that
came out were sobs and tears. So she settled for burying her face in the wet comfort of her grandmother's
raincoat and felt safe for the first time in a month.
Gram straightened but kept on hand protectively on
Missy's head.

"Allie," she said conversationally.

"Hello, Becca. Long time. Things are making more
sense now."

Gram patted Missy and then pried her free from
the raincoat. "Punkin? I need you to go stay by Miss
Gerard for a bit, okay?" Missy shook her head.

"She's scary!" Her emphatic pronouncement drew
a chuckle from her grandmother.

"Oh, she's all right, once you get to know her. I
asked a friend of mine for help, and he sent Allie. I
need you to go stand with her for just a bit until I deal
with this young fella."

Gram gave her a gentle push toward the side of the
passage where Gerard had taken up a perch on a
closed dumpster. O.G. was grooming himself with a
smooth silver tongue as he sat on a cement stoop in
the doorway next to his mistress. Missy stepped hesi-
tantly toward a spot on the wall between the dumpster
and the cat before turning to look back at her Gram
and Prentice.

"You're in for a treat," Gerard told her in a perfectly audible stage whisper. "Not many folks get to
see the White Witch of Denton in action."

Prentice went even more pale in the blue light; his
mouth opened in shock, then worked silently as he
tried to find his voice. "You!" he managed to gasp out
at last as he raised a shaky finger to point at Gram.

"Me, you sorry excuse for a soul leech." Missy had

never seen a smile as cold as the one Gram gave the now shaking mage. Even she wanted to run away from that horrible expression. Glancing to her right, she saw Gerard grinning in unabashed enjoyment.

Whether driven by fear or desperation, the mage wasted no more words. He snapped his hands forward, wrist to wrist with fingers outspread. A rush of cold filled the alley as an oily black cloud shot out from his palms toward Gram. Missy screamed and made to move forward, but some sort of invisible tether materialized about her waist, binding her to the door.

"Just watch," came Gerard's gleeful voice.

The horizontal oil slick rushed toward her Gram leaving frost on every surface as it passed except where Gerard, Missy, and the silver cat watched. Missy's stomach seemed to fill her throat as the gray-haired matron raised a single hand and flicked her wrist disdainfully.

Light that seemed to be drawn from a high summer noon in Denton flared to life in front of the cloud, the vertical pillar of brilliance slicing the chill away and dissolving the mage's attack into coalescing puddles of ink. For a moment, Missy thought she could see the weave of the black spell coming unraveled in the flying remnants as they evaporated in the rain. Just as the last of the casting closest to the mage's hands was about to come undone, though, a hidden glyph erupted from the black . . . the brilliant crimson of the firebird!

"No!" she screamed as she stretched out her own hand. Heat scorched her face as a firebird erupted from her own threads, screaming out to intercept Prentice's surprise scant inches from her grandmother's face.

"Stupid little bitch!" Prentice snapped. Another firebird streaked from his fingertips, this time directed at Missy. Her eyes widened as the glyph roared through the darkness aimed seemingly at her nose. She struggled to find another firebird like the one she had conjured for Gram, but nothing answered her call.

I'm going to die, came the realization. *I'm not even twelve and I'm going to die.*

A wall of pale blue ice appeared between Missy and Prentice's attack. His glyph struck the barrier with an ear splitting crack, but the frigid shield held.

To Missy's left, Gram straightened, bringing her hands up to her chest and then down in a clearing gesture. Ice, fading firebird, and sunlight pillar all disappeared with an ephemeral "pop." Her right hand strayed back up to her hair to tuck a loose strand of gray behind her ear.

"My turn," she said so softly that Missy just barely heard. Prentice, apparently, had heard all too well. He cringed back before turning to run hell bent for the alley entrance.

Her attention drawn by Prentice's attempt to run, Missy did not see what Gram did. A rush of air and the sense of something enormous passing by were unmistakable, though. The fleeing mage bent backward with a crack as some powerful force slammed into him from behind. His feet left the ground as he lofted out of the alley and into the street following a rising arc.

A flash of blue and white appeared on the street from the left, and Prentice disappeared from sight as the impact of a bus radically altered the mage's ballistic trajectory with a wet crunch. Missy stared at the now empty alley opening in shock. Against the background noise of a squealing air brakes and tortured tires, a polite cough came from Gerard's perch.

"That was . . . elegant," said the younger woman as she hopped down with a splash. Panicked voices started shouting out in the street. Missy looked up to see the young witch's wry grin, then looked back toward her Gram. The older woman chuckled and brushed her hands in a gesture of finality.

"All a matter of timing and situational awareness, Allie," the old woman said as she joined them near the dumpster. "And if you believe that, I've got a bridge down in Escobedo I'd like to talk to you about."

Gerard chuckled. "And I think Missy there is a chip

off your block. She didn't even have to weave that glyph before she cast it."

The sound of her name released Missy from her shocked trance. She threw herself back against Gram's sopping raincoat. "I want to go home!" she pleaded. Gentle hands appeared on her head, slipped to her shoulders and held her tight.

"Oh, puddin'," Gram said softly, "I know you do, and I wish I could take you back and make it all better."

Missy pushed back and looked up in disbelief at her grandmother. "You . . . you're not taking me home?" An expression of pain and despair washed across Gram's wrinkled face.

"Hon, I want to, but I can't," she said as her eyes began to glitter in the fairie light. "The folks that varmint worked for have been after me for a long time. I thought that if I stayed low and out of sight, they'd leave me and mine alone, but that doesn't seem to be the way of it. I think they killed my boy and then used that grief to twist your mom up and ruin her life. Reckon they thought that if they caused enough pain, I wouldn't fight 'em." She sighed and pulled Missy into a tighter embrace.

"I'm so sorry that I wasn't there to stop your momma from running off, hon. I never thought she'd do what she did, but now I've got to deal with these skunks, and I can't protect you at the same time. I'm just miserable that I couldn't save her."

"But . . ." Missy began. Gram shook her head firmly.

"Nope. You need to go with Allie back down to Houston. That friend of mine . . . his name's Don . . . he's got a school there. They'll teach you more about your threads and a lot of other stuff to boot." Missy snuffled and rubbed her eyes with the back of her hand. "Oh, don't let it be like that, puddin'. It won't be long, and you'll get to meet a lot of other kids, and Allie here won't let anything bad happen to you, will you Allie?"

Gerard jerked back in surprise, glancing between Gram and Missy in panic. "Becca," she started out reasonably, "you know I'm in acquisitions. I'm not exactly a babysitter."

"I'm no baby!" snapped Missy. "And I don't want to go to Houston!"

Allie held up her hands to fend off a further protest. "Look, Missy, Becca has a point. She can't have you trailing around behind her or hiding in her house while she's out picking a fight. You're better off at the Haven school for a bit while she fixes things."

Missy looked back and forth between the two, trying to find a chink in either woman's armor. A siren sounded in the distance.

"Time's running out, Allie." Gram's voice seemed more tired than Missy had ever heard it. "I'm asking you to watch out for her as a friend, not offering you a contract. She needs you more than you could know, and I have a sneaking suspicion it'd do you some good, too."

"Becca . . ." Allie started to say, but the old woman held up a hand, cutting her off.

"For your Grandpa's sake, Allie. Please."

In that moment, Missy thought that Gerard was going to explode. Allie's face had gone all still and flushed with her mouth working up and down silently as her brain apparently tried to come up with a suitable remark to release the pressure. Then the young woman's eyes fell to the right of Gram and the flush faded.

"All right," she said softly. "I'll do it, but you'd damn well better not dawdle."

A pair of matronly arms reached out to drag a startled Gerard into a none-too-feminine bear hug that squeezed Missy between them.

"Good girl!" Gram told her as she pounded on Allie's back. "He'd be proud of you."

Gerard pushed out of the embrace like a cat. "All right! All right! No need to get soppy about it. Jeez!" The sound of the siren drew nearer and was joined by another. Allie glanced toward the street meaningfully before looking back at Gram and Missy. "I think we need to git."

Gram nodded, then bent down to kiss Missy on the cheek. "You be good for Don and Allie. I'll be along as soon as I can get things straightened out."

Missy wrapped her arms around the old woman and squeezed as tight and hard as she could. Her eyes burned, but the tears seemed to have run out. "I will," she said into the raincoat. "Just hurry."

Strong hands pulled her away to where her Gram's own twinkling eyes could look down at her. "It won't be long. I promise." Then she put Missy's right hand into Allie's left, touched the side of her nose, and disappeared.

A pregnant pause ensued as Missy tried to accept that her grandmother had just vanished. A jerking motion shook her hand as Gerard broke free.

"She just . . ." Missy started to say.

"Yeah, I know, the show off," Gerard muttered. "Doesn't even need to form a portal. Those boys won't know what hit 'em." She shook her head and started back into the alley away from the street, Missy following in her wake. Their quiet steps filled the silence, the clinking of O.G's paws on the pavement providing a soft counter-cadence.

"Well," Allie said as they neared the Tommy's body, "let's get out of here before the cops come looking." Gerard raised a hand, and Missy felt a surge through her whole body as Tommy's body disappeared with a pop.

"Where'd you send him?" she asked.

"Back to the Haven," muttered Gerard. "There's a place in the building where they can take care of him."

"It sounds big."

"Nah, it's just an old hotel. Lots of rooms, though."

"Do you live there?"

"Hmph! As if. I've got my own place."

"Will you come visit?"

Gerard sighed.

"I think I'll be staying there for a while. Seems as though I've just been forced to adopt a little sister." She gestured toward the far end of the alley, and an oval of black rimmed with multicolored threads appeared before them. Missy's left hand crept up nervously to slip back into Allie's right palm. Right before they stepped through the portal, Gerard squeezed, gentle but firm.

"Change is always scary," Allie said before they slipped into the black, "but having friends helps."

NIGHT OF THE WOLF

John Lambshead

THE bus stank of diesel, and the seat dug uncomfortably into her slight frame. She got her compact out of her bag and examined her face in the mirror. The same Rhian as always looked back at her, but she did what she could to improve upon nature. Every few minutes, she checked her watch. She was ready by the door when the bus stopped, diving out before it was fully open.

Rhian ran the length of the road and up the High Street. A tall boy in denim waited by the café door. His smile lit up the road when he spotted her. She threw herself at him and he enveloped her.

"Sorry I'm late, James. They time when you switch the computer off, and the traffic was bad and—"

He stopped the flow of words with his mouth on hers. "Come on," he said, coming up for air. "I'm starving."

Grabbing her hand, he pulled her into the café and found a table.

"What'll you have, love?" asked the waitress.

"The all-day breakfast," James said to the waiter. "With tea."

The waitress looked at Rhian.

"Um, some beans on toast."

"No, you don't." James interrupted her.

"She'll have the same as me," he said to the waitress.

"Then you must let me pay my share," she said

"Nonsense, I earn more than you."

He took her hand and chatted about his day. She wasn't really listening to what he said. She just enjoyed hearing him. He slipped the button on her blouse cuff as they talked and worked the sleeve up.

"Do you want to see the other arm?" she asked, slightly nettled.

"No, as long as you are taking care of yourself," James said. "I merely wondered why you were wearing long sleeves again."

"I ran out of clothes." She shrugged. "I have laundry issues."

"Let's go shopping tomorrow. We'll get you some new sleeveless tops to show your beautiful arms off."

He ran his fingers gently along the thin white scars on her forearm. They hardly showed at all now.

She and James sneaked into the hall via the back doors as they were late. Doctor Galbraith was already standing at the front.

"Order, ladies and gentlemen, can we please come to order?" said Galbraith, running his fingers through a surprisingly thick head of gray hair. "I have exciting news. I have secured a sponsorship deal for us to carry out an archaeological investigation of the land by Rodomon Street."

"The rat-infested wasteland by the canal?" asked a well-dressed lady.

"Um, yes," said Gailbraith.

"Why would someone pay good money to dig up that dump?" asked a sharp young man called Mick.

"It could be an interesting site," said Galbraith, defensively. "The waterway is a canalized river. We could find an historical settlement there, an Anglo-Saxon village or a Neolithic encampment, who knows?"

"Or a place that Elizabeth the First slept in," said Mick.

"Yes," said Galbraith, absentmindedly.

The society members laughed. Every second-rate rural inn in Southern England had a plaque on the wall claiming that Queen Elizabeth slept there. Good Queen Bess must never have spent a night in her own bed.

"Very amusing, calm down," said Galbraith. "But seriously, this is a great opportunity to for us to do some practical work. We can write the dig up in *The Ealing Historical Journal*. Think what that might do for our circulation."

"If circulation is the right word," said Mick. Galbraith affected not to hear him.

James smiled at Rhian. *The Journal* was a laser-printed, stapled-together sheet that society members received as part of their annual subscription. Galbraith also gave it away free to local libraries whose staff put it politely on the periodical shelf. Rhian never read her copy, it was deadly dull, but James liked it. Galbraith used it as a vehicle to promote various ideas that had failed to get published in an academic journal.

"How much money are we talking about?" asked James.

"Ten thousand pounds," said Galbraith, triumphantly.

"Who on earth wants to give a little local society like us ten grand?" asked James, astonished

"Ah, the Rayman Property Development Company," said Galbraith. "They intend to build a block of luxury apartments on the site and, very properly, want to check for any evidence of historical use first."

"Are they not legally obliged to do that anyway?" asked Mick.

"I believe that is the case," said Galbraith.

"And how much would a professional study by, say, London University cost?" asked Mick.

"Ah, I am a bit out of touch since I retired," said Galbraith.

"Roughly," said Mick, remorselessly.

"Perhaps a hundred thousand," said Galbraith.

"So these Rayman people are getting one hell of a cheap deal," said James.

When the meeting broke up, James and Rhian stopped for a few words with Mick who was lighting up a cigarette.

"I have heard a few things about Rayman," said Mick, thoughtfully.

"Like what," asked James.

"He's supposed to have blackmailed a planning officer. People who cross him have bad luck. Their cars catch fire, that sort of thing. Just time for a pint before closing, I fancy," Mick hurried off.

"Maybe we should keep out of this, James," said Rhian, worried.

"I wouldn't take too much notice of Mick. He likes to pretend that he is in the know but he's just a law student, not Perry Mason," said James.

Rhian pushed the wheelbarrow across the dusty archaeological site. She stopped halfway to wipe the sweat from her face and readjust the ring that held back her hair. It was one of those weeks when the wind came in from the east and blew hot, humid, continental air across London. Traffic fumes built up fast, and the air turned acrid. The city was in drought, again, and the short-lived showers of rain that had fallen were insufficient to wash away the pollution. She could taste the acid in her mouth, and her eyes stung. She had abandoned any pretence of femininity for practical combat trousers and a crop top. Her feet felt hot and swollen in the heavy leather boots stipulated by health and safety rules.

Taking a deep breath, she gripped the handle and pushed the barrow up the incline to the earth dump. Tipping out the excavated soil in the humidity exhausted her. She tottered back to the trench.

"You look beat, love. Let's have a break," said James.

"Oh, yes," she replied.

They walked to the portable hut where they stored their equipment.

"Would you like water or Coke?" James asked.

"Water, please."

He took out a bottle of Evian and unscrewed the cap for her. Rhian drank and couldn't stop. The water tasted of warm plastic, but she didn't care. It was the best water that she had ever drunk. It reminded her of summer days as a child when she carried water in plastic bottles clipped to the front of her bike.

Mick wandered over to join them. "I see Galbraith has sloped off again," he said. " 'Who's with me?' the man said. What a joke."

"He's old," said Rhian. "Physical work in this weather must be difficult for him, especially as he never takes his tweed jacket off."

"You see the best in people, honey," said Mick. He prodded James in the arm. "You're a lucky fellow."

"I know," said James. He put his arm possessively around her and she cuddled into him. He smelled of fresh sweat mixed with aftershave and male soap. On him, it smelled good.

"I reckon that we are wasting our time in that trench," Mick said, cracking open a drink of cola. The sun-warmed can exploded in a spray of foam.

"The geophys equipment indicated a structure there," said James, somewhat defensively.

"No offence, James, but I am past trusting cheap, clapped-out, rented equipment operated by a novelty-card shop manager who had read the manual in his lunch break," said Mick.

"James did his best," said Rhian hotly, leaping to his aid.

"Of course he did, honey," said Mick. "I don't blame him, I blame bloody Galbraith. I don't see much evidence that ten grand has been spent on this investigation. He hasn't even provided a poxy diesel generator to power a drinks cooler."

"Let's take the trench down just one more foot before abandoning it," said James.

Mick grunted, which James obviously took as agreement. The boys went back to their shovels, and Rhian went back to her hateful barrow. She was on her way back from a trip to the dump, when she heard an excited yell from Mick.

"I've got something, bloody stone."

"Stop digging and use trowels," said James.

The other men joined him and scraped away frantically. Rhian watched from the top.

"The stonework is completely discontinuous," said James.

"We could be looking at the top of a smashed up medieval wall," said Mick. "Keep scraping but be careful."

Other boys jumped into the trench to help, and the work progressed swiftly. For the first time, Rhian understood why James found history interesting. This was like a treasure hunt.

"Hang on a minute," said James. "These stones aren't connected in any way. They are just jumbled together."

He grabbed a spade and dug deeper. "There is bare earth underneath. The stones form a layer."

"Like a Roman road?" asked Mick.

"There aren't supposed to be any Roman roads here," said James.

"So it's a hitherto undiscovered Roman road," said Mick, excitedly. Dreams of glory were clearly passing through his head.

One of the other boys started to laugh.

"What's so funny," said Mick, aggressively.

"The stones in that layer are smooth and rounded," said the boy.

They gazed at him with incomprehension.

"I can see that you are city folk," said the boy, in an exaggerated rural Norfolk accent. "That, there, canal was once a river, right?"

Rhian still did not understand. She was not the only one, judging by the uncomprehending expressions from the others.

"Streams run down into rivers," Norfolk boy said.

"We have spent all weekend digging up a bloody dried-up stream bed," said Mick, throwing down his trowel. "That effing does it. Get the metal detectors out."

"We are not supposed to use them on an archaeological site," said James.

"This isn't an archaeological site," said Mick. "Right now, it's just a wasteland that some poor bloody muppets have hand-dug a trench through."

"Yeah, you're right," James agreed.

"You use the detector love; I will be your digger," he said to Rhian. "You have done enough heavy work for one day."

James had a modern lightweight detector with designer styling.

"You take that side and I'll sweep this," Mick said.

Rhian had to adjust the phones as she had a narrower head than James. She started the slow walk, swinging the detection ring from side to side. The machine murmured gently in her headphones. After half a dozen steps, the machine chimed.

"What do you reckon, love, a bottletop or a can?" asked James, digging carefully. He pulled something out of the ground. "It's a beans can, super."

They moved on, finding the metallic detritus of a consumer society. After half an hour, the most valuable thing that Rhian had discovered was a 50 pence coin, and Mick had found a broken fountain pen dropped by some ancient schoolboy from before the invention of the ballpoint pen.

"This is a complete waste of bloody time," said Mick, switching his detector of with a decisive flick of his hand.

Rhian's detector changed tone. She waved it back across the spot and it chirruped urgently.

"Yeah, you're not wrong," James said. "Fancy a swift pint?"

"I'm getting a reading of something large," said Rhian.

"Sure do," said Mick, ignoring her. "Shall we pop in the King's Arms up the road or go to the Barmaid's Breasts down on the river? It's a bit of a walk, but it always has a fine flock of tourist chicks to leer at."

Rhian took the shovel from James' unresisting hand and dug down. Every so often, she ran the detector over the hole to get her bearings. When the tone indicated that she was close, she carefully removed earth with a trowel. A strange, tarnished, metal object stuck out of the ground. She pulled it free. It was shaped like a round half-dome attached to a spine of metal across the base.

"What have you got there, honey?" asked Mick. He examined the object carefully, brushing soil away from it. "What in the name of all that's holy is it?"

James took it. "Could it be a shield boss?"

"Dunno," said Mick, taking up his detector again, pub outing forgotten. "Let's see what else we can find."

Over the next hour, they found more strange metallic objects, including chain links and round flat plates of metal.

Rhian's detector chirruped again. James dug enthusiastically.

"Look at this," he said.

It consisted of two bars, connected by a chain link that was rusted into a solid mass. At the other end of each bar was a large metal loop decorated by a cross.

"Do you know what it is?" Rhian asked.

"I think it's an ancient horse bit. The linked bars went in the animal's mouth. The reins were attached to the loops," James said.

"Over here," Mick called a halt. "Everyone bring their finds to the hut."

Rhian and James went over to show their bridle bit. One of the girls had a small cast-metal animal, a wolf.

"That is a Celtic helmet crest," said Mick, confidently.

"Oh, come on," said James. "How do you know that?"

"Because I found this," said Mick. He put an object in front of them. It was pointed, leaf-shaped, and socketed at the back.

"A spearhead," said James.

"Look at the markings," said Mick. Vinelike metal decorations ran down the blade. They were clearly Celtic.

"I wonder what this place was," said James. "There is no sign of a settlement."

"Could it have been a battleground?" asked Mick. "Imagine Queen Boudicca's Celtic war chariots sweeping down the Thames valley."

"There's no recorded battle in this area," said James. "It was London that she burned."

"But there could have been an unrecorded skirmish," said Mick, eyes shining with excitement.

"I guess," said James. He grinned at Rhian. She knew that he was not convinced, but he would not spoil Mick's romantic dreams.

An elderly Ford Escort pulled onto the wasteland, the engine expiring in a cloud of blue smoke. The young people crowded around Galbraith.

"Have a look at this lot, Doc.," said Mick, excitedly.

"Ah, yes, most interesting," said Galbraith. "Perhaps I should take these away for assessment. I still have a few contacts at the university."

Rhian barely knew Galbraith, as she had only joined the society recently after meeting James, but she got the impression that he did not seem as pleased as she would have expected. From the thoughtful expression on James' face, he felt the same.

Rhian held James hand as they left the site. She saw a gleam as she passed a dig hole. Without thinking, she bent down and picked up a small tarnished piece of metal. A spade had caught it on one side, chipping off the dirt and tarnish to reveal the shine of silver underneath. She surreptitiously slipped the artifact into her pocket. James looked at her, quizzically.

Later that night, she shared a pizza with James in his flat.

"So what did you filch from the site today?" asked James.

She blushed and handed it to him.

"Why didn't you want Galbraith to look at it, love?" James asked.

"I don't know," she said. "I just couldn't give it up."

James examined it. "I think that it's silver."

He rummaged around in a drawer and pulled something out. "Silver cloth!" he said to Rhian. He cleared a space on his table and polished furiously. Bright metal slowly emerged from black tarnish. Rhian watched with fascination. James used a needle to chip gently away at encrusted material.

"It's a brooch," said James. 'The pin is missing, but you can see where it fastened." He polished furiously.

"There is a face in the middle," Rhian said. "No, it's an animal of some sort, like a dog."

"Or a wolf," said James. "Remember the helmet crest."

He kept polishing and picking out detail with the needle. "There are letters around the rim. Write this down, Rhian. We have an M, something unreadable, an A—no, it's an R, a G, unreadable, an N, and something I can't make out. What have we got?" asked James.

"M RG N ," Rhian spelled out.

James switched on his computer.

"What are you doing?" asked Rhian.

"I'll try and search for the name on the internet using partial matching."

"Don't bother," said Rhian, amused. "The word is Morgana; it's Welsh."

"What is Morgana?" asked James.

"Not what, but who," said Rhian. "Morgana was the name of the Celtic goddess of war. You'll know her better under her English name. She has a place in the Arthurian legends as Morgan le Fey, sorceress, Merlin's wife and Arthur's sworn enemy. In the Welsh tradition, Morgana was also the goddess of death, fate—hence, Morgan le Fey, the moon and lakes and rivers. Her symbol was the raven."

"So why is there a wolf on the brooch?" asked James, puzzled. He turned back to the computer.

She waited, patiently as he searched through the internet.

"Morgana was also the goddess of shapeshifters," said James. "That explains it."

"Shapeshifters?" asked Rhian.

"Yes," said James, standing up. He made a claw gesture at her and growled. "Shapeshifters, you know, weres."

Rhian giggled. "I have no idea what you mean."

"Werewolves, Rhian. Haven't you ever met a wolf?" James asked. He howled theatrically and leaped on her. She went over backward with a shriek.

Rhian was on her back. James lay on top of her, holding her down. They both froze. She was tiny beneath him. She should have felt helpless, but instead she felt protected and loved.

"It's getting late," he said. "I had better walk you back to your bedsit."

That was her big, beautiful, loving James. He looked out for her. He never pressured or took advantage of her, so she would have to encourage him a little. "I have some things in my bag. I could stay here tonight," she said.

"It's a small flat," he said. "I only have one bed."

"I know," said Rhian, raising her lips to his.

Rhian had taken to sleeping at James' flat. He had suggested that she move in permanently to save money. She probably would give up her bedsit in the end. It seemed silly to pay rent on a place she hardly used. James had given her a key, so she let herself in.

"Close your eyes," James said. He fiddled with something around her neck. "Okay, open them."

The newly polished brooch hung around her neck on a heavy silver chain. "It's lovely, James," she kissed him. "This is the first time anyone has bought me jewelry."

"I only provided the chain," he smiled. "But I'm glad you like it."

Rhian kept the brooch on. She even wore it to bed. That night she dreamt, vividly. She stood by a river that meandered across marshland. Mist rising off the water-soaked ground curled in the air making it difficult to see far, but she could pick out the dark shapes of trees on the edge of the boggy area. There was a glow on the horizon, and the air smelled of bonfires.

She heard splashing and male voices. Half a dozen figures emerged from the mist, threading single file across the more solid ground. Every so often, one slipped into a bog. They wore yellow ochre tunics covered with chainmail shirts and had large steel helmets that flanged out to protect their necks. The metal was tarnished and rusty unlike the polished armor in museums. Some of them had spears and long red shields.

They walked past without reacting to her. She noticed that her feet did not sink into the marsh and that she was warm despite being naked in the clammy mist. I'm a spirit, a ghost, she thought.

Horse hooves pounded in the mist. The soldiers stopped and formed a circle. One of them barked orders in a strange language. It sounded like Spanish or Italian, but she didn't speak either. There was the blast of a horn, and a chariot sped out of the mist pulled by two small light brown ponies. The kneeling driver wore only striped trousers, and his hair was stiffened into a punk-style Mohican. A moustached warrior stood behind him in trousers and cloak. He held a spear with a long leaflike decorated blade and an oblong shield decorated with whirls.

The chariot rode around the soldiers and stopped, the warrior dismounting. More chariots thundered past her until the mail-coated soldiers were encircled by silent, waiting warriors. A wolf howled in the distance.

A chariot moved slowly from the mist. A wolf's head standard was atop a pole fixed to the back of the vehicle. The chariot carried not a warrior, but a woman in a long green cloak fastened by a silver brooch—her silver brooch. The woman stepped down and raised both arms. When she spoke, Rhian understood her. It was Welsh, strangely accented Welsh. The woman said "*Kill the Romans*," and the slaughter began.

"Rhian, Rhian, wake up. It's okay," James said.

"What?" she asked.

"You were having a nightmare." He held her tight. They made love, but all the time she lay beneath him, she felt the cold brooch between her breasts.

Rhian let herself into the hall. As usual, she was late, and James was already there. She squeezed onto a seat next to him. His lips were compressed in anger. "I'm sorry I'm late," she said, worried that he was mad at her.

"Never mind that, read this," he said, handing her the new issue of the society's journal.

The newsletter was open at the editorial page. As usual, Galbraith had written it. She flipped through the main points. "Negative investigation," "Some items found by metal detectors—turned out to be of no interest," "Final report to Rayman's indicates that development can go ahead immediately."

"Gailbraith has stitched us up," said James.

"Order, order," Galbraith said from the front, blinking at them through thick glasses.

Mick stood up. "Who decided that our archaeological finds were of no value?"

"I showed them to other scholars, and they confirmed my view," said Galbraith.

"Where are the artifacts we found, Doctor Gailbraith? I would like a second opinion," said James.

"I am afraid that they are lost. Someone broke into my car and stole them," said Galbraith.

"So our finds have disappeared, and Rayman's gets the go ahead to concrete over the site," said James.

"I know that you are all desperately disappointed that we found nothing of value, but the good news is that society is solvent from the surplus. Because the study was curtailed, we spent only a fraction of the ten thousand pound budget."

"Is that why you did it, Doctor Galbraith? For the money?" said Mick.

"That is a despicable implication, young man. I should be very careful if I were you. Mr Rayman is a powerful, unforgiving man," said Galbraith.

"I always thought that you were a bit of an old twit, Galbraith, but I respected your scholarship. I won't make that mistake again. I resign from this society," said Mick. He walked out.

"I resign too," said James and followed Mick. Rhian went with James, and she was not the only one. Galbraith was left with a few elderly cronies.

Mick was waiting for them on the pavement. He lit up a fag. "I keep meaning to give these things up, but now never seems to be a good time."

"We can't let them get away with it," said James. "This is outright corruption."

"Yeah, but where's your proof?" said Mick. "Who will take our word against eminent citizens like Rayman and Galbraith? It might have been different if we had kept some of the artifacts."

Rhian felt the brooch against her skin. She wondered whether to mention it to Mick, but James silenced her with a look.

"So there's nothing we can do?" asked James.

"I didn't say that," said Mick. "There's nothing we can do legally, but a few words around the college, and I reckon that I could get a pretty good student demo going on Monday when Rayman tries to move onto the site. If nothing else, we can embarrass the bastards."

"Rhian and I have jobs to hold down," said James. "We can't just walk out."

"You could watch the site at night for us," said Mick. "Students have short attention spans, but I can probably keep the sit-in going for longer if we have night cover."

"Okay, Monday night then," said James.

"Why did you stop me telling Mick about the brooch?" asked Rhian, as she and Mick walked back to his flat.

"It has no provenance, Rhian. We could have got it from anywhere."

On Monday night, she and James turned up at Rodomon Street at nine. The road was lined with parked earthmoving equipment. A handful of protesters slouched by a banner.

"How did it go, Mick?" asked James.

"Ace, mate, absolutely ace. We sat in front of the machines, preventing them coming on site, waved placards, and generally made a complete nuisance of ourselves. The local press turned out and even the Standard. Someone had tipped them off." Mick blew on his fingers with mock modesty. "Rayman himself turned up in the end to shake his fist at us. It was glorious. All you two have to do is watch the place until morning. We'll be back then."

"Sure," said James. "They seem to have given up and gone home for the night."

"You two lovebirds have a quiet night," said Mick, with a stage leer.

Rhian found it impossible not to laugh. She and James waved them off, and then they were alone. They wandered around the wasteland for a while. The moon came up, casting strange shadows across the site. Its reflection rippled in the water. Rhian shivered; the air was cold this close to the canal, despite the season. James noticed and took her back to the hut. James hauled an airbed from his rucksack, and Rhian pulled a sleeping bag out of hers.

"I hate blowing these things up," said James. "I always get light-headed. Fortunately, I have a cure for that."

He produced a bottle and two plastic cups.

"I think you will find it a cheeky little wine, with the merest hint of cinnamon, apple and old ashtray.

This was the finest beverage that the supermarket boasted for less than three-pound fifty."

I'm sure it'll be lovely," said Rhian.

They shared it watching the city through the open door, enjoying the wine and each other. Rhian was quite drowsy when they went to bed, but sleep eluded her. James dropped off immediately. The city seemed so close; sound carried easily through the flimsy wood of the hut. She catnapped until something woke her up. She lay listening, wondering if she had dreamed the sound, but it came again, the chink of a bottle kicked along the ground. There were also voices.

She shook James.

"What is it?" he asked, sleepily

"There's someone out there," she said.

"Stay here while I go and look," he said.

She followed him, of course.

Five boys stood outside. One of them had a can in his hand, and she smelled petrol.

"So a couple of snotty students are still here. Rayman will be pleased. He fancied making an example of someone," said the lout at the front. "We will have some fun after all."

"A few more minutes and they would have been fricasseed student," said the one with the can. The others laughed.

Rhian moved, changing her silhouette against the moonlight, attracting attention.

"One of them's a girl," a voice said.

"So she is. We will definitely have fun then," the lout said.

"Run, Rhian," said James, giving her a shove. He charged straight at the gang. James hit the lout in the face. James was a big man and the lout went down with a thud.

Rhian couldn't move. She couldn't think. She was so scared for James.

James was trading blows with three of them now. Two of the gang grabbed him. The gang leader was back on his feet. He had an iron bar in his hand.

Rhian watched it in slow motion. The bar swung high before slicing into James' skull. There was a crunch like a plastic toy crushed by a hammer, and James fell, blood spraying from his head.

Rhian threw herself at the lout, screaming. Her nails raked his face.

"Bloody bitch," he said and hit her in the mouth with his fist, knocking her to the ground.

"He's dead," said a ganger, examining James's body. "His skull's all squishy."

"Then she has to go as well," said the leader. "We don't want no witnesses."

Rhian's blouse was torn. Blood from her cut lip dripped down her front onto the Celtic brooch. It gleamed in the moonlight and soaked up the blood, like a sponge. The silver brooch pulsed red light. It burned against her skin.

Cramp seized her muscles. The pain made her gasp. She couldn't scream. She couldn't even breathe. Her very bones ached. Her teeth and mouth were pulled outwards. The moonlight shuddered, and what little color that was left in it bleached away. The world was monochrome, but the world smelled; it was alive with thousands of shades of scent. She heard everything, from the breathing of the gang members to the cars on the distant M4. She howled with pleasure at the beauty of the city.

She rolled over onto her feet and stood up. She smelled fear; the gang reeked of terror. She chuckled deep in her throat, but it came out as a growl. Her mate lay still. She loped over to him, and she licked his face. James' head lolled. Blood oozed out of his broken skull. The gang backed away from her. One of them held metal in his hand. She could smell her mate's blood on it.

The wolf did not intellectualize; the wolf acted. She gathered her legs under her and leaped. The prey backed away, but her front paws struck his shoulders. He prodded ineffectually at her. The iron bar bounced unnoticed off the packed muscle in her shoulders. She smashed him to the ground with her body weight. Her jaws descended on his face and she bit hard, tasting the rich flavor of hot blood. The lout screamed, the sound fading into a gurgle.

A ganger sobbed and ran. The wolf chased running prey. She brought him down in three bounds, and her jaws snapped his neck as if it were made from balsa wood. The last three stayed together for protection. Prey often chose the illusory safety of numbers. She prowled around them, forcing them into a closer and closer huddle. She howled and leaped in among them, jaws tearing flesh and crunching bone. She tasted blood, so much blood.

The sheets were laundered stiff, and the room smelled of antiseptic. She opened her eyes.

"You're supposed to ask where you are," a woman in white said. "It's traditional."

"This is a hospital, and you're a nurse," said Rhian.

A parade of doctors examined and prodded her. She felt empty. Why didn't she feel anything? The nurse persuaded her to bathe and then gave her a ghastly nightdress to wear. James would have laughed to see her in it. That was when she cried.

"The police would like to interview you. You don't have to see them if you don't want to," said the nurse.

"I can't avoid them forever," said Rhian. "Let's get it over with." The brooch lay comfortingly cold between her breasts.

A CID detective and a woman constable interviewed her.

Rhian ran through the events of the night.

"And you can't remember anything after they hit you?" asked the detective.

"Not until I woke up in here," said Rhian. She looked the detective straight in the eye.

"Did you see any dogs?" asked the detective.

"I don't recall any," said Rhian. "Why do you ask?"

"The gang were killed by dogs, after—" The detective stopped.

"After they killed James." Rhian finished the sentence for him.

"I'm sorry," the detective said.

"I'm very sleepy," Rhian said. "The sedatives, you know." She shut her eyes.

"That's enough for now," said the nurse. She pushed the police out the door.

Rhian pretended to be asleep, but she could hear them clearly.

"We may as well go," said the detective.

"We can't leave it at that," said the constable. "That girl was found stark naked and covered in blood. She was raped."

"And whom do we charge?" asked the detective. "The scrotes who did it are dead, and, by God, they paid. Why rake it all up if she can't remember?"

"But what about Rayman?" the constable asked "He gets away scot free, does he?"

"There's no evidence against him that would make a charge stick," said the detective. "He attends the same lodge as the Chief Superintendent."

"I wonder why we can't find the dogs?" said the constable.

"They must have been bloody big, rottweilers or something. They will be covered in blood as well. They'll turn up. Those idiots must have brought attack dogs with them. That girl was lucky that she was unconscious when the dogs went wild."

The detective's voice faded into the distance. Rhian took from under her pillow the scalpel that she had stolen on her way back from the bathroom. Rolling up the sleeve of her nightdress, she carefully cut her arm, welcoming the stinging pain.

The clouds cleared, and moonlight flooded London. The sun would soon dominate the sky, but for the moment Morgana the moon goddess ruled. The pub and restaurant crowd had long gone home, but the nightclubs were only just starting to empty. Rhian felt the silver moonlight on her skin.

Rayman was arguing with a woman who slapped his face. She stormed off, her high heels clicking on the concrete car park floor. He adjusted his tie and walked toward a Mercedes. Rhian stepped out in front of him.

"What?" he said. "You seem to have lost your clothes, girly." He leered at her.

Rhian stood silently, watching him.

"Cat got your tongue?" he asked, coming closer. "Wait a minute. I know you from the coroner's court. You cost me a fortune, girly, you and your stupid friends. What are you up to now, you stupid bint?"

Rhian studied him unemotionally. Her beautiful, lovely James had been killed because of this shallow, greedy, worthless man. She showed him the razor in her right hand and drew it slowly across her left arm, adding another cut to the parallel scars that already disfigured her skin.

"You mad bitch," he said. "Kill yourself for all I care."

She pressed the blood against the brooch. She intended just to scare him, and it might have stopped at that if he had stood his ground, but he ran.

The wolf did not intellectualize; the wolf hunted fleeing prey.

OPUS NO. 1

Barbara Nickless

"ALEX, he's playing your favorite." My lover moved closer in our private box. "Chopin! Isn't that the "

I smiled and placed a finger to my lips. The cadenza whispered past, a scintillation, and I leaned forward in delight.

She tapped me lightly on the forearm in protest but returned her attention to the stage.

Outside, shadows gathered. These shadows didn't move with the failing sun, but merged into pools of Stygian darkness. After some hesitation, they surged toward the orchestra hall, intent and swift, whispering my name.

A thread of unease wove through my enjoyment of the pianist. I tilted my head, listening to something other than the nocturne.

She noticed. "Alex?"

Now I looked at her. Her blonde hair gleamed in the soft lights from the stage. Her warm skin smelled of lavender and musk. Her perfume was a whiff of the wilds, and I missed the wilds.

She raised an eyebrow.

"It's nothing." I reached for my coat. "A bit of indigestion. I'll take a taxi and call you later."

"Don't be silly. If you're sick, I'm coming too. Daniel can drive us both home."

"I need some fresh air."

"That's usually what a man says when he's leaving a woman for good."

I bent and kissed her. "Later, love."

At the door I hesitated and looked back. She hadn't turned to watch me. Angry. Hurt. I blew a kiss she would never see.

I let myself out of the box, ran down the red-carpeted stairs, and shoved open the door to the lobby. By the window, I hesitated.

Through the glass, the faraway darkness considered me. It was a singular gloom that I could singularly appreciate.

The door closed behind me, and the *forte* section of the nocturne plummeted to the hush of *sotto voce*.

"Call a taxi for you, Mr. Smith?" the doorman asked. "Looks like a storm is coming."

"No, thank you, John. I enjoy the wind."

"Good evening, then, sir."

Outside, a swirl of dust pirouetted on the sidewalk. The street was empty, one of those moments of quiet occasionally visited upon Fourth Street in the early hours of the evening.

The wind rose suddenly, howling down the avenue. It yanked at my coat and threw grit in my eyes. Leaves needled my skin like tiny, golden wasps. The shadows deepened where they crouched between the automobiles and lurked among the buildings.

Perhaps the taxi would have been a good idea.

I strode quickly along the brick exterior of the concert hall, eager for home. But at the alley, I paused. A faint light, a glow of pearl, shone deep in the passage that ran along the concert hall.

A child's sobs trembled on the night air. I hurried down the pathway.

A small girl crouched near the brick wall. A velvet

dress peeked from beneath her navy blue wool coat. Her patent leather shoes were dull with dust, and the wind had tugged her short red curls loose.

"Elise." I recognized the little girl who had moved into the apartment below mine a week ago. I'd never seen her parents. Only Elise, watering the flowers on the balcony and sometimes dancing to unseen music the way children and madmen do.

She looked up. Tears sparkled on her thin face. "Are you the one who made me come outside?"

"No, Elise. I'm your neighbor. Upstairs. The one with the bonsai trees on the railing."

Her lip trembled. "I've never seen you."

Of course not. "I'm one of the good guys."

"You're supposed to say that."

I studied her with new appreciation. The light that hung about her was too faint to be seen in the daylight. That was my excuse for not noticing before that she wasn't wholly mortal.

"But in my case it's true." I held out my hand. "Were you at the concert?"

"Yes."

"And something made you come outside?"

She nodded. "Something in the shadows."

"You can sense it?"

"I heard it. When I went to use the bathroom." She let me pull her to her feet.

"Where are your parents?"

"Mother's inside, listening to the pianist. She thinks I'm in the bathroom. But the shadow-sound was so lovely at first. I had to come outside and see." She looked up at me with light green eyes, witch eyes. "Something magic is coming, isn't it?"

"Yes."

"And not all magic is good, is it?"

"Some of it is very bad."

"Are you the only grownup who knows about it?" She screwed up her face. "The only one who knows about *them*?"

"Are you the only child?"

For a moment we stared at each other in something between fear and delight. I'd been alone for so long, and now here was someone with a touch of Faerie.

She must have wondered what it was all about.

I tucked her hand in mine. "Let me take you back inside the concert hall. You can stay with your mother until the end of the program. By then the darkness will be gone."

"You think it's you they're after."

I shrugged, but she shook her head.

"It won't do any good, for me to go inside. They're after me, too."

"How do you know?"

"Because they said my real name. The name I use in my dreams. Not even my mother knows that name."

Could a seven or eight-year-old guess at the power of one's true name?

Only one with more than a little bit of Faerie about her.

I glanced toward the end of the alley. The dusk had darkened unnaturally to a midnight blackness. "I'll take you to my apartment. You'll be safe there. But we'd better hurry."

She clutched my hand more tightly, stumbling next to me as we hurried along the alley and onto the street. The hairs on my neck rose. Even in mortal guise, my long strides were too much for Elsie. I took deep breaths and made myself walk more slowly, forcing down a quivering urge to shape-shift into a swifter form.

We had a little time, I thought.

We crossed the street to the next block. I glanced over my shoulder. The shadows had swallowed half the road. Street lights and window displays shone like ships' lights through thick fog. A pedestrian walking his dog stepped from neon into shadow and disappeared. I wanted to cry a warning, but I knew that he wouldn't see the shadows or be harmed by them.

Elise's hand sweated in mine.

I bent to place my face close to hers. "What if I carry you?"

She nodded and when I knelt, she clambered onto my back. I could have changed into a swiftly charging horse, and magicked her into forgetting the entire trip home. But something in me protested. A spell would leave her confused and in pain. I would use magic only if the shadows got close enough to strike.

I leaned forward.

"Hang on."

Half a block from our apartments I stopped, gasping for air. I expected trouble, but the building soared serenely in the blue-black night.

Elise gave a little cry.

Something burned against my heels.

I grasped Elise's ankles and sped forward, more wind than man. We were part of a whispering breeze that slipped us past the doorman before he knew we were there. I shoved the door closed behind us.

"Mr. Smith!" Thomas straightened his uniform coat. "I didn't see you."

The pursuing shadows crested against the door. The charms I'd placed there a year earlier glowed a pale blue. Reluctantly, the shadows fell away, a receding wave.

"It's all right, Thomas. Elise and I were playing a little game."

I stood the girl on her feet, but she kept my hand.

"Are we safe?" she whispered as we moved toward the elevator.

"We're safe."

For now.

I made Elise hot chocolate while she used her cell phone to try to reach her mother.

"Mother keeps her phone off during the music. When I don't come back from the bathroom, she'll go into the lobby and try to call me. She'll also tell the man who works there to search everywhere and to call the police. But she won't really mean it, so he won't do it."

"Why won't she mean it? She must be worried."

"She's used to it. I wander off a lot. Mother says it's in my blood. Along with the bad thing."

"What bad thing?"

But the sound of Jane's voice echoed through Elise's phone. Her mother must have reached the lobby.

I checked the charms placed around the windows, wondering how long they would offer protection. A few days, perhaps, now that the shadows had found me.

I found a bag of miniature marshmallows, which I softened in the microwave and dropped into the chocolate.

Elise talked into the phone.

"I'm okay, Mommy. Yes. The man upstairs. Mr. Smith. I'll wait for you."

She hung up and sipped her chocolate, then wiped her mouth daintily with the napkin. "Will they be back?"

"Not tonight."

"Tomorrow night?"

"Possibly. But we're safe for now."

"Meaning not for always?"

I looked at her, trying to find the light that had surrounded her in the alley. But in the incandescent bulbs of the apartment, she looked as mortal as anyone else. Rather thin. And perhaps a bit pale, but that was understandable. "You'll be fine, once I move away."

"Where are you going?"

"To another city. Maybe another country."

"Will they still find you?"

"Yes. I'll just move again. I've done it many times."

"What are they?"

What to say? How much to reveal to this child with green eyes and a secret name? Perhaps she had faerie blood in her from some long-ago ancestor. It wasn't unheard of, as I very well knew.

"I call them the Old Ones. They have other names. They're one of the *tuatha*, which is an ancient word for tribe."

"Tribes? Like the Native Americans my teacher told me about?"

"Sort of."

"Is there more than one tribe?"

I glanced at the shelves around the room, crammed with books and journals and maps, every bit of research and detritus I had collected in order to find the tribes who practiced peace and love and beauty. "Once there were many. A very long time ago."

"But not any more?"

"I'm afraid not."

"What happened to them?"

I pressed my fingers against the heat of my untasted mug of chocolate. "They died."

"How come?"

"I'm not sure."

"Were they bad, too?"

"No. They weren't."

"Why are these Old Ones after you?"

"They want me to play music for them."

She pointed at the Steinway. "Is that your piano?"

"Yes."

"Will you play for me?"

Normally, I would have refused. But it had been years—years!—since I'd played for an audience. None of my lovers had ever heard me play, though all of them had pleaded and teased. None of my neighbors, either, for I soundproofed my walls and closed the windows and placed the charms of silencing.

And none of my people. Not since that terrible war, when I'd realized the horror of my gift and fled, burying myself among mortals, denying myself immortality, suffering the misfortunes only mortals can suffer.

I sat at the Steinway Grand, pushing my tuxedo tails out of the way and poising my right foot over the damper pedal, the left over the *una corda*.

My fingers pressed into the opening notes. The

Steinway returned rich tones as I played *legatissimo*, blending one note into the other like pulling a bow on a cello.

War, violence. I knew Liszt didn't intend that. The Hungarian Rhapsody No. 2 was a piece of joy, a delight of the composer with his country's native songs.

I moved into the *friska*, struggling to keep my fingers gentle. The tremendous speed of the piece offered me no challenge. The lightness terrified me. A trickle of sweat loosed itself from my scalp and rolled past my ear. Under my hands, the Rhapsody became a eulogy to war, an ode to bloodshed.

But Elise felt none of my angst. When I was done, she clapped with delight. "That's the clown music!"

"What?"

"That's what they always play at the circus when the clowns come out."

I looked at her. "I've never been to the circus. I don't know how to play for clowns."

"You'll have to go, then."

"It won't help. I know only how to play war music."

"I bet it will. Haven't you heard about the kittens?"

"What kittens?"

"The ones in the experiment. They grew up where everything had lines that only went from side to side. The ones like the mountains against the sky."

"Horizontal."

"Yes! The kittens had to live like that for weeks. Then the scientists put them in a regular room. Guess what happened?"

"I can't imagine."

"They ran into everything that went up and down. They couldn't see the watchacallem lines."

"The vertical."

"Right. They could only see what they were used to seeing."

My hands played the opening notes of the *friska*. Could one learn to *think* vertically?

Someone pounded on the door. "Elise! Elise!"

I pushed back the piano bench, walked across the polished floor and opened the door.

She stood in the hallway.

My blood ran hot, then cold, and I staggered against the wall.

I knew why the shadows had come.

Jane didn't recognize me, of course.

Her red hair was shorter than I recalled. Faint lines tracked the skin at the edges of her eyes and mouth. Her eyes held a new stillness. But her features were as fine as in my memories of her, her skin like the petals of an ivory orchid.

I'd made love to her on a night long ago. Duty had driven me forth to sire a half-mortal child and deliver it to the warring tribe of Faerie.

But I had fallen in love with Jane even as I convinced her to love me.

After our single night together, I'd stolen her memories and fled, putting as much distance between us as I could. When the Old Ones came after me, I didn't want them to find her.

Deliver a child to war and darkness for all eternity? What father could do that to the child of the woman he loved?

I abdicated my role as war minstrel. Defected to the world of mortals, leaving both love and hatred behind.

But Beethoven had been playing on the radio that night. *Für Elise.* I'd commented on it, whispered the name in her ear. She must have held that one memory against everything else and named the child Elise.

Now she barely gave me a glance before pushing past me into the apartment.

"Elise!"

Her voice was sharper than I remembered. What had become of my once-joyous Jane? Had my betrayal, still buried deep in her psyche, taken the heights from her? Had I taught her to think horizontally?

Or was I giving myself too much credit?

My gaze drank in the graceful fall of her feet, the stir of her hair at the nape of her ivory neck, her straight, taut back.

A glimpse of gold at her throat showed me she still wore the necklace I'd left with her.

Oh, God. Jane.

Elise ran to her. "Mother!"

"Baby, why'd you leave me?" Jane set the girl away from her and frowned. "What made you go outside?"

"When I went through the lobby I heard music from outside. It was very pretty."

Jane took Elise's hand and faced me. "She's always been like that. Can't say no to any kind of song. The wind. The birds. Thank you so much for taking care of her."

"My pleasure."

Elise stopped at the door and tugged on her mother's hand. "Mr. Smith, will you teach me to play the piano?"

That night I poured myself a giant snifter of brandy and prowled the apartment. I was surrounded by the flotsam of a life lived through possessions because I could allow myself nothing else. Persian rugs on the floor, Rembrandts on the wall. Wedgwood crystal and pewter plates and Chinese porcelain. The Steinway. I took them with me every time I fled, leaving behind friends and lovers.

I brushed my hands along the keys in the upper register, creating a delicate tinkle that wafted through the four-room suite.

Clowns. Despite the soreness of my heart, despite the longing for Jane that had arisen again when she stood at my door, I almost laughed.

Liszt, you rascal. How had I not managed to find your humor before? It was there in the tripping grace notes, the marked accents, the rapid staccato. You'd even written it in one place. *Piano scherzando.*

Tentatively, I played the opening measures of the *friska*. But the notes were weak rather than graceful, pale instead of sweet.

Commanding myself to be patient, I moved my hands to the bass keys, shaped my fingers for A-minor. I played the scale in the Russian pattern, and then the cadences, building myself for the composition I had begun after I left Jane.

My Opus No. 1.

Jane, Jane.

A-minor wouldn't serve me. The melancholy notes moved past sorrow and into something darker. Suddenly I was playing a Requiem. Mozart's, arranged for piano.

I slammed my hands on the keys, drawing forth a discordant sound, bringing a bitter, warmonger's smile to my face. Another chord, and another, and a shape began to take form. Black shadows stretched across a battlefield. Bodies crumpled everywhere, bearing stricken faces, horrified eyes, and terrible, terrible wounds plucked at by carrion crows.

I pushed myself away from the Steinway and buried my face in my hands.

I had been raised to inspire the troops. To turn idle thoughts to war. To harden hearts and sharpen blades and strengthen fists. In the darkness of the Old Ones, I labored like Vulcan at his forge.

Seeding black flowers of war, blooms of disease, whole forests of misunderstanding.

But then I'd been sent forth to create a child. A child with my gift for music, but whose genes would add a mortal flair. After all, who better to compose the music of death than those who must—by their nature—die?

I tossed down the rest of the brandy and resumed my prowling. Outside, the shadows retreated. Waiting. Gathering strength.

The Old Ones were on my trail, and for the first time in eight and a half years, I thought they might get me.

I drank more. I plunged into the kind of stupor I had not visited since I left Jane.

But through that stupor, one thought chased me like a hound of hell, demanding that I turn and face it, deal with it, live or die with it.

I was the only one who could save Elise.

Sunshine poured through the south-facing windows of my apartment.

The hammering of my heart separated itself from the beating in my head and revealed itself to be the sound of someone pounding at the door.

I rolled over, dragged myself to my knees.

The knocking continued. "Mr. Smith?"

"I'm coming, dammit." I found the couch, hauled myself upright, and staggered to the door.

Jane wore blue jeans and a black turtleneck and a determined expression.

"I'm sorry, did I wake you?"

"No, no, I was just—" I waved a hand airily toward the piano, "composing. Come in."

I pointed her toward a chair near the windows, where the sunshine could lie at her feet. I scooped up the brandy snifter and hurried into the kitchen.

"Coffee?"

"No, thank you, Mr. Smith. It's about Elise."

Her tone warned me that I might not like what followed. Abandoning my own need for coffee, I took a chair across from her. "She's a lovely girl."

"She is. Talented. Smart. And—" Her eyes finally met mine. "And she's dying."

"Dear God."

"She's in the hospital. She's been sick for months. Early this morning she collapsed. Last night's excitement was too much for her."

"But there must be something they can do!"

"They've tried everything."

Jane must have seen the horror on my face. Where I should have been comforting her, she suddenly reached across and took my hand. "She has time, still. Months! Perhaps as much as two years."

*　　*　　*

After Jane left, I found the footprint in the magic dust I'd scattered on my balcony. Leaning over, I saw the same immense prints on the faerie dust sprinkling Elise's balcony. In front of each pad, a deep impression of a claw.

The Old Ones had no need to rip me into pieces like Orpheus mourning his Eurydice. They'd done a much more exquisite job by luring Elise into my path and then ensuring I would never see her grow. They were the cause of Elise's cancer. *They* were the bad thing in her blood.

There were two ways to save her. Send her into Faerie, where her disease would stop its fatal destruction. Cure her by letting them take her into the darkness, as Hades took Eurydice.

Or I could bargain with them. Go in Elise's stead.

Once they had me, they would make me play again. And there would be war.

In the late afternoon, Elise came home.

I stood at my window and watched Jane wheel her from the taxi into the apartment building. I watched to make sure no shadows leaped.

Just before she disappeared beneath the awning, she glanced up. She couldn't see me, but she waved anyway. I clenched the curtain.

Later, I sat at the piano, frowning at the keys.

What arrogance, to think that I could escape my fate. That I was destined for good, rather than evil. Did that make me evil, or merely Evil's instrument?

I rose and drew on my coat, prepared to make the rounds yet again to see that my charms still held. If Elise had months—maybe years!—then I would make sure she got them. I didn't dare leave her now. She was exposed, innocent, ripe for the taking. But I would give them a greater battle than they thought possible.

As I reached for the doorknob, I heard a tremendous crash in the hallway, followed by a scream.

I threw the door open and raced outside.

Jane lay huddled on the floor just outside the elevator. Beside her, one of the immense black urns had shattered into pieces.

I hurried down to her, but as I neared, I drew back in horror.

She lay curled into herself. Still alive, her left hand clutching feebly at the rug, her right hand pressed to her throat. Blood seeped through her fingers. She looked at me with dull gray eyes.

In the spilled dirt from the urn, I saw a vast paw print.

For a moment I couldn't move. Ice crystallized around my heart, and my mind became a thing detached.

"Mr. Smith," she croaked.

I sped forward and dropped to my knees beside her, pressing my handkerchief to her throat.

"Ah, Jane. What have I done?"

Her eyes showed more worry than fear. "Elise . . ."

"I won't let anything happen to her. I swear it."

The blood soaked through the cloth and poured onto my hands. It ran past and drenched my coat. It puddled in vast sheets on the floor around me, crawled in viscous streams toward the elevator.

Enchanted. They'd enchanted her blood to pour like a river through her wound. Even as I watched, she grew pale and luminous as a tropical orchid. The blood diminished to a drip, then stopped altogether.

She died in my arms.

In the distance, sirens wailed.

The elevator door opened and Elise stepped out. "Mother!"

"Elise, turn around. Go down to your apartment and stay there. I'll join you as soon as I can."

I'd placed my strongest charms around Elise's door and windows. If she were to be safe anywhere, it would be in her own apartment.

"But—"

"Trust me, Elise. You'll be safe there, but only there."

"Mother!"

"It's what your mother would want you to do."

Trembling, Elise turned her back but made no move toward the elevator. Her thin shoulders shook with her sobs.

"Aren't there good tribes?" she whispered. "There must be good tribes. I've dreamed about them. You've got to learn to play for the good faeries."

"There aren't any good faeries anymore. Anyway, it doesn't matter. I can't play music that way. I've tried."

"It's like the kittens. Remember? You have to think differently."

The police took me down to the local station in handcuffs.

I couldn't blame them. I'd been found holding Jane's dead body, my clothes covered with her blood. In my grief, I'd had no time to magick myself with a manifestation of innocence.

They put me in a small, green-painted room with a mirror which I guessed was actually two-way glass, and a metal table with two chairs. The room smelled of sweat and hormones. A detective came in and introduced himself, asked me a lot of questions. It was clearly his role to convince me I couldn't escape my guilt.

He knew nothing of true guilt.

I waived my Miranda rights, and after a time he tired of my protests of innocence and stomped from the room.

Impatient, I paced. What was happening to Elise while I was caught here? If the Old Ones had breached my outer charms, how much longer would the inner spells hold?

If I could have saved Elise by confessing, I would gladly have gone to jail. But to send her into the darkness while I slowly died in the light? Impossible.

I could not condemn Elise even to save her life.

When the detective returned, he was much subdued. He said my neighbors had corroborated my story and that I was free to go.

"Just don't go far, Mr. Smith."

"No."

Only to the depths of hell.

The charms still held, but they had weakened in the
time I'd been with the police. I knew it was only a
matter of minutes—perhaps as much as an hour—
before they failed.

I lit all the candles and turned off the lights. In the
warm glow, I opened the windows and door and released the last of the charms protecting my apartment.
I sat at the piano and began to play. Opus No. 1, the
composer's first—and last—composition.

But it wasn't the Old Ones who arrived. It was
Elise.

"Keep playing," she commanded from inside the
door. "For me and my mother."

My fingers kept moving. "Go back downstairs,
Elise! They're coming."

"They'll come for me no matter where I am."

I touched on A-minor, the melancholy key. Always
my favorite. I glided through a cadenza, the notes
glimmering like pearls strung along the keys.

"That's too sad," she said.

In the corners, the shadows rustled.

"All the minor keys are sad."

"Then play another kind."

She sat next to me on the bench, her feet swinging
free. She was too small to reach the pedals.

From A-minor, up four half-steps to its related
Major, C.

"That's better," Elise said. "But it isn't right."

The dominant tone, then. Onto G-Major. I played
a few notes from Bach's fugue. Without knowing I'd
done it, I went back to the minor key.

Forms loomed inside the door, tall and sinister.
Cold like a breath from the dead soul of winter.

"Stop it!" Elise cried to me. "I saw you at the concert. I looked up and saw you in your box. You were
smiling. You were happy."

"I was."

"Then play what that man was playing."

So I played Chopin's Nocturne in C-Sharp Minor. A composition by a man who knew that the sorrow of night could be balanced by the sweet taste of moonlight. I played the sad tones with a richness and warmth that surprised me. *Tenerezza.* Tenderness.

The creature by the door stepped forward and *blew*, hard and sharp and long like the wind off a glacier. The candles sputtered and went out.

Elise's hand pressed against my arm.

I kept playing. Into the brief *animato*, I captured a touch of abandon.

But the darkness crept closer.

"The clowns, Mr. Smith," Elise whispered.

On to the *friska*. Light and gentle. Up, then down along the full range of the keyboard. Faster and faster. Every bit of concentration to keep my fingers from tripping over each other.

Beside me, Elise clapped her hands and laughed. "Those are the clowns. Can't you see them?"

"Yes. Yes!"

I segued into my own composition. My Opus No. 1. This time in E-Major.

Basso, then swelling upward, a sparkling sound that reached toward the stars. A noise like a chorus of birds, the wind in the trees, the rumble of waves, pale moonlight resting on the river bank.

A man in love.

The candelabra on the floor beside me burst into flame. In its gleam, I watched my hands in the reflection on the fall board, dancing, dancing.

I played for hours while outside, the world turned gray. I played through fear and past exhaustion, driving back the darkness, composing for my lost love. And for our child.

The shadows shattered like ice. Gold and silver ribbons of light swirled across the floor and tossed the shards into the air. Slivers of darkness vaporized in the sudden breeze that made the draperies dance.

Elise jumped to her feet.

The room filled with a hundred winged figures, tall and slender. They smiled on us, and the air vibrated with their song.

"You've done it," Elise whispered, as sunlight streamed through the windows.

The light surrounding her blossomed as I took her hand.

REGENCY SPRITE

Dave Freer

"P SST!"
Either I was being attacked by a leaky gasbag,
or someone was trying to attract my attention from
the dark alley to my left. A sinister alley, you might
say, in every sense of the word. Perhaps it was a snake
with a speech impediment! At this time of night, it
seemed likely, or at least to anyone who had had a
passing-through acquaintance with as many pints of
strong ale as I had had.

It could, of course, be someone who wished me to
step into a place even darker than the vague lamplight
of the mist-swirled street to relieve me of my money-
bag. Tch. There are people with hopeless delusions
everywhere, even in sinister alleys that smell like uri-
nals. How could I so dishearten a fellow creature? If
I'd had any more money I would never have left that
purveyor of my refuge from the vile duplicity of all
the female race. I would have stayed on until I passed
into happy oblivion. I lurched peacefully on.

"Psst!" The leak in the gasmain was more voluble
now, as if trying to convey a sense of urgency.

I ignored it.

And then, by low cunning, an uneven paving stone
made a totally unprovoked attack on my toes (the
cowardly things will do this, but only when you have

drunk more than sixteen pints of strong ale and fair amount of blue ruin). I sprawled into the gutter, which was a good thing, as I felt at home there these days. More at home than in my own home on Grosvenor Square, to be honest. That was merely a trap filled with lost dreams.

The gas leak seemed to believe that I had fallen simply so that it could have the opportunity to go "pssst" at me again.

And I had obviously misguessed its ambition to knock me down and then attempt to rob my now empty pouch, because I was down, an easy victim for the most puny dacoit, and it had made no such attempt. Instead, it hissed at me yet again.

In exasperation I addressed the narrow slit of darkness. "I have no interest in your sister, no matter how fair, young, or clean she is. Nor do I have money to buy anything illegal with. So you can stop making that noise at me. You are disturbing my rest. Go away."

"You stupid human!" whispered someone from the alley, pure exasperation oozing out of the words like Trinity students out of the gin-sluiceries after Oxford boat night. "Do you think that if I could get away from here on my own I would be asking a drunken sot for help?"

There was something undeniably feminine about that whispered accusation. That in itself was enough to irritate me. And I was inured to the bleating of people about my state, anyway. "I have no interest in helping anyone leave this charming locale. I'm happy here, happy for now, anyway, and you are disturbing my feeling of well-being," I said, composing myself for slumber upon the lovely soft curbstone.

She flung a fishhead at me. "You fool," she whispered crossly, and accurately. "You'll be run over by a hackney carriage. Or the mohocks will find you and rob you. They were prowling earlier. Keep quiet, crawl in here, and get this thing off me."

"I have nothing left for them to steal. And a hackney carriage would be a welcome release. Especially from your hissing," I said loftily.

"I'll curse you with a lifetime's misfortune," she hissed.

"Too late," I said, turning my head away.

"I'll give you wealth beyond your dreams of avarice."

"I have already had that. A lot of good it did me," I said bitterly.

I would have been quite content if she had not begun to sob quietly. Even fishheads don't worry me that much.

So I crawled into the darkness. The noisome darkness. With a tumble of spilled garbage and more fishheads, by the bouquet. To think that I'd once been a rather fastidious soul.

Her arm was trapped under the edge of the overturned garbage-bin. At her size, not even all her strength and the beating of her ragged filmy little wings could shift it. The little fey face was screwed up in pain. "Get me out of here," she said, "before the cat comes back again."

I lifted the heavy steel rim off her easily enough. But even in this poor light it was clear enough to see that her arm hung at a strange angle. It needed attention. And her wings too were tattered, perhaps by her encounter with the cat.

It wasn't every day that I encountered a denizen of Faerie here in the grimy streets of London, not even after five years of Prinny.

"What are you doing?" she hissed, between clenched little teeth, as I picked her up in both hands. "Put me down. I've got to get after them."

"I am taking you out of this alley, to find one of those hackney carriages. Then I'll splint your arm. Then I shall probably lie down and sleep off this dream," I said with as much dignity as I could muster.

"Ah!" she gasped as she tried to move, her little face ghostly pale. "No. I have to catch them." She moved. And screamed, despite obviously trying not to.

"You asked me to help. Now I am going to help you. And you need that arm splinted." I put my hand inside my coat. "Now shut up and keep still unless you want to end up in an iron cage at a freak show."

I tried to walk as carefully as I could, wishing that my head was clearer and feet were steadier. A hack clattered towards us out of the mist tendrils as if it had been called, with the steady clip-clop of hooves. "My good jarvey," I called out, suddenly painfully aware of the empty state of my money pouch. "I need a cab to Grosvenor Square."

The coachman lifted his whip. And then, perhaps because of the address, or my accents pulled his horse to a halt. " 'You got any money, Guv?" he asked suspiciously. "Cos I'll see the rhino up front, see."

"Er. I was set upon by mohocks . . ."

He shrugged. Raised his whip to give the horse a tap. "No fare, no ride. I been in taken by you toffs afore."

"Pick up a fishhead and show it to him," whispered a weak little voice from inside my coat.

I could at least throw it at him. And convince him that haddock's eyes were mutton pies perhaps . . . I bent over and picked up the fishhead.

It glistened golden.

"I seem to have found one of my coins," I said, holding it out. The jarvey's whip hand was arrested in midstroke.

"That will do nicely, sir. And where would you be wishful of me to be taking you? It'll be payment in advance, o'course."

I gave him my address and the fishhead. "Keep the change," I said, doing my best to alight one-handed.

As the cab rattled across the cobbles my fuddled mind wondered just what I should do now. My knowledge of medicine was slightly less than my knowledge of faerie-folk, which in turn was greater than my knowledge of females. The little fay was both of the latter. Still, something told me that this was not a case to summons Dr. Knighton to attend.

*   *   *

Through the pain Annwn also tried to think rationally. It had been pure misfortune that the dogs had knocked over the canister of the accursed metal. Still . . . they had saved her from the cat, when they'd returned. And having someone of the old blood come along to rescue her, even if the fool did not realize it, was a piece of rare luck. He was, she reluctantly acknowledged, quite right. An injury inflicted by cold iron was always serious. She could forget what she had planned. The problem was going to be getting back, injured as she was, let alone following Prince Gwyn. The doors between here and faerie were few nowadays, and well guarded. It wouldn't matter how she'd got here, the way back would be perilous. In the meanwhile, every bump they went over hurt. She gritted her teeth and wished for an end to the journey, at least. The human was doing his best to help. It was right that she gave him some form of repayment, she thought, although in the fashion of humans he probably wouldn't appreciate it. In the old days Faerie had tried to shape human society, interbreeding with the noble houses. When failure became too apparent, they'd settled for shutting themselves off as much as possible. Now, it seemed that some—like Gwyn—were trafficking here. Just thinking about him hurt her. Left her with a conflict of emotions. It had been jealousy that brought her here in the first place. Now, knowing the truth, she felt betrayed and abused. Prince Gwyn had not courted her for love.

Still, she did understand his motivation now, even if she would never forgive him. As humans were reputed to be fascinated by the fey, there was a counterattraction, a curiosity about the world above. Most of Faerie looked long and often at the world above. Even a child could create the window-spells required for that. Then there was the food . . . there were some things that magic was curiously unsatisfactory for. Children were told that the food and drink of the land above was poison, or that it would bind them there to the dull earth. Annwn, guiltily, knew that it was not true. Desire might bring them back, but not magic

*   *   *

The hackney carriage pulled up at the door of an elegant Palladian mansion in that most desirable of addresses, Grosvenor Square. I could never look at the house, the home we had dreamed we would fill with laughter and children, without anger. Marianne had insisted on the address. Only Grosvenor Square would make her happy, and to make her happy I would have sold Redmund. I would have given her anything, then. Deep down I knew that I still would. Well, anything but what she said that she now wanted. That I leave London. And her.

I knew that I was not man to play "Cuckolds, all's awry." My pride ran too deep, even if she'd left me to be the mistress of a Royal Duke, and it was the *on dit* of whole town.

The little fay in my arms stirred uncomfortably. She was so frail, and I must have tensed on seeing the house. I shook the feeling away from me and alighted from the cab. I had to be gentle. Kitty would have laughed at me and told me I was too gentle to be good at treating hurts. It was true enough. Even the sight of a small injury always made me feel sick. Kitty had always been the one who did the treating of injuries—from bandaging cut knees to splinting birds wings. She'd been as close as a sister to me once, before I had told her that I was betrothed to Marianne. I hadn't seen her since that . . . scene. Looking back now, she'd been right. And if anyone was the right person to take the fay to . . . it would be her.

Kitty . . . Now that I'd thought of her, it seemed obvious. Well, I was still fairly castaway. That did tend to make one oblivious of certain facts, like her stepfather.

"Jarvey," I said, with as much dignity as I could muster, having just staggered against my own gatepost—which, with alarm, I realized had iron rails, a circumstance I never noticed before. "Wait. I will need you to transport me . . ."

"Ho, you'll not find a place to sell you more blue-

ruin this side o' Tothill fields at this time o'morning,"
said the hackney driver with a snort.

"I need to go to a posting house, not drinking,"

He looked me over. "That'll be a first, for a flash
cove like you."

His comment stung, but it was not without accuracy,
so I left it at that and took her indoors, to a chaise
lounge in the second salon. The little thing had been
oddly still, but I was relieved to see that she was still
breathing. She opened her eyes. They were wide and a
little wild. "This is not a good place for me to be . . ."

"While I have to agree with you, it's unlikely that
any of my staff will have stayed up to see you here.
I'll need something to make a splint . . . and then the
best I can think of is a big bandbox. There's a swans-
down muff still, left from Marianne things . . ."

"There is an ill-wishing on this place. An
unhappiness . . ."

"That's true enough," I said sourly. "Lie there. I
have some sticking plaster, and I must look about for
something to use as a splint. Then we can be away to
someone better skilled than I."

She shook. "Be quick. It . . . hates women."

Well, my Aunt Seraphina had had just such humors.
Forever saying a place was augish or something. A few
people called her eccentricities fey, which had always
pleased her no end. She hadn't like the house either.
Marianne had, and that had been good enough for
me, then. An odd thought struck my still befuddled
brain: Perhaps a fay would be fey.

I found a roll of sticking plaster and some small
scissors. For a splint I looted Marianne's remaining
knicknacks. I found a very elegant oriental fan with
ivory canes that she used to flirt from behind, those
soft eyes peeping provocatively through sooty lashes
above it. I'd been too dazzled to read their true message then. I had been such a fool, I realized, ruthlessly
cutting the silk that held the canes together. I took it,
the large bandbox, and the muff to the green salon.

She wasn't there. Had it all been an illusion? A

strange product of too much drink? I stared hard at
the chaise lounge refusing to accept the evidence of
my own eyes. I'd carried her. Felt the weight of her.
I held the branch of candles higher. And then I could
see her still lying there, holding her injured arm. Her
little face was still pained and much too white, her
green eyes wide and fearful.

Glamor, I realized. Well, glamor or no, I had do
something about that arm. There wouldn't be any
brandy in the house, but some ratafia . . . I had alway
detested the stuff. Even drunk I didn't like the smell.
I went to fetch a decanter and returned. She wasn't
there, but now I knew I just had to look harder.

"Drink this," I said kneeling next to her, holding
the crystal glass of almond-scented liquor to her lips.
"No daylights."

It clattered slightly against her teeth as she tossed
it back. Belatedly I realized that she was actually
quite small.

The scent alone was heady. Earthly fruits steeped
in brandy flavored with almonds. Something for those
of the wealth and power of Faerie to sip. She'd tasted
it once. A gift from Gwyn—she'd thought him fabu-
lously generous at the time. Love had tinged that, as
pain did this time. It was so unmagically powerful that
it almost overwhelmed the pain of the human moving
her arm. Oddly, she could see that he was crying as
he wrapped the white carved canes—carved with an
almost elven delicacy—around her arm. He strapped
it in place, and gradually the pain of his handling
ebbed. His long white face with its high cheek-bones
and clean planes was almost a mirror for her agony.
He'd felt it. She knew, looking at him, what a curse
her kind had loosed on humans, mixing blood and
then deserting them to live with after-clap. Those of
Faerie knew how to block out such magics.

He stood up. Looked at his handiwork. "I think
that'll do. Now let's hope that the hackney cab hasn't
decided to lope off into the night. We'll need to get

your arm properly set, and there is only one person I can trust to do it."

Trust. Annwn knew that that was a rare and a precious commodity, and one Faerie had little of. Less now. They would see her as having betrayed the faith that the house royal had placed in her. They would not see it that she too had been betrayed. But right now she had to get out of this house. She stood up a little shakily. "Then let us go. Now."

"Steady. Unless you have a supply of fish heads, I'll need to find something to raise the wind with."

She blinked a little owlishly. Raised her good arm. The curtains began to flap and flames on the branch of candles danced wildly. "How hard a blow will you need?" she asked, an expression of faint puzzlement on her impish features.

"I meant my pockets are all to let. I'll have to spout something."

The ratafia was definitely affecting her. "I'll never fit in a pocket. Not even shrunk to my smallest." she blinked. "Spout? Like a whale-fish or a poet?"

For the first time in months my impecunious status embarrassed me. "Money. Gelt. I don't have any cattle in my stable any more or an ostler to hitch them up to my phaeton. Actually, I don't have the phaeton either. And I was thinking of transporting you in this bandbox."

"Cattle," she informed me loftily, "belong in a byre. I could call horses for you if you desire. It was one of the powers given me." She looked at the marble floor. "Only perhaps we should do it outside."

"I am surprised at your consideration for my house."

She shook her head. "It's the horses. They'd slip on this, and they don't like fire. Besides, there is an ill-wishing on this place. They might get hurt. Let us go." She'd swayed up onto her feet, into the hall, and was heading determinedly for the kitchen. I followed willy-nilly and turned her toward the front door.

It was a foggy predawn out there. It was also a street remarkably free of a hackney cab. That was probably just as well, as two gray horses were thundering down it toward us. Magnificent creatures. Lovely arched necks and clean lines. They also, to my eye, looked like they might want to kill us. But just before I was about snatch the bosky fairy away to safety, they stopped. They stood, still, barring the occasional restive toss of the head. She looked at her arm in irritation, her torn little wings fluttering vainly. "You will have lift me up onto her."

The horses were beauties . . . "But . . . what about saddles?"

She stamped her tiny foot impatiently. "Dawn comes closer. We must ride."

She didn't look as if she'd stay in the saddle anyway. "You're as drunk as a wheelbarrow."

"Don't be silly, wheelbarrows don't drink. Even barrows only drink souls. Throw me up!"

I was ready to cast up accounts myself, but I knew what she meant. So I lifted her. She threw a leg over the horse if it were something she did every day. Perhaps the Faerie did. It was certainly less than ladylike. I'd ridden bareback myself as a boy at Redmund—but not without a bit and bridle. "Up," she said, imperiously. Her steed stood more steadily than she had. I was still a bit foxed myself and nearly went over the far side of the horse. The mane that I clung to was oddly cold. I was no sooner up than the horse moved off rapidly, breaking into canter. "Yoicks! We're going the wrong way."

She turned her horse with consummate skill and nearly had me off onto the street. I would have fallen had it been anything but the easiest paced beast I'd ever straddled. "Whither?" She demanded. "They'll head for the sea if left to themselves."

"The White Horse Inn, in Fetter lane," I gasped.

"Just point. The names mean nothing to me," she said with a little exasperation.

Wild horses must have raced through half the streets of London that pale morning. I couldn't point very well or very often when it was all I could do to stay on the horse. And her steed tried to stay in the lead. They were like no earthly horses, seeming tireless.

"Slow . . ." I managed to say, when we'd just frightened a lamplighter dowsing wicks (no modern gas lamps in this part of town) out of several years of life.

"It wants scant time till dawn, and the horses must be away by then, back to the water."

"Close. We . . . better . . . go on foot. People about," I said pointing to a wide-eyed flowerseller, who had dropped her posies and was gaping through the foggy swirls.

"True." She halted her horse, and I alighted. I didn't quite fall, as I managed to clutch the neck on my way past. She leaped, graceful as a fairy . . . and landed, plainly jarring her arm. She winced in pain.

"I bid you go. Return to waters," she said to the steaming horses. They did not wait but were away, racing wraithlike through the fog towards the river.

"I'll have to hide you under my coat again," I said. "It'll be more difficult now that it's light. But we can't have people seeing you."

"Oh." She fluttered her wings and blurred slightly, expanding and changing.

Before me stood a young lady of the upper ten thousand, attired in a clinging pale primrose muslin overdress with little puff sleeves. She had a very fine double twist of pearls about her slim white neck and looked ready for an evening's dancing at Almacks. I suspected she even had vouchers for it in her reticule.

Glamor. I had forgotten that, even though she'd used in my house to hide in plain sight on the chaise lounge. "Do you think you could manage something a little more suited for traveling on a common stage?"

"Oh, " she said with just the hint of a pout. "I liked that." She blurred her clothing into a sensible frock of twilled cotton covered by a slightly worn pelisse. It was as well that the seamstresses and snyders of London did not see her do this, or those that did not die of shock would definitely have wanted to hang her.

The innyard was the usual bustle of mendicants and

street merchants, even at this time of day. I felt the
ghostly twitch of a pickpocket and wished the fellow
well. My pockets were still wholly to let, which could
just pose a problem as I had neglected to find anything
I could pawn. I'd become quite inured to that little
indignity. Still, my fey companion could conjure sover-
eigns from fish heads . . . which strangely enough I
didn't have any of, either. There was an outraged shriek
that quite distracted me from my perusal of the sellers
of paper twists of cobnuts. My youthful companion hit
someone—a pockmarked youth in a fawn frieze coat.
Hit him so hard that he fell over. By the way he was
doubled up and gasping, it was not a blow that Gentleman Jackson would have taught in his Saloon.

"Here! What's happening?" I demanded.

"He put his hand . . ." she said indignantly, glamor
briefly hazing.

The young pickpocket had not accounted for the
glamor, it would seem. It might have been his intent
to remove a purse from the pocket of her pelisse, but
he had touched on something more sensitive. I advanced
on him, and he scrambled to his feet, squirming away
through the gathering crowd. A comfortable countryman
bent down and picked up something the pickpocket had
dropped. It was a purse. Monogrammed. With faint
shock I recognized it. "This yours, little lady? That was
a capital hit, that."

I nodded. "She has learned some things from her
brothers. Mostly they are undesirable . . . but, well,
thank the kind gentleman nicely, young lady."

She bobbed him a little bow, but made no move to
take the red morocco purse.

It wasn't hers—but then I felt that I had some claim
on my dear absent's wife's property, and whatever was
in it, by courtesy of the man who had taken her from
me. "You'd better let me keep it."

I took the purse and opened it a little. "I'd better
check that your pin-money is intact," I said, "You
never can tell with these rogues." I was quite proud.
I felt that I was turning into one myself, especially

when I saw a generous roll of soft peeping out at me. "Come, let me get you some coffee after that nasty experience. Give me your arm."

"Well," I said, when we were out of earshot. "That was a lucky accident."

"There are no accidents. Not when someone has woven the fates as tightly as they have around you," she said tersely.

"I wish you would speak the King's English occasionally. Anyway, we have money now for us to travel post. We can hire a decent equipage and let you have more comfort for that arm. And also some coffee." I was beginning to desperately need coffee.

Coffee. Annwn looked at the dark liquid. It was a strange, bitter brew, oddly pleasing after the first few sips. She'd only taken those because it provided social cover. There was an odd weaving of spells about this man. Strange, dark and powerful. Yes, there was some of the old blood there, but since she'd been in his bespelled house, she suspected more. She was seeing part of the weave, not the whole cloth, she was sure.

The well-sprung carriage bowled along the postroad toward Bristol. Now that I was awake, sober, even if my head was not too happy to be with me, I wanted some answers. The little fay was, it seemed, less than willing to provide them.

"Just what are you doing here? Are there others of your kind I could return you to?"

She shook her head. "No."

It seemed she was reluctant to say any more. "I have to get you home," I said, wondering about the land of Faerie. "I cannot help if you will not help me."

"I don't know how to get home." She colored slightly. "It was . . . an accident." she bit her lip. "I was following someone. They . . . did some sort of magic, and I found myself in that stinking city of yours. I was trying to follow them when the dogs chased the cat, which upset the iron bin, which trapped me."

"Follow them? So they came here?"

She nodded.

"But why didn't you call them for help?"

She blushed fully now. "I was angry. I get very angry.
I . . . I was going to kill her. And him if I could."

"What?"

"Prince Gwyn. He . . . used me." A little tear fell from
her sooty lashes. "I didn't realize it right then. I thought
that I had caught them in a tryst. But it was to come here.
I understand now. It's . . . it's almost worse." She wiped
her eyes with the back of her hand and sniffed.

I offered her my handkerchief. She looked at in
puzzlement.

"For you to dry your eyes and blow your nose on,"
I explained.

"Oh." She took it and dried her eyes and . . . held
it away from her nose, looking at the fine mon-
grammed lawn. "It's too pretty for that. I've seen people use them though. We watch you, you know."

"You watch us?" I repeated, feeling idiotic.

She nodded, rubbing the fine stitches. "It is a simple
spell. Even a child can do it. And you humans are
strange and fascinating to us."

"You are strange and fascinating to us too. But I
mean the stories say that there used to be faerie
folk here."

"Once the line between the demesnes of Faerie and
here was a thin one. There were many places where mortals would stray across into our realm, and the fay would
come and sport in yours. But that is all over now."

"Why?"

She shook her head. "I cannot say."

There was something about that that piqued my attention. "Cannot? Or will not?"

She held her lip with her fine white teeth for a
while. "Both," she said eventually. "And I have failed.
I have betrayed my father's trust."

"I suppose I did that too," I said gently. "But my
father alway used to say 'no fences without a fall' . . ."

"If the king finds out that they came through our

demesnes, that I was blind in love enough to give the entry spells into the North March to a smuggler, it will be our heads that fall," she said grimly, and she turned to look out of the window.

We came at last to Tatcham, and as the coach rolled down the raked carriageway, through a neat avenue of young cypress trees, I wondered just how I was going to explain all this. Not to Kitty of course. Explaining anything to Kitty had alway been easy, except for my engagement to Marianne. But I had left rather precipitously last time. I sighed, seeing the great house. It had altered greatly from the comfortably shabby, slightly rundown place where I had run tame in my youth. There were new wings, and the facade had been cleaned. The grass was manicured. Plainly Lord Carandon's enterprises prospered. I was glad for Kitty's sake, but Tatcham . . . it had changed. It was no longer the refuge it had been when I was growing up. The little fay looked uneasy too.

I paid off the postillions, and we made our way up to great door. Plainly we had been seen, because before I could reach for the knocker it was opened.

"Master Arthur!" Wilkins beamed. I would never be Viscount Lord Redmund to him, but remained little Arthur Wolverly from across the water. In his mind, no doubt, I had muddy knees, and a fowling piece that I was not supposed to have touched for him to have cleaned and quietly returned to the gun room. "I will send one of the footmen to call Lady Catherine." He looked rather doubtfully at Annwn.

I didn't enlighten him. This affair was muddled enough. "From that I assume that she's in the stables as usual, Wilkins." Footmen! Tatcham had always been understaffed and falling to bits. "I know my way well enough." I should. The stables had been our play place, until Lord Carandon had informed me that his stepdaughter should no longer be in my company without a groom. Ha.

Besides, by speaking to Kitty down in the stableyard, I might avoid Carandon.

*   *   *

The woman's face lit up as she saw my human companion, and she dropped the foreleg she'd been examining. "Arthur!" She ran toward him, arms outstretched. And then she saw that he was not alone.

Coming to this place, seeing her from close up . . . It was clear now. Well, clearer anyway. The last person Annwn had expected to see was the woman who had been with Prince Gwyn. But all the pieces began to tie together now. Magic was like that. Everything interlocked. Especially when a dark one made such a working. They should never have been allowed to interbreed with humans. Throwbacks such as this were inevitable. And yet . . . Faerie had fought the nag-alfar before. Destroyed their lairs and torn down their castles. Annwn knew them, she knew their smell and their hatred of her kind. This woman was one of the alfar, the dark ones from the northern ice, but there was none of the reek of evil that normally came with them. Living among humans she would not have been raised to evil. The darkness was still there, of course. But . . . not released.

"Who is this?" the woman-alfar asked in a voice that would have frozen steam.

"I need your help with her, Kitty. She's hurt. You were the only person I could think of to turn to. The only person I could trust."

Annwn could see Kitty visibly thaw with the last word. Seeing another woman with him hurt her. And yet . . . she loved him enough to be willing to help.

"Ah, Redmund," said a cool voice from behind them. Turning, Annwn knew things had just become much worse. The doorway was filled by a tall slim man in a many-caped coat, with a whip in his hand—the man she'd seen with Gwyn and this woman back in Faerie. And just behind him stood Gwyn, attired for driving, like a human.

I saw Lord Carandon's whip flick out and the lash twist around Annwn . . . and her glamour vanished as it touched. I tried to move and found myself frozen just there.

"Father!" said Kitty, running forward.

"Stay back, my dear. I have her powerless. I have a series of little magnetized iron beads sewn into the lash for just this type of eventuality."

"But . . . that's *Arthur!*"

"She has him in her thrall, Catherine. A weapon for the evil they plan. I will be able, I hope, to lift the enchantment. In the mean time, Gwyn, I shall require a suitable glamour to get us across to my laboratory. I believe that we were not seen by any of the grooms?"

The man he called Gwyn looked as if he might be sick. But he shook his head. Kitty stood there, twisting a lock of her hair, looking as if she would burst into tears, as we were led away. I did not want to go, but I could no more resist than I could cry out.

Carandon's laboratory was on the second floor. As well as the arcana it was cluttered with, it also had a row of sturdy iron cages, perhaps intended for animals. Annwn was thrust into one of them. I was led to small room off the passage on the far side of the laboratory. Lord Carandon eyed me with disfavor. "Why did you decide to meddle in my affairs, Redmund? I thought you were safely away in London. I will have to dispose of you now." He paused, putting a slim white finger to his chin. "In some manner which will not excite comment from the outside world. I will have to think about it. Come, Gwyn. I see no occasion to delay our visit to town."

"How did she follow us?" asked Lord Carandon's companion, his voice nervous. "She's dangerous, Carandon. Dangerous to keep and dangerous to kill."

"My dear Gwyn," he said languidly, "leave dealing with you fey creatures to me. She is not without value to my work. You may take the compulsion off this one." They turned and left. The door locked, and I was left standing like a waxwork. The paralysis faded slowly, but it was to be some hours before I could move. And I was sure that crying out would bring no help.

The bars were cold iron, and the cage was just that. Bars all round. Annwn could not avoid touching them. They hurt. The darkness and the betrayal hurt more.

And then there was light. A branch of candles and the woman-alfar. Fury and hatred stirred in Annwn, almost eclipsing the pain. If she could get free of here, she would . . .

"Arthur trusted me." The woman was plainly both unhappy and afraid.

"He did," said Annwn, keeping her voice level. "He said you were the only person he could trust. So he brought me here, to my enemies."

"But why?"

"He could not help himself. Your workings enmeshed him. I freed him of the other thrall placed on him, as my gift for saving me, but your magics are too strong for me. It is a pity, for you deserve Gwyn my faithless lover, far more than you deserve Arthur."

"Gwyn?" she colored slightly. "My workings? What do you mean?"

"Prince Gwyn was my lover. And as for your black working, you know all too well what I mean."

Kitty shook her dark ringlets. "Gwyn Morgan has been paying court to me. It was flattering, I suppose. But . . . my heart was given to someone else long ago." She held up a finger. "We . . . um . . ."

It was clearer to her now. "You pledged your troth in blood." The blood that mingled and drove the magics that had been close to killing him.

She nodded. "We both pricked our fingers and put them together. It was children's play, I suppose. His . . . sentiments underwent a change. But mine never did." She took a deep breath. "Even if he loves you now."

"He doesn't. He brought me here because I have a broken arm. He said that you were a healer. He doesn't realize that he is too. He has just never learned to block the pain of those he tries to help."

"You're not . . . you're not . . ."

"His lover," filled in Annwn. "No. But Gwyn was mine. He betrayed me."

A note of doubt crept into her voice. "Papa says that your kind can be very persuasive. Very deceptive."

Annwn shrugged. "But not, as you should know, when constrained by cold iron."

Kitty nodded slowly. "No. That much I have learned. I don't know very much about you. It is Papa's special field of research. He is teaching me."

"He is using you."

"No . . . I just help him a little with his work. He did so much for Mama and me. He says that I have an aptitude for it." She sounded doubtful . . . but she was also busy with the latch. "Do you truly swear that you haven't enchanted Arthur?"

"By the high throne and the low. By Mab and all the princes," said Annwn. "I swear that I have done nothing more than lift the spell that bound him to someone called Marianne. It was killing him, in combination with the ill-magics on the house. Your magics."

The hands fiddling with the lock had stilled. "He was in love with Marianne. He told me so himself. He was enchanted with her."

"He was. Enchanted. A tawdry human spell. Easy to break. Your workings on the house were not."

Kitty looked first incredulous, and then terribly guilty. "It wasn't meant to hurt him."

"It would have killed him but for your shared blood. Why not direct your workings at her?" asked Annwn, curious about this dark-alfar motivations, despite her predicament.

"Because . . . he loved her," said Kitty in a small voice. "I couldn't hurt something he loved. I . . . hated that house."

"It worked on her anyway."

"Did I . . . I mean, the crim. cons. say that she's the mistress of . . ."

Annwn shook her head. "It is a facet of your magic, alfar-girl. You could only bring out what was there. If

she had loved him truly, it would just have been a
house blighted with ill-fortune, and they would have
left it. Now are you going to let me out or not?"

Kitty nodded, and sprang the lock.

Free of the iron, and close to Kitty, Annwn could
feel the tracery of magics that had been bound about
the alfar-girl. Magics of the same sort that had been
placed on her first rescuer. She snapped them like
chains of gossamer. "Now we need to find your Arthur
and get out of here," she said, as Kitty shook her head
as if to clear it and rubbed her hand across her eyes.

I was not going to fit out of the window. Nor, it
would appear, was there anyone outside to signal to.
And then I heard someone at the door, a rattle of
keys. Well . . . there was nothing that could serve me
as a cudgel. But I was known to have a punishing
right. If I could see that it came to handy blows before
the devils had a chance to use their enchantment on
me, well, at worst I could floor Carandon. At best I'd
floor his companion first. Leaping down from the high
sill, I knocked the man down with my rush. . . . to
realize it was neither Carandon nor the other fellow.

It was Wilkins. He sat up. "Master Arthur," he said,
"I've had the grooms saddle horses for you and your
friend. You'd best be gone, quickly. Lord Carandon
is planning terrible things."

The old butler had been at Tatcham long before
Lord Carandon had married Kitty's mother. He'd
been our partisan through all sorts of trouble from
when I was barely out of short clothes. I should not
have been surprised . . . but I was. And touched, especially after Kitty had just let her stepfather take us.
"Wilkins, where is Kitty? I have to talk to her."

"I think she may be in the laboratory, young master.
None of the servants are allowed in there."

"Good. Then that's where I am going. Best play
least-in-sight, Wilkins. I don't want you in trouble over
this business, and it is deep doings. But thank you,
from the bottom of my heart."

"I am glad to be of service, young Master." He smiled. "In the hall we always thought you and Lady Catherine would make a match of it. It was not to be, but I'd always thought that I would be your man."

"You may yet be. And I may still surprise you. First I've got to put your present master to grass . . . I am less than sure how to do that. First off, I must spring Annwn and talk to Kitty. Best be back to your post, old friend."

I walked down the passage toward the laboratory.

"I have been quite blind, haven't I?" said the alfar-girl.

"Bespelled, yes. For many years," said Annwn.

"And now it would seem," said a cold voice from the doorway, "that I will have to redo a great deal of my work."

"Papa!"

He smiled, showing his teeth. "In a manner of speaking, yes. Now, back away from that creature, Catherine. They are dangerously glib if nothing else. I am proof against your spell, fay. I have been studying you kind for many years. I lack your power, but I exceed your skill."

Uncertainly, the alfar-woman moved toward him. She had after all been under his influence for many years. Then, to Annwn's surprise she grabbed his arms. "Run!" she screamed.

But it was too late. Gwyn stood behind him. Annwn knew that he was more powerful than she was. She felt him raise his will . . .

And saw him turn and fall as the alfar-girl was thrown off by the man she called father. The human mage turned and drew a long thin blade from inside his silver headed cane. "Redmund," he said. "I was planning to dispose of you more tidily." He raised the blade.

Annwn could do nothing to the mage. He had indeed protected himself very well. But a faerie blade was hers to call. And Arthur had earned it.

*   *   *

As I faced my death, I felt the swordhilt smack into my palm. It was a long and a very light blade. Lord Carandon dropped his thrust to parry my stroke, and I was forced briefly onto the back foot. I beat at his blade, and then we were hard at it. He was not my master by much, but I was feeling the months of dissipation wearing away my stamina. It might have gone ill . . . but then Kitty thrust a foot between his legs. He fell heavily, and I leaped forward. This was no gentleman's duel . . . and I thrust at nothing. He was gone with a clap of inrushing air.

I looked around in puzzlement. "He has translocated," said the little fay.

I helped Kitty to her feet. "You have to go," she said. "Now. I have seen him do this before. He'll be back with help."

The fay nodded. "We need to be away. All of us. What did you do to Gwyn? He is more dangerous still."

"I gave him a leveler. He is just back there. . . ." He wasn't.

"Wilkins sent a groom to saddle horses for us." I took Kitty's hand. "Come with us." There was much yet to be dealt with, and much that could not be undone. But this I could put right.

"She must," said the fay. "I will need her to get home."

"Only if you want me to," said Kitty, looking down.

I lifted her chin gently. Looked into her dark eyes. "I never wanted anything more," I said, and kissed her, while the little fay stamped her foot with impatience.

ABOUT THE AUTHORS

By day, **Walt Boyes** is a not-so-mild-mannered chief editor of a technical magazine called *Control* and a partner in a high-technology consulting firm, Spitzer and Boyes LLC. Ah, but by night, he transforms into the Bananaslug of Baen's Bar and begins to write. Walt has written ten nonfiction books, articles and columns too numerous to count (Bananaslugs have very few fingers anyway), and has published several fiction pieces, including two short stories in the 1632 Universe and some children's stories. Walt is currently working on two nonfiction books, and a novel (of course—doesn't every writer have one stashed somewhere?). Walt is Associate Editor and Marketing Director for Jim Baen's *Universe* magazine.

Paul Crilley is a thirty-year-old Scotsman living in South Africa with his partner, Caroline, and their young daughter, Isabella-Rose. He spends his days writing scripts for South African television and his nights trying to finish the various novels he has on the go. His first novel, *Night Of The Long Shadows*, was released in May 2007. He and Caroline have just bought their first house. Visit Paul at www.paulcrilley.com

Linda A. B. Davis was originally schooled in print journalism but has decided that writing science fiction and fantasy is a lot more fun. She enjoys creating new worlds and characters that she would like to see become real. Her work has appeared in various magazines, both web and print, as well as in local newspapers. She lives in northwestern Florida with her husband, daughter, three dogs, cat, and rabbit. When she's not dodging hurricanes, she also enjoys softball, reading, jigsaw puzzles, and travel. Many thanks go to Steve, her parents, and her Aunt Frances for their support and inspiration.

Russell Davis has written numerous short stories and novels in a variety of genres under several different names. Some of his most recent work can be seen in *Slipstreams*, *Maiden, Matron, Crone*, and *Under Cover of Darkness*. He lives in Nevada, where he writes, rides horses and spends time with his family.

Eric Flint is a popular star of SF and fantasy. *1634: The Galileo Affair*, a collaboration with Andrew Dennis, was a *New York Times* best seller. His novel *Mother of Demons*, was picked by *Science Fiction Chronicle* a best novel of the year. His novel *1632*, which launched the Ring of Fire series, won widespread critical praise, as from *Publisher's Weekly*, which called him "an SF author of particular note, one who can entertain and edify in equal, and major, measure." He has also shown a powerful gift for humorous fantasy adventure with *Forward the Mage* and *The Philosophical Strangler*, which *Booklist* described as "Monty Python let loose in Tolkien's Middle Earth." A longtime labor union activist with a master's degree in history, he currently resides in northwest Indiana with his wife Lucille.

As a sick brat, **Dave Freer** once found himself trapped in house in which he had had nothing to read. Having read the contents of all the jars and detergent boxes, he started on his sister's collection of Regency romances. As a rugged outdoor fisheries scientist and fish-farm manager, he learned to hide his passion for them in girly-magazine covers until he grew up and stopped worrying about it. Now he is a full-time writer, author or coauthor of ten novels, including *Rats Bats & Vats* (no. 7 on the Locus ranking) and *Pyramid Scheme* (no. 3 on Locus), both with Eric Flint, and the successful *Heirs of Alexandra* series with Mercedes Lackey and Eric Flint. His last solo novel, *A Mankind Witch*, was star rated by *Publishers Weekly* (meaning they considered it a book of outstanding quality). He is contracted to write a further five novels. Freer has written a growing body of shorter fiction too, all of which is designed to avoid him wasting time rock-climbing or diving for spiny lobsters. He lives near Mooi River, South Africa, with his wife, sons, various dogs, and the cats that own him, somewhere close to middle of nowhere.

Esther M. Friesner is the author of thirty-three novels and over one hundred fifty short stories and other works. She won the Nebula Award twice as well as the Skylark and the Romantic Times Award. Best known for creating and editing the wildly popular *Chicks in Chainmail* anthology series, her latest publications are the Young Adult novels *Temping Fate*, *Nobody's Princess* and *Nobody's Prize*. She lives in Connecticut with her husband, is the mother of two grown children, and harbors cats.

Darwin A. Garrison resides in the wastelands of northeastern Indiana, where he spends his days hunting the wily saber-toothed prairie gopher to supplement his family's meager diet of instant ramen noodles and Kit Kat bars. Frequently observed near video retailers stocking anime titles and bookstores with notable science fiction and manga sections, he cannot be easily identified because he looks just like any other middle-aged cubicle lemming. By dint of his disconnect with reality and the miracle of the "infinite typing monkeys" theory, he has managed to write two other stories of sufficient quality for sale to DAW/Tekno anthologies this year in addition to Firebird and Shadow. His dearest dream is to sell enough fiction to fund a recurring Friday night anime-pizza party that will continue until he succumbs to intense mozzarella poisoning.

Daniel M. Hoyt aspires to be *that* Dan Hoyt—you know, the one who writes those cool stories and books. Realizing a few years ago that rocket science was fun but unlikely to pay all the bills, Dan embarked on a new career choice—writing fiction for fun and profit. Since his first sale to *Analog*, he's sold several stories to other magazines and anthologies. In addition, Dan is particularly pleased to announce his upcoming DAW anthology, *Fate Fantastic*, edited with Martin H. Greenberg. Curiously, after a few short years, Dan's mortgage is still outstanding, but he remains hopeful. Catch up with him at http://www.danielmhoyt.com

John Lambshead was born in the English Westcountry surf town of Newquay in 1952. He was educated at Newquay Grammar School, and Brunel University in West London. He took a PhD at The Natural History Museum in London in 1983 and now works there as a research professor in biodiversity. He is married to Valerie, and they have two grown-up daughters. John's hobby was designing wargames and computer games. He is best known for creating the first icon-driven computer game, *The Fourth Protocol*. He has written a number of popular history and gaming books, including David Drake's *Hammers Slammers Handbook*. His historical science fantasy, *Lucy's Blade*, was published in May 2007.

Fran LaPlaca's short story, "Wings to Fly," appeared in the award winning Realms of Wonder anthology, *Fantastic Companions*, and her flash fiction has been featured online at antipodeansf.com. She lives in the rolling green hills of northwest Connecticut with a cat, a hamster, two fish, a rabbit, as well as a husband and two of her three children. A member of the soon-to-be-famous CEvo writing group, she works on her novels while laboring away in customer service. You can find her online at http://www.sff.net/people/fran-laplaca.

Alan Lickiss was raised in the suburbs of Washington, DC, where he met and married his wife, Rebecca. He lives along the front range in Colorado with his wife, four children, and at last count one cat, six parakeets, and one dwarf hamster. Alan spends his days working in software development, writing in the evenings and on weekends. His goal is to give up the day job to write full time. Other work by him appears in *All Hell Breaks Loose* and *The Future We Wish We Had*.

Barb Nickless's short stories have appeared in a wide variety of magazines and anthologies, including *All Hell Breaking Loose*, *New Writings of the Fantastic*, and *Fate Fantastic*. Currently at work on her second mystery novel, she lives in Colorado with her husband and two children.

Kate Paulk takes interesting medication. This explains her compulsion to write science fiction and fantasy and also means you'll be seeing a lot more of her in the future. Her friends would fear for her sanity, but she claims not to have any. She's been published in *Crossroads*, *Fate Fantastic*, and *Misspelled* and is hard at work on a novel. She lives in semiurban Pennsylvania with her husband and two bossy lady cats. Whether this has any effect on her sanity is not known.

Charles Edgar Quinn works buying and selling books at The Book Broker in downtown Colorado Springs, a huge, independent used book store that now faces an uncertain future because of renovations and rebuilding on the block. He has worked there under three owners and three different names since 1993.

Previously he worked managing the metaphysical bookstore section of a new age store, a job he got by virtue of having the right birthdate— they seemed to consider the horoscope the most important part of the interview process. He worked a few years as an independent wholesale distributor, and worked for a while at a North Carolina newspaper, the *Durham Herald*. His unavoidable writer's cat is a large orange Tabby named Scooter.

Irene Radford has been writing stories ever since she figured out what a pencil was for. A member of an endangered species, a native Oregonian who lives in Oregon, she and her husband make their home in Welches, Oregon, where deer, bears, coyotes, hawks, owls, and woodpeckers feed regularly on their back deck. For this story Irene updates her popular Merlin's Descendants Series, bringing her world of magic and wolfhounds into the present.

Laura Resnick is the author of such fantasy novels as *Disappearing Nightly*, *In Legend Born*, *The Destroyer Goddess*, and *The White Dragon*, which made the "Year's Best" lists of *Publishers Weekly* and *Voya*. A long-ago winner of the Campbell Award for best new science fiction/fantasy writer, she has published more than fifty short stories. Under the pseudonym Laura Leone, she is the award-winning author of more than a dozen romance novels, including *Fallen From Grace*, which was a finalist for the Romance Writers of America's Rita Award. You can find her on the Web at www.LauraResnick.com.

Mike Resnick is the author of more than fifty science fiction novels, one hundred seventy-five stories, twelve collections, and two screenplays, and has edited over forty anthologies. His work has appeared in twenty-two languages. He is the winner of five Hugo Awards, has won other major awards in the USA, France, Japan, Poland, Croatia, and Spain and, according to

Locus, is the leading short fiction award winner in science fiction history.

Kristine Kathryn Rusch has sold novels in several different genres under many different names. The most current Rusch novel is *Paloma: A Retrieval Artist Novel*. The Retrieval Artist novels are stand-alone mysteries set in a science fiction world. She's won the Endeavor Award for that series. Her writing has received dozens of award nominations as well as several actual awards from science fiction's Hugo to the Prix Imagainare, a French fantasy award for best short fiction. She lives and works on the Oregon Coast.

Harry Turtledove is an escaped Byzantinist who writes alternate history, other sf, fantasy, and historical fiction. He may be best known for alternate-history novels *The Guns of the South* and *Ruled Britannia*. He is married and has three daughters and the stereotypical writer's cat—although the fuzzy galoot in question hasn't got the brains to make a proper stereotype.

ABOUT THE EDITOR

Sarah A. Hoyt was often disciplined for lying as a child. Being who she is, this meant only that her lies kept getting more complex and inventive. Now living in Colorado with her husband, two teen sons and a claw of cats, she has sold a dozen novels and over fifty short stories. Her Shifters series with Baen started with *Draw One in the Dark*, while her Musketeers Mysteries—with Prime Crime—started with *Death of a Musketeer*. Upcoming is her Bantam Trilogy *Heart of Light, Soul of Fire*, and *Heart and Soul*, which details adventures in an alternate British Empire where magic works. *Something Magic This Way Comes* is her first attempt at editing, and she can't really explain it. All she can imagine is that after four decades of a blameless life she somehow got bitten by an editor, thereby becoming one every full moon.